The
Prentice-Boy

Ray Rumsby

CLARET PRESS

Cover and Interior Design by Petya Tsankova

ISBN paperback: 978-1-910461-60-0
ISBN ebook: 978-1-910461- 61-7

A CIP catalogue record for this book is available from the British Library.

www.claretpress.com

It is the design of the following voyage, to describe the whole coast round Great Britain not merely to give plans and outlines of its well-known towns, ports, and havens, but to illustrate the grandeur of its natural scenery, the manners and employment of people, and modes of life, in its wildest parts.

A Voyage Round Great Britain (8 vols. 308 plates 1814-1825)

Richard Ayton, with a series of views
drawn by William Daniell, A.R.A.

Not in Utopia, subterraneous fields,
Or some secreted Island, Heaven knows where,
But in the very world which is the world
Of all of us, the place in which, in the end,
We find our happiness, or not at all.

The Prelude (1805)

William Wordsworth

May 1820

ONE

Meet me in Millers Yard, young'un, he said. I knows that place—a cobbled square, an all the dwellins leanin-in above you. No locks nor glass. There is but shutters the children swing upon, an dogs gone wild. Folks livin in Millers is dressed in rags, like me. They holds-to their doors with twine, an no way back to daylight but down a alley too small for a cart. You'd fink London was wantin to close the whole place over, stitch it tight, forget it ever was.

From the alleyway I can see him now, waitin—someone what don't belong among Millers people. His garments tells you he's got a job. He don't shovel muck for a livin, neither. So why might a stranger want to meet me in this sorry place? A man what promises pastries, not cash, talkin all the whiles of sugar an jellies an rich fruit cake till your belly rumbles? *No need for you to go thieving today, lad. Big wink. Kept special for you, y'see?*

Out upon the streets the last shower did rinse the air, the dust much settled by it. The alley is different, bein slime-damp. Near the far end come sharp in your nostrils yard-smells of moss, an wood-rot soaked afresh, an muck-heaps. Amid this reek, I smells a rat.

At six o the clock by the bells of St. Martin's I crosses the cobbles into the stranger's sight. He near slips when backin neath the timber of an overhang. Children at their game is quick called within by their mother. Just an echo of little voices left behind. Not right for a whole yard to be so still afore dark. Why did he not come forward? It ain't no errand he wants me to run, no message to some secret lady-love, no pothecary parcel to be buried or picked up, an now I'm close enough to see little raindrops from the eaves upon his shoulders, he ain't carryin no cakes at all.

Sudden he grabs me like you might a hen, turns me about, shoves me agin the wall.

'Just bend forward, son, stay quiet, and you will get your reward.'

None here to stop him. Much as I struggle, he pushes me down. 'Still, lad, still!'

From neath his arm I see the belt buckle hangin loose. I am his prey.

'Still, I say!'

Again, an echo acrost the Yard—his voice, or another's. Loud enough for him to look up, long enough for me to wriggle low an elbow him in the crotch. I got sharp bones, not much flesh on em, an in pain he doubles-up, stretchin out a hand, mouth wide as a Billingsgate cod.

I'm off full-tilt down the alleyway, out from the shadows an along the street, jiggin this way an that twixt the strollers, passin gigs an carriages, till I dares look back. Walk quick by Leicester Fields. Lose myself in the crowd makin its way to the Aymarket.

*

The shower being over, unfold my canvas sketching-seat. Sitting thus by the theatre's footway I am enough sheltered from wheels, spray, and horse-droppings. Pointless to wear the smock for public appearances in the Haymarket—too many insults about milking-stools and missing cattle—but the brass-cornered equipment box, my Old Faithful, is at hand. Pin a fresh sheet to the block. Sufficient advertisement, along with a list of fees, um, prices. Humble portraits, these, which pay the petty costs of our artistic programme.

We have laboured years upon our passionate undertaking: tinted etchings from camera obscura images, capturing the land-scapes and ways of life, region by region, around our shores. Ruth listened close when first we talked, as is her way. *Views by William Daniell A.R.A., Commentary by playwright, critic and essayist, Richard Ayton!* They were newly married then—all was hopeful. And now? Our enterprise scarce two-thirds complete, the remote eastern coasts unvisited.

I no longer put much faith in maps.

Bestow my easeful smile upon those stopping to watch: potential subjects for my sketches. One grows used to it. Today's swift exercises in line-work have earned a few shillings; my latest aquatint, exhibited in Durham at eight guineas, remains unsold. Volume Five of our voyages cannot be issued without Richard's commentary. He maintains that it is *underway*.

The usual, desperate, pre-tour quest for funds. In truth, our venture lacks a noble patron in the old way, to grant us income, purchase volumes, mention our tour in high places. Little has changed: artists still must bow and scrape. How Richard mocks it all!

The weak sun going down, warmth failing. Where are the ready customers for one's portraits? What has happened to human vanity? Before the entrance to a theatre, in Heaven's name! And irksome to sit by this playbill on the wall, without correcting the impossibility of Lydia Languish's hand.

The purse safe in my pocket. Undo the strings. Once more count the pence, though it wastes time to tout for custom like some pie-seller, and needless, had Richard and I been able to agree the finance. The present coolness seems—

A bristled face tilts close before me. Side whiskers and the collar of a heavy shirt, fraying green neckerchief tied loose. Smell of onions, or sweaty woollen stockings, or both.

'You do pictures then, do ye?' A small man, keen-eyed despite the defeated expression. Pushing back his cap, rubs his head with it.

'That is my profession, yes. Do you wish to sit for me?'

'Do what?'

'You wish me to draw your picture, for a fee?'

'Yes.'

'Then take a seat, my good sir. Ten pence for a sketch, I'm afraid.'

'You're afraid?'

Sigh. 'Do you have ten pence?'

The man nods, tapping his pocket.

A pause.

'You pay me before I do it, y'see.'

The grizzled fellow hesitates with coins in his fist. 'What if I don't like it?'

Others stop by to watch me unclasp the felt-lined box, take out a tray of goose-quills, ink tub, glass bottle, brushes, small sponge and a folded cloth, before securing the lid with some style.

'Sir, I assure you that those who purchase William Daniell's services delight in their portraits.' Place the tray upon the box. 'Should you remain uniquely dissatisfied, I return one half of your payment, and keep the sketch. I cannot conjure a Prince Charming; you cannot deny a finished work.'

Smiles among the growing audience. My subject narrows his eyes, twists his mouth this way and that, rubs his nose, counts out ten blackened pence.

'Thank you. Please look toward me ... and perhaps a little to my left ... that way, to my left, thank you. My drawing shall be in ink. No corrections. Kindly stay as still as possible. I shall not long detain you.'

The watchers come near: a mother with her son; a large family at the side; a young woman with a basket. Gainst the nearest column of the footway leans a pale, barefoot youth—sixteen years perhaps, old enough for gaol, gaunt enough to have spent time there—who inclines his head, peering across. Those queueing for the box office turn toward this free spectacle.

A fine brush-head for the outline and the hints of shape; one thicker for this man's heavy brow, his shadowed right ear, the neckerchief's gathered material.

'Try to hold your position, sir.'

'It's these people, they—'

'Your position, sir!'

His lips push forward in childlike displeasure. Of more interest, worth capturing, is that glimmer in the subject's eyes, his shrewd narrowing.

Now, spot water upon the back of my hand. Dip an inked brush into the area of wetted skin and swift establish pale shadows neath the eyebrows, a hint of wide nostrils, his darkened neck.

They shuffle close about me.

Shade below the cheekbones, deeper for his collar. Sponge-dab the top of one sleeve to suggest texture beyond the drawn line. Smudge substance into the hat.

Smiles of appreciation.

That pale street-boy is at my shoulder. His stale garments! With one grubby hand half-raised in imitation he peers at the method as if I were Rembrandt. Meanwhile my subject blinks rapidly, stretches his neck, resumes position.

'Near done, sir.'

'Glad to hear it.'

Lines upon pale wash, streaked shades, produce the chin's stubble. Distressed wave patterns for the side whiskers, shadow-lines for the shirt-collar's hollows.

Nod my head, gracious, gracious, to a beaming admirer.

Enough. Close my hand upon the brush-stems and sit back—a stage Neptune.

'You may relax.'

'Should think so, too!' He points toward the theatre wall. 'Havin to look at that dreary woman the whole time.'

Mere pence, yet more cash in my purse. An adequate like-ness—too heavy about the chops. However, the calculating wari-ness in the man's eyes I have caught, the element which intrigues. Bottom right in charcoal: 'William Daniell A.R.A.', a flourish for authenticity, and the year.

Unpin the finished sheet and set it upon the rest. Several watchers press forward: *A dead spit, that is.*

My subject stamps about, tugs the neckerchief, arches his back: *Oo-aw-w-wh!*

The people closest linger. Sufficient light for another sketch? Slim chance: the lamp-lighter is ahead of the hour. Hurried footsteps along the stone floor at my back. Swish of a lady's skirts, her escort's tapping cane. With a thump the creaking doors of the King's Theatre are unbolted.

Settles the matter: no more clients today.

'Your portrait, sir. I believe you shall, er, you shall...'

Something odd about my subject's sideways look. The bearer of a large bale hurtles into us from the right, losing his balance and grip of the bundle. Straw spills across my shoulders, face and neck. Now this careless porter seeks to haul himself upright against his own impetus, grabbing my collar with his free hand before clinging to an outer pocket, as our graceless dance topples sideways in slow, inevitable collapse.

'Ouf!'

'Sorry, sir. Sorry. The crush!'

Bedding trapped between us where we sprawl upon the damp ground.

'Get from me, man!'

'I was pushed!'

Glare upward between stems of tangled vegetable matter, clutching a paintbrush posy pressed gainst my chest.

'Just... get...'

'Pushed!'

A huge weight rolls upon me.

'This is ridiculous! Puh—!' away a length of straw from my lip.

Others hasten to the theatre's entrance. And does some chasing-game take place—that child, leaping over us, pursued by the street-boy who stood next me?

Chiding family-members haul the bale-carrier away into the Haymarket throng.

Get to my feet. Dignity requires at least a semblance of disdain. Rub the fresh marks upon my better jerkin. Take stock. Brass-cornered box beside. Canvas folding-chair retrievable, though trampled. Flick the scattered bedding's insects from my sleeves and neck. One great sneeze. And um...

Pocket. Pat-pat.

Not there. My other pocket. Try there.

Or little pocket. No. Never used.

Or the... pocket he ripped?

'Thief! Thieves! I am robbed! My purse—stolen! Thieves!'

Step this way and that, arms outstretched, brandishing brushes, eyes wide, watery and blurring. (Must not neglect the brass-bound box.)

'Thieves! Thieves! My cash stolen! Thieves!'

Spectators become passers-by, all smiles gone. Those prepared to observe me now, maintain their distance.

Who spied this theft?

None. *Pickpockets everywhere*, all agree.

Or has there truly been a robbery?

Is this man's pleading a hoax?

I stand a-tremble here as the three Fates assess my own guilt of the crime upon me!

Deranged? These days, cannot be too careful.

Perhaps an actor from the Theatre?

A play about a robbery, yes! That old fairground ruse!

Dispersing, gone: lives to lead.

And I am desolate.

So...

Gather my trampled canvas seat. Slump upon the footway with pounding heart—stricken, faint, abandoned. A day spent in this heat, some performing beast in a travelling fair, to end with less than I had before! Stare at the sable brushes. The familiar pain across my back stems from long hours leaning over copper plates, my wheezing breath from nitric acid. Richard is right: our tour of Britain lacks investment. We must beg wealthy West Countrymen to purchase two dozen tinted etchings of harbours, naval yards, and clifftop Cornish mines.

Yes, and geese may fly, um, pigs.

My embarrassment must not become known. The joke would do the rounds. *Thieves took the pence and left his works!* Doubtless a ribbing from Richard. Constable snorting his great horse-laugh, Turner's usual doleful commiserations, and—

'Sir, ain't this yours?'

'Mine?'

My purse, heavy in my palm!

'Best grip such fings tight in hand, sir—not leave em swingin about for someone to grab.'

'You fetched it back?'

'I chased that nipper. Saw what would come about an caught im afore he could pass it over—an if you would, sir, perhaps put your, er, *fing-what-I-rescued* out of sight.'

'Were you next me during that last sketch?'

The scrawny youth smiles. 'I was followin best I could when you did them shadows, an that stuff was suckin the colour up. Name o Cloud, sir, Jesse Cloud.'

TWO

I ain't got words for how good it feels bein off of the streets. That Aymarket gang would use my skull for a foot-ball. Ain't never lived in someone's home afore. I but slept in cellars or lean-tos where I could, an not get caught. St James's Workouse wasn't homely. Families, not all of em friends, kept in one big room mid the racket of spinnin-wheels. In the schoolroom, governors did give you tests an must go away pleased or else all in trouble. The teacher quick to use his cane, whiles the Sunday churchman said be ever grateful.

Mr Daniell's place here is free floors up wiv solid boards underfoot—the door my only chance to get away. *It is a reward for your helping me, Jesse, after I was robbed.* William Daniell, it is—wrote upon a parcel he got sent. I can read enough for that.

It is just me wiv him: no family, housemaid, nor cook. No pitchers of wife nor chiles. That day in the Aymarket, when Mr Daniell did say *I can give you a roof over your head*, what he meant was, come an clean, light the fire, fetch-an-carry, do the laundry.

In the workouse we was loose-dressed for growin bigger, but was ever Bluecoat Children so all might know us. *It is no prison,* they said. *Ye are not prisoners.* It looked like a gaol, felt like one, smelled like one. It was a gaol. When Nat an me runned away from bein cared for, we rid ourselfs o them blue coats quick. His nibbs here is used to livin free by hisself—a gentleman wivout the means, not finkin to give me no apparel. But I likes it more to wear my own fings, nicked when first out.

I don't know what he does fink of but his pitchers. He will stand quiet in the middle of the room, rub his scalp, lookin at the floorboards for a long time. He cannot be finkin of floors, an don't seem to say prayers, so it is likely pitchers. The man is a proper artiss, though I ain't yet a proper artiss prentice. When I looks at floorboards, I sees dust in the joins, an knots—no foughts in my head at all. This might not be the way to do art. I must make myself useful the whiles, wivout gettin acrost him, an hope the learnin will come.

I am safe for now. Not sure how this will turn out.

*

Jesse stands, narrow-shouldered, ready to add steaming water. He and I are four days met, yet as I stand at the ewer this morning, it is pleasant novelty to be served in the manner of a gentleman whose attendant is, um, attending in the approved fashion.

'No need for more water, Jesse. Pass me the back-scrubber, will you?'

'Sorry, sir, but—Oh-hh-w! You mean that brush fing!'

'Yes, the back-scrubber upon the wall, Jesse. Carved ivory, brought home all the way from Bihar: *that brush thing.*'

My attendant examines the carved handle, smiling before I demonstrate usage.

'Sir, that ivory bein white, like stone but not stone, puts me in mind of whalebones. I have seen a atpin and comb what might be whalebone.'

Wait, wanting to hear more.

Jesse nods his head. 'Yes sir...'

Some shutter in the youth's mind has been let fall. More to tell there, though not today. The resolve in Jesse's eyes and in the set of the face is the gaze of someone hidden, watching from a place of retreat.

In the silence falling, fitful peals and a confusion of bell-chimes from high towers ring the hour across London.

'Sir...'

'Yes?'

'When I looks around an sees ow you live, wiv the pitchers an all, I feels lucky, sir, to be took-on.'

What a frown!

'It was my good fortune that you regained the purse.'

'Yes sir. Can't see why I done that.'

The frown eases. A strange mischief now in Jesse's eyes. This lad is unknown to me. Verbal engagement with company is discomfiting in my own print-room and, and, *home*.

Return the back-scrubber, my hands still acid-stained from working with the copper: never fades.

'Ivory, now, like whalebone, is animal material, though from a land creature. Know of elephants, do you?'

The prentice, arranging the shirt and freshly-ironed breeches on a chair, does not turn.

'In a way, Mr Daniell.' Jesse seems tense, scarce moving, some forest creature alerted to sudden danger.

'I have seen elephants, Jesse, in a region called Hyderabad— massive creatures, magnificent beasts.'

The casement misting. Three storeys below, no yelling costermongers, pin-sellers or tavern drunkards disturb the day in Cleveland Street. All indecorous washing-lines and laundry-poles confined to backyards. No hint of machinist uprisings, yet my spine tingles.

'So, um, shall I tell you of my journey?'

My expectant pause regrettably unfulfilled.

'I well remember the day. I was younger than you must be now...'

No response. With back half-turned, the youth examines the shirt he has put out for me—mark upon the sleeve, perhaps.

By accommodating a street-boy, I put myself at hazard. Low-life people exist among thieves—are thieves, and Jesse doubtless likewise. Why reward his singular generous act with trusted status here? This hidden youth now my responsibility!

Smooth a hand across my scalp.

'Well, before the sun grew excessive hot, my Uncle Thomas and I set forth upon the long road westward, down from the hills of Hyderabad...'

*

Mr Daniell talks to hisself, like what a proper artiss might do. He has got all the paints, brushes an tubs for art, but is in some way a printer besides. His nibbs scolds hisself when mixin colours, or will look sideways at a drawin of a tar barrel, rub his skull, an mumble to somebody in his head. They don't always agree. Such fings can come when you only got your own company, as I knows, though my treasures is ever wiv me to look at.

Mr Daniell lets me sit wiv him for meals. He has got platters, usin knives an forks. I feels stronger wiv food in my belly—for I did once see a beggar fall, too weak to stand again.

Here I sleeps like a Lord, lyin in the kitchen under a blanket all to myself, an top half in that two-hander tray-basket for takin washin to the yard. The basket is osier, wove in-out close, an bound at the top. I borrowed his charcoal to draw the pattern. He might not mind. Its shadow makes a low patch upon the wall. Them little ovals of light is gaps in the wicker, not seen at first, an only known by lookin past the basket. Two patterns, not one.

This might be a safe place if he don't find me out. When I forgets myself, like speakin of whalebone, I can slip-up an start him wonderin. I must stay watchful. You'd fink his nibbs would keep an eye on me, case I nicked his belongins, but he don't, much— just twitchy at havin another around.

A patchwork quilt is spread acrost his bed. Racks of tools along the wall. Also, that back-scrubber. Otherwise, he ain't got a lot worth nickin what easy can be took away. I have looked.

*

Storms the night long, and water gurgling far below. With day-break the rains ceased, the gale vanishing like a faery-tale curse to leave me irritable now, prone to coughing, ill-slept.

And doubts regarding our British venture ruin the appetite. Should grim persons demand payment for board at The Newcastle Groggins, or for the box unused at *Dido Queen of Carthage*, not to mention… well, not to mention. Unpleasantness, harassment, even threats, would deepen my embarrassment. And shameful that a street-boy given shelter and instruction here might witness his Master's indebtedness.

However, the debt of gratitude I can repay.

'Jesse, when my father died young, my mother became so distraught that Uncle Thomas lent our family his support. Now the old fellow himself is stricken, both duty and compassion demand I pay my respects. You understand?'

'You want to go see him, sir?'

'He lives nearby, a former artist, and you may come with me.'

By the doorstep we pause before pools of rainwater and the

criss-crossed grooves of oozing mud. London's dust-haze is less freshened than sunken, silted neath a tide of cool air.

In Fitzroy Square, a vestibule curtain flicks back. The great lock groans. Disappointed, the concierge waves us in. *You know your way, sir, I am sure.* She is too old now to accompany visitors up two flights of stairs. They violate her peace.

Mrs Lambton will have recognised my distinctive rat-a-tat-a-tat, yet opens the apartment door with customary caution. How we know each other.

Heavy of breath: 'Mrs Lambton, greetings after the rains! I bring my prentice-boy, Jesse Cloud.'

Her thin face angled behind the door, a straggling lock of hair over one eye. Remarking the newcomer she smiles. 'Young Mr Daniell, and Jesse, welcome both!'

'My purse was stolen in the Haymarket. Jesse retrieved it, y'see, before a farthing taken.'

Fifty years of age, merely ten years older than I, Thomas's housekeeper calls me Young Mr Daniell. The volume in Mrs Lambton's right hand is spine-upright, her forefinger keeping the place.

'It is *A Tale of the North*—put out of late by a well-connected Lady, persuaded against everyone's better judgement to attempt a work of fiction.'

'Then why read it?'

'A sort of loyalty to a woman-author.' She glances back, smiling from neath the hook of hair as we quit the drawing-room. 'Though I need not therefore like it.' By the door to Uncle's apartment the widow pauses. 'You will find Thomas much the same, Young Mr Daniell, which is to say, unwell. It will please him greatly to see you.'

'Unwell?'

'Seized by a fit even yesterday.'

'Then perhaps...'

'Perhaps introduce Jesse briefly to your uncle?' She beams

toward my prentice. 'You and I shall sit together afterwards, Jesse, and come to know each other better.'

'Yes Miss.'

Mutual nodding and smiling as she stands aside for us both to pass, but the lad's discomfort manifest.

'Uncle?'

The same high-ceilinged room, its long curtains half-drawn. The same water-colours upon the walls, and Persian rug, and russet dressing-gown lain upon the high-backed chair, still pulled close to the bed. The same bed, whose occupant slumbers as when last I came here. Jesse scarce advances within the room, a shadow by the door.

'Uncle Thomas?'

Lean over, wondering whether or not to reach out. A catch in Uncle's throat, an obstruction which bubbles briefly, dies, and revives with each new breath. I retreat to the chair, seized by an inexplicable need to clear my own gullet, to do it for him. Swallow hard.

Bedside, a sickroom's familiar tokens: bottle of tincture, large spoon (surely for equine administration); several paper-twists of powder, water-glass; monogrammed kerchief, neatly folded. News-paper sprawled upon the counterpane. Above the bed hangs Uncle's framed *Lower Slopes of the Nepalese Hills*, from the few works which survived intact our voyage home. The pale building in the middle distance is exquisitely coloured—as one might expect of so skilled an artist—yet the *angle* of the wall! Would have taken a mere moment, a dab of Payne's grey, to adjust that line before the picture was framed. But it was not my uncle's way. Is not his way. Nonetheless, the—

'Aren't ye proposing to speak?'

'Oh!'

'Trappist Monk? You've the hair for it.'

'I thought you slept, Uncle. How are you?'

'Cannot sleep aright: only lie here.' The old man's eyes close for several seconds. The catch in his throat again. 'Purgatory.' And within this troubled quiet, 'What brings you, William? Speak, man.'

'I have my new prentice-boy with me, Uncle.'

'Your what?'

'Prentice. Jesse Cloud, his name.'

'Then I wish him well…Hear me, over there? Good fortune to you.'

'Fank you, sir.'

'May need it.'

Mrs Lambton at the door beckons Jesse away.

I report anything to indicate success, progress, general thriving: the Scarborough painting near finished; the tour of Britain's coastline with Richard Ayton continuing apace; *undoubted interest being shown* by owners un-named of fashionable galleries unspecified; perilous routes undertaken to capture uncommon perspectives, *reminiscent of our journeying from Bombay all those years ago, Uncle*—although now ha-ha without elephants. Also, rumours in London that the Academy may shortly invite a fellow's application for full membership. This fellow, in fact: Constable's sole rival for the vacancy.

'Oh, how entirely unlooked-for.'

He may be sour of mood.

Thirty years ago, it was revelation to accompany my beloved uncle in far-away places. The mountains and wide rivers of India, its peoples, trees and creatures, fascinated me. I watched craftsmen hammer metal, the techniques of dyers, engravers and potters, while grieving little for my father. Only Mother's death when I was fifteen years old ended this beguilement, fetching us home.

Deep-cushioned, Uncle Thomas regards me with concentration, even surprise, rather than pleasure or relief. His useless right arm lies upon the counterpane. I would wish to remember my uncle in better spirit.

'I shall repeat, Uncle, that I remain indebted to you for your guardianship when I was a lad, and, and—'

At last, a smile.

'—for having supported your brother's family generously, given the Admiralty's quibbling allowance to my mother for a husband killed in, um, unfortunate peacetime circumstances.'

A frown clouds Uncle's smile. The one good hand is raised, opens, bids me pause, falls again. Something other than a polite display of modesty. At once a fit of coughing. Bubble-noises, his voice weak and strained.

'Fetch me the water, would you? Must sit up.'

Haul the old man higher upon the bolster, propping with the creased pillows. Pass him the glass. Uncle Thomas's body is less bulky than anticipated, his oiled skin near embalmed.

'So, you have a prentice-boy?'

'Sixteen years of age, he claims.'

'You were younger still.'

'But Uncle, I am not Jesse's guardian; he is not my nephew.' *No, that response rasps.* 'I mean, in the way your brotherly kindness made secure a grieving family.'

With a growl, Uncle Thomas dabs the hand-kerchief to the corners of his mouth. His speech is sour, almost plodding, while he gazes at some far point in the corner wainscot. 'I was ambitious, like you. Chose to regard the voyage east as opportunity, not—'

Uncle's breath subsides. When he gathers himself, the point is forgotten, or evaded. 'Thought to paint charming landscapes. Sell 'em to the rich in Bombay, Delhi, Karnpor. And you'd learn as we went, William. British buyers in those enclaves would take home our exotic scenes; upon returning, we'd sell to galleries.' Uncle Thomas sighs, head down. In his throat a flap is raised, a drain-hole bursting after rains.

'Never thought she'd die while we were there!'

Mention of my mother, or perhaps my thanking him for his kindness to Aunt Amelia, to my sister and to me, darkens Uncle's expression. Why such bitterness regarding events so long ago? My uncle *chose* to see opportunity in the voyage—not exile, or defeat. Blind to any other circumstance, I had thought our Indian venture more heroic.

Uncle Thomas and I returned to England in the cold. My parents had been buried together, the frozen ground settled, stonework newly-engraved. Beside me, poor Mary at ten years of age seemed lost. How could our gentle mother not go on living?

Knew then I must become someone different.

*

It ain't just any old study, but her private study. Neither lock nor bolt upon the door. Mrs Lambton sits in the corner, fixin her jackdaw eye upon me. Cocks her head at what she sees, naught said. They have set this up between em, an I shudders at what she might have spied straightway to bring me crashin down.

'Jesse,' she says, all proper in her talk, 'you tremble. Unwell, perhaps?'

No Miss, playin dumb. I been in studies afore; ever they brings trouble of some kind. You gets to look out for the shuttin-fast. I ain't bout to tell Mrs Lambton what can appen in them places.

She waits for me to say more, an when I don't, nods to her bookshelfs.

'In a study one reads and writes. A quiet place to think.'

Yes Miss. Very nice. Books all different sizes. One shelf bendin.

Mrs Lambton points to a little chair. 'Do sit there. Once my daughter's.'

Fank you.

'What was your home like, Jesse?'

Don't know, Miss. Never been there.

She frowns at me from neaf them curls. 'So where did you grow up?'

St James's Workouse, Mrs Lambton. They did say I was one o them what gets left at the gates.

'A foundling?'

Yes, Miss.

She goes quiet, ever watchin. Her eyes scarce blink. And Mrs Lambton don't wear no necklace nor jewels nor rings, such as I ain't seen afore in a woman of her class. She's got on a plain dress, an them black slippers. Short of cash, perhaps. She might save for books, bein bold to buy her own.

Mrs Lambton leans forward. Her knuckle-bones is swolled. 'You know, Jesse, I am interested to learn of your pursuits.'

I ain't met that word, so she arks somefink else. 'What do you like doing?'

That is one question I can get right: *Drawin fings.*

Next, it's what might I want to do when I gets older. Never fought I had a choice. *Well, if I dint have to work, drawin fings true as they look,* says I, *to help medicine. Like wounds from the wars, an women's insides what died in childsbirf surgery.* I fink it might have put er off a bit. *Plants helps healin, too, Miss. I draws wildflowers livin how they can upon rough ground, much overlooked. Now I speck you know, Miss, how Feverfew is good for insect bites an achin teef, whiles Camomile helps wiv gut-ache an the runs. Well, both them plants got white flowers wiv yeller in the middle. Some folks cannot tell em apart. My drawins, Miss, though done wiv charcoal, shows what's different.*

'Why not become a proper artist, like Young Mr Daniell?' says she.

I tells er I wants to help people, not just paint. Mrs Lambton smiles, sayin no more, but gives me a ard biscuit.

'Is Jesse Cloud your full name?'

What can she be talkin about?

Mrs Lambton jiggles her feet on the floor—got the hoppits bad, far as I can tell.

'Do you have other names?'

No Miss. Two's enough, ain't it? She smiles again. What can there be to smile at? I puts her right. *At the workouse they said,*

Jesse is the name we did give you, but Cloud you must keep safe. Keep it safe for it is your somefink-or-other name, an your mother's. I did not understand at the time, Mrs Lambton. All I knew was I did not have no mother.

She nods her head. Keeps noddin. Scratches somewhere in er hair. I sits tight.

'It was praiseworthy of you to assist Mr Daniell following the robbery, Jesse.' She smiles at me again. 'Many another would simply have kept the purse.'

Fank you, Miss. When I brought it back, his feelins was clear. I am learnin to watch out for her smiles.

'Had you already left the workhouse when you met Young Mr Daniell?'

In the Aymarket, it was.

'Yes, alone in the Haymarket. Therefore, no longer a Bluecoat Child?'

For all her readin an writin, she don't understand. I won't let nobody put me back there. Nobody. Mrs Lambton might tell others where I got to. For tuppence they would easy make mention at the workouse door. More than a year I watched out for myself, an do still. She'll get naught from me.

THREE

Mrs Lambton's swishing arrival is welcome, bringing tea and her unique, brick-bake biscuits. She bends over my uncle to set his tray before him, touches a hand upon his shoulder, pulls close a plain wooden chair.

Uncle Thomas reaches across to clasp her fingers. 'Lizzie.'

An affecting image as she pauses to regard him, the two posed briefly in that way: a Vermeer interior. During the months of Thomas's illness this arrangement of figures, the tenderness of man and woman together, must have repeated itself many times. I see that now. The composition is its meaning.

The widow Lambton has her own preoccupations—forbids talk of cookery or household matters, and of what may be à la mode, the newest entertainment, or place to dine, by demanding: 'What is this nonsense? Why exhaust time upon it?' Whereupon Uncle will either laugh or become seized by coughing. She mentions often her distant cousins, the free-thinking Godwins: the couple's circle of acquaintance is close. In Mrs Lambton's stirring novels, adventurous heroines scale walls, address banner-waving multitudes, or sail with Barbary corsairs. All are well-disposed to the Paine-ite, Jacobin, or Revolutionary tendency. In some quarters, such allegiances would be thought worthy of trial. She does know.

Sitting upright, teacup and saucer in hand, Mrs Lambton brings our attention to an item in today's *Morning Chronicle* (its pages flung upon the bed), which belittles the Marylebone Association for the Rights of Women.

'The author, too craven to identify himself, deservedly remains a nonentity. Yet his scurrilous, prejudicial sneering slights our membership.'

Her eye glints. Uncle Thomas nods.

'Let us acknowledge how important are the rights of women to this country. It is no matter for levity that so many of my sex receive little education beyond the stitching of linen, while those few with access to books are debarred from professional employment or—'

'Excuse me, Mrs Lambton. May I ask what insult or innuendo you have suffered at the hands of this, um, writer's pen?'

Her face contorts with my sentence. She puts down her teacup to rid this child of something he should not be holding: 'Young Mr Daniell, *please!*'

In devilment Uncle Thomas glances upward: 'Marrows. Called them Marrows!'

The widow purses her lips. 'Because of Marylebone, plainly. Weak acronyms must pass for wit. The government having declared public association of any kind illegal, this spreader of noxious verbiage upon the populace suggests that we women play political games. He announces details of our meetings, inviting retribution! To him and to all such grub-street hacks I would repeat the words of my uncle's honoured cousin, Mrs Wollstonecraft: *take away natural rights and of course there is an end of duties.* It is no game we play, sirs. No game at all. We women shall indeed achieve our goals, for—Oh dear, my apologies.'

Fighting talk, dangerous talk, threatening the very foundation of family life. Yet Mrs Lambton seems distressed. I have not seen her so wounded. Pats the buttons at her throat, regarding the floor with concentration until composure restored.

She turns her head—a stiffening, a straightening. 'Young Mr Daniell, as you know, I have talked with Jesse Cloud.' The widow gazes narrowly upon me, her eyes bright beneath the Medusa hair. 'An interesting person.'

Whatever this knowingness may signify is beyond me. Uncle Thomas looks blank. 'Yes, Mrs Lambton, I believe Jesse shows resourcefulness.'

'Just so. The power of, well, the *human spirit* let us say, constantly amazes me. Long may it endure.' The hint of a smile. Mrs Lambton puts her hands together, which ends the matter, whatever it was. 'More tea? We have plenty in the pot.'

*

I ain't much slept.

I fink Mrs Lambton knows more than she will say straight. *I was thinking, Jesse… An artist in oils may paint over an earlier work. The image upon the canvas masks another.*

It was a test. Mr Daniell scarce uses oils, so I held my tongue. *Often, change may indicate altered perception or purpose. Corn-*

dollies, horseshoes nailed to doors: the same material contrived to different effect. However, a portrait which hides another thereby creates the mystery of an alternative meaning. She did give me one of her odd looks: cheeks gone in like worn leather, all cracked.

Yes, Miss, said I, but paintin-over saves waste.

Mrs Lambton smiled whiles her eye in that curl pinned me to the wall.

She knows: wants but proof. What if she tells his nibbs, just when I got safe off of the streets, an bein fed? He would fling me like fish-guts upon the heap. Troublin, but cannot be spoke of when none to tell.

It was night's end afore I found sleep, an dreamed again of Amy. It felt like her beside me where we was lyin, white all around. I have had this feelin many times. There was another, like them shadows upon his nibbs's wall: a sister took away whiles I was left, an none did come back for me. I growed up wonderin what I had done wrong. Where is my big sister? Where was she took? Here I got a proper house to go to, an a chance; I will fight to keep em.

*

Messrs Moulton and Clyne
THE GRAND SCENIC HALL & GALLERY
Oxford Street, London.
May 22, 1820.

William Daniell. A.R.A.
16 Cavendish Terrace
Cleveland Street, London.

Dear Sir,

We are pleased to inform you that, following the season's exhibition of coastal views in The Grand Scenic Hall, including your *Clifton, Near Bristol* (now sold), and *Fishing-Fleet at Aberdeen*, we have received an enquiry from a Lady interested in other works of yours with a view to purchase. The Lady identifies expressly scenes of the eastern counties.

However, we understand that the fifth volume of *A Voyage Round Great Britain,* and the accompanying Commentary by your colleague Richard Ayton, remain in progress. Our meeting last year concerned your Scotch pictures. Thus, on behalf of our client, respectfully we request you communicate any later progress by the morrow, if possible, naming locations.

Should you have further work of potential interest to our client, may it be presented at the Gallery with all haste. Being non-resident in London, The Lady consents to our appointing an agent in an advisory capacity upon her behalf. Naturally, our client remains the final arbiter in questions of taste.

It is in all parties' interest to proceed in this matter without delay, while ensuring due diligence. We enclose our Statement of Fees. In awaiting your reply, sir, we remain your humble servants,

> Messrs A. D. Moulton & J. Clyne of London (est.1792). Exhibitors Valuers Vendors Restorers & Auctioneers of Artworks

Your humble servants, indeed! The gallery's letter holds much promise: I am not forgotten; above all, views are sought of eastern shores—the very coast which our grand tour would next visit!

Lady of Taste… Some Grand Dame of the shires with her little black slave-boy. Gloomy staircases hung with decorated ancestors, or decorated with um, hanged ones, and prize livestock, various long-nosed females wearing lace, somebody's peacock. But this Lady brings the prospect of a cash sale, and cash has priority.

Therefore, by what mischance does Mrs Lambton write me today? Invites me to refreshment as if it were long our custom, when I would press forward with my Lincolnshire scene for an enthusiast!

Mrs Lambton's note, so soon following upon my last visit, and without Uncle's scrawled words appended, may signify Thomas's worsening health.

Perhaps visit?

*

His nibbs ain't glad to get the little note, whiles pleased wiv the sealed message brung to the door. Don't know who from. Mr Daniell keeps goin back to read it again. Less rubbin of his bald scalp. Ever I brushes the bits off of his shoulders. He puts this new message back inside his shirt, so might be good news he wants to show somebody. I can only wait to find out, but his britches is clean ready.

*

My sister's letters near fill this drawer. An ocean away, Mary laments my ill-health—would know more! Neither of us forgets those early years.

Here, the card-supplier's demand for payment. Um, final demand... I have lost track. Bottom of the pile. *Pending*. One has one's priorities.

And here, my sketch of Scotland's coast at Fanagmore. Hold it to the light. Follow with a fingertip the bleak charcoal shore. My last act of record before Richard's fall.

The scene swells before me: our ship harboured in the bay before dark, the air heavy, threatening a storm. Yet by dawn we set sail again. Cannot the ship's Master read the blackness of those low skies, or feel the wind's whiplash? *Get ye below,* his sole response, heedless of Englishmen. And we are off Scourie, scarce an hour at sea, when the tempest's fury flings away our yelling and impels the vessel ever nearer outcrops of black granite.

Get ye below. Though the rolling deck is awash, to get below is to envisage the hull's timbers asunder, an inrushing flood, our forlorn clambering to escape entombment fathoms down. In misery I cling to the deck-rail, fearing to crawl, crouched neath a further onslaught of chill waters upon my back, while Richard scrambles, almost loses his footing, and miraculously is brought sliding to the hatch-cover. He begins to descend the companionway, beckoning me to follow. At any moment a sudden weight of sea may smack upon the deck and carry me helpless away.

When the ship rolls to starboard, I leave go the portside rail and stumble toward Richard's outstretched arm, all blubbering thankfulness. With his guidance I contrive to turn-about, my foot finding the topmost rung. One last glimpse of the ship's bow rising amid the spray, of rocks revealed before living walls of sea envelop them.

Then it happens. A counter-tide amidships.

The vessel falters, all headway lost, as a mass of water throws itself upon us. Wipe salt-film from my eyes, aware now that Richard no longer grips me. I clamber down the companion-ladder into the gloom. He is sprawled upon the lower deck: the ankle-bone splintered, flesh pierced, and blood appearing.

As the ship rears, holds, plunges, Richard cries out. Kneeling in the slop and filth, I seek to dress his wound with my ripped shirtsleeves. A crewman brings him a leather covering. We must have passed those Scourie rocks—gone from my mind. Two hours more at sea, the Scotch venture abandoned. Soon to begin, the writhing agony of our long return.

Richard saved my life by waiting. Had he got below, he would be a fit man now.

Shall not work this sketch further. Shut it in the drawer.

*

Rat-a-tat-a-tat. The door opens cautiously to my woodpecker knock. 'Good-day, Mrs Lambton.'

'Young Mr Daniell, welcome!'

A rich aroma of freshly-ground coffee, poured and served in the kitchen—another of Mrs Lambton's customs.

'Thank you for responding to my note. It is appreciated.'

'No, no...'

'It is appreciated.'

I anticipate a gloomy prognosis from Uncle Thomas's physician; or that Mrs Lambton seeks to embroil me in some tribulation exciting our womenfolk; but chiefly fear that Uncle's investments have failed, ending my free use of his Cleveland Street apartment. Richard Ayton's injury weighs heavy with me, while our disagreement about finance is unresolved. Thus, a relief when Mrs Lambton raises herself upon a stool to say that Uncle's health is unchanged today. Further, she has drafted a paper claiming the right of school-mistresses who marry to remain employed. An irrelevance to me. What then might she wish to broach?

'Young Mr Daniell, I believe we both understand in our different ways that Jesse Cloud—'

'Jesse?'

'—has intelligence. You cannot fail to have perceived it.'

'Well, no. I mean, yes, I haven't. Failed, that is, to...'

A singular, lancing gaze while Mrs Lambton adjusts the lock of hair so that it should fall where it hung before.

A pause as long as Deuteronomy.

'Quite.'

No fresh catastrophe. But Jesse? Perplexing. We toy with coffee cups and slim spoons: social convention does not befit either of us. The hall clock struggles to another quarter-hour.

'Your prentice and I spoke together while you were with Thomas.'

'Mmm?'

'Also, to inform you that our Marylebone Association for the Rights of Women earlier discussed the condition of the poor.'

'Ah. Impressive.' Little wiser, but pertinent.

'Subsequently, I visited St James's workhouse in Billingsgate. Young Mr Daniell, I was shocked, horrified, that people should be so reduced!' Mrs Lambton's neck and jaw free themselves with an arcing motion. 'One reads of landlords who refuse to pay the parish rate for maintenance of paupers, while raising their own rents; but to witness the outcome shamed me. I saw a mother and four children admitted that day, destitute, cast out upon the streets! Once I had reported these scenes to our members, we women passed a resolution upon the subject, now become formal policy.'

'Very, um...'

'Impressive? From the register at St James's, I learned that your Jesse Cloud arrived a foundling, a frail infant, at this same workhouse. Upon leaving, the youngster came honourably to recover your stolen purse, having escaped all temptations to criminality.'

'Well, I don't know about th—'

'Whereupon a course of action occurred to me, which shall embrace our Association's aim to instruct and improve the deserving poor, d'you see, for Jesse is ambitious.'

'Does not education encourage false hopes, Mrs Lambton?'

'In what way?'

'May it not be a form of cruelty to enable people born into pauperdom to entertain thoughts of rising in society?'

Oddly, Mrs Lambton sighs, clasping her hands. 'Young Mr Daniell, it is our civic duty to assist the less fortunate. The cruelty consists in denying others hope! Hence, I believe my role should be to facilitate Jesse's progress toward literacy.'

'You will give Cloud *lessons*?'

An eyebrow raised. 'Do you not regard Jesse as your prentice?'

'*In part*, Mrs Lambton, yes. An unsought responsibility, I confess.'

'And the other part?'

'Well, to attend upon me.'

'Your servant, then.'

A bright-eyed blackbird listening, head inclined to what stirs underground. The dangling forelock sways at an even greater angle. Altogether disconcerting.

'Young Mr Daniell, success in almost any profession requires greater competence in reading and writing than is afforded by any workhouse. I wish to enhance Jesse's capabilities while fostering interest and enjoyment, by reading and discussing appropriate works. And Young Mr Daniell, now that my position is set forth, may we agree the matter? I am persuaded your Jesse Cloud needs and would desire tuition. To offer a few hours weekly is one means open to me of supporting a Bluecoat Child without leaving your uncle's side.'

'Well...'

'Not leaving his side, d'ye see.' She straightens. 'Good! Let me refresh your cup. Should Thomas have wakened, we may go in with him awhile. Often he sleeps until late.'

Not my intention. This taking-on a prentice catches like brambles.

*

Mr Daniell is bein strange bout a surprise for me. Most surprises I have had wasn't nice. *Don't know what you mean, sir*, says I. 'That's why it is a surprise,' he says. Stands there wiv this wet paintbrush in hand, big green smudge acrost his cheek, beamin. He ain't hidin his other hand. *Is this surprise a paintbrush, Mr Daniell?* 'No, of course not,' says he, starin at the brush, 'I am using it.' I looks about. *Is it in this room, then, sir?* 'No!' He is laughin. 'Jesse, you are to call upon Mrs Lambton.'

That ain't much of a surprise. More like a errand.

Mrs Lambton sits in her kitchen, fiddlin wiv them curls. I

speck once they was a great attraction, or leastways she wished em so.

'It is more homely here, for a pleasant exchange. Use the stool, Jesse.'

'Fank you.'

'I suppose you were given lessons at St James's?'

'Yes, Miss.' (Naught said of surprises.)

'Did you enjoy them? That is, did you like learning in class?'

'No, Miss.'

'Why was that?'

(Should 've said yes.) 'We used to get in trouble, Miss.'

'You pupils did not behave yourselves?'

Shallow little questions, what can lead quick into deep waters.

'Sometimes we was put in trouble for bein wrong, Miss. All different ages. Them little ones couldn't make head nor tail o lessons most times. Nor some bigger ones, neither.'

'Did you behave yourself, Jesse?'

'Got bored a lot, Miss.' (Should 've said yes.)

'Well, I grew up with books, and was taught to read them. I offer to teach you. Would you like to begin again with reading?'

'Yes, I would, Miss. But how might I fare? I'd only get more fings wrong.'

'Opportunity is Error's best companion.'

'Don't follow, Miss.'

'Our mistakes may prove instructive. My dear child, do not trouble yourself with it.'

I ain't troubled. I am restless, bein so essited. *Would you like to begin again?* I hope this surprise is true, she to be my teacher, an me the learner. Proper readin! What I do now is more like guess-work. Mrs Lambton ain't arksed of my hopes for art, my drawins of wildflowers an bones. But I can be a artiss prentice besides. I might read stories, an not have sacks to make, though cannot yet be sure.

Back to Cleveland Street. Straightway his nibbs is off to a

pitchers-show. He ain't long gone afore there is a big ruckus in the entry below, boots heavy upon the stairs, an fearsome sounds like devils come furious callin.

FOUR

Two great blows upon the door.

'Daniell! ... William Daniell!'

I am trapped, fox-in-hole.

'William-Daniell-William-Daniell-William-Daniell!'

Workouse men, wantin the Master bout me? This door ain't studded oak. They could soon smash it. Has Mrs Lambton told upon me? Bluecoats ain't never free. If caught, you can get farmed-out to any willin to pay, no questions arksed. Belly-worms wriggles me sick at them foughts.

'William Daniell!'

Two men what boot the door, cursin an makin theirselfs wild, whiles I shiver agin it. What if the neighbours come out to this racket? Not knowin, they might give me away; let on that William Daniell lives here, an his prentice within.

Fills me wiv dread. My hands is clumsy, turnin the key to go stand tremblin afore the men.

It brings em to laugh. One leans on his stave; the other shoulders his.

Yes?

'We want William Daniell.'

Who?

'Listen, fleabite, don't play games. Go fetch Mr Daniell. It is a matter to settle.'

He don't live here, sir.

'What?'

Not here, nor hereabouts, far as I knows. Now, I must—

'Wait, wait lad. Don't you go off like that. Who does live here?'

Mrs Wilby—but don't come in. The shock might do for er.

'Fetch her, then.'

I turns away, callin out: *Do not fret, Ma'am. These men means no harm. They will soon be gone!* I turns to face em. *She is all shrunk into erself, poor soul. Just lost er husband. But if it is Justice or somefink, I'll wheel her to the door. Might take awhiles to get her off of the soil-seat into her special chair, y'see, an—*

'Look, is your Mistress a relative of William Daniell? Does she know him?'

Sir, Mrs Wilby ain't long for this world. Sometimes she don't know me.

The ox of a man lifts his head high, like to bellow. The other turns back to the stairs.

'Be careful when walkin abroad, son. Liars can easy suffer mishaps.'

I slams-to the door, sinkin back agin it. Over, for now. They ain't workouse men; they want his nibbs, not me.

*

With care, straighten-up. Release the eyeglass into my palm, blink some clarity into these strained eyes, and again peruse *A Lincolnshire Sluice-Gate, Following Dawn.*

Succession of dawns, in truth. Winds over the estuary propelled stage-scenery clouds low across the sky, soon darkening it. An easterly off the sea would bring mist to veil the mooring-lines, or else make silver waves amid meadow-grass. Upon the Monday, seafowl wandered the water's margins and mud-channels; by Thursday, ripples lapped the towpath, mud-channels submerged, all wading birds gone.

My fens-sketches and notes do not admit change. Hours spent by the water's edge have brought me to one moment, a single point, and no prospect of compromise. Yet any person familiar with that country would know its magical guises.

Nevertheless, the scene's muted tones appeal: a dulled, distant sea, heavy clouds, the sluice's ironwork, crumbling wood-rot. There's truth in it.

Rub my flaking scalp. Yawn. Stretch once more. Back-ache, not stiffness.

I shall complete.

*

Jesse in the doorway: 'Warm today, Mr Daniell. Will you want your light shoes?'

Richard's message is curt: *Covent Garden Crumpton's Rooms top floor late afternoon, should you wish.* For generations of theatre-people, Crumpton's bare wooden spaces have been the humble nursery of each glittering new Spectacular. I know that Richard desperately seeks better medical attention. Can he be so soon removed from Dymchurch?

Our glorious programme once occupied all creative thought: art with social purpose, a tour depicting lives and customs along Britain's remote coasts! Richard was newly graduated and ambitious, following his marriage to Ruth. Now I, at forty years of age, have hopes of full membership of the Royal Academy, whereas my younger colleague scribbles his impressions of each stage of our travels—falling behind, even with that task. Having confused the catalogue numbers, calls me an insufferable prig for pointing it out!

Our present differences over finance occasion some sourness, yet Richard remains a friend. Sole friend, in fact. An author, a respected critic who knows the worth of one's time. His scrawled note suggests offhandedness, but he is no agency trickster, out to rob innocents.

For this particular innocent has been robbed already.

Unease renders burnishing and etching impossible. A mere instance of carelessness, one wild superficial scrape, would set me back days. Thus am I prised, winkled, engineered from my work.

By Covent Garden, Jesse tugs my sleeve, near drags me from the thoroughfare to crates stacked by a wall.

'Look, sir, over ere!'

'What?'

My prentice sudden wary. 'D'you see, sir?'

'See?'

He peers past my shoulder as I ponder greenery. Ridiculous stratagem.

'Someone you would avoid?'

'Yes sir.' Still as deer before flight.

'And now?'

'They're passin.'

Cannot resist glancing upward: two men, heavy-built, he with the red cap swaggering through the crowd.

'Then let us proceed.' Workhouse clearing men? Jesse must dread them.

Propped gainst the New Orleans Cotton Warehouse, Crumpton's Rehearsal Rooms: three knock-kneed storeys.

Jesse Cloud's light footsteps upon the stairs raise the question: should this youth be, well, *present*? My prentice must gain experience, but to what end? Foolishly not discussed. And Jesse Cloud is not law-bound. His master wished merely to show gratitude, being unused to responsibility.

Pause before the top flight, having attempted the staircase with undue relish. Gulping by this smudged glass, feign fascination with St Paul's Church stonework.

Young Jesse waits.

Phantom odours inhabit the top floor in sorry circulation: old varnish, new whitewash, tallow, liniment, mouse-piss, tobacco, human sweat. Clamber the final steps to the door.

Within, one leg outstretched over a footstool, Richard Ayton reads a manuscript. Motes about him drift in bars of light. His walking-stick kept close. A shabby coat across his shoulders in defiance of the season.

'William, is it?'

'Yes.'

'One moment. Must change this.'

'Of course.' My author-colleague, deep engaged in writing. Or, um, re-writing. As Richard lifts another page, some indisposition cramps his fingers.

Jesse and I gaze upon the awkward set of that leg.

My hesitant advance: 'Ayton, old fellow, w—'

An arm flings out. *Sssh!* Bite the smile. Richard's manner may reflect a playwright's testiness ahead of performance. Late emendations. Yet might he not appreciate his colleague's thoughtful observations? Perplexing.

The quill scratches. Jesse glances toward me, eyebrows raised. Now Richard wipes and pockets the pen, puffs his cheeks, waves the manuscript dry, and with the stick gets to his feet.

'William, my apologies. You bring your servant?' He grins. 'Are you now gentry?'

'My prentice-boy, Jesse.' They nod greetings. 'He learns with me.'

'Benefits both. I was re-working an interlude entertainment. Twenty delightful minutes of *hiss-boo, lawks-a-mercy,* and *ooh-I-say!*'

Jesse chuckles, looks to me, resumes solemnity.

'At Covent Garden?'

'Four days hence.' Richard gathers his materials, wincing as he turns. 'I hope you have a thirst, William. The Barleymow beckons.'

'Jesse, Mr Ayton and I have important matters to discuss. I wish you to call upon Mrs Lambton for instruction, um, if convenient. And here are, oh, several pence. Fetch a pie. But *buy* it, lad. All for you.'

*

I ain't got long for readin lessons. They don't sell pies all night. Fresh-dried laundry piled upon the chair, an though a warm evenin, I must make a fire for the flatiron. I doubt his nibbs will be home to see it. He ain't settled in hisself. Mr Hayton wiv the bad leg is a toper, given half a chance. You can smell it about him.

At his nibbs's uncle's, Mrs Lambton is glad I did come. She shows me into her study.

'Tell me, Jesse, do you read and write?'

'Not heavy, Miss. To write much words on a page takes a lot.'

'But you write your name?'

'Yes Miss.'

'Some cannot.'

'No Miss. Some just writes theirselfs wiv a cross.'

'Do you have favourite tales? Stories you choose to read, time and again?'

It is a test, I sees that. Her beak up in the air.

'For example, is *The Hare and the Tortoise* a story you would seek out?'

She don't understand. 'Miss, I ain't got a book to go back to, see.'

'No, I suppose not. Well, has someone read you the story of the race? It is a fable, Jesse. A moral tale. The tortoise wins.'

'The tortoise!' I can tell from her face this ain't goin well.

'Then passages will have been read you from the King James version, yes?'

'Yes Miss.' She likes this answer. I have got one right.

'Well, there we are. The Israelites' journey to the Promised Land?'

'I ain't sure bout that one.'

'They were displaced from Egypt...' She is waitin. So am I.

'The Israelites, you see, had to leave. Were told to leave. But they knew an ancient story—'

'Oh!' The Bible is a fick old book an hard to rember. Tip of my tongue.

'Yes? You snap your fingers, Jesse.'

'Oh! Did they go by sea, Mrs Lambton?' I got a glimmer then.

'Do you mean the Red Sea?'

'This ol man Noah took all the animals aboard a ark.'

'Well, the Bible records a great flood.'

'They did come in twos, Miss.'

'Yes...'

'They was all at sea, an Noah let this bird go over the water. It dint come back.'

'Signifying?'

What does she mean? I ain't goin to pass her test.

'Jesse, the bird did not return. What did Noah learn from the fact?'

'That they was lost?'

*

Ayton can walk no farther than The Barleymow. With my arms half-outstretched, watch him struggle into the window-seat, the grimace when angling his foot neath the historically impractical, carved table. Our unstated hope is to savour a good meal together for the first time since, well, for a long time; to consume quantities of beer in merry company, and without rancour to enjoy this warm evening.

'Your prentice is scrawny. A meat pie won't detain that one long.'

'He does have laundry to press.'

'Ah. You permit use of a key?'

'Richard, since when were you a stickler for rules and permissions?'

Our converse less a bubbling stream of refreshment than a trickle of wearing challenges, forever dribbling away into an unproductive nettle-patch.

'Tell me, William, you are *sure* of this Jesse, are you?'

'He recovered my stolen purse in the Haymarket. Why should I not be sure?'

'No great reason. Judging books by covers, you know.' Richard smiles to himself. Foxes me. Irritating.

Ours is a fragile peace. When I insist upon buying the meal, Ayton deems it pity. Demands to pay for the refreshment.

'How does your sister fare across the ocean, William? Do you still write each other?'

It is at least an attempt.

'The last from Mary was two months ago. Think I replied. None of your mocking, Richard! At any rate, she continues to make a go of it with Aunt Amelia. The old lady now requires much care, it seems.'

'But Mary is wife and mother also, is she not? Drink up, there's a good man.'

'Doing my best. She mentions her children. Seldom the husband.'

'Not a good sign.'

'No?'

Richard looks at me strangely. 'At times you amaze me, William. Let us have another jug, though I fear you must fetch and carry.'

When I return past the loud tables, so little space between, Richard is slumped vagrant-like, wildness in his eyes: agony, or the medication for it. The kitchen-boy who brings the meal watches him warily, sliding the platters across.

'You seemed well occupied at Crumpton's, Richard.'

'Bless you, but we both know those scripts are bilge— wadding between Acts, and little profit in them. A plot carried by laughing-gas, I ask you! This is beef, is it?'

The faint urinary air about us issues neither from the inn's upholstery nor its musty curtains, but from my friend's unseasonal coat.

'And how is Ruth?'

'Ruth? Distressed.'

(What, I wounded him?) 'Richard, I did not mean to—'

'Without saying so, distressed for my failing health. Distressed that we may no longer walk together, that I mope in the kitchen, that I scold our children, that entertainments and journalism must support us now literature cannot, that we need remove to London. All true.'

'Oh.'

'Guilty as charged, Your Honour.' Shuts tight his eyes. Some grip of pain.

'Well, um, what do the physicians advise for your recovery?'

'*Phys*—?' Richard draws back, staring hard at me. 'William, please try to understand. Advice from physicians wrecked my recovery!'

At this, look about me sharply.

He lowers his voice: 'One of those butchers believes amputation may be needed.'

'Good God!'

'What about that, eh? From a fall! I've not told Ruth. Not mentioned it, you appreciate.'

Ayton peers across, chin slightly raised, eyes wide and unblinking, searching me out. Similar rough-shaven faces, of condemned criminals or Bedlam lunatics, stare from the broadsheets. I study my beer-pot, unable to meet his gaze.

Another polished carriage passes the window at a trot.

'Richard, I am most sorry.' Ought not say *shocked*, or even *ashamed*.

'Do not lash yourself, William; the storm threw me backward, not you.'

'But your medical man's opinion seems extreme. May not others judge differently?' (Again, that Newgate stare.) 'Oh! I see. London fees, is it? Perhaps I should fetch another round, if that's, um, you know...' He waves me onward.

Beyond Richard's shoulder a half-moon hangs above the roof-tops, an arc of pale ochre through the dust-haze, scimitar's edge upon lilac.

Cross to the bar and its foul brume of pipe-smoke. No point in calling for a bar-tender at this hour, the place is a crush. Two more beers for Mr Ayton's slate.

The lilac would need blanking-out in places.

Add a couple of large rum chasers to my own bill for the meal, and here we come, safe portage to table assured! We toast Good Health, Fellowship and All Success to Ourselves, Friends and Family; next come Heroic Enterprises, unspecified; Good Riddance to Bony on Saint Helena; and, without enthusiasm, Here's to Our New King. These important duties observed, the rum is gone. Now might the topic of finance, our dark freight moored in some outer harbour, be more reliably brought ashore.

An old fellow nearby, stroking the whippet at his feet, seems to attend without listening, to remark without looking, as I tell Richard that a provincial Lady, having seen work from our tours, now desires to purchase East Anglian views.

Ayton slumps with injured leg outstretched. Waggling a finger, insists he shall neither embark upon further coastal voyages, nor ride in country bone-shakers hauled by nags; that more journeying would break the terms of our agreement. Money aside, time is short, d'you see. Oh yes, for it seems but one of us has studied the contract!

'Richard, I—'

'Let me speak! How often have you said that your role is to create etchings, aquatints, your *works*, while my function is merely to *come up with some text*?'

'Well, yes, in a way.'

He taps the table-top with his forefinger. 'I have heard this. This you may not know.'

'Moulton and Clyne have—'

Ayton thumps the table with his fist, jumping the cutlery. 'Hear me out, man!'

The whippet scrambles to its feet. Customers glance across. Confronted by such vehemence, I cede the ground.

Richard resumes in less alarming tones. 'My dear friend, gallery-owners tell me that the commentaries largely sell the illustrations, not vice-versa. The public will have forgotten Defoe's tour of the country a hundred years ago.'

'No views in those days. All text.'

'Exactly. It is our concept of original writing with original artwork, and—'

'Coastal locations, Richard, exclusively.'

'Indeed. The written text of our volumes, *rich impressions, modes of life* and so forth, appreciation without self-congratulation, balance of detail with generality—my dear fellow, don't you see? To fulfil the promise of our manifesto, language must be as fully engaged!'

Ayton has gone too far this time. Quite unacceptable. 'Richard, you are not well.'

'Oh, don't start…'

'Not well! Laudanum, is it? And in your cups, for that matter. I worry for you. But let me say, it is my series of views, not your neat comments so carefully balanced between blessing and damnation, which buyers first peruse. My artworks speak for themselves. They do not *illustrate* your writing!'

Upon the instant I get to my feet the room travels sideways a distance, and when I try to follow, reverts to where it was and I am not. But the meeting is yet to end. Ayton's hand grips my cuff, no strength in him, no weight to it. A condemned man's staring, watery eyes.

'William, we have worked together ten years. I shall write what you wish. Yet remember: I am the listed author of these volumes. Wherever your artwork goes, my writing is the…' He swallows some difficulty in his throat, '…reference point. Good God, man, can't you see? Ruth and the children shall soon need that income!'

His hand is let fall. Eyes closing, he rests against the blackened window-ledge.

'Listen, Richard, it pains me to see you like this. Let me arrange safe carriage. Where do you lodge?'

Turns his head, opens one eye, points upstairs. 'Thanks all the same.'

His quiet, suffering smile I shall not forget.

*

Stumble homeward. On a whim, head for Little Compton Street to ask for La Parisienne. *Regrettably, sir, she is occupied.* They bring wine. While twisting the glass stem to and fro between finger and thumb, try to fix the swimming colours of tasselled damask, their arrangement in the musky hangings. An aromatic swath of mint silk passes by, and a black coat, cane and gloves. Vaporous grey-blue layers gather above something in a dish upon the unoccupied table opposite. Subdued murmuring, brief laughter, half-heard in the half-dark. Watch the swinging movement of a woman's ankle as she dangles her shoe by the toe.

And drink on. All know I shall wait.

FIVE

Briefly startled: another within my apartment.

'Is work begun, Mr Daniell?'

'Not quite. What are you doing? Oh, those.'

Jesse stands before the portrait over the hearth-place. 'Family, sir?'

'Yes, my father in uniform. Less tall than I remember him, but I was a child then. You see the round table beside? A hint of it there, look—the polished surface. The artist darkened the tone.'

'Was it in your house, Mr Daniell, that your father got painted? Not aboard ship?'

'Our house. Dark oak, y'see—'

'So the table wouldn't stand out too much?'

More questions.

'Yes. The artist replaced our wallpaper with background wash. My mother was most displeased! I recall my father posing at ease in the corner of our drawing-room: a true Naval Officer on deck in a moderate sea, though beside a card table.'

Jesse Cloud grins, looking from the portrait to me and back again. 'Very smart, sir, ain't he?'

'Father took less care day-to-day. Wore big boots in the fields, striding out with his knobbled stick and faithful spaniel. To call the dog he'd place his fingers gainst the teeth—like this—and make the most piercing whistle. Juno was quite deaf, in fact. Not wandering far, simply watched for Father's gestures. Mary and I covered our ears!'

'I never learnt that whistle.'

'Nor I. But Father would set the hens off, I can tell you.'

'And these littler pitchers: your mother, sir, that right?'

'The cameo and silhouette, yes.'

'Sorry, Mr Daniell, I don't, I can't quite—'

'Oh! Of course, yes. A cameo is a small portrait in a brooch or necklace. It is personal—some precious reminder kept aside, perhaps upon a dressing-table. The solid black shape is a silhouette. Foreign term: French.' (The defeated French. Still brings a smile.) 'Less fashionable now. A silhouette is a solid outline, usually of a person's head and shoulders, as with my mother's. Observe the sharpness.'

'Painted first?'

'A background contrast. Chinese White.'

'Does it look like her?'

'Oh yes, her shadow.'

My prentice-boy draws back. *Shadow* suggests the insubstantial. Have not Jesse's parents ever been shadows?

'I can produce a silhouette of you tonight, Jesse—your own outline. What say you?'

Looking away, Jesse dips his head. Shutters down again. Baffling.

'Ooh!' He rushes to the stone mantle. 'Did you paint that one of your mother when you was a boy, Mr Daniell? Oh *sir*, the green an blue inside of that bark—wasn't you *good*?'

*

Almost dawn. Gather my gown tightly, pull the night-cap down over my ears.

Early morning light is more congenial to detail than a mellow or fading afternoon, however rich in colour. For sometimes it is the promise of colour. Fresh encouragement today, those first bars of sunrise. Sketches and line-drawings stacked along the wall; letter from the Scenic Hall safe in my jerkin pocket.

Often I print by night: rows of flickering tapers, dripping and smoky, set beside the dark form of my press. Its solid six-inch timbers are strengthened with cast iron and clamped; the great press-wheel a mechanism to lower city gates; within its maw, two solid panels as level and unsullied as ever met together.

Peer into its shadows. Sniff the works.

I love this press, its surfaces. Five men were needed to lug the thing upstairs. Told them: *No dismantling, it is my instrument of torture.* Theirs, too. Before the machinery arrived, craftsmen laboured three days to strengthen the floor.

In due course, the pressing.

Remove the cloth from my work. Airs of exhausted acid-on-metal rise, a haze of wax and resin following. Here the gleaming reverse outline of the Lincolnshire sluice-gate, bare thus far of lichen; the ironwork yet unenriched with time-worn craters; the pale tones still to become bronze sky; the distant, Lear-like oak awaiting final ruination.

Hour upon hour, for days, to reach the critical moment: a single sheet impressed upon a polished eighteen-inch plate. The smoked metal drypointed and scored, scraped burnished and washed, the resin crunched to a fine ground and heated; the copper several times bitten in acid, its tones ready for printing. A soaked sheet of heavy paper positioned under covers, held fast for my turning the great wheel evenly, evenly, urging the paper through. Throw back the covers and with tenderness remove the print unblemished. A pearl eased from its shell.

Well, it awaits. At present I have income likely from a Lady of Taste, and perhaps from others. Prospective funds have not afforded good sleep.

Turn to the rack: the burin in its rightful place, to hand. Only resin required.

'Good-day, Mr Daniell. Begun early, sir?'

'Ah, Jesse. I need supplies. Come this way. Something to show you.'

*

When Mr Daniell bids me come see somefink, who knows what he might mean? We are by ourselfs, it is yet darker than light, an I rember that first man. Tuppence for you, says the man, two sound pence if you will do tricks. But the only one tricked was me, an later dog-sick in the street. I went back cryin under the bridge; looked at my bone treasures in the pouch left me years afore. So far, I been safer hid here than in huts an holes. I must stay hid.

Be at ease, Jesse, says he, though little chance when it's me what fetches an carries. I am to be his artiss prentice. Like a job, but not paid. Still to be his Man an keep doin the cleanin. He looks pleased wiv hisself bout this, an likewise I hopes to fare well. I was afeared he might let me go, finkin he had sheltered me awhiles, and so done enough. He ain't that sort, just itchin to go at his works. Calls his paintins works. He will learn me proper art when he can. This might be when somefink comes to him, but is more better than naught.

So I stands beside him wivout much candles lit in the small hours, for learnin. His nibbs wants but to show me a box wiv sand in it called resin. I am to fetch more resin for his works. I don't fink Mr Daniell sees how slow I goes to im for the shillins.

Take naught for granted. They never mentioned that one in workouse lessons. You learned it for yourself. If someone grabbed your bread at mealtime, you got beat-up should you blab. All of us in blue was told to listen bein the main fing. We was many, and they did much tellin. But Mr Daniell don't listen close, or talks crossed-purpose, so I must work out his need.

I have now met his nibbs's friend, Mr Hayton, workin on a play to make people smile wiv a bad ankle an inky fingers. Others so far is his Uncle Thomas the old man painter, an Mrs Lambton what writes stories. Mr William Daniell don't seem to know normal people.

I dreads to tell him two men wiv staves did come knockin.

*

One half of a meat pie spooned with gravy lies fresh in my belly, the remainder jugged until Jesse's return with resin and sugar for the next pressing.

No excursion to Camden fields today: I would persuade Richard to tour those remote eastern shores with me. The leg-wound distresses him. He is prickly about his duty to Ruth and the family, about his writing, and lack of income. He mocks my taking-on a prentice-boy! Hence, a companionable talking-together may reassure him about the costs: my rational calm deployed to ease relations between us. Pocket the encouraging letter from Moulton and Clyne, tie and conceal my purse, and set-off. Hard lessons learned.

Step aside from a passing coal-cart.

Avoid the sailor's stumps and chalked placard, BATTEL OF NILE.

Crumpton's sagging timbers slope into view above the parasols, heads, hats and collars in Covent Garden. Three pell-mell children, lissom as deer, leap wide to pass me. By the cotton warehouse, men struggle to unload another great roll. And adjoining, the Rehearsal Rooms' unblessed odours. Kneeling seamstresses upon the topmost floor glance up, pins bristling in their mouths. Richard Ayton? They shrug. Not here. The troupe may be at the playhouse. Dress rehearsal?

Hasten downstairs, across to the theatre. Doors locked. At the rear, actors rehearse by the wooden steps. One folds her arms when I approach.

'Mr Ayton is gone home to family, sir. You are a friend, perhaps? Taken worse.'

'Most sorry news. Um, when was this?'

She looks to her colleague. 'An hour past?'

'No more. Heading to Blackfriars, I believe: the carriage station.'

'Then I thank you both.'

'You are welcome.' Her hands open wide to the skies, as if to confirm rain. '*Oh Ernesto, long have I yearned for you in my maidenly dreams!*'

*

His nibbs is likely gone off to see Mr Hayton's show, but did not say. I seen Morris Men wiv sticks, an street Mummers, but never a play in-doors. I speck Mr Daniell wants to tell of the gallery's good news—a pitcher sold, might be. *Thus*, sent to Mrs Lambton for more learnin. She will have spoke wiv him of her plan, so I ain't in trouble for comin here.

Miss don't mention how bad I did in that last test. Must have forgot, an I'll not say. I knows to watch my step. Today we have got The Country Mouse an the City Mouse.

'The story ends thus, Jesse:

> *Your living is splendid and gay, to be sure,*
> *But the dread of disturbance you ever endure;*
> *I taste true delight in contentment and ease,*
> *And I feast on fat bacon and charming grey peas.'*

When readin, Mrs Lambton's hands go up-down like to a march. Where did she get that from? She calls it a story, but sounds like a poem. It rembers me how I have lived much wiv dread of disturbance, whiles lackin the feasts.

'When the mouse returns from visiting her city cousin, what does she?'

'She stays how she is, not takin to his ways.'

'Yes. And *she* is?'

'The Country Mouse... Miss, is this a test?'

'But why remain? Better food in the city, after all.'

'Because of the cat.'

'Good. You read with understanding. What does she eat in the country?'

'Fat bacon an grey peas, like afore. Grey peas is very dry, Miss. The same food, but the mouse likes it more now.'

'So, what is the meaning or moral of this fable, as we call it?' (Mrs Lambton plays the games she can win.)

'Eat up or else?'

'Or otherwise, *Make the most*. And what might we call writing of this sort, Jesse?'

'Childish, Miss.'

'Perhaps. The story is slight.'

'At the workouse a-Sunday, we got read poems after dinner. This mouse story is wrote like a poem, ain't it, Mrs Lambton?'

'Yes. Rhyming verse.'

'Like a poem, cept you can follow it. In the city there is much to hide from, Miss. Many folks wiv empty bellies, what steals by night, like that little mouse.'

'Sadly, yes. Is that what caused you to hide?'

Smilin, she waits. I smiles back. I ain't to be fished out like that.

'The city can be frightening, Jesse, so from what were you hiding?'

'You don't always know, Miss, do you?'

Mrs Lambton sighs, fidgetin. Straightway brings in full stops.

Young homeless is judged toys for sale. In that tunnel where I once hid, they did come wiv a lantern, searchin. I lay face-down in the mud whiles it shone about. Their voices bouncin off of the walls brought me to shit myself. Later, I washed in the freezin river. Shivered all night on the bankside neaf some steps. You don't never forget.

Mrs Lambton searches me out also. I fink she has spied me straight off for what I am, waitin like that cat. Should she turn me in from righteousness, I loses all I suffered for. Worser to be took back to the workouse, now I seen what good livin can be. I swear I won't be took.

Yet I would have Mrs Lambton keep learnin me. She is raggy that I ain't been answerin straight, so for full stops I makes out I knows even less than I do: ain't sure what them dots is, don't see they comes every four lines, unawares of countin one-two-free after stoppin. That way she can judge how I learns the readin. Then she comes out wiv a new bit so quick I scarce gets hold of it: *A full stop marks the end of one thought and the beginning of another.*

I have wrote that down.

*

There's the man himself! Amid the mail-coaches at the Old Kent Road staging-post.

'Ayton!'

Horses raise and plunge their heads in billows of drifting dust. Thudding, heavy hoofs pound the gravel as carriages cross and pass. Journeyers and well-wishers stride forward, or pause and look about, clasping children tightly by the hand.

To my alarm, a four-wheeled horse-and-trap springs lively from the throng toward me. At the reins in grey livery stands the red-cap fellow whom Jesse spied at Covent Garden. His colleague behind him faces a manacled prisoner. Their concern is neither the crowd nor workhouse business. Marshalsea prison men, with a debtor. Chills my heart. Turn aside.

Ayton again, about to board a carriage heaped with belongings, ready to depart.

(Run, man, run.) 'I say, Ayton! Richard!'

The fellow is in difficulty. His foot drags horribly, wrapped thick in bloodied cloth. He seems unable to hold the stick firmly to take his weight, each slow step an achievement.

'Richard, here you are at last! Chased across a half of London to find you, I...'

The look in his eye dismays me. That provisional smile, agony in his face.

'William, this is timely. Would you be so kind as to help me up the step?'

'Yes, of course, I—'

'A solid push needed, I fear.'

One space remains in the cramped compartment. Baleful occupants eye his arrival. They have seen Ayton's wrapped foot. Perhaps they envisage the journey, six hours to the coast, and the consequences should this man's seeping wound worsen. Someone tries to create a space marginally greater for, or from, this last passenger. Their aversion would be my own.

As he half-tumbles to the bench, Richard's cry of pain becomes unconvincing satisfaction: 'Aargh-aah, there we are!'

Wince, bite the lip.

'I have left the show, William. Cannot go on like this. I told em all.'

'You return to Dymchurch?'

Ayton nods. Cheeriness performed, both hands clenching, unclenching, clenching upon the brass of his stick. 'Rejoin my wife and family in our cottage. What could be better?'

Again, the fateful look in his eye. And he turns away, turns away!

'Richard, please keep with our British tour. Moulton and Clyne tell us—'

Ayton mimics reverence for the names, dangles an imaginary kerchief with flamboyance, while eyeing his unsmiling fellow-travellers.

'They tell us an offer comes!' Breath short from my exertion. 'A purchaser of coastal scenes. And Commentary, no doubt.'

Ayton's eyes close momentarily, his brow tightening. 'Oh, no doubt.' And as his face relaxes: 'Apologies, William. That was graceless.'

Loud call from above. 'Ready up here! Prepare to be off, one-and-all!'

Fresh, mutual regard between us in these moments: a deeper exchange of meaning.

'Richard, I have this, um, advance payment. Our client is in earnest, a lady of means. We may rely upon her. Take it, take it.' Three guineas of mine thrust into his palm.

Slow in closing his fist, he looks up, his unshaven face pale and weary. 'I shall complete the Commentary for you, William. Do come visit us in Dymchurch.'

Small gestures of irritation among the passengers. Pursed lips.

'Before we remove. Visit us!'

A rap of doom upon the roof. Carriage door shut tight, the boy clambers again to the high board. I stand back, attempting jauntiness. Whip-crack. The mail-coach lurches forward. Raise a hand, *Farewell, farewell*. Grim smile from my old friend. He leans over the stick to look down, adjusting the position of his leg.

*

The Frenchwoman *does not encourage visitors today,* according to Madame. *Women's matters, sir, as I am sure you understand.*

'Oh, yes. I see. Most unfortunate.'

I own to lacking confidence in that respect. Aunt Amelia, having taken Mary into her care after Mother's death, I believe gave my sister instruction while I was to occupy myself with fence repairs. I suppose a married fellow would acquire sufficient understanding, where needed. My life so far has followed a more solitary path.

However, La Parisienne *may be willing to reach some accommodation* with me this evening, at half the standard fee.

So it proves. Having witnessed my absolute need at, um, first hand, the Frenchwoman's delicate touch and close personal attention contrive highly effective means of accommodation. No activity required as she leans forward. Merely observe the curve of her back, caress the shift loosened to her hip.

Now we lie calm and settled, La Parisienne part-clothed beside me. Faint draughts from the curtained window, shadows flowing and receding across the subdued outlines of our flesh. The lamp's fumes drift upon the air, mingling with a lemon scent. Yet the staleness of old carpeting and hangings, of decaying plaster, and something from this worn bedcover, haunt the place.

La Parisienne smooths lengths of her dark hair. Though she smiles, conveys distress. How to capture that inner contradiction?

'Thank you, sir, for your consideration.'

'In what way, consideration?'

For long moments, the Frenchwoman regards me with seriousness.

'I ought not speak of it, sir. We have house-rules. Yet some men show no restraint, forcing themselves upon us even at these times.'

La Parisienne releases the lock of hair. Nods her head. Some private truth.

SIX

'Take care. This acid bath eats metal. Think of your skin. I use wooden tongs.'

Jesse nods, sleeves pushed back along thin wrists, peering forward as in the Haymarket. For that day's self-indulgence, I am become responsible for a prentice's welfare.

'By the way, Jesse. The two men from whom we, um, sheltered are debt collectors, not workhouse clearance men. They do not seek you.'

'Yes sir. Fank you.'

'You are not relieved?'

'Oh yes, sir. Much.'

'Good. Now lad, watch what happens, but do not approach close. You are ready?'

'Yes sir.'

Concentration. Quiet.

'There, completely covered. What do you see?'

'Might be bubblin.'

'Now let us count twenty.'

Jesse frowns. '... Free, four, five...'

'It is time for the water, Jesse. Jesse, the water!'

'Oh! Oh yes, sorry sir.'

'Good. Pour there... And perhaps... Good. Now, one wipes clean—entirely clean, with vigorous wipes. And again. Just so. Now, what d'you remark about the base of our etched gatepost?'

'Oh, well, there's... It's hard to find the words, sir.'

Look to window, to ceiling, back again. 'I see changes in the metal. Do you?'

'Like patches, Mr Daniell?'

'Yes! Good. Awaiting ink, but what sort of patches?'

'What *sort*?'

'Tell me what they are like.'

'Well, nibbled away sir, I would say myself.'

'Yes. Nibbled away. Why?'

'Because of the...' Jesse's eyes brighten, widen. 'Oh! Oh! The wax don't—the wax upon it hides the stuff, um the metal, the—' Fingers clicking.

'Copper, yes.'

'Hides the copper, sir, so them bits under ain't burnt. That right?'

'Indeed, bitten. The acid bites, as we say.' At this response, my prentice-boy stands taller. 'Now, what do you remark about the patches?'

Hard taskmaster! Jesse regards me with high seriousness, near reproof.

'Them crackly edges?' His fingers exercise themselves in illustration.

Have to grin, cannot prevent myself. 'When we stand back to observe the copper strip, what do we remark in our gatepost?'

'All roughed up, sir. Looks rotten. Old timber, that is. You can tell.'

*

Today I begun learnin the right way to do art. Mr William Daniell, what I am artiss prentice to an very proud, did tell me bout this sand called resin an I was to fetch some. Tastes horrible. You spread resin on a metal plate to keep acid out. Resin makes wood fings look rotten. *Thus* they calls it technique.

An we had food again. I got this belly-ache so ain't been hungry, but did eat what was given. All holy-holy in the workouse they would tell us: *Be forever grateful*, tho it was but gruel an we had to sit an pray whiles it went cold. I eats all he does give me, fearin he should stop or go broke. Mr Daniell is most clever in his work, but what sort o nitwit is it, beggin his pardon, what strives hard for cash, an even on the promise of it, starts spendin straight off? Where did he learn that?

Wanted for debt, but skips it in his head.

*

This May breeze cooler than anticipated as we near the end of Berners Street. With Jesse's help, *Scarborough from the Headland* and *Lincolnshire Sluice-Gate, Following Dawn* (back-to-back, boarded, tied, wrapped in cloth layers and re-tied) are borne forward. I have promised Moulton and Clyne delivery prompt this afternoon. For my finished works, left unframed, two ivory card mounts are cut.

Pause at the corner with Oxford Street. Peer twice each way, cautious fox sniffing at the brake's edge.

'Here upon our right, Jesse.'

The cash to Ayton was proper, entirely proper. Likewise, proper to undertake Jesse's maintenance for several weeks, or even longer, from gratitude. Doubtless proper also not to seek a loan from Uncle, who suffers enough. The outcome of this public propriety has been personal embarrassment. Unless a work is sold today, no further glass supplied on credit. It would be humiliating to make no sale once invited to submit. Do such failures reach the Academy's, um, ears?

The gallery's grand facade of Portland stone and high windows overlooks treacherous polished steps. I take the lead, crouched and cautious, raising high one end of the frames.

A liveried doorman advances. 'You have an appointment, sir?'

Once upon the top step: 'Yes. I am invited by the gallery's owners.'

'Invited to what, sir, if I may ask?'

'Well…'

'Just doin my job, sir, you understand.'

'I am William Daniell A.R.A., requested by Messrs Moulton and Clyne to bring some of my work here. A certain Lady has expressed an interest.'

The doorman smiles, nodding his head. Information provided matches information possessed within. Permission to proceed.

With chevronned cuff he waves us onward. *Through the double doors, sir, along to the office in the near corner, where you will find...*

The office door opens upon the knock: Ambrose Moulton, a smooth, dedicated professional with the manner of a funeral director. Rising more slowly from his office chair and the accounts books is Jeremiah Clyne, who occupies himself occasionally in rediscovering the gift of speech. Lastly, Douglas Cromarty, a little tufted grebe whose head has popped up from the waters of Agency in previous encounters. His presence increases life's complications. A sombre gathering: weak smiles by all at none in particular before resuming the guise of polite mournfulness, as befits all significant money-making.

Jesse Cloud and I exchange glances, his eyes widening to express—well, what? Excitement? Were Jesse a friend, at this point one might wink, show cheeriness. Instead, the slightest shake of my head forbids my prentice-boy's uttering a word. His presence goes unacknowledged. It is obvious what Jesse is.

My work unwrapped upon the table. Ambrose Moulton, unfolding a magnifying glass, bends to examine the etching's detail, the quality of fine print. He regrets *the apparent absence of a populace in Lincolnshire* to enliven my sluice-gate. His colleague Jeremiah measures both works, compares their titles and dates with what he has already, confirms the signatures, levels a little finger at the squiggle beneath W, and records the facts in a desk-book. Nods toward me, signifying authentication.

For each print, Cromarty praises the coloration and composition, use of perspective, my handling of light and shade, landscape features, flora and fauna, the appeal to potential buyers, possibilities for gallery display, location and viewing distance, the—

A look from Moulton quells him. (Whose agent is this?)

And, Good Gracious, Jesse is beneath the table to stow the board and wrappings out of sight! In the silence he reappears, child at a wake, peeking from beneath the cloth. Something about the line of that linen-fringed face?

A gentle tapping at a side door in the recess. Two young children, the smaller pushing the end of a plait into her mouth, are ushered into the room by their mother, with maidservant in close attendance.

Moulton clasps his hands. 'Aaah! Greetings, children. Greetings, madam! Gentlemen, today we are honoured to welcome Mrs van Brielle, worthy daughter of the celebrated artist, John Crome of Norwich.'

A considerable surprise, although plainly not to Moulton and Clyne. We have moved from mournful assessment and sober authentication, to a well-planned state of brisk relief from glumness, almost approaching good spirits.

At once the children spot Jesse Cloud, on hands and knees beneath the table. They try not to giggle. One seems about to bend down and perhaps even to join the game, though held fast by the maid's grip upon the broad ribbon about her waist.

In restrained desperation, I beckon forward my prentice. Cromarty grins as Jesse crawls out. The Lady, unperturbed, extends her wrist for Messrs Moulton and Clyne to bow before. She has the sweetest of smiles. Twenty-eight years, perhaps?

'Mr Cromarty, of course,' she says. 'Good day. And this must be...'

'Yes Madam, our artist, Mr William Daniell.'

My right fist closes tight. *Their* artist? Am I some sculpture? Struggle to hide my annoyance. Definitely *not* their artist. The audacity!

'Please allow me to introduce him, Mrs van Brielle.'

'Yes, why not?'

Was there a hint of irony in that delightful young woman's— and oh, those eyes! Blue-grey crystal clear on porcelain white. God, wh—

'Mrs van Brielle, Mr Daniell, an Associate of the Royal Academy.'

'So I understand. Though of provincial stock, one endeavours to stay well-informed.'

'Indeed, Madam.' Ambrose Moulton leans forward to an exposed pearl ear-stud, his voice like his eyes, lowered: 'This one may even attain full Academy status at some point, who knows?' And for public purposes: 'Madam, the artist whose exhibited works in our gallery you have admired!'

Mrs van Brielle walks ahead of Moulton's ushering palm. 'Good day, Mr Daniell. Such a pleasure to meet you. My dear father in Norfolk speaks highly of your work.'

'I too am most delightful—pleased—to be um, to meeting … Not forgetting also to give, or pass, greetings to Mr Crome.' A fiasco, mercifully of little consequence. She shakes my hand. Warm gratitude, not tepid greeting.

'The quality of your aquatints impresses me, Mr Daniell. Plainly they require dedication as well as talent.'

Ambrose Moulton, curator and provider and close by, gracious inclines his head.

Her attention is not swayed: 'My congratulations, Mr Daniell.'

'Thank you, madam.' Throat-clearing. 'Each work demands many hours.' At the room's end, Jesse Cloud nods in affirmation.

I keep hold of the Lady's hand. She withdraws it. Prolong the moment, take it back!

Cromarty's tufted head bobs up from the shallows: 'Naturally, madam, all those hours of dedicated time are reflected in the sale price.'

(Yes, whose Agent?)

Moulton winces. The feathered quill ceases to flutter in Clyne's claw.

Mrs van Brielle glances across her shoulder: 'Agata, perhaps the children would like to explore the secret garden?' The word *secret* sprinkles magic. Yes, they would. The maid leads them out to a rear exit. Audible struggles with a lock; more giggling shushed.

Watching the children depart, Mrs van Brielle and I find common reason to smile, a minor blessing. *Agata* is the Nursemaid, whereas *she* is English. Her husband is Dutch or Flemish or something. A Low Countries emigré? Aren't we still at war with them? On and off?

Now Mrs van Brielle regards me steadily. Upon her neck just below the ear, a delectable mole. 'Mr Daniell, your Coastal Tour is a pleasing idea: thematic unity, working lives, and the sense of a long quest of discovery. Each view unique, is it not? No other prints?'

'They are known as fine prints, yes, madam.' Left ear.

'*Fine prints.*' A little nod to herself, quite self-possessed.

Moulton interposes, certain that de Heer van Brielle would be pleased to acquire whichever works madam should happen—

'My husband runs a shipping company, Mr Moulton. I am your client.'

Hurrah for thus clipping his wings! Ambrose Moulton swims against the tide: the Lady of Taste knows her own mind, and her inclination does not extend to Scarborough.

'Madam van Brielle, most may discover little similarity between a bustling seaside township in the light of a golden sunset, and a broken sluice-gate rotting by a muddy creek under heavy cloud at daybreak; but Madam is a person of refinement who doubt- less appreciates how ill-judged would be such reservations. May the Director of a celebrated and long-established London gallery humbly suggest not a *matching* pair, but a *contrasting alignment* of tinted prints? In one's family home, such a pairing of achieved contrasts would grace the walls upon either side a chimney breast, perhaps?'

Madam looks downward, lips pursed. She is decided. Further comment unnecessary.

She wears a fine-linked silver chain. Mrs van Brielle's slender neck needs no grand adornment. I suspect Dutch Lutheran influ- ence upon her taste. Otherwise, the Lady may simply know what is fitting.

Cromarty swims by this elegant presence. With thumb upward, little finger extended downward, he indicates the fine quality of each etching. Displays his technical terms: use of the burin *here*, and again *here*, and the colouring as much textured in the glorious Scarborough sunset as in the Fenland clouds. And may he mention the complete *delicacy* with which features of the beach resort are rendered within the composition? Church spire *there*? The tiny flagpole with its brave Jack *there*? Coach and horses by the hostelry? All gainst the blue-grey of the sea, lit from the west?

They are magnificent features of the print, she concedes. Mrs van Brielle mentions also the raised surface of the ink lines. A characteristic of the process itself?

She looks my way!

'Oh yes. Yes. Yes indeed.' Stepping forward. And, and, stepping back.

Cromarty persists. 'I declare, these fine prints are not merely a *contrasting pair* of great charm, but also, even paradoxically, *matching* in levels of artistic technique. Madam may be willing to concur with me upon this point?'

'Well...'

'Yes indeed, Mrs van Brielle. I thought so. And—'

A pencil clatters to the floor from Jeremiah Clyne's desk. Now in Cromarty's direct view as he bends to pick it up, Clyne's head swivels owl-like, eyes wide behind his spectacles, full gaze, hostile and unblinking.

Cromarty, startled, ruffles the tuft above his brow. 'Madam, I believe these good gentlemen may be persuaded to offer a reduced fee for the prints as a pair, should you so wish.'

Smiling, Moulton consults Clyne at his desk; Clyne returns his gaze. The thought had not occurred to them. Each ponders it. Moulton rubs his chin. With eyebrows raised, Clyne twiddles the pencil between his fingers. Some adjustment possible? Yes, after all, why not?

No! This is not wanted—not what *she* wants! I have had no part in it, as artist. The artist merely, um, hasn't! They are wrong so to belittle her.

My prentice at the far table shakes his head. Jesse misses these subtleties; not his role. The artist alone must intervene upon the lady's behalf, offer an arm, suggest alternatives.

However, uncertain quite what to say.

Mrs van Brielle advances amid us, at an angle before me: 'Thank you for these contributions, gentlemen.'

Tender, the pale nape of her neck in the divide of hair, above that glittering chain.

'You are considerate in giving of your time. Now, plainly I am not alone in admiring Mr Daniell's work.' (Turns her shoulder, a graceful inclination of the head toward me.) 'I confirm my wish to purchase the Lincolnshire scene. I find it expressive also of landscapes in the Low Countries, familiar to my husband and to me.'

Murmurs of gratitude, especially behind her right shoulder.

'However, you have no firm price as yet.' She looks toward Jeremiah Clyne, his visage a perfect inexpressive blank. 'I know that artworks vary in size, scope and medium. One may not be comparing like with like, although exhibition catalogues and published volumes of the British tour provide some guidance.' The gentlemen nod their heads: *Reasonable, reasonable.* 'This Fenland print is unexhibited. However, on the basis of earlier works—the Aberdeen Quayside, Lindisfarne, and also Blyth—I offer eight guineas, with three for any Commentary.'

Nine, Moulton is willing to grant. Clyne regrets that ten may be needed. Cromarty thinks eleven. Mrs van Brielle smiles. 'Gentlemen, I do not haggle: nine guineas plus three settles it.' Sideways glances. Brief pause. Nodding heads concede. 'Excellent! Perhaps Mr Cromarty, as my agent,' a slight emphasis there, 'shall fetch me your invoice by Monday, let us say? Thank you.'

No hands shaken. No need of confirmation.

To conceal my childish smirking, briefly contemplate boots and carpet, observe the hem of her skirts swirling to rest. A deep ultramarine, purple undertones. And anyway, silk.

She smiles toward me. Does she know the effect?

'Thank you, Mr Daniell.'

'No, I thank you, Mrs van Brielle, I—'

'Do take my card. I need merely sign it.' She reaches over for Clyne's retrieved pencil, scribbles something, and passes me the calling-card. 'Now I must return to my children and Agata, poor girl!' The pencil replaced upon Clyne's desk, farewells to left, to right, and gone.

Grinning, Jesse Cloud approaches with the boards and wrappings under one arm. 'Fought I'd keep these, Mr Daniell. We might need em again.'

*

I takes care not to say too much wiv Mrs Lambton—well-meanin, but watches me like a surgeon what can saw your fingers off for your own good. She says, are you happy to read, Jesse? *Yes Miss, course Miss.* Then let us begin with something from the news-paper. All friendly. When she says let us begin, she means me. I'm to begin. People say one fing, meanin another. This I have met afore. My big sister Amy, all white in the bed-box aside of me, was sudden took away. When I was old enough to speak of her, I ever got the same reply: *You never had no sister.* Said simple, for bein believed. Yet not true. We are kin.

In the news-paper, a green parrokeet flies out the winder where kept an not found for nine weeks till it does come back from whence it did start off from. There is some reasonin to this tale what Mrs Lambton talks of: how to be sure it is your bird when there is much parrokeets kept in homes, but I gets fogged. It pleases her I can read most words, sayin If you wish to know something, Jesse, be not afraid to ask.

Then she sits back all straight wiv her little black shoes wigglin like she's got small creechers in there. Her eye comes up afore she says, Jesse, you learn from Mr Daniell. What sort of works does your Master produce? It is a test. *Prints, Miss?*

Wrong, but I ain't told to stand a hour upon a stool or in a corner like for school. She means ackertints or some name said like that, an when I arks Mrs Lambton how is ackertints wrote she says it is not wrote, Jesse, but writ-ten. So not much use me arksin.

SEVEN

Decorated lettering, van Brielle's card between my finger and thumb:

THE NEW HORIZONS PACKET COMPANY.
Harwich-Helvoetsluys est.1801.
Great Hall, Ardleigh, Colchester, Essex.
Greetings
Willem van Brielle.

Across it, in pencil: *Please write via Mrs Crossman at 8 Maddox St, nxt. Dickenson's Drawing Gallery. Ellen v. B.*

She is sincere. Otherwise, why pass across the calling-card at all?

Allow her message to be what it seems. No assignation or indiscretion implied. Mrs van Brielle, Ellen, intends what she writes. The card signed in full view. Her business-like request for a response follows our meeting.

Response to what?

Assume the husband to be author, other factors omitted. Thus, Willem van Brielle, who owns a mail-packet service out of Harwich, leaves his visiting-card while far from home, desiring the artist to write to her lodgings, um, his.

Quite.

My own image in the glass is somewhat ragged—at best Bohemian. Not wealthy; older than the Lady; perhaps her husband's senior; and this itchy scalp resembles a worn cricket ball.

In that light, absurd even to contemplate a reply betraying bold enthusiasm. Possibly misconstrued? Hence, to put much in writing seems presumptuous, offensive.

Refrain from communication, therefore.

Refrain? Such gross bad manners toward a Lady of Taste who purchases one's work! Also, unlikely to secure further offers. It would displease Messrs Moulton and Clyne. Their fashionable gallery is much prized for exhibitions.

In view of these arguments, one must reply to Mrs v. B.'s unassuming request. Her delicate beauty, self-possession and grace, her eyes of such a clear, searching blue-grey, her slender neck of ivory-white beneath the gathered hair, the necklace glittering, and her judgement sound despite all these feminine qualities—such things matter not a whit. For business reasons, an answer must be made, out of *respect*!

*

'I found a bread roll, sir.'

'Good!'

'Fresh. Back o the market.'

'Yes, well... Here, take half. You deserve it. Have you been running?'

Jesse grins.

The bread tastes wonderful, newly-baked and pulled apart, still with a hint of warmth from the oven—as good as any I have eaten.

'Just to say, sir, better if you takes your time over it. Chew it around a bit, since we ain't ad vittles for awhiles.'

My downy-cheeked prentice demonstrates the method, chewing happily before me.

Ungracious to question how this bread was come by.

And plain rashness to have handed three guineas to Richard Ayton, however pure my intent. Two guineas might have sufficed.

One would have shown sympathy. I carried the cash in perverse defiance, because my purse had been stolen at the Haymarket. Is that not the truth? Fearing to appear parsimonious while possessing a sizeable sum upon my person, I gave it away!

Most shaming is the small change I retain—an inner pocket of half-pennies and farthings kept close for the deserving poor: grooms, messengers, country-girls selling goose-eggs. I little used to consider the fact. Today, instead of expending those last few pence to purchase provisions for ourselves, I have avoided mention.

Pointless to pretend ignorance of my hungry young prentice's actions upon leaving the building at that hour. It is but sly stepping-aside from responsibility.

What if Jesse had been caught?

*

A violet sky, the day darkening. My belly's hollowness is now become thorough frailty. Limbs, shoulders, neck: weakness, lassitude. Insufferable to envisage twelve more hours, hunched like a destitute, hands returning constantly to nurse the emptiness neath my belt, too off-beam to work. I have laboured months; ought not the mood of triumph, of just reward and joyousness, outlast one day? Summon fresh energy from excitement! Strike out along a different path!

There is much to celebrate. The sale of my *Sluice-Gate* shall enable several debts to be settled—um, reduced—once Moulton and Clyne have claimed their gallery-fee. They are well pleased. Ayton shall receive official payment for his Catalogue contribution. I am encouraged to continue the coastal tour. And Mrs van Brielle's, Ellen's, card has assisted Cupid's arrow to speed most surely to this fellow's unprotected heart.

The last woman I adored may have been the Reverend's daughter: Arabella? Abigail? Perfection at the pianoforte! Such spates of hapless devotion arrive unsought, sudden Nile floodings to hide all ugliness and begin some deeper renewal; whereas my wilful attempts to, um, invite greater intimacy have proved calamitous.

Appalling misunderstandings may occur in vicarage music-rooms.

Might light-headedness from hunger bring bad judgement? My selfish priorities deprive Jesse and me, yet we suffer neither malnourishment nor, God forbid, prolonged starvation. The fee for one's artwork shall be paid soon. Or in due course.

Hence this further visit to Little Compton Street is justifiable. Consolation. Some pretence of mannish devil-may-care, but consolation for such misery.

Gain admittance in the remaining natural light. Remove my petty coins from the inner pocket and hand them to Madame, every last one.

Insufficient, of course: her face contemptuous as she leads me from the company to the desk in the alcove serving as her office. She places the coins upon its polished walnut surface, spreading them with a sweep of her hand.

'What is this, sir?'

A temporary embarrassment, my explanation. Soon to be resolved. A Lady of Taste, currently residing in London with her family, has promised before witnesses to purchase a work of mine forthwith.

Madame little moved. 'Ladies of Taste notwithstanding, even so favoured a client as yourself, sir, must be aware that the sophisticated, skilled and altogether delightful company of a resident of this establishment ain't customarily granted for a matter of *pence*!'

Yet finally, as anticipated, Madame is persuaded to consider her client's faithful relationship with the establishment and with the resident in question; previous responsible conduct taken into account, alongside promised repayment within the week; plus a half-crown in consideration.

'You are fortunate, sir, to have caught me in a generous moment.'

Madame approaches more closely. 'Honour obliges me to explain the terms.' Along with the lavender scent, a whiff of something quite disgusting.

'Terms?'

'Namely, if the establishment makes a temporary reduction in fees on the client's behalf, it entails the resident-in-question's rent being regarded as unpaid by a corresponding amount. Costs must be absorbed, one way or another.'

'Madame, I regret that, um, I rather fail to—'

'If you cannot pay the bill for her services, the remainder we deduct from her rent.'

'You reduce her rent?'

She shakes her head. 'The resident pays rent in advance. We take what you owe us from the rent she has paid. Puts her in debt, y'see.'

'Oh.'

'Good! Finally, sir, residents who fail to pay rent outstanding for seven days or more, especially the long-term ones—in a word, older—put themselves in peril of dismissal. No shortage of girls becomin residents. This must be understood ... sir.'

'Yes.' Quite straightforward. Very plain. Acceptable arrangement.

One has a pressing need, the truth of it. The coins swift counted, noted, accepted, and put somewhere in Madame's attire. I am to linger in this smoky salon while she goes upstairs.

Shortly afterwards: 'La Parisienne awaits you, sir. Let me escort you to her boudoir.'

At first it seems I lack opportunity to appreciate detail, although of course there is time. Most unseemly, immediately the door closes, to fall upon the Frenchwoman in the grossest manner. The circumstance requires greetings, polite enquiries after well-being, remarks upon the changing seasons—just as at a social gathering near-neighbours might mention family events over sherry.

The aim is to facilitate an effective service in which the client feels at ease. Also, the resident may make polite enquiry to elicit a client's requirements, since needs change with circumstance or state of mind, while clients at times display particular, variant tastes. An element of improvisation called for. In the company of La Parisienne, one dare not mention one's hunger—for fear she should laugh.

My own needs may be limited in range, but the Frenchwoman soon discovers their specific nature. Hence this evening, while our polite conversation sustains itself passably at one level, a series of subtle and less subtle activities takes place at another.

Despite etiquette, despite the half-light theatrics in which the resident is discovered *en déshabille* playing Patience—despite everything, I seem to lack time. Difficult to utter witless remarks about the history of intaglio, to gaze with apparent fascination upon shadows rippling the ceiling's surface, while a social acquaintance encourages with her hand the engorgement of my reddened member, and soon, with light delicate touches, brings her lips to its gross emergence as if to the brow of a new-born child. Difficult to show consideration for the unexplained bruises revealed on this woman's ribs and left breast when time presses, when in my urgency all that matters is to expose that triangle of hair, part her thighs, and enter the depths of her practised, welcoming embrace.

The oil lamp upon the dresser hisses, stutters, flickers, before resuming. When the whole desperate engagement is over with, soon over with, all grows calm: a restorative stillness beyond my pounding lungs. La Parisienne has helped banish something forest-wild and dark, though it belongs with me, and will return. The roundness of her calf is cool and smooth upon my thigh as we lie together. Her hand moves in the warm yellow light, generous along my upper arm and down again to the elbow: a mother's soothing nursery rhyme.

In this warm, close sanctuary, hints of lemon balm or citron rise from whatever scent she has applied to her neck. The henna dye in her hair ceases near the roots. Her handsome face is lined more deeply than I remember.

Lacking nourishment, unpractised in energetic pursuits, I cannot ease my racing heart. Hunger mines the goodness from my very marrow, bringing faintness upon me. Sweat and semen, and liquid matter, whatever it may be, lie cool upon my skin. It appears that nothing out of the ordinary occurred just now. La Parisienne duly smiled encouragement. The 'O' of her mouth as usual indicated surprise. She rose above me, arched her back in most accommodating fashion; her customary, absorbed solitude as she gripped my shoulders. Nothing out of the ordinary neath the fluttering shadow-play upon the ceiling.

Now her lips touch my neck: lightest of gestures. I have found a desperate peace in this Frenchwoman's company, a fleeting forgetfulness of hunger. She is yet to learn of the rent she owes.

*

His nibbs has sold a pitcher to Mrs Veebee, he calls her. But a pitcher ain't sold til the cash comes, an we got little in our bellies. He ain't a man of the streets. Now we are up the creek worser than whence we did come from. *Whence...* Mrs Lambton says that. Fink that's how you use them words.

This day I am trusted to take a letter to Mrs van Brielle in a big house wiv high winders an tall chimbleys in Maddox Street. Mr Daniell says she lodges in rooms, which means stayin there like a inn, cept the entry where you wait don't smell like the inns I knows. A maid takes the message.

'It is for Mrs Veebee, Miss, by hand.'

'Yes,' she says, 'by my hand.'

Wiv that she shoos me back down the steps.

Mr Daniell is fretful, arksin what reply, but there ain't no reply since her sort don't come to the door theirselfs. Mrs Veebee is pretty an quite young, but a married mother up-country, an rich besides, so naught to be gained there. His nibbs is all a cluck-cluck fussin, though he won't have wrote her what he was doin in Little Compton Street last night.

*

The window bay overlooks Cleveland Street, warmed by a May morning's sun. Pleasant to observe the tree's pattern of branches, to remark how it briefly speckles passers-by in its gently-shifting shade. At the dog-cart, the dairyman pours a full measure, a rich creamy frothing, into a family's jug. Even from this height, I can feel how much cooler is the china to the child's touch as she bears it homeward.

Have to turn away. All would be gladsome if coins were in my purse, if I might stand awhile in one spot without fear of sinking.

Jesse Cloud is forbidden from going out alone. Given my own recent conduct, to adopt a high moral stance concerning a bread roll may seem perverse. Yet one's sense of responsibility for the young prentice grows with the passing days. Theft remains a crime. For the moral stance, better late than never.

Jesse, ever more pallid, sits on the wooden footstool by the door, hands clasped about knees, in an attitude of patient lack of expectation. We shall eat once the sale of my *Lincolnshire Sluice-Gate* is confirmed and the fee paid. Soon paid. Also, Ellen may reply as to her purpose. Causes for optimism.

'Are you to attend a class today with Mrs Lambton?'

'I was forbidden, sir.'

Context changes all. 'Jesse, to lack shillings and pence is an embarrassment to me. Years ago, Uncle Thomas proved generous to my dear mother and to our family. Later, he granted me this apartment. One hesitates to seek further favours. With that in mind, I mention in strict confidence that I have encouraged him to believe my standing as artist grows substantially—which is broadly the case, if little rewarded. My elderly uncle suffers poor health. It would cause needless hurt were I to, if I should ever, um, disabuse him of that impression.'

Jesse crosses to me. 'Sir, ain't you well?'

'Perhaps just sit awhile.' Allow myself to topple into the armchair, hands flopping upon the worn fabric. At once dismiss the image of Ayton's collapse within the mail-coach.

The prentice clicks his tongue. 'That's how it gets you.'

'But Mrs Lambton's lesson, Jesse: were I to go with you, Uncle might be told the good news about the client's offer, and—'

'—about Mrs Veebee?'

'—about the *sale*. And, um, during our visit perhaps refreshment might be offered us, as natural hospitality, without our having to—'

'Ask for it?'

'—confess a brief shortage of funds and I will thank you to let me finish my sentence!'

Head lowered, the youth mumbles something.

'What was that?'

Jesse looks up, eyes bright. 'I said you need a full stop for that, sir.'

Audacity? Presuming a role above his station? Mrs Lambton's unwelcome seditious influence already evident. Scowl, though Jesse's attention has turned to the casement.

'Jesse, have you strength to seek a lesson today, however difficult to study when hungry? We need merely turn the corner into Fitzroy. Should go the distance. I trust the Lady to make this purchase; less confident of the gallery's transferring my payment with equal promptness. And there we are. What do you think?'

'What do you want me to do, sir?'

'Go to your lesson. But remember, when with Mrs Lambton: *confidentiality*.'

The prentice frowns.

'It means keep it under your hat, Jesse. Under your hat.'

'Well, I fought to put a few biscuits there, sir.'

He returns the footstool to the wall. Jesse does not seem to have intended humour. Those little remarks: coincidence, that it?

EIGHT

Mrs Lambton opens the street-doors herself to my knock. 'Oh, Young Mr Daniell, you are welcome, indeed! Such good fortune you are come to visit. Your uncle has been most poorly.'

In disregard of her years, the widow's soft black shoes skip and ease themselves up the flights of steps. Halfway, I pause for breath. Plunge onward with Jesse close after.

'I have witnessed how fast the elderly may fade,' Mrs Lambton says over her shoulder. 'Poorly, at sixty-three! Please come in, both.'

The faint breeze entering Uncle Thomas's apartment fails to dispel the mustiness of old clothing left in cup-boards; of long-hanging drapes; of used air and yesterday's vegetables; and mingled sweetness from bedside tinctures, syrup, and ruby laudanum. By his doorway we pause, listening with up-turned faces to the troubled breathing.

Mrs Lambton's sharp nose approaches my cheek in unwelcome proximity. She does not blink. The curled tip of her bootblack hair sways at the corner of my jaw.

'Your uncle wishes to speak with you, Young Mr Daniell. His strength fails.'

'I had not fully understood.'

'On occasion, signs of delirium.'

'Mm...'

'None can know the future, but Thomas has asked for you. It is fortunate you bring Jesse today.'

'Yes.' (Fortunate?)

'Doctor Phillips is aware.'

'Thank you, Mrs Lambton. Most helpful.'

Her demeanour assumes at once a more public aspect. 'Then I shall leave you with him. Come, Jesse.'

This is not how it was meant to be.

The widow's chair is beside the bed, close to the pillow. Fetch another and sit awhile, grateful to be off my feet, waiting for Uncle to move; waiting also to find in myself some self-assurance. The room's furnishings and walls swirl slightly. All my speech-words gone.

Hard to recognise in this old man the bold fellow who took me at ten years of age upon our venture across the seas to India. *Signs of delirium.* Has opium always been supplied to this house? How much laudanum does Uncle Thomas consume? Who determines the dosage? Possibly not Doctor Phillips.

Reach forward. Dab Uncle's perspiring brow, his crooked fingers, those bloodless nails. Lay my hand upon his, not knowing what else to do.

'That you, boy?'

'Yes, Uncle.'

'We are alone?'

'Yes.'

'Something to tell ye.'

The furring in Uncle's throat has come to resemble a low growl. Brief gasps as he attempts to move his position.

'No. Stay there, William. This will pass.'

Each time Uncle's struggle for breath begins, my hand more tightly grips his liverish flesh. Faint with hunger, nausea and fearfulness all together, I need fixity.

The tumbling in Thomas's throat exacts some scouring effect, his mouth gaping. 'Phillips says it cannot be long.'

In the quiet, study the deep-scored flesh of Uncle's face. Thomas has lived peacefully in comfort in later years. He was not born to labour from boyhood behind a plough, yet a fibrous, blue-black vein pulses unevenly over his left brow. Force of will remains, little more.

'Sit me higher, will you?'

On my feet again, unsteadiness flooding me. Rearrange bolster and cushions, plump and tug about, until Uncle Thomas seems more at ease.

'Any water there?'

His gravelly murmuring and glance upward show gratitude as I return to my chair.

Uncle's chin is down upon his chest. From there, pins me with his low, direct gaze. 'Phillips is right. Must ready myself. Lying here like this brings back what happened—long ago, but want you to know.'

A confession? Press my hands together, trying for priestly calm.

'Your mother, now...'

Oh God.

'At nineteen, Clara was a fine young woman to behold: sensible and modest. Prettiest smile I ever saw. We both wanted her, John and I. Other suitors, too, though Clara's family was not wealthy. But I proposed the first.'

It is gulping speech.

'She would have chosen me, William, would have been mine, but all came to naught. Her family thought my brother the steadier man. Promising naval career, and the elder one inherits, whereas I *dabbled* in art, was *prey to enthusiasm*. At the last my dear Clara became persuaded, also.'

'Well, follies of youth.'

'Wait. More to be said. Loved your mother with all my heart. Simply knew, have always believed, that she was sincere for her part. Our parents would not commend one son before another; Clara's family preferred John. Scarce a matter of the passions, they thought, but best interests, common-sense.'

'Uncle Thomas, I do not wish to con—'

'Not their love, though, was it? It was ours to keep!'

'Uncle, you speak of forty years past! I have no need to know.'

'Oh, it is for my sake, William. My sake, doubtless.'

His good hand flails about for something.

'Your kerchief, is it? Do not over-reach yourself.'

(Sudden giddiness.)

'Thank you. Something wrong, William?'

'No-no. Stumbled gainst your bedside table.'

Uncle wipes both rheumy eyes, dabs his nose.

'We did not dispute, William. I was very, what's the word, *sporting* about it. And we all maintained the pretence. Attended the wedding; no sulking; kissed the bride; waved them off upon their journey. Guests in-the-know were impressed by my maturity. But I was quite broken. Afterwards, found it impossible to remain at home. Rode alone about the country, looking for subjects to paint. I would become an artist, y'see—confirm the flaw they all suspected! None troubled what might befall me. Journeyed far and wide.'

'A rambling artist, even then!'

'Akin to self-pity. High upon some hilltop, yet hiding. When my circumstance became unbearable, I removed to London. Sold water-colours here and there in small galleries.'

'Did my mother, um, meet you?'

A brief smile. 'During John's last voyage, Clara came to me in London. Unaccompanied, consider that! But please understand, she would not visit my lodging. Insisted we meet in some public place. Arm-in-arm along Oxford Street, New Bond Street, Hanover Square! So proud, no matter the route, this strolling to me was wonderful. She still loved me, William; told me so.'

My own Mother! Bile rising. I am no priest at shriving-time.

'I wanted us to recall our first walks-out together, until Clara explained. Went to a coffee-house—doll's-house cups, all very dainty. When I reached for her hand, she withdrew it. Knew then,

I think. No plan besides the here-and-now! It was my selfishness.'

His weariness shows: head lowered, eyes closing, furred breath.

'Uncle... Uncle, what did my mother say?'

'Told you: that she loved me. Always would love me. But her duty was to John and the family. Your Aunt Amelia stayed at the house with you children. Remember that, William? Well, there we are. Ever close, those two. Amelia would have known. I was the fool in all this, willing to disgrace myself and my family, to make a cuckold of my brother while he was abroad serving the King!'

A slight shake of the head; helpless appeal in Uncle's look, drifting away.

*

How to respond to what Uncle tells me? This false man first betrayed the family's trust, and now has poisoned the well of my childhood memories. No shame of mine, yet it sullies me.

The thought worsens my own empty-bellied nausea. Bend forward, attempting not to swoon. The pattern of the Mughal rug swells, then shrinks, before my eyes.

A groan somewhere.

Clearly now, from close by, the old man's wretched sobbing.

'Your mother was a good woman, William,'

Plainly, that was the difficulty. The meeting in London must have exposed Thomas's appalling misjudgement. What followed? Once more obliterated.

'Weeks later, heard from the family. Y'know: *Regret, your brother's estate...* I was required to—' Uncle no longer in control of his speech. A great sigh brings silence for a while. 'George Morris, legal man, to execute the will. She did not wish...'

Uncle Thomas lies back for long periods, head to one side, eyes closed.

Reach forward once, twice. Touch that blotched skin.

A slight half-flinching movement. Life refuses to quit him, or he it.

I cannot stay. No more possible to censure one so ill than to contain these roiling passions. But even as I steady myself half-upright, Uncle begins to speak.

Sink upon the chair.

'Loved my brother, you understand. Wretchedness to be taken young that way. The family needed me then, oh yes! *Could you do this, do that? What is the Navy's response? Won't she get an Admiralty pension?* They challenged me: *You have written, have ye not? Cannot afford a Maid—not now! How will Clara live, Thomas? How live?*

His liquid speech again, contemptuous: 'A Maid!'

Hints of other actions: 'But also my chance. Had the money, the means. And she did not de—'

Something or other, unclear. Mumbling into the pillow. She did not demand? Decide? Demur? The laudanum's bedevilment.

'Clara, I understand to wait. In due course, yes.'

Conversing with my mother thirty years ago, as if she were here in the room! Chills my blood.

'Promise you, dearest, never the Navy for William. And the girl still too frail for travel, I agree.'

My mother's hand in his. Little Mary's delighted shriek from the kitchen-garden: *Another butterfly!* Was I there? Is this a memory of mine?

The mounting clamour of hour-bells across London rouses him. Bewildered, Uncle raises his good forearm high with fingers outstretched, as if drowning.

His gaze falls upon me, becoming aware.

'Meant no harm, William. Believe me, loved Clara with all my heart. She promised to join me in her own time. But no time allowed. Hoh, she died, and I was not there! Not there!'

Those last wailing words fierce with exhaustion. By degrees Uncle's fingers close, his arm withdrawing beneath the white bed-linen into fathomless slumber.

*

I can tell Mrs Lambton ain't keen to learn me today, just pleased I am here upon her daughter's chair. The hoppits is kept, an that big curl acrost her eye, but in herself Mrs Lambton ain't the same, bein long in the chops. Her eyes is red, not skewerin.

'Jesse,' she says, all proper wiv knobbly hands, 'Today I have little of use to your instruction, but shall hear you read.'

I likes listenin to people what read, showin the meanin by how they says it, an doin the voices. She is the one wiv her beak in books, not me. She can't want to hear me stumble about in words not seen afore. I speck she is troubled, now the old man might die. Mrs Lambton an his nibbs's uncle ain't a couple in name, but in fact. Names and labels don't mean a lot. That daughter she speaks of, long gone, is hers by whatever name.

'Miss, don't you mean to do readin today?'

'Well of course! Why should I not?' She looks away. 'Now, Jesse, what may we find for you?' Mrs Lambton opens a book from the stack by her elbow.

'Let this suffice: the journal of John Wesley, a holy man. In girlhood I heard him preach. He toured the country to speak from the heart, as your Master journeys to paint.'

(Did she have that curl a-dangle in them days?)

'This entry, Jesse. It is no test. Merely read it aloud.' She leans her chin upon one hand.

I can but try.

'March 1788, Bristol. On Thursday to hear my address upon Slavery, the house, from end to end, was filled with high and low, rich and poor. I preached on that ancient somefink-or-other, God shall enlarge Japhet. And He shall dwell in the tents of Shem. And some-one-or-other shall be his servant.'

That don't promise to draw crowds, if you arks me.

'*About the middle of the dic—dics—discourse, a* somefink *noise arose, none could tell why, and shot through the whole con—greg— whole congregation. You might have imagined it was a city taken by storm. The people rushed upon each other. The benches were broke in pieces. In about six minutes the storm ceased. All being calm, I went on.*'

Mrs Lambton don't dig wiv more questions. All bein calm, I goes on.

'*We set Friday apart as a day of fasting and prayer, that God would remember those poor outcasts of men, and make a way for them to escape, and break their chains in sunder.*'

Outcasts might mean slaves. Sunder I speck is in Africa.

'Miss, there is big words in Mr Wesley's book, but also big fings what he tells people... Miss?'

She looks up. 'I apologise, Jesse.' Wipes a finger acrost the corner of an eye.

'You ain't got to pologise to me, Miss.' Her jaw is gone wobbly. 'Don't I?'

She is deep. I have learned two readin fings: entries is in books as well as buildins, an readin when people is up-set gets you more biscuits.

*

A boy with his little sister, playing skittles in the yard, scratching alphabets upon slates in the nursery room—what might we ever have gleaned of love-rivalry from before we were born? Father was Master of his own house, Uncle Thomas an occasional visitor, though seemingly ever welcome. I saw no sign of strife between the brothers. Had there been looks exchanged at table, subdued remarks to my mother, hurried whisperings in corridors, they were beyond my comprehension.

I recall there were silences—winter evenings, especially. Long silences, in fact. Mother would take up her sewing by candle-light. Father stood in that characteristic manner by the hearth, coals glowing at his back. I would paint uniforms on clothes-peg soldiers and sailors, or sketch the dog while it slept, or turn the pages of some illustrated volume from the shelves—but in any event, venture nothing which might disturb the quiet, and thus remind my parents that I was not yet abed.

Thomas was the beloved uncle whose impromptu tales inspired Mary and me; who once caused my little sister to laugh so much that she fell off the roll of an armchair. He it was who repaired yo-yos and dolls' furniture; who could write backwards swiftly and accurately upon steamed-up windows; whose watercolour brushes jiggled above his top pocket like a moorhen's nestlings peering out at the world. Yet when my father attained the rank of First Lieutenant, Uncle Thomas, the promising young artist, was not invited to portray his brother for our dining-room; the work given to a journeyman instead. That decision carries more meaning now.

Just before my ninth birthday, Mother told us that our father was to join the frigate Amphion, bound for Bermuda—a source of great pride and honour. The parting was especially grave. Mary curtsied, offering Father her posy of wildflowers. How lightly his hand touched her cheek, how simple the gesture, and the love in it! When proudly I saluted him, he responded with due solemnity. I presented Father with my painting of HMS Amphion in full sail. A Lieutenant with a spy-glass stood alone upon the deck. I had taken a long time over it.

In the weeks following, Mary and I kept the promise to remember Father in our prayers. Sometimes Mother would remind us of his portrait, the look of him, there upon the wall. The dog pined; the hens were less raucous; no gunshots in the woods; no rabbits hanging by the scullery door.

Our uncle scarce visited.

I remember Mother's going to London while Father was at sea, and the strangeness of being cared-for by Aunt Amelia. Mary and I were fond of her, so greatly impressed by our drawings, ever available, hopeless at games. The next day Mother returned, gathering her skirts to step from the carriage, hand upon bonnet in the breeze. When Mary and I rushed from the doorway ahead of Aunt Amelia, we saw from Mother's wet cheeks how much she had missed us. Such unguardedness was not her custom. In her fierce embrace that day, I felt proud to be a son so loved.

Still no Uncle Thomas. My sister and I ceased to expect him.

When a naval Commander and six sailors brought Father's body home from Portsmouth, without forethought I sprang to attention and saluted as I had done upon his leaving. Little Mary clutched my other hand as the casket passed. It seems the sight of us caused both maids and the few neighbours present to become tearful. I had thought the loss of a much-respected Naval Officer was affecting them deeply, but no.

The funeral swift followed. Upon the day, Aunt Amelia explained that those attending Father's final homecoming had been moved by my solemn salute alongside Mary's innocence. I was flattered and surprised. *So shall I do it again?*

Aunt thought not. Possibly some loss of spontaneity. No mention that respect for Father fell short of affection. Without fully understanding, I followed her advice.

'And what is that brown frock-coat man doing here?'

Mary and I witnessed Mother listen to Lawyer Morris's guidance. She had little time to join our games because the papers upon the table needed untying, poring-over and talking-about with Mr Morris, before being tied together again with black ribbon. We remarked Mother's pallor, how she would gaze at Father's picture, would scarce eat, how differently she sang to us at bedtimes, and sat so rigidly in Church. Only Uncle Thomas's visits lifted our spirits, seeming to admit fun and laughter again. There was business to conduct, but whenever he took a seat indoors, Mary went to sit upon his lap.

Now those memories, so fresh despite the years, appear false—less than the truth.

In dismay my sister and I beheld our strong, capable mother become downcast, long engaged in earnest talk with Aunt Amelia. They would emerge together sighing, and then smile. *Pretending, aren't they?* Mary once whispered.

It was arranged: with Uncle Thomas my guardian, I would venture upon the high seas to the land of the Hindoos. An artistic education abroad would benefit me, Mother said. Yet Mary and I belonged together, spent all our time together! I valued what she brought to my attention or found amusing. Sought to protect her, so small for her age. Neither of us imagined how long this separation would last.

When the day came for Uncle and I to depart, Mother seemed broken. By the doorway, she kissed me, smoothed a hand along my cheek, instructed me to be a good boy, and to write home. She folded Mary in her arms, reconciled to my leaving. Yet we all wept.

Never saw her again.

Weeks later, the hot bright colours of Bombay stunned me. Uncle sold his sprawling watercolours to people who occupied palaces and fortresses. To pass the hours of journeying across that great country, he told beguiling stories in ways that my father, solitary hunter in the fields, had never done.

June 1820

NINE

8 Maddox Street, London
1st June.

Dear Mr Daniell,

Having admired those works of yours which thus far I have chanced to peruse, it was gratifying to make your acquaintance at the Scenic Hall.

I am pleased to confirm that today I have authorised twelve guineas payment to Messrs Moulton and Clyne, regarding their invoice for the Lincolnshire aquatint and its accompanying commentary. Delivery of the work is anticipated this afternoon. My husband shall convey it upon departing for Ardleigh. Thus, your clouded sky, your sullen mud channel and water-sodden landscape shall adorn our home in future!
My second reason for writing to you concerns a matter quite separate from Gallery business. I am contemplating the possibility of further investment in your work. Should you agree, I envisage your continuing the Voyage of Great Britain into eastern counties, so as to portray the similarities between English coastal scenes familiar to me from childhood, and my husband's native country.
In brief:
1. To produce three aquatinted fine prints, from sixteen to eighteen inches in length by eleven to fourteen high, to include a Suffolk port, the Essex port of Harwich, and a river, estuary or waterside of your choosing.
2. The task to commence this summer; each work to be finished and mounted, before framing to specification within the twelvemonth.
3. Further prints not to be sold elsewhere.

4. The gross fee offered is £39 (non-negotiable), including all expenses, payable in three instalments viz. £12 upon commencement, £12 at November's end, subject to a Review of Progress, and £15 upon successful completion (31st July, 1821).

I do not know your present engagements or commitments, but must attend to matters in London for a further three days. Therefore, a prompt reply to the above address, indicating your general response and putting forth any questions you may have, would be much appreciated.

Mr Daniell, in offering you my best wishes for continuing success,

I am
Yours sincerely,
Ellen van Brielle

Ellen's letter I have read, re-read, read again, considered for a while, picked up to ponder, and studied further, akin to an actor with some ambiguous play-script of Ayton's. She has *admired* my works. My acquaintance is *gratifying*. Mrs van Brielle, Ellen, feels thankful for the occasion when I held her hand. Mere chance, cruel fate almost, denies her opportunity to study more of me in detail—my works, um, in detail. One brief meeting and already two communications from the lady's genteel pen to her *Dear Mr Daniell*. Hold the sheet close. Perhaps a faint hint of perfumed aroma from her wrist? Hers would be discreet. Merely the first sentence, and yet such intimacy!

Ellen declares boldly that she shall remain in London while her husband departs into Essex. Not an invitation, exactly, but implying an encounter. Also, this splendid lady indulges in teasing banter: *your sullen*, what was it, *sullen... mud channel!* How perfectly coquettish, so soon in our acquaintance, and again raising the question: Does she know the effect she has? Upon me, that is. Set aside the Dutchman at present. Of course, paragraph three's innocent guise in fact admits *a matter quite separate from Gallery business*, opening wide the doors of possibility. The Lady of Taste has a subtle mind! Perilous.

The beginning of an 'affaire de coeur'? She may assume a man of mature years is more experienced in the conduct of, um, informal attachments than is the case.

Consider the letter's conclusion: Ellen, Lady of Taste, enquires of my *present engagements or commitments*, while confiding her own intention to stay alone in London for three days. And she seeks *a prompt reply*. Well! Titillating details, couched in commercial language. One reads of well-bred women, sadly neglected by their husbands (doubtless some of them Hollanders) who have commissioned artists to portray them, and after hours in the seclusion of private rooms have indulged them with far more than financial reward. May not the Lady's, Ellen's, closing words, *I am yours sincerely*, confide incipient passion?

Banish such thoughts! Try to recall my delicious dream earlier of whoever-it-was.

Stretch. Rise from my bed. Forty years old; balding; irritable scalp; short of breath; wrists that crack. Hardly Byronic. Ellen is a wealthy young married mother, showing no sign of, um, neglect. Caution needed, in order not to rise from the proverbial phoenix into its ashes. Plainly disastrous.

Shuffle bare-foot to the doorway. Call for Jesse and a ewer of water.

Without warning, the face from my recent night-fantasy acquires chilling identity. La Parisienne, and her rent!

Yes.

Mrs v. B.'s letter promises payment soon; but cash needed now.

*

'Aah! There you are, lad. What are you d——?'

Upon the lower landing my prentice-boy kneels rear-upward, sketching. Jesse stands in haste, head a little to one side, tossing back a length of hair.

'Mornin sir. Dint speck you quite this early. I did find stale bread at the market, and a clean shirt is ready for you today. I'll go——'

'What are you doing down there, out here?'

Jesse looks to the floor as I descend the first few steps. Some dead creature lying outstretched, black, smearing the boards.

'Dog sir. Likely felled by a carriage wheel. I brought it in to do a drawin. It don't smell yet. Reckon it's new took place, sir. Next the entry.'

The hind legs spread impossibly wide, meat after a butcher's first hack. One side of the animal's head is not how it should be, the teeth smiling thus. Gather the gown about me, peer over, aware of my exposed feet.

'Mmm. And why bring this mangled creature next our apartment? My apartment?'

'Like I said, sir, for drawin. More private.'

'Show me.'

'Beg pardon, sir?'

'Show me your sketch.'

'Well, it's——'

'Show it me, dammit!'

That was unfortunate. Strive for the calm, appreciative discussion of another's work which the Royal Academy often preaches, seldom achieves. The prentice regards me with a hunted look.

'Jesse, you are not in trouble. I wish you to pass me your drawing, that is all … Good Gracious! Come.'

Matters too important, too confidential, to be said in public—even upon the landing. Matters for the kitchen, where voices do not echo and dead dogs are never brought.

'Jesse, listen carefully. The lady whom I encountered at the gallery, the one to whom you delivered a note on my behalf, Mrs van Brielle—'

'Got two young-uns, sir, ain't she?'

'Yes. Yes, as it happens. She wishes to buy one of the prints we carried to the Scenic Hall.' Jesse nods. 'A fee is paid to the gallery's owners; ours shall arrive shortly. But most significantly, Jesse, Mrs v. B. offers to purchase three additional works from me.'

'Well, there's quite a few to choose from, sir.'

'New works, Jesse.'

'What, *more*?'

'Known as a commission.' Wait for the severity of one's tone to be fully assimilated. Prentices must learn. 'From time to time, artists of note are offered commissions—advance payments, you see, warranted income—to produce new works. Mrs van Brielle has made such an offer, which on this occasion I accept. She commissions three new aquatints of scenes in the eastern counties. It enables me to conduct the coastal tour's next stage... and in fact, to sustain myself.' Jesse frowns. 'Shortly, I shall write my reply, and your important task is its delivery to Mrs v. B. at her London lodging. Eight, Maddox Street. Is that clear?'

'Two steps up, an a fox door-knocker, sir.'

Sighing, scowl at the empty cookpot. Even as I half-turn, the prentice makes a slight movement. I catch the look of strain upon the youth's face—a wincing reaction, soon gone.

'Something wrong?'

'Oh no, sir.'

'Jesse, come now, I saw you clutch your midriff.'

'Gut-ache, sir.'

'Lack of food. You look most pale. I promise we shall eat a good meal this evening. I shall have cash by then. I shall, Jesse.'

'Yes, Mr Daniell. Fank you.'

Have I given offence? In my state of personal undress, how may another's confidence be won? Tighten the gown. 'Jesse, it is good news. And I thought, well, that you might be pleased also.'

'Oh, good news about the food, sir, and the fee, no doubt. Hoh yes.'

'Then...'

Nothing. Jesse stands unmoving.

Look down to the floor. Jesse's disappointment is not about the dog. Perhaps we should have gone to the front window, to stand in the bars of warm morning sunlight? More cheerful there. Jesse frets, unwilling or unable to explain. The kitchen too enclosed? Cannot seem to strike the right—

My prentice sniffs. Wipes a hand across his nose. No tears; not quite. 'See, Mr Daniell, I fought it was my luck to save your purse. I saw ow it might appen, an it did. An you was good enough to take me on, where another might have tipped thruppence or somefink an sent me away, though I would've took it right enough. See, an you bein a artiss an all, I hoped, I just...'

'Jesse, I did not wish to distress you.'

'An Mrs Lambton doin all the readin wiv me, I was happy, sir. I was. But now you're goin away, an me back upon the streets, Mr Daniell—after I come that close!'

'No, you misunderstand. I wanted to tell you, your animal sketch is well-proportioned. Strong, free-flowing lines. You have talent.'

Jesse's head comes up—a sudden flare of defiance. 'You got no idea what it's like!' Facing each other now. 'No idea!'

A terrible silence, broken only by footsteps upon the stairs. Murmurings without.

'Jesse, understand that I do not under any time—circumstance—brook disrespect, or insolerance—*insolence*! Yes. Not. Is that clear?'

Jesse holds aside, almost in dismissal, before turning to face me again, his wrists half-raised in a strange gesture of resentment mingled with fending-off. Some habit learned.

How little can I have understood! Move toward the youth.

Not wanted: Jesse draws back. Swift alter my gesture: comb fingers through the thin growth of hair upon my scalp.

'Jesse Cloud, the plan is not as you may think. A prentice course demands months, years of training. I am an Associate of the Royal Academy, not a caulker of barrels!' Extemporising, thrust forth an arm. 'I am no mere *decorator*! Any prentice of mine shall be expected to undertake at least...'

(How long, exactly?)

'Two years, to the conclusion of Part One, that is. Note well. Commissioned to tour eastern England, Jesse, and all I hear from you is displeasure!'

Jesse is half-smiling now, still sniffling, but enticed little by little into participation. Richard's troupe might approve my performance!

'Who else but Jesse Cloud to prepare our baggage and resources for journeying? Who to undertake hire of carriages, coachmen and chambers, and fetch and carry, pack, launder, set out our light-box and tent, accompany expeditions, and thrive upon expert artistic tuition, equipment, practical experience, and, and, I know not what? Who but Jesse Cloud to divert thieves and villains, hmm? Can you deny me, sirrah?'

I become a Bragadoccio onstage, a parody demanding applause, fairground showman, Henry the Eighth, arms akimbo in all his swaggering pomp. We are both grinning. Perhaps this time Jesse's raised hands are about to applaud.

Rap-rap upon the apartment door.

'Not yet. Just one moment, Jesse. As I mentioned, your sketches show much promise. In your next, *paint* the shading. I shall provide instruction, and um, demonstrate techniques. Outlines in charcoal, lad, otherwise colours henceforth.'

'I only got blue, Mr Daniell. An cochineal.'

'Cochineal?'

'From Mrs Lambton. She—'

This time, several fist-thumps upon the door.

'Let us see what can be done when the payment comes. Now, please apologise to our neighbours, and rid us of that wretched cur.'

Cochineal... Very strange.

*

The gallery's doorman leads me to Clyne's office, taps, opens, addresses the silence beyond.

'Mr Daniell to see you, sir.'

The doorman's face reappears, beaming: 'Please enter, sir, if you will.' A sweeping gesture of welcome with his free hand.

The door closes behind me. Approach Jeremiah Clyne's desk, pausing a few paces distant. He does not look up. The stillness of his whole being indicates profound attention to something else.

'Um, good-day to you, Mr Clyne. I thank you for granting this meeting without prior appointment.'

No response.

'It concerns your sale of my work to Mrs van Brielle.'

'Yes.'

'Firstly, I appreciate that various deductions shall have to be made from the overall payment.'

'Yes.'

'Fully appreciate, in order to—'

'Thirteen per centum.'

'—effect a satisfact—Excuse me?'

'Thirteen.'

'Oh yes, thirteen.'

'Per centum, including Cromarty.'

'Yes. However, I come to you this morning in somewhat un-fortunate circumstances because—'

'How much, Mr Daniell?'

'Beg your pardon?'

'How much do you seek in advance?'

'Oh! Oh, um, well, let me see...'

'Fifty shillings enough? We Partners retain a float, Mr Daniell. Pays a cleaner. Buys fish for the gallery's cat.'

My fist clenches, heart raging. *Fish for the cat?* Stand up to this sneering puff-adder! This smirking, obnoxious Hogarthian parody of a—

'Well, Mr Clyne, if you could possibly arrange perhaps four guineas it would be, you know...'

Clyne positions the nib of his pen against one line of figures in the columns. A sudden smile, as sudden withdrawn. He settles himself, contemplating me with reptilian stillness.

'Oh dear *me*! Bad as that, is it?'

*

Ill-prepared for rainfall in early June. Even the short walk from the gallery to Little Compton Street is dampening. To have sought the advance from Jeremiah Clyne, though humbling, does enable the purchase of victuals. Repayment of what was withdrawn from La Parisienne's rent scarce constitutes Good Works, but at least shall make amends.

Perhaps a lack of forcefulness explains my bungling with finance, and, um, general life arrangements. Might not a wife and family in some way secure a man at his mooring? Such timidity! I rage at my Uncle, would despatch Clyne to his snake-pit, yet utter not a word. Must take hold, become firmer of purpose. I am thought a dreamer, a *hermit-crab*, according to Richard. Why so little gained from forty years' experience?

The door is opened almost as I knock. A young woman, aproned, her hair pushed up into some temporary scarved arrangement, regards me from the doorway. Unwelcome, I can tell. Out-of-hours. She is busy. By daylight, and without the heavy eyebrows and rubied lips, scarce more than a girl. Bright droplets of rain gather upon us. The resident half-leans upon an upright besom in an attitude of exasperation. We recognise each other, but that is not enough.

'Sir?'

Her hair is organised differently. Almost a different person. 'I would like to—'

'Sorry. Closed till seven.' No pretence of respect.

'I would speak with Madame concerning a financial matter.'

'This ain't costume, sir. I am cleanin the downstairs. My turn this week, see?'

'Be that as it may, my girl. I seek to meet your Mistress, and if you offer further insolence, believe me it shall be reported, and shortly no cleaning at all shall occupy you here. Do we understand each other?'

The resident looks over her shoulder, and with a toss of the head, beckons me within. Flattens herself gainst the wall as I pass. That single response jangles the nerves. I walk onward in embarrassment, buttocks tight, some Music Hall prancing gentry.

Damask chairs pushed back in the gloom; bare tables stacked one upon another or folded by the window. A miscellany of glassware and candle-holders lines the mantle-shelf. Beyond, the plum-coloured curtains withdrawn expose a cracked, limewashed wall. Everywhere the smell of boiled fish.

Madame is not at her desk in the alcove. Ring the small handbell, and wait. No response. Ring again, more loudly, and turn upon my heel to find someone seating herself in the far corner. Or himself, as it may be. Once seated, re-lights a long-stemmed pipe of white clay, lip-stained red.

'Good afternoon.'

'Good-day.'

Whiskers down the sides of this person's face, which is framed by a long blonde wig. A sort of kirtle the most interesting item of clothing, short enough to expose male blue-veined legs, large feet in Roman sandals, and toenails painted cinnabar. Rings and bracelets flash here and there in the dim light.

Clear my throat. Once more, clear it.

'You meet some odd types in here.' The blonde has a deep, smoker's voice.

'Yes, I suppose so.' Still no sign of Madame. Consider the handbell again.

A prolonged draw upon the clay pipe, grey vapour expelled. Must be a man. A man in sheep's clothing, waving the stem-curl to disperse the fug.

'Take you, sir, for example. You've got what I might call—if I wished to be rude, which is not the case—*monastery hair*. And it strikes me, just as an idea, you know, a mere suggestion, that you might look well in one o them Scotch things, what's the name? Tam something? Tam o Shanters, that's it. Tartan. Rob Roy. You'd look well in one o them, in my opinion. Upon the tilt, to one side, sort of like so? Keep your head dry on a day like this.'

'Indeed?' Ring the handbell with vigour; manage to knock it over when replacing it; grab the thing before it rolls to the floor.

'You've come at the wrong time.'

'I can see that.'

'She don't get up till five, most days.'

'Oh. You, um, work here, do you?'

A shake of the head, amused beneath the wig. 'I own it.'

'Well... very good.'

'Yes, not bad.' Heavy footsteps upon the staircase. 'You're in luck. I expect Madame comes. Don't miss much. As a man of commerce myself, I know the worth of a private meeting, so shall take my leave of you, to conduct your affairs as you will.'

He stands slowly, seeming to do everything with admirable calm. Flicks away strands of tobacco from a sleeve. A downward movement of the wrist to smoothe his dress reveals a number, no longer angry, as they say.

'This apparel is for my days off. We all appreciate home comforts, don't we?'

*

Upon goin out, Mr William Daniell said I must wait for the cash to buy paints wiv, an left me some pence for a cheese roll. By chance, one fell off of a baker's basket straight into my hand this very mornin. I bought some black an yeller.

There is a little piddlin place called Maresbrook. The stream is much covered-over wiv builders' rubble an muck from the homes nearby. It is ever damp, an comes back wiv the rains. Besides midges an toads, wild plants is down there. I took a red dead-nettle from a patch of it to do a pitcher of, like a proper artiss prentice. It is hard to mix blue an yeller to get the right green. The right green ain't the same all over, bein faint near the tips. I fink them leaves is called *mosake*, from little dark lines all over; hard to do wiv a brush or they stand out too much. The red upon leaves next the stem looks like their little flowers has bled into em. It is interestin when you gets close, but I worked too slow an the nettle bent over. I chucked it, bein left wiv colours half-done.

It is a start.

His nibbs did take silver coins wiv him. He don't always rember to go out wiv cash, so is set upon some secret purpose, or if not secret, then closed to me. It will come clear.

*

When Madame enters through an inner doorway, the young woman ceases her cleaning and hastens to the back of the house.

No bargaining. I owe the remainder of the bill for rent outstanding, plus twenty per cent, plus dislodgement—legal term, apparently, for a standard fee applied in circumstances such as these, to compensate the lender for the inconvenience of providing cash at a high rate of interest. Dislodgement. No choice but to pay, thus easing my conscience about La Parisienne's rent. Taking newly-acquired coins from the neck of my purse, add the half-crown and push it all toward Madame's waiting hand. At once she begins counting.

Dislodgement shall not prevent my buying food today; may threaten pigments upon the morrow. However, should the weather improve, I do not intend much painting. I shall advance Jesse's instruction, and prepare us for the next phase of my artistic tour. Therefore—

'...house, sir?'

'Oh! I beg your pardon. What was that?'

'I was enquiring if the person with whom you have just spoke chanced to mention this property.'

'Yes.'

'Yes, he did mention it?'

'Yes. Owns it.'

Madame winces, looks down at the polished desk-top, drums her fingers. 'Tells everyone that.'

Seize whatever initiative remains to me. 'So, Madame, please pass me your receipt and I shall depart.'

'Receipt?'

'For my records.' Keep to one's course.

Madame searches for paper in a side drawer. Merely to glimpse her surprise confers a sense of achievement. One lesson learned: forcefulness brought her response.

'Furthermore, Madame, the bill is paid in full and on time. Hence, I understand that your resident, La Parisienne, is likewise deemed no longer in your debt. And, um, therefore not faced with departure.'

Red-cheeked, Madame hauls herself upright in her chair. 'Oh yes, sir. The Frenchwoman stays where she is—for now, that is.'

Look down sharply, but Madame has dipped nib in ink, attending to what she writes.

TEN

'Jesse, how do you fare with that light-box? Is it not heavy to be carried far?'

'Mustn't grumble, sir.'

(Stoicism of a veteran Fusilier.)

Even before Camden, my intended walk to Hampstead Heath has come to seem over-ambitious. Lean the folded tent-poles against the ironwork of the bridge across the new canal. Stretch one's back. The water's viscous surface slops and heaves, gliding between its banks.

When did I last visit the Heath? Panoramic views across London; sites for artistic demonstration. Memories of Hampstead are imbued with the spirit of the times, so attuned to the natural world.

My past readiness to explore hidden groves partly derived from thoughts of Miss Aurelia Carrow and her sister, Dorothy. Earnest readers of literature, they desired to clamber the Fells while poets declaimed verse, to bathe in rock-pools beneath misting waterfalls, stroll the Cobb at Lyme, become wood-nymphs— do almost anything in fact to escape the dreariness of a country house in Belsize. Pending, the sisters devoted themselves to the mystic wisdom of youthful artists such as William Daniell, late of Bombay.

Yes, well, that came to nothing of course.

Hampstead Heath, mirage-like, remains distant. Blustery weather. Hence, having set out for the Heath, we arrive at a change of plan.

A narrow-boat, boxed within her gates, rises in the lock. Close by the roaring weir, the Midland Lass yaws in what space she can. The boatman stands aft, head lowered. With thumbs hooked in pockets, he looks to one side from the corner of his eye, aware of passers-by upon the towpath: a sly glance of pride. The boy in the middle distance leads away their horse to graze.

However, the constant passing of riders, carriages, curricles and heavy-wheeled carts upon Camden Bridge renders *camera obscura* demonstration impractical.

'Jesse, let us walk on. I promise you, no great distance.'

No sooner does the long incline of Haverstock Hill begin to pull upon one's calves, to nudge nose nearer to knees, than a site suggests itself: a buttercup meadow, edging woodland along the rise.

It will do.

*

'Rickety, this tent, sir, ain't it?'

'Weight the exposed side with stones, Jesse. My demonstration shall not take long.'

Two sheets stretched about eight poles tied in a conical shape, tall enough for the occupant to stand near-upright: a wig-wam as depicted in news-papers, save the woollen cap perched atop to exclude light; save its manufactured canvas replacing stitched animal hides; its function observation, not habitation; and for an individual, not a family.

'Ain't this tent leanin forward, Mr Daniell, on the tilt?

'The meadow's slope assists our purpose, in fact. Now let us set the folding table.' *Jesse, please set the folding table.* 'Push the rear legs into the ground a little, because it, um, inclines... Good. And now for our crowning glory.' *Jesse, please fetch the light-box.*

'Called a light-box because it permits light to enter through the small hole, here.' With a flourish indicate the lens. 'However, the apparatus is known properly as camera obscura: a dark room. Thus, we begin with contradiction.'

Thus? Wherefore and whence this *thus?* I seem to have become a pompous school-master, enjoying the sound of his own voice!

'Um...'

'Go on, sir. I am listenin, honest.'

'Yes-yes-yes. Lost my thread, just now... Oh! Light. I am no engineer, Jesse, but by twisting the lens fitted to this small hole, one brings it forward.' Demonstration. 'Or indeed, backward.' Demonstration. 'Now, the lens gathers light entering and throws it, but—oh yes, ah now, the mirror is a vital part of our light-box, kept flat on a small tray which slides out from the rear.'

Strangely, Jesse makes no move.

'A small tray which slides out from the rear—Jesse!'

'Oh! Oh, me to do it.' Jesse squeezes past. Unused to the idea of participation?

1. Open left hinged side-flap (g) by turning screws (c) and (d) anti-clockwise.
2. Insert mirror on rest (h).
3. Set angle of mirror using brass adjustment knob (i).
4. Re-close side-flap (g) by turning screws (c) and (d) clockwise.

'D'you follow?'

'Can I try puttin the mirror in, sir?'

'Well, I suppose so. But no finger-marks upon the glass, and above all don't drop it. Understood?'

'Yes sir.' Jesse removes the mirror, re-sets it, and repeats the exercise. 'Well sir, what's it all for, this light-box?'

'I come to that.' From the tent's gloom, look out upon the meadow, past the belt of trees, over the road, onward to Chalk Farm. Sheep graze in unfinished yards where new houses rise. 'Should an artist wish to portray this landscape, the light-box is a means of taking what is out there and putting it in here.'

Jesse looks doubtful: mouth twisting, right nostril twitching; touches the box as if it might disappear.

'In here?'

'Yes.'

Jesse shakes his head.

'Let me show you.'

5. Open hinged box-lid, using catches (a) and (b).
6. Insert tracing-paper of appropriate size upon rest (e). Remove lens cap (j).
7. Ottewill's Patent Blacking Cloth ensures reduction of ambient light.
8. Use view-finder (f) to obtain focused image by adjusting lens (k).

'Now look within, lad.'

The prentice frowns, steps forward, bends to the glass plate, and at once starts back. 'Well how—?'

'Do you understand? Taking what is out there and putting it in here. How may I ensure my picture's safe return to Cleveland Street?'

'What, we got to carry it in the box, sir?'

Shake my head. As Jesse bends to the image, I cover the lens.

'Aah! It's gone! It's gone, sir! I dint do it, honest to God, never touched it!' Wild-eyed with alarm, the youth checks with the meadow, which is still there.

'I told you, Jesse, it is a matter of light. I simply closed our dark-room door.

If I open it, that is, remove the lens-cover again, what now?'

With great suspicion, considerable caution, eyes narrowing and head a little to one side, Jesse edges forward to peer neath the lid.

A pause.

'What do you see?'

'I dunno, sir.'

Jesse emerges, a frown creasing his forehead, assures himself of the meadow and buildings beyond, before bending to re-examine the image. Finally, from below the lid's shadow: 'Hmm...' Solemnity, as if diagnosing acute windiness in an ageing ewe.

'It ain't a pitcher in there, sir—you can see it's all crawlin about.' Jesse hunches, almost shuddering.

*

We pick-nick together, social station being less important to affirm here. Clipped to a board, our newly-traced outline of the slopes. Bread and cheese unwrapped.

'Though costly, tracing-paper allows us to bring back the image, and thereafter to work within-doors.' Jesse nods, chewing. 'However, you prefer to sketch subjects close by, the fine detail, that so?'

'Yes sir.' Jesse swallows, wiping mouth on sleeve. 'Wild plants for medicine, mostly. Might just be a nettle, like that one, or a poppy. I done oak galls. An I draws flesh.'

'Flesh?'

'Yes sir. Lots o people draws fine houses, don't they? But flesh close-up, now that ain't so common.'

'You refer to your dead dog, animal carcases?'

'Not always, sir.'

The prentice watches me with utter frankness.

Flesh? If neither fish nor fowl, then... Frankness need not imply innocence. This workhouse youth lived months upon the streets. No call to deceive oneself about Jesse Cloud.

'You, um, observe human flesh in detail?'

Jesse nods. 'Shall I say more, Mr Daniell?'

'Please do.'

Two thrushes bob through the daisies and buttercups, pausing with heads raised, before setting-off again a few yards more. A pretty meadow.

'Well sir, the Thames goes a long way. At low tide, when the water sinks back an mud lies bare, in special places you might find a body. At the right time o day, or wiv a lighted taper, you might see somefink stickin out the mud, an you'd know what that is. No matters how it did get there. The river gives em back.'

Crack of timber in the trees. The thrushes flee to other grounds.

'Shall I go on, sir? Or is that, you know, enough?'

'No-no, continue.'

'Well, folks poor like me might crawl out upon the mud an take a look. Searchin for someone gone missin, might be, but mostly for coins or rings, bracelets, knives—that sort o fing. No good to the dead, is it? An them what goes out there, riskin their own necks, or usin planks, well they might have the shirt off of em, too, y'see, if enough desperate...'

Such desperation showed itself after Waterloo. A pair of epaulettes hacked, it was, that the fellow touted in Goodge Street, each bearing its blue cotton threads.

'But Jesse, you merely sketched those bodies found, did you? Wounds, and so forth, for medical study. No robbery involved?'

Eyebrows raised, he regards me with sorrow; pity, almost.

'Surgeons is too high for me to show pitchers to, Mr Daniell.'

'I mean to say, as a boy in Calcutta I witnessed sights so shocking and frankly degrading that I could not sleep. By day, kites circled overhead. Even now, the very scent of almond blossom! So much beauty in that country, yet horrors, too. In darkness the smallest sounds threatened. And from Manchester, not a twelvemonth ago, have come reports (doubtless exaggerated) of military action gainst gatherings of our own citizenry. But Jesse, I did not, had not...' Hands open to the heavens. 'After all, this is England!'

Jesse avoids my eye; hugs knee to chin as the moments pass.

'Sorry, sir, if I up-set you.'

*

'Now, Jesse, as we return, recall the scene we traced, and notes made. A fence crossed the high part of the field. Was there a gate? ... Good. And beyond, the trees: what hues their stems and branches? ... Yes. When the wind gusted, the meadow-grass flowed like a river. How tinted then? ... Silver? How may the artist's brush suggest silver? ... Excellent! Now, consider the field-path...'

'...In a landscape, hues change with distance. Greens become blues. An artist shows this journey from near to far through his use of tone, that is, depth of hue. Bright sunlight plays upon shadow, revealing greys, purple and tan. And *show* irregularities, Jesse. Untidiness. Gaps. We remark them in life; hence, record them in artwork...'

'...for a single aquatint demands many days. Each scene minutely observed, *learned*, that afterwards one may recover the subject to life. And—What? More questions? Certainly, I can ask you more questions. May have wandered ... Oh, well thank you, Jesse! Most generous. Gratifying that you find my comments worthwhile.'

*

I liked what Mr Daniell did say bout little fings or gaps what makes the pitcher real. I seen that wiv teef. Ain't never straight, an no two jaws the same. His nibbs knows a lot when he gets goin, clever wiv the paints, an sharp to make out how them colours change. But he ain't so sharp as to spot my eyes crossed, what I did in lessons when bored, countin how long you kept em crossed. He is clever in narrow ways—like that canal-boat, not easy turnin about.

*

Message pushed neath my door. Quell this leaping heart! Wait. Not written in Mrs van Brielle's hand—not Ellen's, seeking an assignation, but Mrs Lambton's, urging a meeting. Does Uncle Thomas's condition worsen further?

Mrs Lambton writes with needless mystification.

Perhaps avoid telling her so?

I shall visit—once this work is complete.

ELEVEN

Inky-fingered, Mrs Lambton opens the door. 'Young Mr Daniell, welcome! And welcome, Jesse!' As if our visit were unexpected, when we come at her request.

Good day, and the familiar rest of it. Mrs Lambton bears the wide smile of an ancient sun deity: manifest, simplified, fixed.

'Your uncle's health is much improved! He is out of bed, by the window in his chair—yes, by the window! I do not suggest that beforehand all hope was gone, but this transformation is either a latter-day miracle, or the happy result of Doctor Phillips's ministrations!'

(Miracle, then.) 'I am relieved, Mrs Lambton.'

Is that my response? Chance, and the passage of time, exposed Uncle Thomas's disgraceful conduct: a beloved's untimely passing, the restless conscience of an old man fearing the future. Impossible to envisage my mother as he described her. What turmoil raged within those civilised exchanges, all the contrived jollity?

Mother, nursing little Mary through frail health, must have expected her brother-in-law to protect me. And Uncle Thomas honoured his promises, keeping secret their fruitless, hidden love-longing. He has borne this burden since her death. Such passions were beyond my youthful understanding. Even in adulthood, I have little considered the quiet outlay of funds which surely followed. Without Uncle's concession to me of his Cleveland Street apartment, how might I have supported my ambitions?

The old Cavalier showed me love in ways a growing lad might not have recognised, but love nonetheless. My disgust has come later. Having readied myself for Uncle's imminent death, his living-on seems, well, almost contrariness.

As we walk the corridor, Mrs Lambton instructs Jesse to wait in the study. She places herself before me with a hand raised in warning.

'Despite this improvement, Young Mr Daniell, there remain

his limited mobility, lack of appetite, and shortness of breath. His powders and tinctures have been administered. I bathe him, y'see, change his clothes, make him comfortable; do all in my power.'

Only then am I struck by a surge-tide of regret for my own selfishness, the long hours of the widow's watching-over. Her swift footsteps precede me into the room, where Uncle sits in the moted light and warmth of the sun.

'Thomas, you have a guest today.' Smiling, she leaves us.

Wait with hands clasped, swallowing some unexpected lump in my throat: apologetic, moved, smiling, not relieved at all.

'Good-day, Uncle. I hear you enjoy better health.'

In his chair, Uncle's body droops forward, propped with cushions. A grey-striped nightshirt loose about the shoulders. Rapid, shallow breathing.

'Made a fool of myself, William. Being under the weather, put myself in disgrace. But thought—well, thought ye needed to know.' Head down, his voice strained as whey.

'Well, you are here still, Uncle. Recovered.' My smile quite false.

'Here, yes.'

'And, um, the sunlight does not distress you?' Irritable sensation in my throat.

Uncle Thomas reaches a hand to the lifeless arm, smoothing the fore-part up and down. 'Spent days looking from my bed to this window. Days! Means much, just to enjoy a view upon the Square. And that wheeziness of yours, William: too long, too often, fanning resin. Gets upon your chest. Nitric acid, I ask you! Ye should know all this.'

'I thought perhaps hay fever.'

Look out upon the elms in Fitzroy. Strive to quell the conflict within.

Attending to the sick must be a talent. I have chanced to observe others who find simple, necessary words of comfort—those small acts which prompt sufferers to respond. Theirs is a quality of

Grace, whereas I stumble in embarrassment. My own attempts to show concern lack some dimension. They rankle, unsettle people; they unsettle me.

A few days ago, it was moving to witness Mrs Lambton and Uncle together. Do I feel for him now as I did then? Am I not changed by his confessing?

Birds in the wild cherry. Cannot discern their kind or number.

'William, please go to the chest by the wall. Middle drawer there.'

At once recognisable, the beautiful box of inlaid wood studded with ivory, the Maharajah's gift to Uncle for the portrait of his family in Delhi. Later used as a paintbox. Brushes and charcoals upon its shelf. The drawer holds jars and bottles, pigments, sponges, long-handled squirrel-hair brushes, a much-stained mixing palette, and paper and card. All to be taken.

'The Maharajah's box is yours, William. The rest to encourage your prentice-boy.'

'Do you not want them, Uncle?'

'To what end? My arm is dead. You are the celebrated artist, William. Make use.'

'Well...'

'Sentimental value, I know. And good times, but useful things.'

'Thank you, Uncle. On behalf—' Sudden dryness of the throat.

'And William...'

The one good hand beckons me forward. Perhaps I should have been more demonstrative just then?

Uncle reaches out to my shoulder, wanting me downward, closer to his thin whisper, to that foul breath: 'William, look after Lizzie for me, won't you, when I am gone? No money in what she writes. Clever, but too political, too close-to-home. Publishers won't take the risk.'

*

I looks acrost the books in Mrs Lambton's study, reachin out a finger to touch one or two. Books have got their own smell. Some have gold on. Works, she calls em. Mr Daniell calls his pitchers works. Don't see how they can both be right.

I am gettin used to not knowin a lot. There's fings I never knowed of afore like ackertints. I always knew I didn't know what they was. But there's fings I fought I knew in a general way, like pitchers an books, what turns out to have different names as well as the same name. Not knowin what you fought you knew can easy make you look daft. We all knows them livin off of the river, what crawls out over the mud-banks, must watch for deep waters; but there's also parts along the banks—safe ground, you might fink—where poor souls fall in an never seen again. You can be trapped when learnin, likewise.

Mrs Lambton begins all fussy wiv her papers. She is still diggin.

'Jesse, do you know of Simple Simon?'

'Yes Miss. We done that in lessons.'

'A popular piece of nonsense.'

'Met a pie-man, Mrs Lambton.'

'Yes. On his way to the fair, was it not?'

'Too poor to buy a pie, Miss, though off to the fair. Called Simple Simon, so we knows not much up-top. But some people ain't good wiv cash, are they? Can't keep it when they got it.'

'Indeed.'

'An some just penniless anyway. I seen plenty o that.'

'Have you?'

'Yes Miss. I was sorry Simple Simon went hungry, but fishin in a bucket is stupid.'

'Don't think I know that version.'

'You don't know it, Miss? Does that mean I knows somefink you don't?'

'May we get on?'

'Yes Miss.'

'Simple Simon is an old verse, Jesse. Popular for many years. Were you aware it can be sung?'

Mrs Lambton ain't simple. She won't catch me singin. Pull them shutters-to straight off. 'No Miss, I can't sing. Terrible, I am. I only does readin.'

Miss goes quiet afore tellin me there is biscuits in the kitchen, so she can talk wiv his nibbs in here. They got their secrets too.

*

'Thomas is most grateful for your visits, Young Mr Daniell. I feared we had lost him.'

'Yes.' Between us, the unspoken thought that I am here because of her note slipped under the door.

'Sixty-three years cannot be such an advanced age to have lost use of a limb.'

'Perhaps not, Mrs Lambton—though some are struck down earlier in life, as we know. My own parents, for example.'

'Indeed. Perhaps more fitting to be thankful for the mercies granted us, and not to bewail what is gone.' (She dabs at her eye. Some mote) 'Our speaker at the recent Marylebone meeting alluded to this very point. Mrs van Brielle called our attention to—'

'Mrs van—'

'Brielle. Ellen, our speaker, gave an altogether rewarding talk upon family life and domestic interiors in artwork of the Low Countries. Why, do you know her?'

With her head tilted, the dark lock of Medusa hair serpenting about the bridge of her nose, she studies my discomfort.

'Oh, um yes, I do, a little—in a wholly professional capacity, of course.' Collar-fiddling, trying to clear my throat. 'Mrs van Brielle has bought a print of mine, and I am now commissioned to—'

The widow closes the door.

'Young Mr Daniell, I intend no impertinence, but between ourselves, may I mention that delightful term, *a bachelor's wife*. It refers with generosity to male fantasies of impossible perfection in women, to unrealistic expectations, and dreams of the unattainable. Born of inexperience, you see. Wishful thinking.'

The broadest of benevolent smiles; a single eyebrow arched.

I need no instruction in managing my affairs, um, professional dealings. Forty years of age! No man accepts guidance unsought from any woman, save his mother.

'Mrs Lambton, every artist envisages perfect achievement before each new work. However unattainable in practice, the ideal inspires creative endeavour. Is this not what the ceiling of the Sistine Chapel portrays, the reaching beyond? As for inexperience, Mrs Lambton, how does one know where experience begins?'

Mrs Lambton looks down, smiling less broadly. Some personal recollection?

'Young Mr Daniell, this pamphlet of mine addresses the matter: *The Search for Perfection*. Its argument may assist you. My own copy. You are welcome to borrow it.'

'Thank you.' (Dammit.)

Mrs Lambton rests her finger-tips upon the desktop. She may be standing upon one leg. Her strangeness.

Having determined to be forceful, yet become the object of a widow's homespun wisdom, I shall not contemplate retreat. 'Regrettably, Madam, time presses. Jesse and I need make preparation.'

Mrs Lambton stands full upright, clasping her hands. 'It concerns Jesse. I have visited St James's workhouse in Billingsgate, to view its records. The date of Jesse's admission is written in the old-fashioned way—February of the forty-fifth year of the late King's reign—that is, eighteen hundred and five. The child's age is listed as *six months or thereabouts*.'

'So, no more than sixteen years now?'

'Quite. There was a second child, whose age is given as *about eighteen months.* And Young Mr Daniell, one detail caught my eye.' Mrs Lambton regards me from it. 'In each case, the child's age is estimated; other children's ages are given exact.'

'They could be approximations also.'

'Unlikely, for the same hand made every entry on that page; the same careful person, trying for accuracy. Mothers entering the workhouse come with their families. They know the children's ages. But for foundlings, estimates are necessary.'

'Hmm...'

A gleam in Mrs Lambton's eye. 'I do know a little more.' She leans forward—a willow bending, but with greater intensity of purpose. 'This I learned at a meeting of our Marylebone group. Touchingly, when circumstance compels a woman to abandon her baby at the workhouse gate, commonly some token of the infant's identity is left with the child. A trinket, small piece of embroidery, badge, or sewn beads, which only the mother would recognise or match. A parting gift, y'see, in the hope of one day reclaiming her little one.'

I am captive to Mrs Lambton's unblinking gaze.

'Young Mr Daniell, the lists at St James's record items of carved bone left with both these foundlings. Also, a note of their forenames had been pinned: the mother was in some measure literate.'

Did not Jesse once refer to whalebone? The back-scrubber involved, before closing himself away? Carved bone is plentiful enough.

'At St James's, I asked to be shown the note. Sadly, it cannot now be found. However, the children's names were entered by our careful record-keeper. Has Jesse mentioned a sister called Amy?'

'I do not think so.' Hatpin. A bone hatpin, I recall.

'There was no sister. Jesse has, or once had, a brother called Emil: Emil Cloud. A middle name began with 'S'. That is all we have. His name was later crossed off, leaving Jesse's, but no date marked, and without record of his death or burial.'

Mrs Lambton raises her chin. A response required. But my

forcefulness and readiness for manly assertion are faded, leaving me unsure what to think or say.

'Touching, indeed, Mrs Lambton. Thank you. I did not know of possessions left with abandoned children, and, and I shall take good care of Jesse.'

May have promised too much, there. Why add such a commitment? It is poignant that Jesse is a foundling whose brother has left. The carved bonework, also affecting. Such knowledge increases my sense of wardship for the lad. Did not Uncle Thomas care for me? I was no more his child than Jesse mine.

Yet to shelter the prentice indefinitely burdens me with responsibilities ill-fitted to one who seeks membership of the Royal Academy. I have debts enough! Those Academician greybeards' notions of style and subject lead public taste. Financial embarrassment and the boy's protection divert me from the true path. My own possibilities must not be scotched by, um, thwarting.

What of Jesse?

And why always this guilt?

*

Another visit to Uncle before leaving. Perhaps our last. My deceiver-hero asleep, snoring in the chair, the pale flesh of his neck become livid scarlet. Lay my hand upon Uncle's shoulder: merest touch.

'Thank you again for the gifts, Uncle Thomas. And for, um... We must—'

His struggle to waken.

'I was thanking you, Uncle. I must depart—prepare for the next coastal tour.'

'Going now, William?'

'Yes.'

'Pass on my best wishes when you see your mother, will you?'

Oh God.

*

7, Syracuse Row,
Shenstead Lane,
Lambeth St Mary's.
7th day of 6th month, 1820.

Dear Mr Daniell,

Such doubts attend my writing this letter that even now I question whether it shall be sent or at the last be consigned to some dark corner, in token of my impertinence. I hesitate to address thee less formally, therefore, notwithstanding those earlier occasions when, as I well recall, grand projects were devised in the garden of our former home. Sir, my husband Richard, long thine associate and still, I trust, thy friend, speaks much of thee in high terms. His recent return to us at Dymchurch, bringing thy most welcome gift, was earnest enough of thy Christian charity. Truly sir, upon that eventide our family did give solemn thanks at prayer.

It has not gone well with us since Richard's injury amid the storm at sea. The wound, being swollen and as yet unhealed, brings him continual pain, and thou wouldst find us much reduced. We are removed from the coast to the above address in London, for that his ankle requires the ministration of physicians better-qualified. Further, my husband's spirits have declined into the melancholy. Richard no longer writes, lacking all vigour. I am not privy to our standing with banks, landlords or lenders, but I believe a theatrical company owes him payment for a script performed, whilst the fee for his latest Commentary upon the British tour is yet to arrive.

At gatherings, the Friends enjoin me to be prayerful, to trust in His ways, and to seek solace in the quiet of our meetings. As a newcomer in Lambeth, I find such companionship comforting. Also, a few months past, Richard and I were blessed with the birth of a third child. Yet I fear our domestic circumstances may underlie an infant's afflictions, for the youngest now suffers the croup.

Mr Daniell, on reading this list of woes I anticipate how dreary the struggle of our lives must seem to thee! Doth not Philippians offer wise counsel when we are instructed to ready ourselves for abundance as for need? I have readied myself, sir, and with God's Grace we shall indeed abound. Should this letter reach thee, it is but to ask that thou might visit our lodging as soon as may be convenient, for my husband's sake. Sir, 'twould do him good.

> In sincerity in confidentiality and in all faith,
> I am Ruth, wife to Richard Ayton.

How long since last I saw Ruth? Four years? The boldness of this sad request suggests someone changed from the self-effacing young woman whom Richard first introduced to me. It was Richard, naturally, whose talents shone—known equally for his satirical verse and squibs in news-papers as for his plays and sober art criticism in journals.

Upon that cloudy September afternoon, we sat in the cottage garden. They were much in love, and I believe remain so. I envy him the security of knowing it. Sketched them there, at the table neath the apple tree. Merely a few swift lines in charcoal, but I recall he did get it framed. When Richard confided his beginning a comic playscript, Ruth dipped her head. She was ever of a serious, indeed old-fashioned, cast of mind. Richard's mother doubtless hoped that Ruth would steady him. Even so, whilst hatching a campaign of Napoleonic ambition, he and I consumed formidable quantities of ale and liquor in nearby hostelries.

Smooth a hand over the letter's creases.

Our burgeoning plan to illustrate *modes of life in the country's wildest parts* appealed more to Ruth's notion of worthwhile endeavour than did Richard's humble theatrical entertainments. I did not foresee the full extent of our journeying. Increasingly, Richard missed his family. Neither of us could have anticipated the manner of his bringing-down.

Images rear of him at the crowded south-side staging-post: a grim, defiant vagrant lacking strength to haul himself into the carriage; the obscenity of the bloodied bundle about his dragging foot; the fellow-passengers' disgust.

Little wonder that Ruth's serious-mindedness has become earnest Quaker commitment, and so obvious a source of strength. Indeed, what else might she contemplate? She does not resort to begging. That she writes *in confidentiality* must mean without Richard's knowing. Mentions his melancholy, also. I am trusted. She asks of me no more than to visit: *'twould do him good.*

Shameful that I cannot go.

My freshly-ironed attire is piled upon the armchair. Jesse opens the travel-trunk to gauge what space remains, shakes his head, closes the lid, and hurries away. Nearby stand the camera obscura and brass-cornered box, topped by the Maharajah's gift which Uncle passed to me—beautiful, tainted. Bottles, rags, water-jars...

The printing-press stands covered and pinned by heavy dust-sheets. With those hidden appurtenances, big wheel and feed-tray in sombre stillness, the bulk upon its solid legs resembles some confused, defeated beast brought to the zoological gardens.

A day-and-a-half before we depart, the tripod here tucked neath my arm, and Ruth Ayton's letter seeking my assistance has caught me off-guard. I owe it to Richard. Now that our partnership's brightest hopes are dashed, to be reminded of one's responsibilities within friendship is wounding.

Dust afflicts my chest. This time it is the dust.

TWELVE

Along Oxford Street, to the polished steps of the Grand Scenic Hall. Particles from London's streets assail my lungs—subtle, warmed layers like the resin for my prints before the burn.

'The very best of the day to you, Mr Daniell!'

'Good afternoon.' Forcefulness.

'For Mr Clyne once again, is it sir?'

The doorman and I are acquaintances, it seems. Nod my head.

'Mr Daniell, please for you to exercise carefulness within the Grand Scenic Hall today. We are in the midst of a turnaround. Big ladders, stepladders, hooks and fixings, paintings high and low...'

'Oh?'

'A new gathering-to of the old collection, sir, so far as I understand. I think that's what's happening.'

I am escorted wide of a full bucket and mop, wider still of a quivering fifteen-foot ladder. Someone at the top, upon instruction from another upon the lowest rung, straightens Canterbury Cathedral. Hammering. Tapping. *Three, two, and ... lift!* In a far corner Ambrose Moulton inclines his head as two workers consult him. They point to the warhorse staggering neath the tonnage of a triumphant medallioned General. Along one bare exhibition wall, the faded outlines of works which have been removed create a ghostly cemetery, four rows high.

Usual procedure: polite knock, hand gripping the office door, murmuring within, invitation to enter.

Forcefulness.

'Mr Clyne.'

This time, something about the manner and pace of my entry, my newly purposeful advance to stand before his desk, causes Jeremiah Clyne to respond differently. He does not continue to write or calculate, but without raising his head, watches from atop his spectacles, strokes the pen's plume between forefinger and thumb.

'Ah...'

'I do not seek another loan.'

Clyne smiles. 'No. You have not long received payment for your Lincolnshire sluice-gate, Mr Daniell.'

'Nor do I come to offer other works, at present.'

'Then your purpose?'

Forcefulness. 'To gain information: to be told whether or not the fee owed Richard Ayton for his latest commentary in the, um, the—'

'Volume?'

'—volume, descriptive volume, yes, has been paid.'

'No, it hasn't.'

'Because I have evidence that—pardon?'

'It has not yet been paid.' Jeremiah Clyne places his quill in the groove of the account book, wriggles back into the arms of his chair. 'We received the completed manuscript from your author-colleague yesterday afternoon.'

'Only yesterday?'

Beaming, Clyne jabs a thumb backward to the shelves behind. 'There, should you wish to see it.'

Clear the throat. 'Oh.'

'Now we have to examine it for the printers. Pernickety, they are!'

Jeremiah Clyne is almost laughing.

'When shall Mr Ayton be paid? He is unwell, his family lives in distress.'

My forcefulness blunted.

Clyne shakes his head, sighs, taps a fingernail thrice upon the desk. 'Come, the text from your colleague shall be read with great scruple, to lessen the risk of mistakes when type-setting. A necessary process, Mr Daniell, *as you know.*'

'What I *know*, Mr Clyne, is that Ayton's family sorely needs those three guineas. They cannot wait.'

The gallery-owner gets to his feet. 'If we were to pay for everything in advance, sir, we would shortly find ourselves insolvent, I assure you!'

'Look, three guineas, dammit! You have your coins in the drawer. *I in-sist! Don't stand there, man! Open it!*'

Is that my own voice yelling? Whence this sudden rage? Grab the villain! Why has Clyne retreated to the wall, raising an arm across his face? End this!

'Three miserable guineas! What is that to your fancy gallery, Clyne, eh? Small change, you know it! A pittance! Give it me! Give it me right now. I shall not let you go. You–shall–make–that—*Aa-aah-ah-rgh!*'

From behind I am hoisted squirming into the air. The stuccoed ceiling grates my nutmeg scalp along its rope-work. Beneath me, pen-quills in the stand, the stand itself, the blotter and cash-book, are scattered by my thrashing legs.

'Put me d-ow-wn!'

Gasping, Clyne stumbles forward across his accounts, clutching his throat.

'Where shall I deposit him, sir?'

'Oh, just over here will do.' Moulton's smooth tones from the doorway.

'Yes sir.'

Thud.

'Thank you, Mr Winch. I am sure we are all most grateful.'

'I do my job, sir. Trust you understand, Mr Daniell. We cannot be having a rumpus. Thank you, gentlemen. I warrant the smears up there shall be wiped clean following this appointment.' Mr Winch takes a last look round. A nod of satisfaction. With order restored, and tugging a sleeve, he returns to his post. The office door closes quietly after him.

Moulton smiles with saintly beatitude, clasping his hands as if to bless a marriage. 'Good! Jeremiah, are you fair recovered? Yes? Excellent. And, er, your spectacles. That is better. Now, Mr Daniell, from the sounds reaching us in the Hall, I fear you may have become agitated on behalf of your dear friend and colleague. It appears you suffer neath some strain. Might that be the cause, would you say?'

Both feet off the ground!

Blood upon these fingertips, having touched my scalp.

Forcefulness? Utter humiliation! Thank goodness Jesse is not here.

*

Mrs Lambton has brung me to her study again for readin. She dusts and fans dry what she has wrote, afore lookin at me out o that hair-curl. Beckons me to a seat. 'Now, Jesse, shortly you shall accompany Mr Daniell into Suffolk, I believe.'

'Fink so, Miss.'

'Well, I have something for you. Do not frown so, child, it is no punishment! I retrieved this unused day-book from the back of a cup-board, and pass it to you, Jesse. Upon your travels you may record your thoughts within it, y'see. Whenever you please.'

'Fank you, Miss. Very kind. You mean it's for me to do writin about me in, Miss? For my own self?'

'Indeed so. You may write your name inside the cover, there.'

'For me, not you?' I ain't said it right. Her eyebrows is gone up into her curls somewhere, an her lips wrinkle. 'I do fret, Miss, case of a test.'

'What a strange notion! Not a test but a gift, Jesse, to use as you decide!'

'Yes Miss. Fank you, Miss. So, 'ow much have I got to write?'

Her head drops quick to one side. 'As much or as little as you wish. And Jesse, I trust you intend no impertinence.'

'No, Mrs Lambton, such words is beyond me.' The book is full of empty pages. If she don't want it back, I can use them pages for my *art* as well as writin. 'Well, Mrs Lambton, bein as it ain't a test, an I ain't got to fill-up the whole book, truly I am grateful.' I flicks its sheets. 'Them's … nice pages, Miss. Fank you.'

She is near grinnin, now.

'It is no trouble. One wonders what may be considered education within those benighted institutions. Now, Jesse, I have some news for you from St James's.'

'What!' *They knows where I got to. They are still comin for me!* 'No, I ain't goin' back, Miss, never!'

'Do not alarm yourself. None seeks you out.' Her ink-stained hand pats my wrist. 'None. The news concerns your elder brother.'

'Brother?' My heart is batterin like a volunteers' band.

'Yes. There was indeed a child next you, as you have said. A boy, Emil, not a sister called Amy. And I believe you are a special person, Jesse, two people in one.'

Mrs Lambton is beamin, like two-in-one is a good fing, an to have a missin brother yet to be twice a person is a puzzle solved. Can't make no sense o that.

People can mean different from what you fink. What is Emil? I knows I was wiv another. I heard little feet kickin, nor will never forget, along wiv my treasures. An I missed company all my life. Can it be that even your best memories ain't true? I am that mouse hidden away, believin itself easy-livin, whiles the city cat watches an waits.

*

Mrs van Brielle will have returned into Essex, to the Hollander who quit foreign bulb-fields to pluck a choice English wife from John Crome's garden. They say van Brielle, having played ships, fancies himself a lordly patron of the arts.

In this life the pitiless gods may deny our love; bliss in the next? One regards with suspicion Greek tales of metamorphosis—distraught lovers becoming a pair of sea-horses or something. *Charming twaddle*, Richard's view.

At some point during the tour, perhaps contrive a diversion past her Essex home?

Once only have I dared look long into the living irises of Ellen's blue-grey eyes, down, down, to discover the calm intelligence which waited, beholding me. And if our boat should roll with the swell would not Ellen, daughter of Poseidon, lean against my arm beside me upon the deck? Would she not respond to my passionate adoration, cling to me with each movement of the moonlit Aegean?

No. She is gone to Ardleigh.

*

At nine of the clock, the flying-coach to the eastern coast departs The Saracen's Head at Aldgate. We passengers wait in the sunlit yard as Jesse and others with the coach-boy store items aloft. The horses are led forward for harnessing, and we are invited aboard. Our bold project, commissioned by my beloved! The setting-forth upon every coastal exploration brings pangs of apprehension.

Today, Jesse is my Man. Since his presence within the carriage may give offence, he shall ride above, remain close to what must be watched over. Also, servants with the luggage go half-price. Overhead are my brass-cornered box and camera obscura, its precious mirror at the mercy of each lump or pit in the road. Nothing to be done.

Near nine hours to Harwich, pausing merely to change the team every dozen miles or so. Jesse and I shall step down in mid-afternoon at Dedham, and take another carriage to Southwold. My prentice-boy seems content atop our conveyance: *Don't you fret for me, Mr Daniell. No need you should bother, not one bit!* Nor shall I: the day is warm. A family's liveried servant, bigger than Jesse, kneels upon the mail-coach roof. Space enough for both up there. They do have a low rail.

No sooner the whip-crack than an express enters the archway at the gallop, scattering pigeons and scullery maids, causing the terrier's endless yapping. Cries of 'Hold fast there! Hold fast!' bring us sharp to a halt, the carriage being thrust back and forth with violence.

An exchange with the coachman before the rider, guiding his horse in two delicate sidesteps, turns to regard us.

'Message for a Mr Daniell?'

Open the door. 'I am—' Liquid in the throat. 'I am h—'

'You're im, are ye?'

Nod, thumping my chest; water in my eyes.

'A message of import for you, sir.'

She has written! A love letter, terms of endearment, secret courier to ease the pains of Cupid's twanging bow, my dearest Ellen! (Singing. Singing bow.) Hold out my hand.

But the messenger taps the package gainst his fingers' ends, regards it, winces respecting it, and shakes his head in regret. 'Sir, let me explain. I have undertook to ride at the full tilt on this one 'orse acrost London, to bring you a private message. The seal is unbroken, as before others you may witness. And I must return the same way, upon the same animal, though it be a spanker and mine, sir, acrost them self-same smoky places.'

'Yes-yes, I understand.' My Ellen is gone to Essex. The package sealed. This man holds me for a fool, everyone listening. 'How much?'

'Sixpence, sir.'

Sharp in-breath. Reach for my concealed purse. 'Well...'

'And a ha'penny for the bridge-crossing twice.'

'Of course.' One is accustomed to travel, tolls and so forth. Cannot disentangle the purse, that is all.

The rider sits back in the saddle. Broad grin for his audience within the mail-coach, and for others peering from the roof-rail.

'Thank you, sir. Much obliged, I'm sure.'

The seal is black: my forewarning. Come, unrip the thing.

THIRTEEN

The message is in Ruth Ayton's upright, formal hand: *Thy neighbour in kindness having advised me of thy departure...*

'Oh-h-h.'

Richard is dying. Cannot be. Cannot be!

*...might thou visit him... severest blow to my heart that Richard
shall soon be with Our Lord...*

Slumped now gainst the carriage.

'Mr Daniell, sir, you got bad news?' Jesse Cloud at my side,
eases me down to the running-board, cups my lolling head. Cool
fingers to smooth my brow, rest my cheek.

I must lean upon Jesse. Just for this moment, propped by his
slim shoulder. No longer forceful.

'Does he go or not, son?'

The carriage shifts with each small movement of the horses.
Somewhere distant, beyond, luggage passed down is set beside us.
Jesse's pale hand.

'Now, Mr Daniell, let us try standin, shall we?'

Swift behind me the carriage-door pulled shut, and they are
gone.

*

The little row called Syracuse is hard by the Thames. Eastward,
the docklands' constant clumping-and-thumping. A slow dance
of mast-tops above the roofs. The river is present in the air of
these streets, in the stench of brimming cess-pools, of black mud

and rotting vegetation, which one assumes become as familiar to a long-term resident as a well-worn shirt across the chairback.

A barefoot child of perhaps three years answers the door, sucking his thumb, saying nothing to my greeting. An older girl carrying a little one at her shoulder joins him.

'Yes?' A striking likeness of the eldest to Ruth in her serious gaze.

'I am William Daniell, a friend of your father's. Do you remember me? I saw you when you were just a little girl. We—'

'Possibly, sir.' She turns away. 'Mother!'

The frowning boy and I regard each other until Ruth Ayton appears in the narrow hallway, tucking a length of hair behind one ear. She rests a hand upon her son's shoulder.

Shocking how much older and more care-worn appears Richard's young wife now. Visage blotched and drained of colour, and in her eyes the fieriness of one facing great extremity. Her dress, high-buttoned, fits slack across the shoulders and arms.

'Um, Mrs Ayton—Ruth, I came as soon as, that is, we were near.'

'William Daniell, God bless you for coming.'

She smiles, turns her little boy about, and walks him to the parlour entrance after his sister. *Go join the others, now.*

Follow into their lodging. Shut the street-door, putting my shoulder to it, pressing hard with my foot. Neither tears nor wild release of feeling from Ruth: hers is the same quiet personality I first observed in the cottage garden, years before. That gentle spirit one associates with womenfolk now tinged with bitter endurance.

'Oh, I brought these—in case you were, um, finding difficulty in fetching provisions for... Bread, it is. Oh yes, and sausage. Just, you know, and, um, edible.'

Her quiet children watch from the room beyond.

Look down. Fiddle with the flap of the leather bag, mumble-fumbling, cheeks red.

'Sir, it is a kind and considerate gesture.' Others might have curtsied; Richard's wife does not. 'Sadly, our circumstance here is little changed.' As I pass the items to her, Ruth puts them into her gathered apron.

Behind, upon the wall, my sketch of the young couple in the cottage garden.

'Happier times, were they not?' Ruth has remarked the direction of my gaze: her brief, sad smile.

How casually I took the food when departing!

Wait now, a captive animal to be led away and brought to Richard's room, not knowing what to expect or utter or do.

'Richard, we have a visitor.'

Long moments of quiet. The pervading aroma, at first of butterscotch, becomes over-rich, then heavy and sour in the nostrils, and finally sickening.

Richard's head lifts scarce high enough. 'Aah... was hoping.' Sinks back.

Not at first a welcoming expression on Richard's swollen face. Perhaps even now, mistrust persists within our friendship. Corrosion which neither can repair. Should Richard's eyelids flicker so? And his panting breath—is that, um, *right*?

Ruth seems calm.

His fast breathing rasps. Unsurprising, as the poor fellow is d—

'I came to see you, Richard, when I heard.'

'Mmm.' No words. Weak.

The stillness broken by a sudden convulsion of Richard's body. We are compelled to watch his gasping reaction, mouth working, eyes widening in shock, followed by a struggle which drags ugly noises from his throat. Ruth reaches out her free hand to Richard's shoulder. Again, no words: merely the lightest touch of her palm. Perhaps all that his flesh may bear. How many hours must she have sat by her husband throughout his suffering?

My own breathing too shallow for comfort—wild, conflicting passions close to panic.

'Our good friend William brings food, Richard. I have it here. Shall I prepare it?'

No response. Ruth's reaction is the merest lowering of her shoulders, swift recovered. Her distress is evident from across the sickbed. And hunger in her face.

'Then I shall go cut bread for the children's supper.' Using the chairback, Ruth steadies herself before turning away.

Now he and I are alone. In spite of my clumsiness, I have been entrusted with something precious.

From closer to the bedside, the exposed areas of his body have an egg-white sheen. Their clamminess to the touch is repulsive. One swollen purple hand in view. Woeful to contemplate these changes, to witness in succession the marks of my dear friend's affliction. Step back, bring up a chair. Lean forward in hollow amiability.

Richard does not, perhaps cannot, speak.

'We were about to travel today, Richard: Jesse Cloud and I. The message reached us even as we boarded the coach for Harwich. And so, here I am to see you, now that you are unwell.'

'Mm.' Richard is listening; possibly comprehending.

Something to say, something to say.

'Jesse is my prentice. You and he met at Crumpton's Rooms. A useful assistant. Shows artistic promise. Quite uneducated, of course, and little can come of it, whatever advance in capability the youth might make. We must accept social realities.'

Tinkling in the background somewhere, a musical box. *Little Nut Tree*. Delicate chimes. *Nothing would it bear.*

Richard's pumpkin face is smiling.

'Martha... loves that box.'

*

Mr William Daniell has been long-faced an deep unhappy, an no surprise for his friend is dyin. He got the news from the orseman out of Lambeth. Also, his plans is spoilt for us goin to Southwold an do sketchin. Now Mr Daniell is again short of shillins an pence for vittles, much bein gone to that messenger. At Cleveland Street all we got on the shelf is dry bread. He ain't ate it, but straight out on foot wiv a sausage and a hunk o that bread for Mr Hayton's family, sayin *I leave you to your own de*-somefink-or-other. There is all the unpackin to do, so I speck that's what he meant. Didn't say no more. In hisself he mixes the good, the clever, and the daft.

In my hat was one o Mrs Lambton's biscuits what can still be split acrost a table's edge. You must chew slow. If I goes there, she might give me a lesson in the readin. An cake, you never know. They all tries to be kind yet turn out in some way useless, an shall never understand. If I told more bout myself, what next? Bein straightlaced, she could easy take agin me, an get me flung out.

*

'This is unexpected, Jesse,' says Mrs Lambton.

'Well we din't really go nowheres, Miss. We was called back. Mr William Daniell went out straightways, sayin I might do more book-readin, should you be willin.'

'Most willing. Mr Thomas Daniell maintains his improvement, though fatigued. But Jesse, I have no lesson prepared. That is, I have no plan for today.'

Don't know what to say to that.

'Do you follow?'

'So this what we do here, you plan for it?'

She ain't best pleased. Shifts the curl over her eye.

'I shall find something. Now then... Yes, this may serve. Let us begin. And Jesse, what is it?'

'You just took that book off of the shelf, Miss.'

'Yes?'

'Like you knew what was in it.'

'I do know what is in it.'

'An you put your hand on it straight, like you knew where that book was.'

'I did know.'

'So, does that mean you know what's in all them other books?'

'Broadly, yes. They are my possessions. A few are my own works.'

'An you'd know where to find any book up there?'

'I think so, more-or-less... Now, may we begin?'

'Yes Miss.'

'Thank you!'

May we begin? said in that way, *Fank you!* ain't her meanin. I knows when to stop arksin questions.

She picks Old Mother Hubbard—*Once purchased for another*—what I rember from St James's, an can read quite easy. The poor woman's dog is too clever for its own good. A handsome little dog in the pitcher. It sits up, begs, smokes a pipe an dances till it dies. Old Mother Hubbard don't find no meat-bones in her cupboard. I seen street-dogs lost the use o their legs, an hers don't look starved. Cannot plan if you got no cash.

Mrs Lambton has heard enough from me, so keeps my foughts to myself. Them books is hers, an so *possesstions*. I ain't truly got much *possesstions* cept treasures in the pouch round my neck. At times I takes em out to look an fink upon, same way she does wiv books. When we was very little, that child kept beside me they called Amy, an if a boy with a like name wouldn't make no difference. I still got Amy in my head. We would yet be family, growin-up together, belongin in kinship all our lives. But we is both lost instead.

Old Mother Hubbard is a silly rhyme for young'uns.

*

'The Flying Coach was full, Richard. One or two may have been journeying to Harwich for the packet crossing. But there is a halt at Dedham. I was to break the journey there, boarding the mail-coach to Southwold.'

Footsteps on the wooden stairs. Ruth takes the children their supper, and perhaps shall tell them a bedtime story. Voices from the neighbouring room; a cradle's rhythm. She may not soon return.

Fine droplets of sweat upon Richard's face and neck. Wipe them? Is that a responsibility? Perhaps pull back the bed linen. Is Richard feverish, or merely hot? His outstretched arm lies upon the sheet. I would first need to lift the poor fellow's reddened wrist. It might, um, disturb him, if he sleeps—or dozes, which seems to be the case.

'Richard...'

No response. Clear my throat. How aware is he of his surroundings? My voice may be comforting.

'At any rate, our journey to the coast is delayed until, um, later.'

The perspiration from Richard's brow has formed a trickle, meandering from temple to cheekbone. A touch with the side of my finger smears it away. Richard's skin has the feel of warm poultry, fresh-plucked. No reaction.

Difficult to know the hour—so little light penetrates. The sun is below the city's horizon of rooftops, the yard's high wall. Eight of the clock? Cannot abide the stench from Richard's bed. Sit back.

Quite alone together, this last time.

A sound: some faint murmur.

And again. *William*, was it, the word Richard mouthed? Trying to—

'Yes, Richard? I am here. William. Your friend. Here.'

No words from the man of words, but Richard's hand cranes over and tips downward, pointing, wanting me to do something. They have no bedside cup-board, chest of drawers, or low table. Again, the finger points to the floor, urging me to understand.

Does he need the chamber-pot? Please God no.

Nothing for it but to kneel. Lift these coverings, fumble about.

Neath the bed a large liquor bottle, hidden by the tumbled sheets. Unstop the rich aroma of rum. For all its sweetness, it bites the noxious air. White rum: a long-kept Carib plantation luxury.

Honey and alcohol are suitable for treating grim flesh wounds. Must have read that somewhere. But when injuries fester, alcohol neat is required before an amputation—foremost by the physician, as the wags would have it.

Richard is watching me. Will not let me go. No pleading in that prolonged, effortful gaze. And I know what must be done. Should Ruth not be here for this, um, part? *Meet thy Lord in solemn sobriety*? Some such enjoinder of hers, doubtless.

Bring the mouth of the bottle to Richard's lips. Rum spills from the sides, staining the pillow, yellowing the sheet. He shudders, eyes closed, showing the desperation of a needy, suckling child.

A contrary manner of parting. Richard has never acted predictably.

A long hour or more of stillness, save his shallow breath. Ruth has returned. She bathes Richard's ankle and foot as well as she can of the buttery pus, replaces the leno gauze with a fresh piece before resuming her sewing in the corner. We settle once again.

Silence suddenly present, an intrusion, and we both look up.

Richard stares at the ceiling.

All is over.

I have seen death depicted in galleries: the solemn gathering about an elder, positioned in mellow light upon his pillows, having bid farewell to all, blessed by an attendant priest; an ancient who succumbs gracefully, beneficently, the bearded Father of Generations at peace with the world, in the presence of his grieving family, of wise physician and loyal maidservant.

Not so.

For here lies a man of thirty-two, having died with his jaw agape like a vision of Hell, whose body began to rot while he lived, whose young children newly abed shall wake upon the

morrow without him. The wise physician is not arrived. There is
no maidservant, no mellow light, no arrangement upon pillows,
no speech, no blessing—solely his widow, who weeps now, seeming near to anger. Her trembling fingers, at first unable to close
her husband's staring eyes, must work out the means of caress
down his damp brow to shut the sight away, leaving her with
Richard's hand to hold, uncomforted.

This is how it happens. And all I want to do is creep from here.

*

A neighbour in Syracuse has called—an older woman, a friend,
Ruth tells me, possibly meaning Friend, who steps into the hall
from the encroaching dark. Dismay, murmured expressions of
appalled sorrow, the words themselves not carrying. Below, the
two hug each other. An interesting angle: grief shared, seen from
above, the play of shadow upon heads, arms and shoulders in the
dim hallway. Baffling, too, that such a painterly notion should
strike me. Why? Not an artist of interiors, to set myself apart in
this way.

Turn from the landing to stand by his bed.

Richard, we travelled many hours together in all weathers
until the accident, long before financial matters tainted our companionship. No more rich descriptions from you of grey homes
low beneath the cliff, of cooked fish-heads, of three-masters
rounding the headland. And what of Ruth and your children?

I feel a responsibility. What is done in such circumstances?
How bewildering! I am the innocent who stumbles onstage, the
flaring lights full upon him, and everything come to a stop.

Footsteps now upon the stairs; low voices conversing. Ruth
and her companion about to tidy the chamber, to pull the soiled
linen from the bed, remove the medical powders and laudanum tincture, and dress the body—*for in the morning*, one says
distinctly, *will come the children.*

Richard's rum.

Yes.

Kneel again to retrieve it. No need for Ruth to become aware, or be reminded, of her husband's thirst for oblivion. The bottle two-thirds full. Turn its dimpled surface this way and that in my hand. Squeezing the stopper tight, slide it into a pocket—for his sake.

FOURTEEN

Sobbing against La Parisienne's shoulder, my head in her hair, plantation rum long gone. This woman of the shadows contemplates me, Andalucian sherry sweet upon her lips, seeming to understand my need for forgiveness. Her soft heartbeat. The merest touch of her mouth dips upon my neck, chaste as motherly love. A familiar aroma of citron accompanies swirling greys and blues in the tenebrous air.

No mention of the, um, brief loss of her rental payment. Would she not know?

The bottle we shared lies in my hand, close at her back. Must have consumed the carafe of Burgundy while waiting below.

'He died y'see. Died. Just… not long ago. And I wronged you… wronged you.' Burbling.

La Parisienne's slender arm closes about me in the near-dark. *Ssh-ssh-ssh… Compose yourself, M'sieur. We all have our secrets.*

I have dozed awhile, for La Parisienne is at the low table, head-down, brushing her hair with swift strokes; in her other hand, a small white mirror. Both brush and carved mirror seem to match.

Cease the attempt to button my shirt. Struggle to sit up, to form words. 'Those things ivory? Or wh- whalebone?'

She holds them to her, shakes her head. I am not sober, and she seems unwilling to show much consideration.

'Very fine work. Fine work. May I 'xamine your glass?'

La Parisienne lets go both items, puts hands together in her lap, resigned. Surely, it is no violation?

The backing of the mirror-glass is smoked at the margins, its delicate frame of bone, not ivory. Near the oval's base, amid clinging ivy: *Quis separabit?* Who shall part us? The hairbrush, also: crude bristles forced and glued, but the back is carving of high quality. An identical message inscribed within the leaves.

Mentioned before. Before somewhere. 'Part of a set, hnnn?'

'These are all I have from my husband.'

'You were married?'

'Your countrymen made sure he would not survive.' She stands then, crossing to open the door. 'You wish to dance, m'sieur?'

My time is up.

Attempt to recover. Put aside grief. Forcefulness thus far ineffectual, being overcome by self-pity. When lying with her, the greater my exertion, trying for true masculine vigour, being afforded all possible encouragement, the less accomplished. Our return downstairs signals defeat: *You wish to dance, m'sieur?*

It seems I would, for I am brought to the stairs, backward downhill. One foot, the other foot, pause; steady; next step, brass rods of the stair carpet rising into the shadows.

Jaw hooked over the base of her neck, amid the loosened waves of her hair. My arm about her waist, the outstretched other clawing at emptiness. Those rhythmic swooshing sounds the movements of her hip and thigh, pressed to the wall by my weight.

Music rising from below. Not for us. Grief-drunk.

Cannot change how I lie at this angle. My head rocks upon her collar-bone until released gainst the wainscot, two steps above the salon floor.

I am part within, part beyond the swirling liveliness of Madame's salon. They seem not to need my presence. Amid the smoking flares a solemn drummer-boy taps a rhythm. Fiddler plays, sleeves rolled. My head reels out of time.

La Parisienne sits next me, one step above. Painted toenails; ankles and calves exposed. She is not dressed for dancing—scarce dressed at all.

Madame's salon: hardly the Assembly Rooms. Rich opiates assail the senses, not cordite fumes from fire-crackers across wide lawns. Hissing tallow-fat replaces chandeliers and girandoles. No English country dance, but daring couples who waltz, spindling close together, fondling in public, rat-tat-tat, rat-tat-tat, rat-tat-tat.

With long red gloves a-glitter, lips of crimson lake, and promise in her eyes, the young floor-sweeper makes the rounds to replenish glasses. A Dutch tulip ready to open! (Well, perhaps not Dutch.) Roars of encouragement, studious gambling, uproarious companionship, ribaldry! Madame la croupière in the corner with her be-ringed partner, if that be his role: tonight's creation, a black wig à l'égyptienne.

Now Madame escorts Fine Gentleman toward us from the card-table. A high white collar starches the fellow to the lobes of his ears. Ruffled sleeves above fluttering gills, polished shoes a-squeak, everything about him a parade.

'Greetings, my dear,' says Fine Gentleman, 'My game being ended, I am assured you have at once made yourself available to me, and—but I declare *what* a treasure! What rare beauty we have here! And so fetchingly attired! Madame, your establishment excels itself.' And over his buckram shoulder, 'French, you say?'

'Yes sir.'

'Well-well-well...'

Fine Gentleman extends a fingertip, lifting the chin of La Parisienne, to raise her upon it, as it were, from the step. He peruses her cheekbones, studies her eyes, commands that she smile, inspects neck and bodice.

Whatever sort of behaviour? My Parisienne! She cannot want! *M'sieur?*

Propped here against the softness of the Frenchwoman's calf, I feel her leg become tense where she stands, though her arms are let fall. Lean gainst the citron coolness of her wrist: the room a storm-tossed ship and I its ballast, swilling about below. Clutch her knee. Do not let her go.

Opposite, fingers click-clicking. *Yes, you.* Madame's tone severe, telling me to make way for higher company, though I too am unwilling. Shall refuse. Fine Gentleman's cigar-fumes irritate my eyes. Cannot yet get upright. Down by the plunging waves cling to La Parisienne, this proud unmoving figure at the bow.

Fine Gentleman stands over me, obscuring the salon's glow. Mingled aura of tobacco and cognac as he murmurs sweet obscenities in her ear. Beside my face, brushing my very cheek, a stranger's fingers raise my companion's shift, discovering swift opportunity in her unresponsiveness upon these stairs.

'Obscene! How can you?' Hauling myself upright upon the deck, listing to starboard in a raging storm, three sheets to the wind and going under. 'Leave her! She—'

'Get him out of here.'

'She is mine! No, y'shall not! Shall not quit my post! Not take her, hnnnm? Richard dead! My friend, he was! Mine. Cannot take her also. No, she shall not, you shall *not!*'

They do not follow my meaning. They have stood back, or I have lost balance. My arm outflung strikes something. In recoil, find myself by the wainscoting, all my weight upon one buckling knee. Yet Fine Gentleman looks the more startled: sprawled below, hapless beetle, knees and shiny shoes thrashing the air.

Madame is angry. Vile insults. Points at me!

All confusion. Gasping, try once more to stand. This cannon-ball head of mine rolls.

Looming muscular from the sea-mist, Cleopatra hauls me by the shoulders. My feet trail across Fine Gentleman's belly. That Egyptian wig: horsehair. The smell of it!

'Well, if it's not old Tam O'Shanters, out to cause more mischief! As a man of commerce myself, sir, I must observe how some of our clients don't quite cut the mustard.'

'No, I—'

Slowly, easefully, his grip hauls me from the staircase. The number branded upon his wrist plain before my nose. 'Because first you demanded a loan, didn't you, sir? And hoh yes, I recall how in making payment you demanded a *receipt* of the creditor!'

'No-h...' Knees sagging, feet dragging, body suspended, tilting the deck.

'Perhaps this establishment, smelling trouble brewing, might have taken action straight. But not so, y'see. We forbore. Nor have you took the hint, sir, but have come again, bringing but chaos, inebriety, and protest. Before witnesses, and unprovoked, you have felled an important client! Something must be done, sir. Like this—'

'*Aagh!*'

Sudden blow to the stomach doubles me, would pitch me to the boards, save that I dangle from Cleopatra's winch-arm.

Forcefulness. Lean forward as far as his reach permits. Snarl, contort my face, half-winded, fist raised, trying for menace:

'You. Should. Not. Have. Done. That.'

The second blow sends me crashing.

'Nor thap, in fac. Oh-h-h...'

Somewhere nearby, rat-tat-tat, rat-tat-tat and merry violin dance me to oblivion.

*

Last night I gets woke by thumpin on the door below. The side o someone's fist bash-bash on the shutters sets the dogs off all around. Is the Marshalsea men come back? The people within is cussin. An when I looks out the casement, big feller stands there wiv a animal, an on its back a body slung acrost. Cept the body is callin out an singin for glory, deep in the middle darkness when all else sleeps, an safe nowheres. Fink I knows who that body is, what ain't got back yet.

This place is a fortress—you'd not break-in here to sleep under the stairs. Though I nips down there sharp, by the time I heaves that door open, the big man has chucked off his load like muck from a waggon, an wiv the ass alongside is soon gone from sight. Heaped in the dust is Mr William Daniell like to what I never seen afore, what won't shut up yellin. I gets him within doors, locks it again, an drags him up the stairs best I can.

I fink Mr Hayton might be dead of his bad leg he had a long while, an bein Mr Daniell's only friend, is bein much missed. My Master in sorrow must have gone to that molly-house in his cups, an *thus* is come back strung upon a ass like some poor madman sent to Bedlam. By candle-light, his lips is fat an bleedin from a split. It is very sad.

Come daybreak, all quiet save the honkin from his chamber. Today I tried sittin in his chair whiles playin the proper artiss, starin at floorboards an mumblin bout tones.

I got meat stock bones much boiled to get the goodness, savin the stock for myself. His nibbs is slept most the time when not throwin-up, an don't fancy much. Them big bones is a good shape, wiv knife scrapins here an there, if you looks close. I have set em out for to do a paintin of wiv the new brushes from his uncle, since art is my purpose, not service.

*

Momentary glimpse of Ellen in a summer garden, her dress mallow-white, shades of ivory, lemon, before all swept into darkness. My heart's fast beating its only memory.

Jesse beside my narrow bed. A disturbance of air. Gone.

Brightness. My eyelids tighten. Daylight warmth on cheek and neck. An iron pain clamps my head, drags me from where I lie into another giddy dark, my gullet rising.

All twisted, having retched into the pot. Mostly, into the pot.

Awkward how I lie here, or have pondered the wall until staring has borne me down.

'You're awake then, Mr Daniell.'

'None break-fast, Jesse, thanks you.'

'Well that's a good fing, sir, since you missed it.'

'Where? What... now hour it is?'

'Gone twelve, sir. Noon.'

'What!'

'Now that was a mistake, sir—tryin to sit up quick like that, I'd say, wouldn't you? Let me help settle you back. There we go.'

'Cannot... seem to...'

'Fink straight?'

'Move my, um, this move.'

'Shoulder, sir?'

'Mmm.'

'You come off of the ass's back a bit funny, sir, when brung home. You was let go of too early, you might say.'

'Let go?'

'Perhaps we can leave it till later, sir? Oh, an in the kitchen I still got beef brof in the jug, should you happen to—or would you like me to pull out the jerry from under the bed, sir, seein as you are so dickery?'

Stillness now, save the thumping dry-dock in my head. Mouth swollen, jaw bruised, cheek fat. Blood upon the pillow.

Back of an ass?

Madame and her Cleopatra like to know where each client lives. Doubtless, to recover debts.

*

Yes, cooked food, that smell. Also, the ceiling's whiteness above a shade duller than... the last time. Turn my head.

Jesse holds a small jug and wooden spoon.

'Beef broth, is it?'

'Yes sir.'

'Don't give up, do you?'

'Past sundown, Mr Daniell. True, you was queasy, but might not be so sick now. It don't do much good to go the day wivout.'

'Mmm.'

'I made the stock fresh this mornin, sir, wiv old cattle bones off of the market. Boiled up a treat, Mr Daniell, once the gristle had—oh, well I'll say no more now, bein as...'

'No, please don't.'

'...Only, I got big bones on the table out there, sir. I can paint the ends.'

'That's very, um...

'Yes sir. Them colours I got from your uncle. I thought as how I could do the same wiv hogs' trotters, or bits of fish, you know, or tripe. Now *tripe* would be good, sir. Looks much like—'

'Jesse, do you amuse yourself at my expense? Do you mock the fact that I am not, um, at my best today?'

My prentice raises an eyebrow. 'Me, sir? *Me?*'

Ignoble, the whole circumstance. Close my eyes, adrift, slightest shift of tone between sea and sky.

The stool creaks in the next room. Jesse must have returned to his arrangement of bones. Familiar tunk of brush gainst pot. Spends all his spare time at practice.

Fat is gathered white on the surface of this broth—left for too long. After a few spoonsful, my stomach threatens revolt. Set it aside. The smell lingers.

Meat-bones boiled for sustenance are now a subject for watercolours. I have glimpsed the precious love tokens, carved in bone, sent to La Parisienne by her husband. Metamorphoses. Other hints and indications, bone memories, transformed without knowing the whole.

*

If Mr Hayton is dead I speck we shall go to the burial, not to the coast, meanin I must unpack this lot an put back tidy for several days. No tellin what we might need by then. His nibbs goes in so deep wiv his works, he can't quick come out an be company. I begun to see how that happens. For now, I can get more learnin wiv Mrs Lambton.

Livin here feels safe, but ain't. If I did open up to Mr Daniell, I might need help in later days, which bless him he could not provide. He would get a big shock, an not forgive. Mrs Lambton, bein shrewd, might be but bidin her time whiles makin me sweat. It would be worser for me, should he hear fings from a clever woman what reads a lot. I will not let her peel me like a honion.

At times I did go see how Mr Daniell fared. Once he sicked up all around the piss-pot. I got it wiped now. I did have fun about him not eatin—his fault alone. It was good stock.

Them new gas lights in the market alleys makes a stink. In darkness you can see to run, though others chasin can see your path likewise, an little gained all round. Should them costermongers come searchin, none yet knows I got a proper house to run to.

FIFTEEN

Good news from the publisher. Two volumes of our British voyages supplied to orders from Edinburgh and Exeter. My earnings *paid direct to the bank, as required by its management.*

'Jesse, I wish you to accompany me to Mr Ayton's funeral. What manner of ward-robe have you?'

'Don't have no ward-robe, sir. More of a box. Small, sir—size of a dog-kennel, if you finks of a small dog.'

'Yes, I understand, b-'

'Like that Mother Hubbard wiv the bare cup-board.'

'Yes. I was referring to your apparel.'

'She had a small dog. It did sit up an beg till it died.'

'Jesse, you saw a drawing of a dog.'

'I know, sir.' Frowning neath the fringe.

'A drawing of a small dog.'

'Yes.' Nose-wrinkling.

'The dog's size is an artistic choice.'

Quick head-shake. 'No, sir. No-oh! That dog was never much higher than her ankle.'

'Jesse, when next we discuss artistic matters, please remind me to inform you of scale and perspective. The image of the dog introduces those concepts.'

'Pusp-'

'But I shall begin with scale, Jesse, scale. And for your attire tomorrow, here is a shilling. That should be enough to—oh, my purse not to hand.'

'In your room, sir, by the bed.'

'Ah yes. Take a shilling from it. Purchase a jerkin of sober colour—gun-metal grey, perhaps—one you may wear on other occasions. D'you see?'

'An get some soap, Mr Daniell?'

'Not needed. Borrow mine. Have you not been using soap, sirrah? Is that why you, um...? Be that as it may, find a suitable tailor.'

The prentice frowns again. More going on than may appear. 'Yes, sir... Yes.' A glance aside.

'I say again: a tailor.'

'Mistress Gant's. More of an exchange, it is, on the Clerkenwell Road. Somefink wrong, Mr Daniell?'

'Wrong?'

Lips, fingers, sudden trembling. Images of Richard lying in his coffin, the lid propped upright; of his face pinned in an approximate smile; the long, troubled gaze of his children in the parlour at Syracuse as I pass; and below me, afterwards, Ruth and her neighbour clinging to each other in the narrow hall.

Alone. All alone. And where forward now?

'I ask you to leave me awhile, Jesse. I was thinking of Mr

Ayton's last hours. I am not—that is, take the shilling, go to your Mistress Gant, say why you need the jerkin. Tell her, one without obvious repairs.'

*

There wasn't no shillin, so went wiv eightpence. Over on the Clerkenwell Road Mrs Gant hangs fings up an takes fings down, movin em about so you'd say new stuff is in the shop. She finds me a grey jerkin. Plucks the ticket off afore bringin it acrost, an so can name her price. The jerkin don't much fit, bein big at the shoulders an long in the arms, though a good colour. Sixpence she arks, but I gets her down to five. *You got a bargain, young'un.* What she always says. So I says, what about some soap for payin cash. *I only takes cash,* says Mrs Gant, *an I can tell from here as you might need soap, but I sells apparel, see. Got it?* I pays up. Hobson's choice, bein no choice. Mr William Daniell wants me lookin tidy.

I don't speck she'll miss the black cotton an buttons I nicked from that bowl whiles she took the ticket off.

My hair is growed all over my eyebrows an ears; I might cut it.

An I don't trust Mrs Gant even more.

*

City streets surround this country churchyard, so small and over-full. Carved lych-gate, stone tower, yew branches darkening a low-hedged wall—elements of elegiac rural splendour, now themselves over-built. The riverside thumps faint here in St Mary's, whose grounds retain a sense of calm. No more lowing herds wind slowly o'er the lea, no weary plowmen.

The curfew bell sometimes still rings out.

To walk about the graveyard scarce encourages mourning—too many burials close together, some sunken, most with simple wooden crosses. Care needed at almost every step. Jesse stoops to examine borage plants; plucks a sample.

Richard's mother confides: 'Ruth and I asked the curate to conduct the service. A promising young man—something of a firebrand!' Neath the black veil, she murmurs: 'More suitable than the vicar.'

'I believe the choice would have pleased your son, Mrs Ayton.'

'Oh yes. Richard ever delighted in mish-mash.'

Within a few miles of Lambeth Palace, her brusque non-doctrinal stance is engaging. '*Mish-mash*! Brings to mind my childhood, Madam.'

'Oh?'

'Cromwell's men had lime-washed the interior of our village church many years before. When someone began mopping-down the north wall, images appeared of men and women in strange garb, of furrowed fields painted in green, brown, or slate-blue. The scenes held no religious significance. They were left part-revealed.'

She smiles again. 'It suggests uncertainty more than compromise.'

'Yet it puzzled me, Mrs Ayton. If those scenes were thought so out-of-place within a church, why leave them visible? Not politic to erase them?'

Now it seems I amuse her!

'Decision by indecision is highly political, Mr Daniell: the essence of mish-mash.'

'Then I suppose Richard would have approved, also.'

She rests a gloved hand upon my arm. 'Thank you. You comfort me. My son prized your friendship, Mr Daniell, as he did your art.'

Mrs Ayton moves onward. Family trait to blur edges, perhaps?

No mish-mash within the church: Richard's family to one side, Ruth's to the other. Wearing black but unveiled, she sits with her children, the neighbour from Syracuse, and possibly brother and sister-in-law. Young Martha holds her mother's hand. Jesse and I sit farther back: a fellow beside his prentice, unremarked.

'Have you attended funerals before, Jesse?'

'Yes sir, at St James's. Some folks got brung in for their last days, to get a proper burial.'

'Mm.'

'But that was the workouse, sir. Down by the fish market. I speck it's different here.'

A group of young men and women, seated along one row, look about them. Richard's acting troupe for the Interludes, at a guess. Polite nods to the critics from the journals.

Oh. And Moulton.

Mr Ambrose Moulton, black tail-coat, gloves, cane and all, to represent the Grand Scenic Hall. Moulton's presence was foreseeable: Richard wrote the commentary for our previous volumes. Why permit myself to stumble upon it? In truth, I neglect consequences.

Two other gallery-owners with Moulton; and Murray, our publisher, who issued Richard's articles in *The Thespian Cabinet*. In this company, Ambrose Moulton chooses not to heed my presence. Awkward. And the tall, fair-haired man with the toothy smile? Seems to know everyone.

'Mr Moulton wiv them folks over there, ain't it, sir?'

'Yes, it is.'

'You don't like him, do you?'

'Jesse, your hair needs cutting. It is a floor-mop above your face.'

The young curate's service treads carefully, seeking to balance subdued Church of England formalities with bold rhetorical appeals to Wesleyan righteousness, the defeat of hypocrisy, and silent Quaker contemplation. Nonetheless at its end we are surprised by his beckoning forward those in the front stall; to see Ruth Ayton, with the infant awake at her shoulder, and the older children beside, leave their places and turn to face our gathering.

What is this? Is it not the committal next? Why an address? By the bereaved—the widow, that is—by a woman? Unheard of!

We gaze about us.

So frail, Ruth and her young family stand beside Richard's coffin. All is still.

'I, I would like to say something. I cannot let him leave without.'

Silence. Can only wait.

'Forgive me, I am not used to speaking thus.' The baby reaches to Ruth's face. She takes the little hand in hers. 'Yet I am thankful for the opportunity.' She nods to the clergyman standing by. 'And our family is grateful for your coming today to pay respects, for I know some thought my husband, well, waspish—his writing, a certain sting to it.'

A degree of relaxation among us. Someone chuckles in recognition, others nod their heads: the man we knew. Ruth appears surprised. Martha, her eldest, smiles.

'At any rate, I have always read deeply in religious works, seeking to follow the true path. Sometimes, nonetheless, I failed to understand Richard's meaning in his writings.'

Just as well.

She gulps, head down. 'I wish to say that my husband was a good, loyal man who loved us all dearly, and whom we loved as much. For months after his fall at sea Richard suffered greatly in body and mind, until by God's Grace released from all pain, for which we must give thanks... My apologies, I cannot—excuse me.' Martha moves to comfort her, but Ruth gathers herself. 'At times my husband's writing may have seemed sour, even cynical. That was not his character. Richard was a spirited, moral person. A loyal companion. An earnest man of good faith. And I loved him. I simply... simply wanted you all to know.'

She glances to the coffin. One last, tender touch upon its bare surface.

'Thank you. I, er, that is all.'

Ruth's sister takes the baby. Martha leads her young brother back to the pew.

Unsure how those about me respond. Unable to look.

*

It appals, the gape of the burial pit, how mourners find themselves staring into its depths, how in those few paces from church to graveside the barnstorming curate converts himself to sonorous reciter of lyric in his clean white smock, at ease amid the opened pages of his Book of Prayers. Appalling, this collective pretence of fittingness.

Ruth does not cry. In public and beside the children her expression is restrained, eyes narrowed, mouth taut because of the struggle. At times she looks toward Martha and Bobby, offering a weak smile before breathing deeply, closing her eyes. Mostly they conduct themselves in that unnatural, constricted way children have of trying to still themselves because they are before elders. Bobby Ayton looks bewildered. The little one has begun to cough and then to cry. Ruth's friend from Syracuse leaves the graveside to carry the child up and down by the rustling trees.

One last, murmured amen; handsful of crumbled earth slither across the wooden lid.

Manage to mouth my farewell to Richard—gratitude, mostly, the essence of it. His words to me at the Barleymow: *Thanks all the same.* He would have noted my self-pity imposed upon sorrow, would have approved the blurred edges.

*

Moulton at my shoulder as the mourners depart. 'Mr Daniell, so pleased to have caught up with you.' The tall man with prominent teeth stands beside him.

'Yes.'

'A sad business. Sad business. The poor fellow was unwell for many months.'

'Oh, indeed. Richard's long illness brought hardship to his family, as I sought to explain to Mr Clyne.'

'Well now, it is regarding Good Works that I come to you. We propose to raise funds for—but no, I shall leave this in the capable hands of Willem van Brielle. May I assume the two of you are acquainted?'

What?

'No? Well then, my apologies, gentlemen! Mr William Daniell, this is Menheer Willem van Brielle, a noted man of business, a purchaser of and discerning investor in artistic works—including your own, Mr Daniell. I declare, your celebrity precedes you.'

Incredible! *Good-day to you.* To be greeting my adversary warmly! I am affecting pleasure in looking up at this fair-haired Dutch giant, who utters platitudes as his vast hand encloses my own, pumping it without cease. A little too much warmth and affection abounding, perhaps? It is a solemn occasion, the burial of my only friend, who remained so despite our disagreements. Caused most of 'em, must be said. We ought not grin like fools in a gin store.

Moulton smirks as he takes his leave. The trap of obligation set. Doubtless it shall involve my own outlay—apart from the obvious difficulty that here stands one's rival in love, this over-friendly wolfhound, and no more welcome. Are my feelings for Ellen so obvious that Moulton perceives them? Written upon my brow? My wrist branded with a fool's heart?

Jesse, solemn-faced, watches apart. He seems anxious, often glancing toward the gravel path and waiting carriages.

When finally van Brielle lets go my hand it becomes possible to concentrate.

'Yes... Um, could you offer a little more detail about this proposal, please?'

'There is no more detail, Mr Daniell. That is all we have, all we need. We put our monies together for the good lady and widow of your friend.'

'Who comprises this group you speak of, Menheer van Brielle?'

'It is Willem, please. Call me Willem. Our group is made from owners of the Covent Garden, and editors of journals, and my wife and I, of course, er...'

'And the Scenic Hall?'

'Mr Ambrose Moulton will fetch it all together.'

'Ah.' Not putting one farthing in the hat, then.

'I trust that also you will help our cause, Mr Daniell?'

'Well, Menheer, um Willem, Richard and I were friends and colleagues. I have made some initial provision for his family which—which I intend to sustain.'

Van Brielle bows his head, smiles courteously, about to retreat. He means well. Why should he not? 'My wife will be most pleased. Ellen is concerned for the childer-en. And I shall inform Mr Moulton of your plans.' Willem leans over me, confiding to the top of my head, 'I liked Mr Ayton's entertainments. Such good humour.'

Oh, hilarious. A most gracious parting between us.

But Jesse points to the gate: Ruth leaving shortly. She stands at the carriage door with her boy, the sickly infant at her shoulder as Martha half-walks, half-runs along the L of the gravel paths, bringing me a note from her mother.

They are to remove from Lambeth and shall reside with her brother and sister-in-law near Winchelsea. A generous invitation. Fears they shall be too many, but at least a roof over their heads, and *the children safer than hitherto.*

When I look up, Richard's eldest daughter watches me closely, waiting. Such an earnest child's face beneath the dark bonnet.

'Any message, sir?'

'Yes, Martha. Merely, that I understand. Um, and tell your mother that I shall communicate with her in due course—no, *soon.* Soon, Martha.'

'Thank you, sir.'

Throat-clearing embarrassment. 'Soon respond to your mother's note.'

'Yes sir. Thank you.' Martha hastens away.

My distant gesture of farewell to Ruth possibly too informal for one so lately widowed. Gathering her skirts before stepping into the waiting carriage, she may not have seen me through the lych gate.

It is over, thank goodness. And unexpectedly comforting to have uttered my regret, appreciation, love, whatever it was, at Richard's graveside. The wrangle about publishing rights, payments and so forth finally did not much matter, did it?

Or did it? Perhaps more honest to recall those jags and burrs, the inevitable smudges and patched repairs to our friendship during those years of collaboration. Ayton newly in his grave, and I'd dispute with him still!

More cash may be needed. Pride will not permit Moulton's Dutch squadron to outmanoeuvre me.

*

Mrs Lambton opens to my rap, pleased that Thomas's state of health has not deteriorated. She prepares a further public pamphlet on women's intellectual pursuits. (Brief, one assumes.) But how am I after the funeral? How is poor Mrs Ayton? Warm greetings, also, to my prentice standing by. Is Jesse prepared for another lesson in reading? The widow has been baking again, although her biscuits *this time may be somewhat crisp.*

A source of hesitant relief to me that Thomas survives. Generally, naught changed, and I am glad of it. Too many, um, dislodgements.

Uncle sits by the window overlooking the Square. Rubs his forearm—absorbed in thought, perhaps, since there can be no feeling in it. Still a catch in the old man's breathing. The rasping voice painful to hear.

'Such a pity about Ayton. Man of many talents. Used to read his pieces in the journals—fizzers, he called 'em. So they were. Seemed able to turn his hand to anything.'

'It is odd, Uncle: until the funeral, I had not appreciated how highly Richard was regarded.'

'A mercy not to have found himself in court, I'd say.'

'Actors, journalists, editors—it was a sizeable gathering at the service. Ruth gave tender tribute, also.'

'You underestimated him.'

'Perhaps. Ambrose Moulton played Master of Ceremonies, of course.'

'You don't like him?'

Must it be so obvious? 'No. Oh, and the Dutchman.'

'Ah, Willem.'

Uncle Thomas cannot know Ellen's husband, surely? Perhaps knows of him? The sick man sits with head back, eyes half-closed, the one good hand spread upon his chest.

'Well-wishers are invited to establish a small fund on behalf of Ruth Ayton and her family. Moulton to act as banker.'

'Moulton would. He shall leave the work to Clyne, of course.'

'The Hollander asked me to contribute. Told him I have other plans.'

'Do ye, William?'

'Why, yes. Sell a work at Wardle's or somewhere. Ruth Ayton shall have the profit.'

A fly wanders amid the white hairs of Thomas's wrist. Plainly, Uncle cannot feel or perhaps even see the creature's presence. Flick my hand toward it.

'If I were you, William, I'd go with Moulton's group. Stay in the lee of the Dutchman. Bought your picture, didn't he?'

'Well, I—'

'Willem knows a good many people. Academy members. Fancies himself cultivated for liking blue Delft and pictures of brigs—his own, mostly.'

'That is no reason.'

'And his English wife is one of Old Crome's daughters... Made you sit up!' Uncle's private grin. (What can he know of my Ellen?) 'A good man, John Crome. Does oils, mostly.'

'So—'

'The Academy once invited him, but John buries himself away in Norfolk. Likes Gainsborough for coloration; squabbles with Constable. Crome won't vote. Doesn't have a vote. But others heed him for that reason. If the Academy must choose between John Constable and you, Crome's son-in-law has the money to, well, change minds, let us say.'

'Bribes! Uncle, what can you be thinking?'

'Not bribes, no.'

'Certainly not! Members of the Royal Academy? A gentlemen's club it may be, and pretentious, or dogmatic, um, unwilling to embrace change...'

Uncle's face mildly impatient, waiting for a rain-shower to pass.

'...but not *corrupt*!'

'William, you have touching faith in our institutions. Which Academy members' works do you think your wealthy Dutchman might choose to invest in *after* they have voted, and which not?'

'Oh.'

'Yes. Oh.'

Have come to loathe his knowingness.

'But are not the votes in confidence, Uncle?'

*

R. Morris, Solicitors and Land Agents,
Quarry Street,
Guildford,
Surrey.

W. Daniell A.R.A.,
76 Cleveland Street,
London.

24th June 1820.

Dear Mr Daniell,
re Estates of Lt. John Daniell RN and of Mrs Clara Daniell.

According to the instructions of the above, the late Geo. Morris of these chambers produced Wills attested on behalf of Lieutenant Daniell in 1789, and of your mother in 1795. The will of each was executed according to the provisions and dispositions therein.

Upon Mr Rupert Morris's inheritance of the Guildford practice, a wide-ranging review was begun of historical files in our safekeeping which are yet to be closed or put into the vault. Sir, one such unclosed file pertains to your family. Last year, we reviewed the actions then taken in executing your late father's will, and subsequently regarding your late mother's. Some significant anomalies remain unresolved.

Previous attempts to communicate with you on this matter (viz. 10th September 1819 and 16th March 1820) may not have succeeded. Forwarding to a relative's address twice brought no reply. Fortunately, a recent exhibition at Fuller's Gallery in this town displayed several works of yours. They had been supplied by a London auction house, Messrs. Moulton and Clyne, who kindly provided your address.

We advise that after such a passage of time, this final attempt from our office exceeds legal requirements.

I have meetings with clients in the City, commencing July 3rd. Sir, if this letter should happen to find you, a suitable appointment between us may be arranged.

I am yours sincerely,
Henry Garner, Senior Clerk

Doubtless some legal hocus-pocus seeking to exact consultation fees.

Enough of long-gone calamities! It tore my heart to witness Richard's bringing-down at the last. Has this not renewed my tremblings? I have the future to embrace: fulfil my east coast tour; meet again my beloved Ellen; extend artistic horizons; become a Royal Academician; and train the prentice-boy, dammit! Are these trivial matters? Must one forever be shackled to the past?

Soon I visit remote eastern shores with an untried lad. May write from there, suggesting a later date. Stow Garner's letter in the luggage somewhere.

July 1820

SIXTEEN

A relief to be safe arrived in Southwold, if merely to straighten one's back. Below my casement the North Star swings upon its chain, screeching, tugging at the wall of the inn. Even in this forlorn, distant settlement I am foredoomed to disrupted sleep.

Music and light spill briefly into Gaol Street. Heads and hats, pig-tails and shoulders of five staggering sailors. Richard's harlequin presence amidst them somewhere, the spirit of mis-rule. Singing into the night, they seek to advance in a jigging row across the cobbles.

What o'clock?

Ten yards managed: they are capsized in the dark with all hands.

Pull-to the shutters of my chamber. Set the bar across.

*

'It ain't over-crowded in Southwold, is it, Mr Daniell?'

'Mmm?'

We walk head-down, harried by the onshore wind. It pulls at our boxes and bags, flicks the under-feathers of gulls upon nearby posts. Campion stems and clumps of sea-lavender are taken aback by the onslaught. A rissling of low grasses.

'Sir, you said they had this sea-battle here, didn't they? An they seen off all them ships comin their way.'

'Dutch fleet, it was.'

'An the townspeople left them cannon upon the Green, like to carry on if need be.'

'Culverins, Jesse.'

'An in the meantime all of em's nipped off for somefink to eat.'

'Um, the sea-battle was near a hundred and fifty years ago.'

'Yes sir.'

'Generations before our own time, y'see.'

'Yes sir.'

Proving longer than expected, this low, worn path across the saltmarsh toward the harbour. A thunderous sea crashes alongside.

'They've all gone back home, I speck. That's why there ain't so many folks about.'

At once, turn to glance at my prentice. Innocence in Jesse's expression, gazing upon the low outlines of distant buildings.

'Jesse, the light-box you carry: today you shall have opportunity to capture an image with it.' At once the demeanour changes: quickness in his eyes.

'Sir?'

'The harbour is of no great size, the land low-lying. We have these magnificent skies to behold, lad, and enough light despite the gales, yet little sense of unfolding distance. Perspective shall be the challenge in this work.'

'Pusp—'

'Mrs van Brielle requires a print of Southwold. To present her with a view of cannon upon the clifftop, untimely emblems of the repulse of Hollanders, would be—'

'Complete culverins, Mr Daniell.'

'Quite. Once our exercise in using the camera obscura ends, I shall explain this concept of perspective, as you were promised.'

'Pusp—'

'When returned to our lodging, perhaps. Meanwhile, it shall be my purpose—' (Sneeze.) 'Pollen, Jesse, nothing more. Where was I?'

'Pusp—'

'Purpose, yes, my purpose in drawing preliminary sketches. How I go about my work. Also, occasional notes upon—but let that suffice, Jesse. We are near arrived. I do not wish to swamp you with information. Y'see the arm of a winch there, below the masts? The Gazetteer tells us Southwold harbour is a distance from the town because tidal action closed-off the original port.

These heavy seas eat away the land, carrying with them stones and silt and much else. Thus, with time the Blyth River has journeyed southward parallel to the shore, in order to, to, breach into open water.'

'Sir, you look very hot. Do you want to stop for a short while?'

'Almost there, Jesse. Your equipment must feel heavy, also.'

A sudden gust throws a whole flight of birds into the sky. Their wings beat fast, stilling as they swoop along currents of air before rising again. Not chaos: a chance to explore possibility. The scene fast rearranges itself, beyond any means to render it.

*

The masts visible from the town are those of the Lowestoft packet, the Lucy, driven gainst the quayside by the gale's force. She cannot pole free. Four rowers are set off in a dinghy from the nearby pier, a line cast back to the shore.

An illustration of coastal life, but difficult to set the viewing-tent without its blowing-away. In any case, a scene's depth of view demands our distance and some elevation: by then, the Lucy may have left harbour.

A sketch? Swift water-colour, perhaps?

The lineaments of the composition are clear in my mind. Leave it at that.

More interesting is the group of cabins along the Blyth's north shore, beyond the dock, before the river reaches the outer harbour's jetties. The wind now in our faces reeks of fish and tar, smoke and middens, dung and lime. The lot of most is hard graft; nonetheless, those scraping an existence in this squat row of pitched timber cabins, huddled below the dyke passing for a coastal wall, must in their isolation share a singular identity. No homely bedcover pegged to the first washing-line: repaired canvas.

Sketch the scene inwardly. The frontages of most shelters rest upon short stilts. Their different heights and positions above the sloping river-bank cast pentagonal shadows upon the sand. Also, movement amidst the lines of shingled planking, splashed with grey and green and tarry brown.

'They're at sea, sir, most on em.'

This fishwife means to speak with me!

'Oh, they are? Thank you.'

The woman's seat is an upright half-barrel. She stabs a length of coarse sacking with a long needle resembling those Mother used. *Summer stitches for winter britches*, she would say. Proper to bestow a kindly smile upon the fisherwoman, as between fellow human beings, give her good day, and move on. But no.

Look…

Exposure has reddened the flesh of the woman's arms. Her head down, attending to her task. Mineral grains fleck the folds of her skirt, faded to the hues of a worn Bible, and so much suffused with the dark patchwork of hammered cross-pieces, timber ends and heaped nets behind her, as to be near indistinguishable from it. Now children come from the hut, from behind, from the space below. Five, six of them: rabbits at a field's margin, cautious into the daylight.

Could be a Rembrandt: *The Needlewoman*.

'Um, your husband is at sea, madam?'

Jesse sets down the equipment.

The fisherwoman dips her head to one side. 'Out on the water, over there.'

One of the woollen-hatted rowers in the dinghy. And as I hesitate to respond—in truth, staring somewhat—she addresses me in bold, near discourteous terms.

'You ent voyagers, the buth on yuh, thass plain tuh see.'

Jesse's hand at my elbow. 'Mr Daniell, sir.'

'Yes-yes-yes.' In turning aside to respond to the prentice, I glimpse the needle's long, triangular taper. A step closer. Still the woman does not acknowledge my nearness, but folds and examines an edge, her decorated box of needles and pale bodkins beside.

'I am an artist by calling, and this my prentice.'

'Artist? We do git a foo turn up every now an agin.' From her tone, she might speak of hornets. The woman looks up. Fierce, fine, weary eyes. 'An this what I do here they call makin a burlap bolster-cover for the children's beddin.'

'And you have lived here all your life?' (The hut, the wind-scoured shore...)

'Not yitt.' Her little jest. Very dry.

Even the youngest ones, playing amid the shells heaped beside the hut, draw close now—not to protect their mother, it seems, but from curiosity.

'Is that so, madam? I note the polished bodkins beside you.'

'Thass bonework, sir. He fashion it, whiles away at sea.'

'And the box, also?'

'Yiss. When he was out o Loowstuff, that was, for the Baltic fisheries. Wood-carvin or old cattle-bones, mostly—whatever come tuh hand.'

'It is beautiful work. Those different shades.'

She nods—simple recognition of fact. 'The men are gone a good while. Thass like convicts on the hulks, or prisoners o war. They git time on their hands, all on em. An they think o family.'

A ragged, barefoot boy runs a finger lightly along the box of needles, exploring its contours.

'You compare yourselves to convicts?'

'You seen what we got here: we ent locked up, but we're prisoners just the same.'

*

MY RITIN BOOK   J. CLOUD

It is closin dark
I rember NORTH STAR is rote upon the wall
a gide star to them at sea & safe place to aim for wen drinkin ale

in the nite I had a bad dreme
big Nat & me had run out the workouse just like afore
I told him we must not look like wot we are but use disgize
& in my dreme we was runnin in mud & they cawt him agen
& it was wurse for wot I noo was to come
Nat was a pore sole not nowin mutch at the best of times
I cannot forget wot they dun to him
& I was alone again upon the street.
Full stop for that I do not want no noo forts like them

I ain't got the candle to put more on paper, bein weary besides.

This day his nibbs did let me use the light-box for to trace a SOUTHWOLD pitcher. I was proud. I watched him sketch quick the fisherwoman & her needlebox and the hut at back, then some of her little ones what stayed by her knee. He ended by payin her fourpence to keep the drawins hisself, which is the wrong way round. In his hands cash is but water in a fish-net & he will not learn.

We crossed the river in a row-boat an took free different tracins off of the light-box glass, what should be enough. Mr Daniell says he will use mine of a fisher-boat reachin harbour, an dandies watchin from the jetty, holdin their big hats to their heads. He made more notes, talkin the whiles bout movement an stillness, and what he called grey hues needin free bites of acid at the printin stage, an I near understood it, for that he is a proper artiss after all.

SEVENTEEN

Cleansing, invigorating Dunwich! The tide-wave rushes inward, flooding my mind. That moment of pause to hold breath before sinking away amid the shingle captivates me.

Something for the published volume? Note this, as with observations before an etching. Best acquire the habit. How many words for an Introduction? Richard's Commentary for the northeast voyage would provide an exemplar, had I dared bring it. Too precious. Indeed, I recall smoothing my hand across the print. Such a pointless, fond gesture!

Cries of gulls high upon the air. The moderate wind upon this low cliff might permit a camera image, *The Clifftop at Dunwich* becoming yet another in the British coastal series. My beloved Ellen's letter does not preclude other scenes. Indeed, the Royal Academy expects candidates to submit new works.

Ayton would merely raise an eyebrow at my daring. Wry amusement more his style. The rhythm of that great mass of water breaks upon the shore, each arrival felt before seen—perhaps the reason my eyes begin to moisten, blurring the edges.

'Jesse, to look upon the North Sea from here, its might cannot fail to impress—um, what is that in your hand?'

'Lobster claw, sir. Found it next the steps when we was comin up.'

'Mmm.'

'Sort of blue an green, ain't it, sir? Not red.'

'Yes.'

'Thus, Mr Daniell, never boiled alive—even if caught.'

(*Thus!*) 'Yes. Now, Jesse, while we sit upon this mossy outcrop, perhaps you should learn something of the history of Dunwich. Few residents today, but once a mighty port upon the Eastern coast...'

My history of the place seems to expand of its own accord: *coins of Ancient Rome discovered glinting in the sands.*

'...the ceaseless action of the sea brings rocks and mineral southward to Dunwich, which in earlier times began to obstruct the river-mouth. Worse, the very ground was in retreat. Is it not strange that an entire coast may move?'

Jesse's eyes widen. His mouth forms the silent question: *Move?*

'The ocean's powerful current can undermine a cliff-face. In Dunwich one stormy night, buildings fell into the water. Lives were lost.'

'When was this, Mr Daniell?'

'A very long time ago.'

'Oh-hw!'

'But this coast is still being washed away.'

My prentice sits up, alert, nose twitching—again, so much like Father's spaniel!

'And Jesse, d'you know what people say?'

A youthful expression of wonderment, perplexity, anxiety.

'Do they talk of ghostly spirits, sir, what roam the burial ground where we are sat this very moment?'

'Well...'

'Or phantasms, cravin human blood?'

'Whatever next! Please, Jesse, let us not indulge Gothic excess.' Spate of coughing. Blustery winds snatching one's breath. 'Dunwich was a great township, yet when winter brought high tides and gales, whole streets would slip without warning into the waters below. Altogether terrifying. It is happening now, Jesse.'

The prentice looks about him.

'What is it people say, sir?'

'I beg your, um – this is about Dunwich, is it?'

'Much as I know, Mr Daniell. You said that streets fell in the sea.'

'What? Oh yes. They say, Jesse… Lean closer, I don't bite.' Lowering my voice, darkening the tone, heightening the sense of mystery, as Uncle Thomas was used to do when telling wintry tales. 'They say that upon certain nights the bells of sunken church towers may still be heard, sounding sorrowfully beneath the waves.'

Sorrowfully has crept in there. Storytelling.

We walk out beyond the old Friary wall. Below, sand-martins wheel and call across the air. Jesse peers over the cliff.

'Spied something, lad?'

'Bones, sir, in the cliffside. I can see a leg-bone stickin out. Can't reach it, not from here.'

'Human remains from the burial ground. We ought not move them.'

'They been moved already, sir. That bone will slip again.'

'Jesse, we have work to do. Fetch the viewing-tent and set it in position. We may be able to capture the scene southward along the clifftop, and include the fisher-boats.'

'What is that, Mr Daniell, near the gorse on the cliff-edge?'

'You have keen eyes, Jesse!' Above the shore, a cut gravestone lichened yellow, overgrown, leaning against open sky. Faint indentations to the touch: *Ioh*, and below, *th*, *yrs*.

'Very helpful. It shall become a feature of our composition.'

Inspiration! No need of the Greyfriars gateway. No Gothic symbolism. No prettified ruination. My Dunwich aquatint shall concern time and tide, and land's instability, and what the sea changes. It shall depict loss and absence, um, with all bells silent.

I can use this melancholic scene: sulphurous headstone at the cliff's edge, North Sea beyond. In the composition's lower third sand-martins on the wing, stark gainst tumbled rocks and bleached strand. Those steep shingle-banks which slip underfoot shall lose themselves in the grey, restless waters of my work.

Richard appears to me, raising his eyes to the heavens: *Spare us!*

We are berry-pickers wandering bush to bush, in places halting to sketch thistle or sedge in dry ground. A few swift lines before the slender band of sea. In my prentice's work, one feels the wind tugging leaves and stem. Admirable!

Jesse leads our descent by the narrow path, tangled with briars and nettles, slippery with loose stones, and dead moss clinging. Fallen rock in clusters below. Clutch tight the viewing-tent and brass-cornered box. Lean landward, away from the edge. And to bite upon my lower lip in this manner is of no practical use whatever.

I may portray the heath inland, where insects hover at the vetch. Less striking, yet the pink thrift, ling, and bristling gorse quiver with each gust. Dry leaves carry upon the air. The turf is springy, a thin matting of soil underfoot: flesh over bone.

An image at knee-height, perhaps? Material for Commentary wh—

'Jesse!'

Slipped. Stones skittering away. Clatter and tumble below.

'Hold fast, lad!'

Startled face, head and one shoulder above the ledge, an elbow's crustacean clawing.

'I have hold upon you, Jesse! Here—'

'Don't worry, sir. I ain't let anyfink fall. Light box… still up wiv you.'

'It is your safety concerns me!'

Immediately, the prentice slips further. More stones loosened from his crumbling ledge.

Heave and haul, and heave again, the agony of arms and wrists pulling me downward, urging an end to the desperate scrabbling of my boots for a foothold upon the ground behind, to ease the scream in my head, to be released. And a voice within the scream, above the agony, *Hold! Hold!* Prised stone and earthy pebbles clatter downward. My face in the dirt, roaring. The prentice clutches my arm, elbow, wrist. Grit enters my yell. Weakening. *No! Hold!* Heave and haul to the very fingers, lungs tearing every breath. Clasp again, inch by inch, an elbow, a forearm, until Jesse's knee can claim ground, until he can roll forward upon the path, and I can let go, and we lie panting here, safe under the sky.

Strange smile the prentice has.

'Loose stone, sir, slid from underfoot.'

'Your luck held. Oh-h!' Can scarce breathe. 'Shock, it is. Suddenness.'

Nothing but to lie here, the two of us, upon our backs. Nothing but the tide's thunder below, flights of birds patterning the sky, to calm this tumult in my breast.

A fraught, shambling silence.

'Sir… Back in the Aymarket, why did you make me your prentice? I would have took a few pence.'

'Hoh, I don't…'

The gulls' sad cries are soothing and rhythmic, wave-like. My breathing all out of time.

'Well… In Calcutta years ago, my uncle and I were waiting by the … Dispenser General's office door. Very important man, Jesse. Six Company clerks and a supervisor in the outer office, writing, writing. It was during the heavy rains they have in that region… Uncle Thomas and I watched a street-child wander in barefoot, half-naked, skin glistening. Drips from her hair were dampening the carpet. Simply stood there; looked about… I shall never forget how she regarded each of us in turn. Those dark eyes, so solemn! Starving, of course. She had nothing. Counted for nothing, A great embarrassment. What to do? I looked to my uncle… the supervisor… clerks. None spoke. Scarce a glance.'

(Can hear my lungs: worn bellows of an old church organ.)

'Our business with the important man was soon done. Uncle handed him a watercolour of Fort William. The permits were duly signed, stamped, passed across, and we left his office. Still the clerks were eyes-down, writing; the child was gone… She had been taken back to the streets, returned to the rain. Shameful, y'see, for visitors to witness the Company's callousness… With you, Jesse, I could not bear to let another slip away.'

A pale hand reaches out, before withdrawing. 'Nor did you, sir. Fank you. I reckon none else would've cared, neither, if I had fell straight down.'

'But see, blood upon your shirt, Jesse! Can you move this arm?'

'Yes sir.'

Not much, and in gingerly fashion, but movement nonetheless. Shirt-sleeve torn.

'Good gracious! How your thigh bleeds!' Long gash across it. 'Sit back, Jesse. Sit back, son. Let me—'

'Oh no, sir! No.' White-faced, unable to sit upright. 'Don't fret yourself, sir. This is fine, this is. Long as the 'quipment ain't broke, all's set fair to carry on.'

'But you bleed, Jesse, and I offer help! We carry in our box simple remedies in case of mishap when journeying. Jesse, let me examine the wound. Needs binding. The bloodstain is spr—'

'Sir, I will cope.'

Defiance in his frown, while the tide thunders below.

'A short wait, then, before we must leave.'

We lie back, half-propped gainst the slope. Not to panic, solely that. Shut my eyes. Ease this thudding heartbeat. Yet each onrushing wave brings the sudden slip and slide, moments before, of cliff-face stone; and in the brief stillness following, the horror of Richard's fall.

Breathe. Breathe.

Greater calm returns at last, and more colour to Jesse's cheeks. The fallen lobster-claw reclaimed. Right this and pick it up; check the straps and shoulder that. Single file down the uneven foot-path, subdued, knowing what so nearly took place.

Now the welcome fret of coarse-leafed plants about our ankles. Yards beyond, the water hisses as it withdraws.

*

The waggoner has seen our distress. Jesse is sunk to the ground. Bloodless lips, cheeks consumption-pale, dark stain spreading upon his thigh. We make the lad as comfortable as possible upon two haysacks propped gainst our equipment in the back. *I shall be right as rain soon. You just see if I ain't.*

The waggoner and I converse a little, sharing the afternoon's warmth. His brother is a glazier in Brantham, whereas he prefers the company of horse and open road, life along the shore.

'And you, sir?'

'I am an artist and print-maker, the lad my prentice.'

'Oh yiss? I just got the one boy, the rest all girls. He's larnin it. There ent a whole lot tuh pick up, though that do help if you loike workin wi horses.'

An agreeable quiet. Refreshing. Upon the board up-front, we smile companionably.

The route to Southwold skirts the wide bay up-river. Blythburgh's church rises high over the marshes where we pass, before the waggon rumbles coastward. A heron takes flight from the shallows, wings wide-spread. Sky and ocean merge in the haze. Image upon image.

'Small wonder, your contentment to journey these roads.'

The waggoner nods his head, still smiling. Behind us, perhaps wearied by his injuries, Jesse has been lulled asleep by the rhythms of heavy wheels, the horse's gentle trotting. She is Bluebell, a springtime foal, now six years.

*

The heavy air of The North Star's uppermost floor clings to every surface.

Tap-tap.

'Jesse? … Jesse, it was unfortunate today. I understand your need to rest. The equipment is safe. I shall have it brought to my chamber. D'you hear? Safe. A maid shall fetch you my Aitken's Medicinal Preparation. Smear the ointment upon the wound. Be not over-concerned for economy—um, that is, use it, Jesse. Use plenty. And tie a rag tight above for a while. Your meal is set aside in the kitchen.'

Turn in the dark by Jesse's door, mindful of sagging floorboards, gaps, changes in level. A mincing progress—cannot risk more injuries. Past a second room to the top of the staircase, without candle. Old timbers under the eaves, old beer and old pipe-smoke. The filth in these back-stair places! Grip the rope, head-down. My reaching for balance sweeps a sleeve against the wall, cramped as a cathedral turret. Descend twelve uneven, clomping steps to the door, which opens upon fresher air and the landing's lesser gloom.

Now which pocket the key?

*

My leg hurts. Bleeds when I move. I wrapped a strip round tight, like he said. He would have bound it, had I let him. My britches is all tore besides. They shall need washin an stitchin when I gets time an hot water. His nibbs is much up-set to be turned away, yet I had no choice, fearin to be flung out straight. I might have some chance in London, but on this coast would be done-for. Mr Daniell is good-hearted: he did climb the service-stairs to speak at the door. The ointment much like cream but tastes bad. Wet marshes in your mouth.

The lobster-claw stinks high, but only like seaside, an near cleaned out. This claw is a new treasure. It is green to look at, yet bluer by day. I will draw it when on the mend. Sketch it. A artiss prentice is above drawins.

I am weak from finkin what might have befell me this day. Sets my heart goin quick.

*

Four barrels upon wooden cruxes, musk of barley-hops and pipe-smoke, straw spread over uneven pamments, and the spittoon: nothing about the North Star's tap-room suggests an area used by the gentry. However, an artist draughtsman and maker of aqua-tints is not quite a gentleman—especially one without land or family name of note, save the gentlemanly proclivity to indebt-edness.

Sup my quart of porter without Jesse. Alone this evening at the quiet corner-table. Though I intend to review my sketchbook and notes, the first blank page appears in short order. And what insights gained? This mish-mash, this *rag-bag*, identifies few possibilities!

Mind not wholly upon the subject: wretched tremblings. My prentice wounded, my uncle a shameful disappointment, bills owing, the Academy a dead-weight borne.

This beer is mellow. Good as tincture for affections of the throat and general distempers, so the publican assures me.

Begin again upon the sketch-book, though the prentice-boy's injuries seep into my thoughts. The sudden defiance in those eyes when I sought to bind his thigh! An unhappy quiet befell us upon our return: I had crossed some boundary.

The first sketch, now...

Has he no care for himself? Following Richard's carrying-away, I dread to neglect my prentice-boy's leg. Oil, ointment, powders, alcohol, leeches? Death may follow the slightest wound.

Sup polite mouthsful of porter, then three, and four, anxiety rising. Close tight my hand upon the pot's solid, reassuring shape.

Oh, set aside the sketchbook! I have time.

During those wondrous travels in India, Uncle Thomas seemed invincible. He taught me the discipline of landscape painting, and means to live by it. When the coastal fever struck, he gave me water, told stories, nursed and washed me, changed my sodden clothes, impressing upon me that I must stay with the living. Now, Thomas cannot hold a fine brush—stricken by a malady which stole upon him in Bloomsbury, not Bombay.

How to depict this morass of reawakened feeling? Few apprenticeships in that particular notion: ancient landscape figures, blurred, part covered-over, daubed upon a nave wall. Let the prentice sleep. Jesse does not welcome my solicitude; and young limbs heal with rest. Finish this porter. Clutch the pot, my hand a-tremble as might the foreleg of a month-old pup.

The publican, wiping palms upon apron, picks up a Toby.
'More beer, sir?'

'Um...'

Sit back; near invite it.

EIGHTEEN

The North Star creaks upon its chain. Another north-easterly,
following a ruinous night of yells, boot-stomping, pot-banging,
table-thumping merriment.

Goodbye me darlin, goodbye me dear-o
Bold Riley-o's gone away.

Sung by all with spirited melancholy. At last Gaol Street fell
silent under a half-moon sky. I dreamed of Ellen, crouching helpless upon the cliff-side. Mournful tides of confused sound. Boul-
ders strewn below, stern gulls screaming.

Shakily down the morning stairs to table.

'Good-day, Mr Daniell, sir.' A pale, halting spirit in the corner.

'Jesse! Surprise, indeed! How is that leg?'

'Passin well, sir. More better than yesterday.'

His countenance changes.

'What troubles you, lad?'

'You did arks how I fared, sir.'

'Yes.'

'Don't rember none else doin that afore.'

'Ah... Yes, well, um... Did you apply Aitken's Ointment
overnight?'

'Yes, sir.'

'Good.'

'An fowl-fat over the top.'

'What?'

'Kitchen maid let me have some, sir.'

'Did she now?'

'Brown kelp, they calls it—boiled seaweed mixed wiv goose-grease. Smear it on, wrap a clof round. Her grandmother swears by it: ninety-free.'

'She does?' Say naught, say naught. 'Could you manage some break-fast, Jesse?'

'Fank you, Mr Daniell, but I was fed a little whiles back.'

In the kitchen. Taken under their wing.

'In the kitchen, sir.'

'Bread and cheese?'

'Rusks an butter. I had more than I should.'

'How many was that?'

'All of em, sir. They was *warm*.'

Signs of recovery.

*

Gentle exercise may assist Jesse's thigh-wound to heal—maintain flexibility, prevent muscle-wastage, counter loss of feeling from the binding's tightness.

Reason suggests some easing of the knot.

Perhaps refrain. A gentle coastal stroll the safer prospect. Make a slow walk with limited equipment the two hundred yards to Gun Hill, overlooking the North Sea. For Jesse's sake, forgo the wooden steps to the shore. I too would need pause for recovery, both down and up. Jesse may benefit from using the inn's roped staircase to the servants' chambers before we depart.

Along Gun Hill to inhale the salt breeze. A top hat here, striped parasol there, *Good-day*, and *A fine morning*, and *It is fresh, indeed*, while passing the Naval Guard with politic deference. Beyond the last residences, a gentle slope seaward. Inshore fisher-boats at work. Here we may sit undisturbed.

Jesse grimaces, without complaint. When might he ever have dwelt in self-pity?

Bring forth the primary pigments, two brushes apiece, charcoal, raw paper, notes. Paint freely from sketches already made. Practise! Extemporise! The locality offers inspiration: activity, depth of scene, perspective, light upon the water's surface.

Perspective, now... Some instruction promised, was there?

*

'Jesse, soon we journey to Harwich. I prefer to depart before the sun is high. Therefore, today I wish you to prepare our luggage ahead of nightfall. I trust...?'

'Yes, Mr Daniell.'

'Now, three mail-coaches to Essex during the course of—um, did you wish to say something? Good. We shall use the second, at eight. We must quit our chambers by—Jesse, you shook your head. Yes, you did. I saw you. Just once, shook your head, and that is an end of it. Now kindly disclose the matter.'

'It is but the mail-coach, sir.'

'Mail-coach?'

'Beggin your pardon, Mr Daniell, but Harwich is a port, and Southwold a port along the same coast. We could sail, sir.'

'And?'

'Cheaper and quicker, sir.'

Kitchen maid, meddling.

'So the kitchen maid did tell me.'

'Fond of you, is she?'

'*If the tides is right*, she said.'

'And what about the wind's strength? You saw how the Lucy strove to haul away. Does your kitchen maid make particular recommendations for sailing—that is, tacking, into the wind? And sandbanks? Does she consider the harbours at Aldeburgh and Orford? The vanishing of crewmen when a Preventive Officer appears?'

The prentice looks toward the great cast-iron anchor: a giant's pick, buried spike upright above the highest tide-line.

'Then I must disappoint you both, for mail-coach it is.'

'Yes sir.'

'I have lost enthusiasm for sea-going since Mr Ayton suffered his terrible injury. Near ten years we voyaged together upon our great tour: from Poole to Appledore; the Channel out of Bristol; and Pembrokeshire, onward to Liverpool. Ayr I well recall. Mr Ayton was a keen sailor, Jesse. Did you know that? Lost his footing, as you did, but in a storm at sea. It unnerves me to recall the incident, and what followed.'

Narrow my eyes gainst the bright water. A white-breasted seabird flies with steady wing-beats low above the incoming tide. It follows the shore just below the horizon, heading south.

'Ten years' partnership, y'see. As long in adult life as when young I was granted with my mother. And one does not forget.'

At this, the lad seems discomfited.

Set aside our watercolour tasks, weight the corners. No distractions, barring the wind's bluster, the weight of surging water at landfall, the long sigh of its retreat. Jesse leans back, head lowered. His outstretched leg, tight bound, swells his britches at the thigh.

'Your movement was stiff, Jesse. Does your wound bleed, despite remedies?'

'At times, sir.'

The Nancy Belle, first hauled from frothing shallows to shingle, and thence to the shell-strewn beach, is being made fast. Family members begin to sort the catch. Sudden thrashes of silver, slithering sequences. Fifty yards out, massed gulls squabble over the boat's last scraps.

'Jesse...'

'Sir?'

'When next we travel, perhaps you ought not climb atop the coach.'

'Sir, I—'

'To impose strain upon the thigh muscles may worsen your wound, if not staunched.'

'No sir, it's—'

'I am decided. Two tickets to Harwich via Manningtree, and your place beside me in the carriage, um, on this occasion. Not a servant, y'see: prentice.'

Spread nets hang amidships from the Nancy Belle. Fishermen pick them over for rips and tears, gathering as they go. A performance, in its way: aware of being watched. By the stern, a boy of perhaps twelve years thumb-tests the edge of an eight-inch bone-handled gutting-knife.

Jesse looks across. 'If I may say, sir, I fink you an me sees fings wiv different eyes, bein who we started as? But I am grateful for bein took care of.'

'Thank you, Jesse. And yes, almost different generations.'

Out on the water, rising and dipping with the swell, the gulls have largely settled.

The mail-coach from Southwold journeys beyond Ipswich, onward through Colchester to London. However, after crossing the River Stour into Essex I propose to transfer—head twelve miles east to the river's mouth at Harwich. Jesse may not know these particulars, and hence, that the Stour crossing-point is little more than a parish-distance from the country residence of Mrs van Brielle at Ardleigh. A blessed *rencontre* may yet be contrived!

Benevolence toward Jesse. Indeed, beaming as we mend our metaphorical nets.

'Then shall we resume our painting, Jesse, and your further instruction?'

A performance; each aware of being watched.

*

MY RITIN BOOK   J CLOUD

This day my leg aint so bad bownd wiv ointmints & from
a nights rest & kindly he got his creem sent me wiv a little

pitcher

of hisself all sad faced even looks like his nibbs but I still got a limp.

full stop for a noo fort

I am prowd to be his prentice wot he called me & not his survunt

it did come as a shock to fink he mite care for my hurts

when so far below him & little carin for myself

I got tawt puspicktiff in a speshul seaside art lessun

wot he dun was clever & simple at the same time

he sed look at that bote owt on the water & wen I fownd

the rite wun it wos a fisherbote nere gon from site

make yor finger & fumb into a lobsta claw sed he

I fort he mite hav gorn off of his hed but no he ment it

so I did hold out my hand like I wos a grate creecher

to pick up that pin-hed fisherbote wiv finger & fumb then he got

a stick & made marks to show not mutch gap twixt em

next we dun the same for a diffrent bote nerer land

makin a sekund mark lower down the stick & it was a bigger gap

& larst of all he pointed to the fisherbote upon the strand nere us

how bigg agen he arkst & this time my claw hand just spanned it

so he made a mark much furver down the stick & sed

now wy the diffrent sizes wen them fisherbotes

is all mutch the same in hite & lengf not big wuns & littul wuns

I had to fink bowt this nor wood he tell me

is it bein far away I sed wot makes fings look little

yes he sed so that is wot you draw you hav dun well Jesse

& I wos prowd for now I no bout puspicktiff tho not how it is rote.

Full stop for a noo fort
I have run owt bein tired & leg bindin come loose

*

'Medicine is my vocation, Mr Daniell—rooms of specialist character, scientific attention to life's common ills. Our enclosure overlooking the shore is a crucible of social fusion to soothe feverish
distempers.'

Reasonable fellow, this Purchiss. Reasonable enough. Brown
eyes; nostrils flaring above a little grey moustache; long mournful
side-whiskers, sloped shoulders. An alert mountain hare.

'Southwold has no spa. Your practice does not use—'

'Oh, a *summer visitor*! Sir, Southwold's residents know that
the Hector Purchiss Medical Treatment Rooms afford routes to
health—unlike those discredited spa towns. Bath: nauseating,
filthy pools! Trustful patients brought to imbibe quarts of sulphurous waters following their eggs, veal and Sally Lunns.'

Purchiss's nasal movements conduct his whiskers in a distract-
ing sequence. One capacious, toothy muzzle.

'Discredited?'

'Indeed, Mr Daniell, some practitioners extol the supposed
curative powers of water dribbling from cattle meadows! Yet one's
body is a temple, sir. My Attended Essential Immersion method
uses Southwold's beneficial natural resource, the sea.'

'Ah. Bathing.'

Jesse chews a fingernail.

'Mr Daniell, shrewdly you question its efficacy beyond an
early morning plunge, whereas it begins a sequence.'

A sliver of nail propelled *sppt* to the floor. Lacks all social
nicety. To be mentioned later.

Next, Purchiss's Swaddled Steam method *dulcifies acrimoni-
ous fluids in the blood*, relieving rheumatism and hypochondria.
Finally, his Unique Hot-tub method assuages and constrains

patients *made hectical through distemper and oppressed spirits.* I must have long suffered one of these afflictions; without acting upon it.

'Anybody can do a few pans of ot water.'

Purchiss has heard. Oh, the embarrassment! Yet he smiles.

'Mr Daniell, we may demonstrate gratis upon your prentice how our water-pumps of arbitrary violence impel vapours into every private orifice.'

Jesse resumes the nail-chewing.

'Unnecessary, Mr Purchiss. It seems a professional approach, compared with, um...'

'Buxton?'

'I suppose.'

'A man-trap, Buxton: full of jades. Come this way, sir. We shall assess your condition.'

Thus encouraged, entirely reasonable to subscribe.

Purchiss's advice combines principle with pragmatism: *Submit to the sea's embrace... Anticipate jelly-fish... Avoid co-immersion with submarine varieties of loose bladder.*

Jesse resists the offer to join me. However, an economy.

One's hired swimming apparel is mostly woollen with an arrangement of webbing. Its black and tan hoops have run. The thing sags. Mercifully, few witness this feeble humble-bee's setting-forth, cautious feelers outstretched. Despite the air's warmth, a strong north-easterly breeze creeps into the, um, sag.

An Attendant awaits yonder.

Forward!

'You have not been under yet, sir?' A giant before me.

'Partly.'

'Then hold your breath, sir. Ready?'

'You see, one's diffic—'

My head's contents swill between my ears. Salt-choked. Folded in two, bursting lungs, nostrils filling. This fiend cannot distinguish mortal danger! Fragment-streams of coloured light. Brine curdles my innards before broadcasting them upon the waters.

'Better out than in, sir, don't they say?'

*

I sees him get pushed underwater like givin heavy shirts a soak. When he is took to the quack's rooms, I follows. Nobody ain't said no.

His nibbs is wrapped in a flannel blanket, sat over a spirit lamp like a slow-roastin bird. They swab up fat what's dripped from his skin, makin sure his bum ain't charred. I should fink the heat would draw all the gravy out of you. Next, the hot-tub. Mr Daniell is scraped an scrubbed clean as a new tater, nor let out till lookin proper poorly.

This means the water-cure is doin its job.

Now we both limp out the place. His nibbs can scarce drag hisself along, leanin upon my arm, an walls, an posts, down Gaol Street. To feel this bad he has paid a guinea to Mr Whiskers, an might ave to sell a paintin or somefink. Best not say.

All the way he's tellin me how well he fared, an full fit by mornin. In the Norf Star kitchens they call such folk turnips. I'll not mention that, neither.

Later, Mr Daniell ain't so hopeful. Pokes at his dinner, leavin most to me. He's shivery. I would fetch a blanket, but no, he heads upstairs painful slow. All I can do is help him to bed.

'How pitiful.'

'Don't fret, sir. Lie back.'

'Humiliation.'

'Is that like a bad cold?'

'Humiliation lasts much longer.'

All quiet. He might doze.

'Sir, can I say somefink?' His white face turns to me. 'Well, Mr Daniell, I knows you are a clever man…'

'But?'

'There is more ways to be robbed than gettin your purse stole. Some in grand houses is crooks, too. I would beware them folks, sir, if I was you.'

Not a word. He is crossed the border into sleep.

NINETEEN

A cramped journey with the mail at modest cost is popular—hence unfashionable. To enter Southwold's decrepit mail-coach one mounts wooden boxes slid into place; high upon the board, the ancient coachman stamps the timber to assure himself and others of its lasting another journey; our post-boy yet answers to 'postilion'.

Jesse seems enthralled with the carriage, following with one finger its painted contours, the cushion's cracked leather. With choirboy composure approaching sanctity, my prentice breathes upon the glass before finger-writing JC there.

Opposite, a woman holds a white goose upon her lap; substantial presences, difficult to ignore. The fowl exercises its neck in long self-regarding movements. Only when disturbed by the carriage's jolting does the creature stagger upright, flapping those great wings and pitching us all into head-down chaos.

The woman looks to her companion, sitting stiff and unmoving with a wicker basket of covered something-or-other upon her knees. Interesting pose, hinting at distance.

'No harm to er wings, far as I can tell.'

'No. Else we could all go hoom.'

It is open country. Beyond the gorse and ling upon the heath, a long brushstroke of water meets the sky. An empty gibbet stands upon a low rise within sight of the road.

Onward, ever closer to my beloved's home. Good fortune needs planning. Otherwise, Richard's death has robbed me of all taste for voyaging and travels. I have told him so.

Soon Jesse and I shall be safe returned to Cleveland Street, our preparations done. Not home-sickness, but a simple wish for good order, for there to be no more woe; indebtedness; night tremors. Matters as once they were, free of complication.

Since childhood, have I ever known such times?

Steadiness needed.

*

'Mr Daniell?'

A weighty bundle lies across me. Another bundle, not of straw; scented, holds me down. Heavy lavender. And the world must have started up again; can hear it moving about up there, outside. Violets, in fact, rustling. Not lavender, still heavy. This side my ear hot, and awkward angle of the neck, which cannot be got out of, must g—cannot get out of, since the warm heaviness pressing my chest too much and my face brushed or wiped and tickling nostrils across; yet not the breath to sneeze. Also, voices wh—

'Sir?' Somewhere else, on high.

Cautious, open one eye: flutters, fills with water, mixing all the hues. Both eyes watering, but no brightness now, just ribs depressed, darkness rustling. Incomplete darkness: streaks of damson there, warm clouds across purple. Neck hurts.

'Mr Daniell, sir?'

Know that voice. Push hard, shove with open hand into the plump purple, shrink from a sudden loud shriek in my ear. Open both eyes. Part of another face, horribly and shockingly close, shows equal disgust. Folds of creamy flesh, fine pale hairs. The quivering iris of a large bloodshot eye searches mine.

'Remove your hand, sir!'

Goose-woman. Her face a long goose-egg, tinged with an angry flush. And, um, no longer opposite: here. Soft bosomy up-against. And I red-cheeked with embarrassment. Cannot explain how this has happened.

What has happened?

Leaning upon my shoulder, gooseless, the woman thrusts herself upright and removes the bonnet crushed against my jaw. Thin strands of greying hair unpinned above her ear. She glares scorn upon me. Horrible.

Someone's voice: *Not the conduct of a gentleman.*

Conduct? Stare upward, frowning, dazed, pinned.

Tap-tap. Jesse's face in the skylight beyond the woman's shoulder. 'Mr Daniell, sir, can I help?'

Not a skylight. The carriage door open, or off, the angle wrong. Where once a sandy landscape trundled by, all is vanished into azure. Buzzards mewing up there.

Dammit, we have gone over.

*

Propped gainst a mailsack, the coachman clutches his shoulder. The cleric lies pale by the bole of a tree, a clump of couch grass tipping his hat. Goose in the ditch, fleetingly visible, goose-woman searching the bushes.

Where is my art box with the brass-bound corners?

Good God, Jesse!

'Jesse!'

'Sir?'

'Are you…? Where is the…? How…?'

'Rest awhiles, Mr Daniell. You was knocked out. You was all fell upon.'

'Your leg, um, not further injured?'

'No sir, fank you for arksin. It aches, naught else. The door fell off, so I got out.'

'And the, the…'

'Just scratches to the light-box, Mr Daniell.'

The mail-coach lies upon its side in the dust, a giant stricken beast. One wheel off, the front axle shaved, splintered and finally split, having been dragged along twenty yards of stony road before its dead-weight wrenched the team to a stop. Then the quiet, the violets, brave flutterings of small birds' wings; roadside grasses and dusty air.

A wheelwright, fresh-summoned, kicks the wreckage. 'Where'd they get this one from, then?'

Shaken passengers watch from the verges.

'Dunt think I sin the likes o this ol boonshaker since Bony was a sucklin babe.'

Forlorn, the coachman tugs at his torn stockings.

'A lot o people might look at that strake all hangin off an they'd say, thass a bust rim. Yiss, an I can tell you they'd be wrong...'

Flat in sickness and shock, we examine cuts, bruises and injured limbs. Someone shivers within a blanket. Our fascination with carriage-wheels little apparent. Yet Jesse looks from wheelwright to wreckage and back, edging forward, frowning, as once in the Haymarket.

A grainy quality of the light, muslin, gauze, or thinnest tarlatan, hangs in the air, catches in the throat. Jesse half-turns to consider my chestiness. Turns back, chewing a fingernail; wipes swiftly at the blood-stained trouser with the side of one hand. Is the prentice's wound re-opened?

The Cleric replaces his hat. Re-positions his spectacles. Regards us while sitting apart—customary to his calling, one assumes.

Goose-woman has re-captured her fowl. Its feet paddle air as she strokes the plumage before looping a length of twine about its neck. Slip-knot, preferably.

'...An all of a sudden you get *WAP!* Them strakes useless but for kindlin.'

The original coach-wheel *uncommon broad*; three days to fashion another.

Stranded.

*

I was begun to fret, what wiv time passin an my leg bleedin anew from the coach goin over. Then this farmer on a big horse does stop to give his nibbs an me a ride farther along. From high up he pities us for bein stuck; also, for not bein from where he lives. My Master is slumped like a spud-sack upon the horse's hindquarters.

'No need to put your arms about my waist, Mr Daniell.'

'We just seem a long way up.'

'Grip the saddle-back, good sir,' he says, 'Ye won't fall. This horse has only accepted one pace since the Frenchies got to Moscow.'

The horse is pullin me, the luggage, an his dog in a two-wheeled market-cart what rattles over every bump. Our gear safe beside, if judderin. They use dogs to drive sheep to market in London. It's just whistles, but how do them dogs learn?

Five miles at most, but brings us to the river. Livin upon the Suffolk side, the farmer is to go right at the fork. I climbs down from the cart, ruffles the dog's neck-fur one last time, an unloads our luggage.

'Jesse!'

His nibbs needs help to fall dainty off of the orse. The farmer is grinnin. Wants no cash, but come dinner-time *hopeless City folks* will be a family story.

'Even you Londoners should discover the creek across the way, in that hollow. Morlake and his barge skulk in the reeds. Cannot think why they advised seeking passage of such a man.'

'What is your concern about this Morlake?'

'Morlake and his woman. You won't have heard what they do to witches round here.'

*

'They sent you?' The merest flicker of an eyebrow. Morlake, upon the creek's bank below the road, restrains his mastiff by a shortened chain. Behind him a thick, black-tarred mast divides the copse. Breezes off the water tug at dipped sallows.

'I was thinking a man might find peace here.'

'If he need not work.'

Forcefulness. 'Oh, an artist must work! This my prentice, and our equipment. But as you see, lacking transport.' Weary smile.

A slight nod his reply.

'I am William Daniell, of London, with young Jesse here.'

Bare acknowledgement. No other movement. Morlake's manner is wary, his barge moored up-river in this solitary reach.

'We carry corn and coal, not passengers. Where would you be headed?'

'Harwich.'

'Harwich, straight?'

'Well...' Jesse no surer than I. 'Yes, um, straight.'

'Can't.'

A weaker light now, the afternoon passing. Silence, save the harsh rooks gathering, the weeting of fowl among the reeds, water lapping the barge's hull.

'Can't be done straight. We call at farms, far as the Ipswich Mills. How we live, you understand, and it's the morrow I talk about.'

'I see.'

Jesse squats, plucks a stalk of grass, grips it between his teeth.

'But I could cross the river afore dark. You'll find an inn there. Save you three mile.'

'Oh!' A change of heart. We are forgiven something.

'Mistley, they call it, on the lower road to Harwich. You can see it. The tide's agin us, mind. Not bein my true work, I ask four shillin. Three, should you help us out the creek.'

The mastiff, yawning, stands. A sharp click of its teeth. Discussion over.

*

Swans upon the far bank? The barge seems to make little headway, yet we are half-across. Up-river, cormorants rest upon stakes in the mud-pools by the Cattawade Bridge. Square-riggers downstream. Harwich out of sight. Plant my feet firm upon the deck, despite the Tasker's mild, rocking motion. Beyond its shrouds, the sad smile of Richard's shade.

Catch the bargemaster's rare grin as my prentice-boy hastens from port to starboard and back, eager to embrace the fullness of everything. Morlake neglects to address me as *Sir*, according a perverse respect. Social niceties disdained. Nothing said, but we share an understanding as plain as this coil of oakum, coarse under my hand.

Morlake knows what we will have heard. His bitterness shrivels all it meets—when a youth in Bristol, had heard old Wesley preach on slavery. And now, as wife and baby join him on deck, part of their marriage-story is told: how his woman does not belong, could never belong. Claims of unholy chants, malicious witch-craft, blighted crops, spell-songs, curses upon the unknowing... and the corpse of the basket-maker's boy, hooked by an angler at Lower Brantham Reach.

Godless perpetrators should be ducked!
How can Morlake have made her his wife?

For she is wild-eyed, bought from slavery. Seen upon the river; seldom ashore.

Jesse frowns. 'Is that what took place, mister, bein got from slavery?'

'Faith is her name. Ask her yourself.'

'Mrs Faif, I only ever heard tales of slavery afore.'

'It is no tale, but truth. The Santo Domingo cane-fields.'

Hispaniola. A rich Carib curling of the tongue in Faith Mor-lake's speech. Her skin gleams ruby-brown.

'Born a slave, twice bought from slavery.'

Therefore, once betrayed. Something wrong with her shoulder—not seated aright. A slash-wound long-healed.

'This good man freed me from what they been doin. I was seventeen years old.' She lowers her eyes. 'Thirteen when first taken.'

I have tended to think slavery wrong. Political controversy does not in general appeal to me. Yet to look away gives others licence: Faith Morlake the living proof. How many slaves, far beyond our shores?

Jesse reaches a little finger into the baby's wrappings.

'Look sir, how this tiny mite's gripped hold o me!' Delight upon the prentice's face. 'Do come take a peep, Mr Daniell.'

Smiling toward Jesse, Faith Morlake pulls back the shawl from her baby's cheek.

But the bargemaster sees my response: 'You would remark the child's pale skin?'

No answer. Nothing.

'Why, he is our son. What did you expect? Not like we're dyeing cloth.'

All watching me.

'My sincere apologies. Um, to you both. I am slow in understanding such matters. Beyond my experience. It humbles me.'

'And you the London artist?'

TWENTY

Harwich and Manningtree Standard
Wednesday 19th July 1820

COLCHESTER'S NEW ART GALLERY

Those who appreciate the capability of artistic works to enhance the cultural life of our great nation have cause to rejoice in the forthcoming opening to the public of the Shore and Sail Gallery at North Hill, on Saturday, 22nd July at 11 o'clock.

The initiators of this splendid venture are Mr and Mrs van Brielle, of Great Hall, Ardleigh, whose endeavours in fostering discourse upon works of aesthetic appeal, and encouragement of artists, sculptors and printmakers, have been as consistently attested as they are justly lauded—in this locality and (we hear) in London.

The opening exhibition, entitled New Horizons, displays for sale the maritime works of six artists resident in the eastern counties. Private viewings by invitation shall take place at the Gallery on Friday 21st from 7.00 pm, with an introduction by the artist John Crome of Norwich. A representative of the Standard shall attend the event and thereafter report to our Readers.

We further understand that a garden party is to be held on the lawns of Ardleigh Great Hall in the afternoon of Sunday 23rd, for family members, exhibitors, and those friends of the arts who have subscribed to this commendable venture.
On behalf of all Readers, we offer our heartiest congratulations.

Aelwyn Goddard

*

The Stour at Mistley is an agreeable location. No great cliff-face here, though I struggle for breath by the upper steps, resisting a wild urge to cast myself into the expanse of greenery below. Set down my baggage; Jesse likewise. At once a promising composition appears of the bay with its moorings and activity in the foreground, the low fields of the Suffolk shore beyond, and the sweep of the river eastward, approaching its estuary. The scene arranges itself.

Morlake's barge steals past below, its rust-red sail near fully raised.

Fits of shivering seize me in the warmth of late afternoon, hours after the mail-coach was flung upon its side. Unease prowls within my breast. Upon the day Richard fell, the Scotch vessel did not founder. Of us all, he alone died. Now Jesse's thigh proves slow to heal.

Our arrival fully laden from the Mistley shore surprises the landlady of The Good Harvest Inn. Mrs Tumulty remarks our labours with equipment, my own stained apparel, Jesse's limping gait and mended breeches (the dull blood-streak not fully out-washed), and with reluctance accepts us for two nights' initial stay, *should a satisfactory deposit be paid.*

Next the river though forty feet above it, Mistley's inn offers limited amenity. One of the two bedchambers is occupied. For my prentice, Mrs Tumulty suggests the hayloft at a penny the night.

'Madam, the single chamber shall suffice. Others' lads may bed unprotected in your hayloft, but Jesse is not someone's lad, some harvest field-gleaner. I am an Associate of the Royal Academy, and my prentice shall sleep with me.'

How Mrs Tumulty's eyes widen!

'Um, not my intention to employ so imprecise a term.'

'Oh sir, I promise you, your meaning was quite clear.'

Fool-fool-fool!

A relief to have arrived, to lie in the half-dark, well-fed but sleepless, as the last swifts of summer follow their hurtling paths.

Jesse is silent, motionless upon the floor. What must he think of me?

*

MY RITIN BOOK   J CLOUD

I did sit in a coch next his nibbs not atop of it wiv other folks
& felt like gentree a big coch yet verry old wot hit somefink
& split a weel it was bad for my leg but worser for Mr Daniell
she was a big woman fell all over him in the corner wiv her
frend

& he is much shook by it the goose muk upon his sleeve
shood wosh owt the gear not spoilt the glass in wun peece
you can tell Mr William Daniell aint never rode a horse
the farmers dog was black & wite wiv a wite paw & frendlee
a slow barge ride in the end so we did go by warter if not far
I never seen a witch but hear tell they wurk spels & hav cats
not babes nor can Missus Faif be a witch-woman they will have
made up stories

she aint no old hag but kwite yung her chile took my finger
he had a good strong grip wen Missus Faif lookt at me we did
not speek nor did need to just that look atween us

it wos like we new eech other for wot we wos, in spite of all
the bad part is his nibbs & me must sleep in his bedchamber
it was but Hobsons choyse for we did come to The Good
Harvest withowt the missus here bein told afore & them two dont
get along

I did not much sleep bein full drest fearin how the nite mite
pass

this leg full tender & swolled up but must not be shown
his nibbs more perky to be here in Misslee not Arritch I cannot
fink wy.

Full stop for I got no more

*

Mid-morning. Ripples of heat rise from the ground before us as we walk. The sky is smeared. Haze along the river, misting the horizon. Lines quaver, blurring their edges. Another dream last night of Richard, dragging his bloodied foot to the carriage step. He was shaking his head. Some further sign.

Set it aside. I have a day's work ahead. Make progress and report to the Lady—soon, perhaps. Simply to behold her.

'Jesse, you look pale.' *Even more pale than usual. Deathly.*

'Do I, sir?'

'That wound in your leg: healed over, has it?'

'It's on the mend, Mr Daniell. Underneaf.'

'Loss of blood can cause faintness.'

'Yes sir, so I heard.'

'And you seem to have eaten little since we, since we arose—um, separately.'

Blank.

'You slept sound upon the floor?'

'Not *proper* sound, sir, no.'

'No... Nor I, in fact.' Some distance between us.

'Just to say, sir, our belongins is unpacked.'

'Mmm.'

'Yes sir. And in your jerkin to be cleaned I found a note from a Mr Garner.'

'You have been reading my correspondence?'

'No sir. It was fick paper for writin on. Looked important to be washed and run through the mangle.'

'Indeed so. A legal matter I am to attend to, at some point. Deliveries are made to London from here. And I was thinking, Jesse, how it may prove fortunate to have arrived at Mistley. Mrs van Brielle requires views of Southwold and of Harwich, the third scene left to artistic preference. The banks of the Stour may furnish us with choices of subject-matter, and suit us altogether well.'

'So you want to get on wiv it, Mr Daniell?'

'Yes. I suppose that is the gist.'

'Then I'll—'

'And because it is part of your artistic education, Jesse, I thought that today, for novelty's sake, we might indulge in games.'

'Games, Mr Daniell?'

We have both stopped walking, for some reason.

'Practical activities. Playful challenges. Games, Jesse. For example, standing here...'

'Yes sir.'

'Why do you adopt so ridiculous a posture? I do not ask you to pose! Now then... while we stand here, Jesse, I wish you to consider which view in any direction you would choose as the most likely to appeal to the public. Also, which view may be the most unusual, yet highly interes—*Don't-tell-me don't-tell-me*! I have further amusing activities to explain to you.'

'Feels more like a test, Mr Daniell.'

'Secondly, each to complete a swift water-colour of any part of this landscape, to include but three charcoal lines of any length serving the composition, drawn in any direction. For example, I observe that the arc of the bay here is greater than I first thought.'

'Serve the comp—?'

'A curved line freely drawn would assist me in reproducing its shape. Lines are mere guidance, the brushwork our emphasis. Thirdly, we apply the knowledge gained to make three contrasting light-box images. These we shall carry home with us as outline sketches for etching, tinting and print-making in later months— for my report.'

No mentioning *to whom*.

*

'You are not painting, Jesse?'

'I did stop awhiles, sir, to watch how you manage to work so quick.'

'Comes with experience. My career began when young. Also, I find with pigment that the final effect is not necessarily improved by working slowly.' That frown again upon Jesse's forehead! 'Cannot explain, but seems often to be the case.'

'Not always?'

'Not always, no.'

The youth's eyes narrow. 'How do you decide, Mr Daniell?'

'Well, it has to do with the difference between confidence and cockiness.' Jesse looks across sharply. A sudden smile, a nod of the head, followed by a pause. Hidden mechanisms at work there.

'Sir, I know it ain't my place to say, but I do fink you got them leaves and branches of your line o trees just right.'

'Thank you, Jesse. Development of taste! And why might you think that?'

'The shadows on that side; how it slow gets darker the furver you looks to the right, wiv the greens and blues. But you let in light sometimes, too, sir. I fought it was clever, to see it first, and then to know what to do—plain white, ain't they, them gaps? Clever.'

'Thank you. The gaps left unpainted. You have observed closely my manner of working.'

'Now I know why you was bitin' your lip over it, sir, like this— not cocky at all.'

'Mmm.' My turn to frown.

*

'I am done, Mrs Tumulty.'

'Would you wish more tea before I take these, Mr Daniell?'

'No, thank you.'

'Then may I mention that if you have mail to send, the coach for London shall be here the morrow, first light? That is their day for us.'

'I see. Of course.'

'Dependin on the weather off Harwich, and the tide for the Dutchman's packet comin from foreign. Do you have anythin to send, sir?'

'Um...'

'I keep a mailsack by the barrels, should you wish.'

'Yes. Thank you, Mrs Tumulty.'

She gathers the break-fast cutlery in one fist, stands them, and strides away.

It is as well to be aware of these arrangements for correspondence. Professional etiquette demands at least some reply to Garner, Guildford legal man, office clerk. Reward the fellow's persistence. I shall write forthwith.

*

My arrival at Ardleigh Great Hall is scarce dignified: set down near the side-gate from a passing carter's waggon heading for Colchester. A faint reek of soiled straw and Friesland bullock accompanies me. (Mother's remark, *Unbecoming, William,* as she passes my shoulder.) No gatekeepers here. The wicket entrance opens upon the latch for household gardeners, tradesmen and higglers. Birdsong in the heavy air. Follow the pathway's arc toward my beloved's home.

The Hall's dark mass half-hidden by shimmering beeches. Small orchard to my right. Dearest Ellen may reach on tip-toe for an apple, exactly there, her loveliness as she gazes upward into the foliage—this whole Eden now so bright in mind that I need never imagine her grounds again. Captured, clasped.

Behind me, sounds of trotting hoofs upon gravel. Some village turn-out, bringing two dozen children crammed upon the benches of an old haywain rigged for the day with canvas stretched across hoops, and lengths of bunting. The horses' bridles gleam, their tails brushed and gathered. The children wave Union flags upon sticks as they pass. It might be the villagers' harvest horkey, though most cornfields remain waist-high, awaiting the reapers. Few stalks cling to hedges hereabouts. And the Dutchman is no farmer.

Ahead now, beyond these overhanging branches, the children's *Hurrah!* Some grand celebration. How fitting that by chance I visit on such a happy day, once more to meet my beloved! Her trees give me shade in this close heat.

Hunched with age, Ardleigh Great Hall possesses the remains of a moat, overgrown; split trunks of ancient trees; sunken pond titivated with lilies and tufted reeds. No carriages where I arrive— simply the haycart which brought the children, now deserted, and the horses led away.

Mild apprehension tinges my excitement, edges blurred. The day celebrates someone's birthday, or some alien Dutch festival, or God forbid, a wedding anniversary. Family and friends at croquet, or sipping lemonade upon the lawn. Humble village children and the young van Brielles, released by Agata, a-skip in their shiny shoes, shall consume quantities of never-to-be-forgotten iced sponge cake. And in the quiet drawing-room, its windows open, shutters half-closed against the sun, Mrs van Brielle and I may exchange looks of unspoken longing as I relate my coastal under- takings, striving not to blush. The mild aura of bullock about my person shall not impair the scene's general glory.

Pull upon the bell.

Pull again.

Step back, peer into the windows each side the door.

This smudged sleeve is immaterial. Um, irrelevant.

At last, movement within the house! Echoing footsteps. Soft leather upon flagstones. Advance again to the lower step.

'Yes?'

'I am the artist, William Daniell, come to visit—'

'Artist? Oh, you come to the wrong door!'

'—Mrs van Brielle.'

'Like I say, sir, wrong door. We get all sorts this side. If you go along left out of here, that take you to the main entrance. Where all the guests get welcomed, see.'

'But I have come to visit Mrs—'

One hand to an elbow, the other to her chin, conveying public politeness despite inward irritation.

'I know who you've come to visit, sir, and I'm telling you where you'll find her. The artists is round there. Now I'm closing this door, on account the comin squall go right through you with the main one open. Thank you.'

A little bob before she slams shut.

Strenuous doomed attempts in the marquee to sing hymns in a unison of children's voices. Sequences of crockery and glassware to and fro across the lawns. Carriages to one side; liveried footmen in earnest talk. Dogs chase one another in and out of the dry moat, in and out of the arranged chairs, into the shrubbery and out again.

In the Great Hall's vestibule stands a sombre presence, the Head whatever-he-is, Rock of Ages, purchased with the house. I am not upon his list.

'Look, I tell you that I am an artist from London, wishing to meet Mrs van Brielle.'

'Yes sir. So it may be.'

'So it *is*. She would meet me if she knew!'

'Very likely, sir. I have to do with the on-going celebrations, which occupy us fully, as you might imagine. The guests are all arrived, sir. The name Daniell is neither listed as visiting artist, nor close family.'

'Look, how shall I say this?' *without throttling you.* 'I have indeed met Mrs van Brielle—in London, as a matter of fact. I have here,' pat-pat, next the heart, 'her signed request for my work. Also, I tell you a print of mine has lately been acquired and must even now be displayed somewhere within!'

It brings a sour, suspicious look, but perhaps sufficient doubt to require action. The old man sighs, putting aside his list.

'Await, sir, if you will.' Shuffles down the hall: 'See if I can find her, I don't know.'

Time's machinery in the slow gloom. A ticking, also, of ancient wall timbers in this Indian heat. My shirt clings.

Who are these guests? Some Dutch names, including a Kontesse Karolin van Dorfe-Mecklenburg, no less. The Reverend is Gelnay. Also, th—

'Mr Daniell, what a pleasant surprise!'

I have been watching down the hallway; she has entered from the terrace.

'Oh yes!' Stuff the list into a pocket. 'Mrs van Brielle. Most pleasant, yes.'

From below the brim of a straw bonnet, once again those blue-grey eyes regard me. The beginnings of a smile. Her fond amusement part-concealed.

'Indeed. So, the reason for this unexpected pleasure, Mr Daniell?'

'Um, well...' Dumbstruck. Our precious converse underway, leaving me ashore.

She wears a summer dress, displaying more of her neck and shoulders than when in London. Pale lilac cotton, patterned with white rosebuds in raised outline akin to intaglio. The fine chain about her throat. I am learning her look, the hue and how of that face, each grain of shadow. Must not be thought to stare.

A maid bearing an empty carafe, sugar-bowl, and spoons upon a tray appears in the light of the doorway, hesitates, is beckoned through.

'Why this visit?'

'Ah! Yes, um...' *Please do not incline your head, your soft cheek, in that way. Do you not realise?* 'Madam, happening to be in the area, I thought you might wish to hear of my progress upon the eastern coastal tour.'

'Oh! You persist with your programme, nonetheless?'

Nonetheless? Some chest obstruction. 'Yes, I—' My voice unnaturally high.

'And still your poor throat! Mr Daniell, I hope you understand my predicament as a wife. I fear I must apologise for that letter, and my not being able to—'

'Ellen!' The Dutchman's voice, from within the house. 'Ellen!'

'Shall be with you shortly! Just one moment!' She faces me once more. 'And Mr Daniell, I wish to say also how distressing it was to hear that your colleague has died. Such a talented writer! Please pass my deepest sympathies to Mrs Ayton. But this is a most busy time, as you will have gathered; an important social occasion, because Willem and I have opened a new gallery, and the Mayor of Colchester soon—'

'Ellen! Miss Deemes is much discomfited and would speak with you. Please to hurry!'

'I am gratified that all goes well with you, Mr Daniell, but our guest needs my attention.'

'Oh. Um...' (*Letter? Predicament?*)

'Thank you for calling. I do hope your work shall prosper, Mr Daniell. However, I must hasten away. My goodness, was that thunder in the distance?'

Half-stoop to kiss her hand, but already she turns toward the inner rooms. The swirling dress brings a memory of perfume. Merest touch of her palm.

I stand here, casting about in this hot, shadowed hallway. Difficult to grasp, that is all. Came to report progress regarding her commission, thus renewing our treasured association. Yet the Lady proved, um, unaware... Further, she was surprised at my tour's continuance. Some strange explanation.

Creak of a heavy door. The Dutchman pumping my hand, hail-fellow-well-met, graciousness, hospitality, his bear-paw upon my shoulder to show me the direction required, which is the Great Hall's doorway, *most welcome to visit our exhibition in Colchester New Horizons.* We emerge into the glowering daylight. Snatches of song from the marquee. A maidservant bobs when passing. *Also pleased you did contribute for Mrs Ayton and her childer-en so sad so much up-set to the heart and your sluice-gate painting shall grace the Hall but my wife's offer for the tour I could not endorse might sluice the whole moat for that price ha-ha these headstrong women what shall we do with them for as you know a letter is no contract though if you proceed to Harwich and paint my Beatrix setting sail then I shall buy it from you and which is your carriage Mr Daniell oh at the side is it sensible man avoid the crush sensible man how much I anticipate the revelation of your further works but must leave you being required by guests please pass my best wishes to your wise Uncle and farewell Mr Daniell until another time.*

Stumble head-down past the great windows, to the corner and beyond, into shadow, to the Hall's side doorway and the gravel path. Cannot bring myself to leave by the main gate. With the celebrations begun, the lodge porter would witness my forlorn departure. Heavy iron scrollwork closing behind me would scrape the gravel, its clatter audible at the Hall.

There by the orchard, peering at the apple trees, someone turns to greet me.

'William! I believe we have met at the Academy.'

'Oh yes. Pleased to, um…' John Crome, must be. Her father.

'To be brief: the storm nears.'

'Oh yes.'

'My dear fellow, are you unwell? This humid air: terrible! I wanted to say, Ellen wrote me of her attempt to commission works of you. Most unfortunate. The whole affair caused some discord, you may imagine, but a father cannot interfere. I happened to glimpse your arrival from the library. The matter seemed… Well, I know how I would have felt in your place.'

Hands me a small item wrapped in a napkin.

Lightning blazes the upper fields.

'Come, withdraw from these trees. What you have there, please open later. Done in haste, you appreciate.'

'Oh yes, thank—'

'Glad we have met again, William. You are in favour at the Academy. Farewell now!'

TWENTY-ONE

Nearing the side-gate, unseen by the Garden Party, my pace becomes the absurd gallop of an ageing eight-mile hunter delirious with exhaustion, about to crash the final hedge. Stagger a few yards along the roadway before collapsing. Leaden air thick upon my skin.

Panting, panting. Head side to side. Close my eyes a few seconds more, brought down, faint, awaiting the gunshot.

Lying here, minute by minute my bursting heart becomes enough quelled to hold the Guest List above me: *Kontesse Karolin van Dorfe-Mecklenburg, Mr and Mevr Zonderkerk with Miss Stefania, Miss Henrietta Crome and the Hon. Jenner Warburton, Sir Lancelot Writtal…*

How could I have been so foolish, not to see?

No contract. Whisper it: I was forgotten.

*

The kind couple from Little Bromley made space for me, scarce able to speak, in their gig. Set me down in Manningtree. A mile from The Good Harvest, Olympian thunder-cracks cleave the air. The first drops spit-spat upon neck and shoulders, garments soon bedraggled. Along the low riverside road, I stumble breathless from the misery of this day. Mrs van Brielle would not be, could never be, my beloved Ellen. The deadness of her response halted all my careering expectations. The young wife thought herself a patron in the old way, and I the object of her Good Works—neglecting merely her lack of access to Willem's funds.

And this from John Crome's daughter!

Last few yards to the inn as fresh rivulets cross the hard ground by the Stour. A first volley spatters the expanse of wide grey river beyond. Whiskered heads in the barley fields dip as if stung.

Fling open the inn door. A dramatic entrance in a flashing storm, as befits the creative temperament, the self-regarding blubbery, childishness, and social incompetence to which any respectable artist must naturally strive to conform. Fetch me liquor, ye balladeers, for that I am undone by heartless Ellen of Ardleigh, Lily of the East.

Drenched, silent, pass these staring faces. Forcefulness.

Do not shake your head, Richard. Does not help.

Such a fool!

*

My chamber. Our chamber. No Jesse. Wipe neck and face, bare head, wrists. Tweak the collar to free my back of soaked cotton.

Upon the small table a fresh watercolour, risen in places like half-baked pastry, left to dry. A deeper hue gathers in its moist hollows. Paper too thin for the medium: naïve technique. Yet this small plant, Jesse's subject, is most observantly recorded. The angular lie of it, from ground to observer, and the pigment enough precise in tone to resemble a page from an illustrated natural history: *Heartsease* (Wild Pansy). The lad shows promise.

What of this weighty object passed me in a napkin? Five guinea coins, wrapped in notepaper! *Cannot put all to rights, but enclosed may help. Say naught. John Crome.*

Help? More akin to salvation.

*

'Have you seen my prentice-boy of late?'

Though reluctant to respond, Mrs Tumulty cannot prevent herself from glancing toward the side door.

Once again into the downpour. Gutters issue upon the yard—little torrents which run awhile, merging to pools across the cobbles. Flanks of nervous, stabled horses thump the stall-sides. Both water-butts overspilling. The area sweats a haze of milky vapour from the ground, confined by sheets of rain to a few square yards, and no beyond.

In the kitchen garden Mrs Tumulty's daughter hunches shoulders against the rainstorm, stumbling to pile sheets into her basket. Someone assisting crosses to the second rope-line where women's rags are pegged, plucks each one straight from its wooden fork, each time the line rebounding.

Difficult to identify this dark-haired other, glimpsed briefly between the bobbing lines, whose pale glistening arms reach for, um, personal feminine items not spoken of. Sweep clear the droplets from my eyes. But the shock to my heart has told me: the helper in the rain is Jesse.

*

My return to the chamber assailed by weariness and bewilderment. Close to collapse from what occurred at the Great Hall, now to discover that one's effeminate prentice engages in womanly occupations!

Is this how he thinks of himself?

Adopt a mantle of calm, masking my fury to have harboured some corrupt molly-boy. There he stands, this horror, pale as usual, mess of black hair dripping over his brow, shirt clinging gainst arms and shoulders.

'Close that door, Jesse, will you?'

Wet footprints gleaming upon the floor.

'Somefink wrong, Mr Daniell?

'*Close that door, will you?* is not a question.'

'No sir. That pitcher don't belong there. It was only me avin another go, so—'

'Jesse, leave it. Leave it!' Clear the throat. 'Now then, now. Huh! It comes to my attention that, which is to say, I am made aware that circumstances, as we have them, both of us, have them, between us, are not fully compliant with the terms, loosely defined, of the arrangement.'

'Sir?'

'The understanding we agreed in our agreem—contract, informally understood. It appears you are in breach.' More throat-clearing.

My prentice frowns.

'Namely, that you are not whom or what you say you are.'

My thrust has slipped neath his guard. The fellow seems unable to speak.

'Jesse Cloud, I have been grossly mis-led.'

'Mis-led? By me?'

'Of course, by you!'

'But I have done your biddin, sir. An proper, far as I know. Please tell me if not.'

'I do not question your service.'

'Well so long as my honesty, an care wiv the dockyments, an seein to your wants, an faithful carryin of your light-box an luggage, tryin alongside to learn how to be a proper artiss prentice, then—'

'It is not to do with those matters, I have said.'

'I don't, I don't—'

'*Listen to me!*' The Furies within, screaming all hellishness. Unseen, unknowable, fearsome beyond control, my hands their claws.

An insufferable silence of my own making descends, intense

as the storm. The casement-glass dribbles colour. No escaping, and we must stand exposed in it until the darkness passes. Cannot look each other in the eye. Hands on hips, Jesse peers to one side, as if searching for something lost.

'Now then, now then...' (No more of that. This youngster has fled the workhouse.) 'Listen to me, Jesse. I saw you remove, um, personal items from the washing-line.'

My prentice looks about the room in helpless appeal. 'Washin?'

'Women's things. Don't lie, Jesse, it is enough trouble we have here, as it is. I saw you take them from the line. And where are they, by the way?'

'Downstairs, sir, wiv Mrs Tumulty.'

'With Mrs Tumulty? Those women's rags, um, feminine personal th—Ah! Then you were not indulging in some sick fantasy. You were assisting the innkeeper's daughter, an act of kindness, however much contrary to manly nature! Of course, of course! Just for a moment I feared—well, I'll not say. A laughable suspicion of mine. I owe you an apology, lad. You are not, or rather, there has been no—'

'Sir...'

'—deceit at all.'

'Sir...'

'The old artistic principle: *First essay may lead astray.* Avoid leaping to conclusions. Closer examination—'

'Mr Daniell, sir, I am a woman.'

'—or as my uncle used to say, *when first observing a subject, look twice,* and—'

Wipe a wet sleeve across my face.

'What?'

'I am a woman.'

Look up, look away. Consider that spider threading the ceiling's corner.

'Hah! A joke. Cruel joke. Hermaphrodites. Some mischief of

yours, Jesse. I heard what you said, lad. You told me the washing was returned to Mrs. Tumulty.'

'It is mine, sir, what she looks after for me.'

'Then—'

'Yes sir. Mrs Tumulty knows. Has done from the start.'

'But she is such a dull woman!'

My prentice smiles.

'Don't know if it will elp for you to hear this, sir, but I was born a girl. My mother must have brung me to the workouse wiv Amy, what turned out to be a boy, and French. This Amy, what I fought my sister, got took away soon after, an I never saw im no more. But I knew there was young orphans worser off, an I wasn't no orphan since my mother's keepsakes was left for me. At St James's I grew up as a girl, wearin girls' garments, was put wiv girls, an was spoke to as a girl. Boys was lucky, I fought. Boys got to leave when younger, an do proper paid work, learn a trade, get respeck, whilst girls got taught ever to obey, stitch neat, scrub steps, how to lay table, an prepare for childsbirf an God. Them fings did not look to hold so much promise. I was all mixed-up inside. Nor did I let on, for that none sees inside your head.'

'They are roles which God Himself assigns to us – the foundation of a sound society! Has Mrs Lambton preached sedition to you?'

'I wouldn't know, sir. It is above my understandin.'

'Look, we cannot defeat our essential functions. They define us.'

'No, Mr Daniell, we can't: I am as I was made.'

(Mixed-up?) 'Or, um, purpose in life.'

'Beggin your pardon, sir, but I am past childhood. I have a woman's parts. I speck you understood that, Mr Daniell, from what you did see out-doors. I am sorry if it up-sets you to talk of it, sir, but some o them was my rags, new-washed to use again, gettin rained on. It is a pity how you did learn the truth.'

(I am the very last, it seems, brought to perceive it.)

'Once out the workouse I swapped my girl's apparel for fings off of a scarecrow in the alms-ouse grounds. To cut off my hair an be a grubby boy was but a guise, Mr Daniell. Like somebody alongside. A mask so as to get work, an not have to sell myself nor nick goods, though little work comes if you got nowhere to live. In all that time I never fought I was a boy. D'you see that, sir? D'you see? Alongside me, not standin for somefink else.'

'Jesse, you make light of your long deception, but most surely it represented something to me! To me, it did! Here was I parading, some simpleton thinking to have my prentice-boy by my side, when others, uneducated people, some of them—Mrs Tumulty— could with one glance *know* straightway what they were looking at, um, whom, were looking at. I, William Daniell, discerning artist patronised by gentry, an observer and etcher of fine lines, who speaks in high terms of looking beyond the obvious, I alone it seems did not could not distinguish, see or descry, was blind to, oblivious of, all detail without any kind of inkling suggestion token or tell-tale hint of a sign or least indication some detectable signal flagged that the prentice-boy sharing my chamber *was in fact a woman*! *How, dammit, how*?'

'Sir...'

'Not even an hermaphrodite! Quite *fail* to comprehend!'

The scritching of the shutters has begun to ease. One final brilliant flash illumines the river, before thunder booms across the sagged rooftop thatch.

Cannot breathe. Cannot breathe for it.

'Have you been with men? Speak true, now.'

'No sir.'

'Ah...'

'Men have been wiv me.'

'My God!'

'Oh, Mr Daniell, your hands is shakin. I must stop. It don't really matter, all this. I knows you ain't pleased wiv me for keepin secrets. I speck you got much to fink upon. An whiles you was away, I fretted how you might fare at the Dutchman's house—so now, Mr Daniell, might you want to sit back an rest a little? Like that? You ain't well. I can go fetch weak ale, should your chest be bad.'

'Yes. Fear so. Brought upon me by up-sets.'

The skies clearing. Amid the last rumbling-away, Richard's voice in my ear: *No theatre manager books two melodramas for the same week. But two in the same day, William, and a thorough drenching to boot? Truly, you are impossible!*

Sweep a hand across my hot scalp. 'The tour must be suspended. I have lost heart.'

'They say twelve miles to Harwich, sir. It's—'

'No! No more wisdom from your kitchen-maids!'

Yelling my despair, and this creature, my prentice, driven back.

'You must pack, you hear? There are no funds! Never were. Begin packing. We return to London forthwith.'

TWENTY-TWO

Supper at The Good Harvest, conducted without converse—my prentice watchful, my anguish nearing dejection. Mrs Tumulty's early contempt for me shows no sign of mellowing to hostility. This evening, serving the table with bitter efficiency, she bestows Fairy Godmother smiles upon my cherubic companion: *Poor mawther, that ought do you some good.* The youngster dips a forefinger in the gravy and licks it clean.

Repulsive to behold.

To retire upstairs after dining seems inappropriate. Only by force of circumstance have certain truths concerning my prentice been disclosed to me, his employer and instructor, though casually apparent to a provincial woman innkeeper.

Her employer. *Hers*, dammit!

Sit back upon the bench, head gainst wall, keeping my own counsel.

The prentice moves the stool aside from our table's edge. Observes the room.

The tap-room benchers are adamant: Reverend Gelnay and his pox-faced curate may disapprove, but many country-dwellers must work long hours a-Sunday. Brings a thirst, all agree. Even the mournful waggoner, solitary in a corner with his hat, smiles. Pots raised with solemnity to this accord. Another barrel lifted upon the cruxes.

Mrs Tumulty's daughter, doubtless party to the womenfolk's kitchen conspiracy, arrives at our bare table.

Request brandy along with porter. Brandy has quickening effects. Good for the heart, denoting a person of discrimination— one with sufficient cash, having postponed his going to Harwich. Not to journey-on brings an immediate saving. In future, accept advance payment solely: a lesson learned. My prentice says nothing.

But no brandy! The girl shakes her head: No longer kept, sir. Some rigmarole about supplies once held for a regular, later discovered dead at the foot of his staircase. The remaining liquor finished-off by the hop-pickers, in honour of the malthouse.

The inn admits to Creek Rum, dark and odorous from the cane. A sort of special purchase, carried weeks across the Atlantic, rowed ashore by night to a mooring up-river in the reeds, onward to a safe stowing-place, and parcelled out thereafter... sir.

Rolls her eyes for the prentice's benefit.

'Oh?'

'Shall you order some?'

'Um...'

A toby of porter and two pots set before us, followed by a bottle uncorked of this precious creation, somewhere between tar and liquorice, and two small glasses. The prentice and I glance at each other, but my unforgiving countenance shields inner wounds. A single glass filled, one pot. I am brought to deny all generosity, any concession or movement toward reconciliation, for fear of seeming weak. Yet weakness it is to show nothing, to become nothing except unloved, and await sympathy for it.

An hour gone. The long clay pipes are re-filled. Certain fluids ejected upon patches of straw with impressive accuracy. Voices are more raucous now, the chorus to songs-from-the-floor more universally engaged. Boots and clogs stamp and step the boards with greater fervour, jokes are increasingly ribald, skittles more violent, the pouring of beer less fastidious, its consumption more immediate, the steaming black wall outside more fully occupied and oftener visited.

The prentice watches me. Furrows of sustained questioning to which I cannot respond.

*

His nibbs did say there is no cash, an this journeyin was all a mix-up. I fear it won't be long afore he turns me off. I might get sent away at any time to walk the streets hungry again. It is only so long afore you gets caught.

Him an me ain't talkin. I have hurt him. Lost his trust. His lady-love must have done besides, on the same day, an he has gone into his shell. We sits together here, like neither knows the other, wiv all the singin an swillin of ale an merriment goin on about us.

For deceivin him I am in the dog-ouse. Mr Daniell finks I was actin a part, but he is wrong. I tried to say how I did come to put on men's apparel. I was never bein anyone but me in britches, an it was me wiv hair in a tangle, an me carryin his light-box to put safe atop the coach. I ain't two people. Others must fink what they wish, though some is sharper on that score. I wanted to tell him but feared the worst, an by not tellin him, have brung it on, wivout no hopes of readin or bein a proper artiss prentice doin pitchers.

I cannot go upstairs for fear he will read my purpose wrong, so must stay here, waitin for him to speak. But Mr Daniell is too angered by what I done: will sneak a glance at me, then look away again if I do turn to him. Didn't fink grown men played them daft games. How will he be, back in Cleveland Street, knowin it is a woman deceiver in his house? Bein found out, I lost my chance of freedom—what I ever dreaded.

It ain't slavery, what I got now, nor yet a prison: there is bright days when you spy somefink how it might be, like peekin in past a rich man's door. But it ain't freedom neither. Everyfink hangs upon what my Master does feel, or say, or meet wiv. To cross him at the wrong time would easy put me back upon the streets, an when that rich man comes out his door, it's just another starvin beggar in his way.

This night I would look at my treasures for comfort, but must sleep in the chamber wiv his nibbs. Seein me different now, he might demand fings of me—his price for keepin me on. Don't speck he would treat me so unkind, but Mrs Veebee must have brung him proper low.

I wait for the hours to pass, no more.

*

The maltings revellers straggle homeward, the mariners gone as a boarding party to seek female company. In the tap-room the bargemen savour their pipes, considering the dominoes in silence. Such stillness, as if posed for me! Mrs Tumulty's show of heartiness flags; she stacks washed platters with undue force, one by one upon a shelf. I shall take the air.

Shadows have lengthened across the yard. Wan stars. Movement and snuffling within the stables. The hour holds warmth despite the downpour; bears the odours of old beer, of hay and animal-straw, of barley malt, and sometimes the faint fragrance of mauve evening stock drifting from the window boxes. Stand for a while, hands clasped, aware that in fact I am wearing carpet slippers.

All is finished here, in more ways than one. Tomorrow, journey homeward.

One slow, deep breath in this last of the day.

A gate slumped against the wall invites me forward. Shuffle over, cautious of soft soles on wetted cobbles, to glimpse what I can of the river. The tracing, sketches and notes are secure in my satchel, their composition and tones in my head. *The River Stour at Mistley, Essex,* when realised in its printed glory, shall mark a polite incursion by William Daniell A.R.A. upon the painterly hinterland (the *Country* indeed) of John Constable, my Academy rival across the Cattawade. Yet everywhere I look could be a Constable. Topple him from his realm!

Mischievous thus to dismiss a rival artist at fashionable London galleries. Smirk, nonetheless!

Full moon, pale in a wide sky.

A watery light the colour of ewes' cheese lies over this ground, suffusing the shadows of blackberry bushes, ageing wild grass stems, whitening stalks to a new prominence. From the tree-tops below my feet, the river's span reaches northward to the cattle-trampled ings along the Suffolk shore, becoming obscure now. With the dawn, those higher slopes across the water will rouse themselves, shake off their purple, and shimmer with nodding barley until the reapers' coming.

And this dampened footwear must be packed.

From behind, someone approaching.

'Just wonderin how you fared, sir.'

'Yes...'

A scene's features do not last, neither the dimming day nor its residual light a quarter-hour onward. Small occasions pass without record: so customary, yet so striking! I cannot work speedily enough in these transforming shadows; possess no medium, no means of capture. I must rely on memory, knowing I shall somewhere fail.

The prentice steps forward. 'Sir, forgive me for arksin, but I ain't sure as to packin your green weskit. See, for the journey. Will you be needin it for the coach, Mr Daniell?'

The shape and structure of the young prentice's face remain visible—the skin little blemished; the jawline rising high at each ear; slightness of the nasal bridge. How searching those dark eyes!

'I shall wear it. Risk of airs.'

'Then I shall lay it out, sir.'

'Those, um, coaches. Falling apart, wasn't it, falling apart, which lost a wheel? Axle? And breezes following rains bring agues.' Rueful smile, shake my head. 'Lacking the confidence in life I once enjoyed.'

The prentice nods, as if more is to be said on that subject, although not just now.

'An might I mention, sir, it would help me to be told if you was plannin to keep me on, knowin what you do now.'

Cannot reply. Thought-words missing. The understanding I had believed was mine—working-knowledge, fundamental truths—altogether washed away. Why this sudden fearfulness?

'Well I—'

Somewhere a door slams shut. Bolts made fast. The answer lost.

Grievous to stand here, incapable of taking hold upon reason, quite unable to decide or speak, trapped. Put my fingers to these moving lips. Hide. Rub my growing beard, wave a hand to disguise its quivering. Grass-hoppers in the nearby shrubs, grass-hoppers without cease, grass-hoppers-grass-hoppers-grass-hoppers. Beset now by panic, all my moments gone.

'Somefink wrong, is there, Mr Daniell?'

'Wrong?'

'I speck it was a proper up-set, what happened, sir. I am sorry for it.'

'Mm?'

'I fought I might stand beside you awhiles, Mr Daniell—not gettin in your way.'

'Oh-h.' Half-sob, half-sigh.

Quiet settles between us. A different quiet now, perhaps encouraged by eventide.

'I, um… I am grateful you join me here.' From fellow feeling, not chance. This much understood. 'I meant to say, before the recent—beforehand, that your painting of heartsease shows fine variation of painted tone. Gradual shading, rather than dark or light.'

'Fank you, sir. I do try.'

The day fades and cools. Behind us the inn-yard lamp casts a brighter beam. Only the nearest bushes still visible—swelling, losing definition, hosts to flitting creatures. Above the line of trees, the furled topsails of two ships down-river.

Breathe, breathe. Ease the grip of my fingers, grasping nothing. I remain in good general health, for all the insistent sound of grass-hoppers eats into me. No accidents akin to poor Ayton's. I have in large part taken care. My parents were cautious in their ways, also, yet neither reached forty years; what of myself here in the fancy, embroidered, Bengali slippers? What prospect?

Long sigh. Not sorrow, exactly.

The prentice's slight frame is stark gainst the encroaching night. Those billowing sleeves, the calico drooped at the waist, the loose-fitting, rounded collar—all emphasise rather than conceal the wearer's vulnerability. Her vulnerability. *Jessie*: a mere stroke of the inkpen, the young woman beside me whom I failed to see.

My prentice is steadfast, lively and intelligent, loyal, willing to learn, artistically able. Those fine qualities reveal themselves despite an abiding struggle against circumstance. For most surely the youngster is vulnerable. So little apparent before, it is obvious to me now: Jessie is precious, not because she is a woman, but because of the frailty we all inherit. So simple is this thought, I cannot encompass its dimension.

The prentice watches me askance—studies me, perhaps.

Therefore smile: 'I am weary, naught else, and your recovery from the fall is not complete, Jessie. Let us pause awhile here this evening, before we go in.'

Almost without thinking, not protectively but in silent fellowship, reach out to her—a brief, light touch of assurance upon the shoulder, as if it were the most natural thing one might do, now nightfall has borne away all superfluous shapes and shadows.

*

Since the rains, everything in nature seems to have a hang-dog air. Shrubbery leaves bend low, flexing in light breezes off the Stour; a sudden soaking as my legs brush dock leaves and hogweed. The land is quiet with the memory of what passed hours before, slow to lighten, to regain pale streaks of the aura which comes with dawn. The morning star low above the horizon, the sky more grey than blue.

Such early rising may again become habit once back in Cleveland Street, my implements close by.

The mere prospect excites fresh life in these fingers. To spread careful notes and sketched possibilities before me, removed from all distraction, darkness slipping away as first light inches along the workshop wall! I yearn to take up a gleaming copper plate, inhale the familiar, inky smell of the press stripped of its covers, to contrive an impression of the soft thin metal, weigh it bright in my hands. The lines begin to reveal themselves. My fingers are light upon the contours, the blade keening away fine layers to gain the required precision, consistency of pressure, and depth. To have it all in mind; to struggle with the love of it, lying ready there, awaiting only my beginning. I would feel more secure.

Pause, eyes closed. Merely pause. Hands slack. Breathe in the new day.

From time to time, droplets strike the rain-pool at my feet. River waters lap the Mistley shore. A few yards away, the seventy or more swans gathered here are loth to abandon sleep. Distant bells in the sheep meadows.

Beautiful, but changes nothing. Deceived and self-deceived, a fool to others still, and ill-prepared even for this early morning's excursion to make a sketch or two, should the spirit take me. I have the charcoal, just here, but no pad or surface. Solely her letter from Maddox Street: the ache, the shame of it hidden deep, folded close as sin against my heart.

Use the blank sides. Put them to some purpose.

Breathe. Breathe again. Set all else apart. Today we return.

TWENTY-THREE

Holdin his travel-bag, Mr Daniell goes in-doors at Cleveland Street an wiv one hand lifts the sheet off of his printin press. A little smile to hisself, rocks the wheel, runs his fingers along a beam, sniffs the greasy metal smells, picks up the acid jar to see how much, afore goin over to his rows of tools, checkin they ain't got themselves set out wrong whilst we was away.

It is his home. He will not keep me on. If I runned from here now, I would be no better-off than afore. I got to seek out another way. I wonder what he finds different in me now, from what he found in the Aymarket. The belly-ache an bleedin now quite gone, fank God. It gets you down.

I been glad to see places way out yonder, the animals, woods an fields, whole flocks of birds, an folks too few an wretched to husband it all. Along them shores I did sketch plants an creatures I had never knowed of. The boatmen catches fish in hundreds straight out the sea, big ones what struggle, flung into tubs. Women comes to the strand an buys em fresh-caught for their families. In London you do not see them fings.

Comin back, from far out it was a brown cloud acrost the city, like bonfire smoke mixed wiv a cannon-blast, but is dust an dry muck mostly. I got sight of masts pokin up over stretches of the river, an church spires an factory chimbleys. London is what I know.

Yet the city ain't safe, an his nibbs is ever short. He frets bout Mrs Hayton, sayin we mus go sell pitchers at Wardles or else-where—raise cash for her family an for ourselfs. He would neither let down his dead friend, nor show hisself up afore the Dutchman. An pitchers is one fing we ain't short of.

*

My prentice transfers the frames from neath one arm to the other.

'It hums round ere, don't it, Mr Daniell?'

'An artists' quarter, in fact. Flaxman and, um, that coterie.'

'Beggin your pardon, sir, but the other free-quarters is what smells, then.'

The very ground emits a charnel-house stench. All inward-facing doors and windows shut, as if Hanway Yard itself were im-prisoned.

'Here is Wardle's, Jesse.' (Jessie. My presumption of her male-ness proving difficult to unpick.) 'Can you read the sign?'

'No sir—well, *Arts* I can make out. Oh, an might them first ones be *The Hanway* somefink? Is that what it says?'

'Correct. You make progress in reading. For here,' finger out-stretched, 'we have *The Hanway Emporium* top row, *& Arts Agora* beneath.'

'Cor!'

'Yes, a mouthful.'

'Wardle's ain't wrote there?'

'No. Wardle is the owner's name. Would you wish me to explain *Emporium* and *Agora*? From the Latin and the Greek?'

'Not here an now, Mr Daniell, if it's all the same to you.'

Buttermilk-painted doors, lined with mustard: a caution in themselves. Once within, Jessie waits by my shoulder, nostrils twitching. Father's old hunting-dog would stand motionless at the great wood's edge, sniffing the air with like anticipation.

'Hush awhile now, we do not want an auction.'

The youth raises an eyebrow.

'You know what an auction is?'

'Yes sir.'

'Good.'

My prentice's reply near voiceless, with exaggerated lips: 'When people die, it's, they sell off their belongins.'

'Mm, well, today we do not seek an auction.'

(That frown!) 'No sir.'

Wardle's customary, ill-lit display: leftward, framed art-works cramming the walls; rightward, household furniture, crockery, toys and books. Midway, a bazaar of gleaming vases, oriental some-things-or-other, and ceramic milkmaids. A mish-mash, indeed.

Mrs Wardle emanates wraith-like from between the curtained recess and a suit of armour.

'Ah, Mr Daniell once again!'

'Good-day, Madam.'

Mostly, public recognition gratifies artists of standing; Wardle's of Hanway Yard recognises artists in need of cash. Differ-ent, um, kettle.

'I perceive we have an associate. Wonderful! Which is?'

'Jessie Cloud, my new prentice.'

Which is introduced, and which bows before royalty. Today I signal successes in taking an apprentice, and in bringing works for sale with charitable purpose.

'Perfectly delightful, Mr Daniell, I am sure.'

'Jessie, unwrap.'

Mrs Wardle is much taken with my corn-mill's great sails, admires cloud-shapes, billowing clothes upon a washing-line, saplings arched.

'The etched lines and print quality are superb, delicate tints upon the sail where sunlight becomes shade: such accomplish-ment, Mr Daniell! You may blush, sir. I declare, you may blush! And all for charity. Well!'

Jessie grinning for some reason.

The sweep of Mrs Wardle's arm indicates the prominence awaiting my *Corn-mill and Garden at Weston*. 'The fox-cub pictures can go, Mr Daniell, I assure you.'

(Go? Should be drowned like kittens.)

Shellfish-Gathering was an afternoon's work in youth when new returned to England. Done with a flourish that has deserted me of late. I am become more hesitant. Do others remark my trembling?

Mrs Wardle greatly admires my daubs suggesting human figures—shore-delvers, their ankles enfolded by wet sands.

My prentice is overcome by coughing. Turns away to peruse works upon an upright beam. Mrs Wardle purses her lips.

'So, Madam, what is your offer?'

'Offer?'

'Um, sold for charity.'

Mrs Wardle's warm glow fades to dismay. 'Mr Daniell, we speak at cross-purposes. Artists hire the Hanway exhibition spaces; we obtain profit from purchasers. Were the Emporium to purchase these works, would it not thereby accept responsibility for selling-on? Visitors might not discern excellence; might prefer fox-cubs to tonal technique; decline highly-priced fine prints, and leave them unsold. Which is regrettable, not so? For who then bears the cost but the Emporium, though wishing to support charitable causes?'

The emanation adopts a studio pose—possibly, *The Sorrows of Niobe*.

'What do you offer, Mrs Wardle?

'Two pounds ten shillings, sir, cash in hand.'

'And for the water-colour?'

Mrs Wardle hesitates. Some change of mind? Cannot fathom her discomfort.

'Let us say three pounds for both, Mr Daniell.'

Jessie frowns.

Forcefulness. 'Um, three guineas?'

'Done.'

Which is accepted with mutual regret.

'Mr Daniell!' Jesse getting above his station. Um, her.

'One moment!'

The money changes hands. We smile: *Younger generation. Whatever next.*

'Mr Daniell. Somefink for you here, sir, if you please.'

'Yes-now-what-is-it?'

'Ain't that—?'

Oh no! 'Mrs Wardle, how came you by this watercolour?'

'Someone brought it in, Mr Daniell, seeking to pawn it. Which is what we find can occur.' A certain needle in her tone of voice.

'Um, did you know this person?'

'We had not met previously. Slight, but which hopped about. Now, my sisters and I when children were taught deportment. The back kept straight, thus. Which is the key point. And one advances, so… It is *glissant.*'

There she glides, a fluent swan. With a fixed smile, Mrs Wardle pauses mid-stream to extend one wing in a gesture of refinement.

'Living as we did in Totten-ham, such accomplishments did not extend perceptibly the range of marital opportunity available to us. But I declare once learnt, never forgot.'

'The work is signed.'

'Several Academicians are known to Wardle's, Mr Daniell. May we suppose your familiarity with this work of your uncle's?'

'*Procession into Madras*? Madam, when a child, I watched that very procession!'

My prentice straightens, frowning.

At once Mrs Wardle's mood improves: 'Splendid! A significant item of personal history. Confluence of time and chance. Good reason to regain your uncle's work, not so?'

'How much?'

'Two pounds, Mr Daniell, if you will; upon the ticket.'

Jessie steps closer, away from Uncle Thomas's painted *Procession*. Tight-lipped: 'Sir, I was just showin you them elephants.'

'Two pounds. Done.'

*

Mr Daniell can't help bein opeless wiv money, not seein how others is keen to take it off of im. I feels bad, for tellin him of the pitcher in Wardle's wiv elephants by his Uncle done years back. If I had kept my mouf shut his nibbs would not have seen the pitcher, nor known from whence it must have come from. *Thus,* has he come home wiv but twenty-free shillins for Mrs Hayton, not free guineas. He might have to make it up hisself, though ain't yet got all the way to knowin it.

*

I have Uncle's *Procession* here with me in Cleveland Street simply because Jesse chanced upon it. That stately palanquin, done in haste! Better paintings were sold to local potentates and Company administrators. No matter, Uncle would say, some artworks open doors. My prentice had recalled our previous exchange concerning the—what was it, ivory back-scrubber? Picked up in some Bihari market-place!

Many a hungry fellow-artist has needed to sell at Wardle's. Indeed, one of Richard Ayton's fizzers launched the phrase, 'Gone to Tottenham', uttered mournfully of celebrated names. Wardle's Emporium is the place for a quick deal with few questions asked— akin to the Vauxhall Gardens after nightfall in that respect. Yet no mention of burglary at Uncle's apartment. *Procession into Madras* was not stolen goods. She who presented it at Wardle's, who hopped-about, must have been Mrs Lambton.

The widow is exceedingly intelligent, for a woman: has published novels (however fanciful), pamphlets upon women's subjects. Education and so forth. Not a thief. When she laid her hand upon Thomas's shoulder he clung to her, struggling for breath; clung to her. *Look after Lizzie for me, won't you, when I am gone?*

Uncle Thomas continues to provide my accommodation. Only after his passing shall new responsibilities befall me. Would a middle-aged artist then be more secure of circumstance than a widow-housekeeper of fifty?

'Jesse! … Jesse, are you there? … Jessie?'

Footsteps upon the hallway stairs. 'Ah, at last.'

'I been down to the yard, Mr Daniell.'

'Well, both works sold at Wardle's put three guineas at-hand for assistance to Mr Ayton's family.'

(That familiar frown, head lowered. His silences may convey doubt. Or her.)

'And my original intention to send funds to Winchelsea is abandoned, Jessie. I shall pass the sum for Mrs Ayton to the collection at the Scenic Hall.'

'Yes, Mr Daniell, and—'

'You were about to say?'

'No matter, sir.'

'Do please go on.'

'It's cheaper, sir, ain't it? I can run to Oxford Street and give it over quick. To send a package brings a cost.'

'Mmm. Uncle's watercolour belongs within the family, Jessie. Glad it was regained.'

'Do you want it hung along the corridor, Mr Daniell?'

Yes, keep it here! Why not, after all? Had little considered what to do with it. Was I thinking to return my uncle's work to Fitzroy Square? Wardle's bought it in confidence: why fetch back the owner's abandoned pup?

Weariness brings weak decisions. Thoughts of Richard and his family flood my head, subsiding, rising again.

'Mr Daniell?'

'Mm?' (*What now?*)

'Do you fink Mrs Lambton told him, sir? Does your uncle know he is broke?'

TWENTY-FOUR

'Young Mr Daniell! I recognised your knock. Do come in. And dear Jesse, too—welcome! You were not expected so soon.'

'No, I...'

'The task completed ahead of schedule? Your uncle shall be most pleased! His health no worse, no better. One finds so little respite. And our nonsensical government outlaws free association! The poor souls last year in Manchester, seeking universal suffrage, were slaughtered by our own Hussars! I declare we women of Marylebone shall continue to decry such abominations. Do not those barbaric men-of-means provoke the very revolution they would avoid?'

'Um...'

'Yes, Young Mr Daniell, yes, they do. Also, Thomas mourns for your collaborator and friend, Mr Ayton. His poor wife and children, consigned to Winchelsea! And regarding your own east coast travels, not to know of your whereabouts, frankly, has been quite—'

Mrs Lambton's speech is arrested, her head a little to one side and the curled lock a-dangle, through which an eye peers—a toy dancing figure whose mechanism is without warning broke.

'Have I misunderstood?'

'Perhaps.'

'Your East of England visit, not...?'

'Not entirely, no.'

Mrs Lambton rights herself, re-animates herself. Affability

recovered. 'Fortunately, I baked yesterday, and have lemon biscuits in the barrel, which may appeal provided they are well soaked. Therefore, let us take refreshment with your Uncle Thomas, and you may tell us the excitements of your travels!'

A little skip or two, full working order restored where she stands.

'Mrs Lambton, I have a prior question, um, first. Were you aware from the outset that my prentice-boy here was not as might appear? Was it confessed to you?'

Widow and prentice exchange glances. Guilt apparent: further conspiracy! It is an entire game of gossips goes on about me. I am the blindfold guardian, swishing in the dark, there to be poked at amidst women's giggles.

'My own surmise, Young Mr Daniell, nothing more. We did not discuss it.'

*

'I have been seeking to sketch with my other hand.' Uncle's snort—brief, bitter—becomes a lengthy liquid cough. 'Passes the time.'

Thomas lies pale, slumped into three large cushions, his stricken arm lifeless upon the counterpane. Silk bed-jacket over the buttoned nightshirt. Linen sleeping-cap. He has lost weight. Less appetite, perhaps, or less cash. The presence of the Madras painting at Wardle's remains to be explained. What can be done?

'Never too late to learn, Uncle.' The most dreadful humbug.

Despite an opened window and swaying drapes, the same stale, malodorous quality deadens the air. Journal and magnifying glass; medicinal powders wrapped in paper twists; water, laudanum, horse-spoon. Removing a book, Mrs Lambton seats herself upon a small wicker chair by the bed. It is where she and Thomas might share a news-paper once the morning is well begun. Everything seems much as before.

However, all is not as it was. My prentice stands still, gazing from *Lower Slopes of the Nepalese Hills* displayed above the bed, to *Bathers in the Indus River*, and from one person's face to another. Jessie has that familiar frown, and still a boy, one would say. Without change in appearance, the transition hard to accept.

A random lemon shortcake: *May I keep it for later? Thank you.* Choke an early-morning pigeon. However, my prentice gnaws with relish—gamesome as a teething terrier. Mrs Lambton has set hers adrift. She passes a bowl of tea into Uncle's palm, watches while he sips, before putting it aside for him.

'Well, William, your travels. Tales to tell us?'

Where to begin? Not with the folly of my embarrassing betrayal in Ardleigh. Best avoid the failure to discern that my own prentice is a woman, one whose artistic capability is striking, despite low birth. Indeed, little I dare report to Thomas save artistic endeavour and the hazards of the road. At forty years of age, still beholden to my uncle, still needing to impress.

*

'Tom-boy, are ye?'

'*Thomas!* Tut-tut, to say such things.' Mrs Lambton smiles toward Jessie. 'It was for her self-protection.'

'Beggin your pardon, sir, but long skirts all gets in the way when you dig-up spuds.'

'Hah! By Jove, a youngster of character!'

Whose were the potatoes in question, more to the point.

Lean forward. Forcefulness. 'Um, may I say, it is not clear to me where one goes from here. That is, perhaps discuss it? At some point, review one's options?'

'Young Mr Daniell, do you refer to an apprentice's learning at the artist's elbow, or to male and female biologies?'

'Both. For example, when shall this new identity be revealed?'

Mrs Lambton stretches out her legs where she sits, her feet

protruding beyond the hem of her dress. She regards them thoughtfully, wiggles them to-and-fro in opposite directions.

'Jessie's identity is already revealed. Moreover, has it not always been hers? Is not everyone here aware of the fact?'

'The lad cannot continue sleeping in my apartment now he is a woman!'

An awkward silence. My folly of biblical proportions, writ large upon the wall.

'Oh dear. More tea, anyone?'

*

'You need not fear to be alone, Jessie. Do you understand me? You are not alone.'

Thus Mrs Lambton, when ushering the prentice into her study. Women's talk, is this? At first so simple, on second thoughts signifying more. How may my prentice, given lodging and protection, fear to be alone?

Nevertheless, seize this opportunity.

'Uncle, to mention another delicate matter: I am aware that your finances are somewhat stretched.'

'Aware?'

'Yes. Over-stretched.'

'What has Lizzie told you?'

'Nothing. She has told me nothing.'

Cringe beneath his scrutiny, as if nine years old and in trouble again, before at last Uncle Thomas sighs and leans his head back further into the bolster.

'The first banking collapse, William, you remember? Mob riots? Miller somewhere, strung up from his own sail? The Fusiliers summoned at one point. I split my savings between two banks when that happened. Near halved my losses.'

(*Losses.* Then I am correct.)

'Crosby's Bank failed at the end of last year. Rebellions in the Caribbean, ye must have heard. The slaves killed Crosby's brother, burned the crops, sank a ship in harbour, and fled. Most were caught, of course. Flogged or hanged. But the Bank collapsed, and I lost all I had there. At the time, you and Ayton disputed your own project's funding. Thought best say nothing.'

'Uncle, better to have told me! I would have understood.'

'*Understood*? What would ye have done from your understanding, eh? There was nothing left, man!'

'And now?'

'Now? Lie here. No more fancy watercolours with this arm, William. Dead limb. Not that I trust physicians, even Theo Phillips.'

'Uncle, you have maintained me at Cleveland Street all these years. Please allow me to—'

(Allow what? To do what? I need those rooms in Cleveland Street. How can I remove the printing-press, so carefully reassembled? Evict myself?)

'Allow me to, um, rent it from you, Uncle Thomas.'

*

My return to London brings fresh perspective upon the catastrophe at Ardleigh, begun by my risible, middle-aged passion: Ellen van Brielle as willing wife or lover. Such beauty, for my gaze alone! Those blue-grey eyes watching me; her dresses at eventide, graced by silver about her neck. Ha!

Naïve to expect the lady's feelings to mirror my own, captured in some light-box image. And gross to dismiss the existence of husband, family, home, reputation, security, virtue—she would as soon go with the Raggle-Taggle Gypsies!

My dreams do not conjure Ellen now: Old Crome's daughter, of Norwich. An occasional buyer of my work, she upholds the family's artistic tradition merely as her wealthy husband permits. This Beauty may expect men to fall at her feet, may fashion chains of their daisy hearts to feed the goats, for aught I know. Grown used to privilege, she sidesteps the wreckage of a broken promise to send me upon a fool's errand. It is her father has saved me from the bailiffs.

Forego desire, persisting unbidden and half-acknowledged in some dark corner; all my crimson shame. Give the mind to higher matters.

Yet I feel the lack of a wife. Perhaps to take one would provide, um, focus? Unmarried maids and widows are enough abroad in polite society, God knows: virtuous women, loyal, even pious if required. Some must be suggestible to reason. But *take one*? Suitable females of one's slight acquaintance show little inclination toward so one-sided an arrangement. Richard and Ruth shared more than the marriage-bed. Might he not have suggested to me how one proceeds from acquaintance, through friendship to, um, marital harmony? I did not much confess these matters to him. Feared mockery. He may have known; was but waiting.

And now it is too late.

Richard pauses from his journal to regard me, smiling, generous. Gone.

Jessie's deception shows how narrow yet deep the chasm between the sexes. She has outwitted and outrun a group of thieves; has concealed her feminine functions and, and… *form* from me, and previously upon the streets for many months; she has witnessed without undue excitation a fellow in his under-garments when conducting his bathing requirements; has lugged our equipment high and low; suffered significant injury without recourse to restorative salts; slept in a fellow's chamber undisclosed; learnt the camera obscura's workings, and even grasped basic techniques of engraving, if as yet unskilled in it—all without vanity, simpering, or hysterics.

Is she not admirable, so to conceal her feminine nature at sixteen years?

A draper's carthorse snorts below.

Jessie has prompted these observations regarding the fair sex. This close personal experience, though subverting my previous understanding, may yet prove in some measure beneficial within marriage. Had I property and a secure income, a suitable woman's family might even consider me, um, worth consideration.

*

Mrs Lambton prods me into her study like pennin a sheep.

'Jessie, you need never be alone.' His nibbs will have heard her sayin that. You can't trust em what is above you. Can't never trust em, specially when keen like she is now.

To be alone is not my fear. People comin in upon me when alone is what frightens me. I do not make sheep's eyes at boys. There is handsome men what likes to ramble, an can put you in much trouble. Wiv Mrs Lambton, it is yes dear, no dear, free bags full dear, all smiles, nor even as much hoppity as usual, so I knows straightway it ain't a chat she is after. All I can do is let it happen.

Did you enjoy yourself, says she. Wasn't no seaside summer visit, she knows full well. I had more work than ever, just to go an come back. Under them words she wants to know what went wrong, offerin for me to show disrespeck behind his nibbs's back. She might be testin my loyal service, so I lets it pass. Household Maids have got sacked for less.

Instead, I tells Mrs Lambton of chance fings: me bein saved after the fall, an tendin to the hurt myself, an of the coach what lost a wheel, an the ride acrost the river in a barge. She ain't proper interested till we gets to Mrs Faif an witchcraft. What cane fields, she arks, what the injury to this woman's shoulder, how was she bought free, how fared the chile, an what spells? All such fings, but safe ground. I tells her what I can, so not much. Mrs Lambton clicks her tongue, reaches up to one o them books, then changes her mind.

I don't mention his nibbs goin to Mrs Veebee's an bein sent

packin by his dear lady-love, nor how he did drag hisself back, tail atween legs. I tells her how I was discovered a woman when fetchin-in rags from the storm, an ever since, how much is the Master holed below decks an like to sink. Also, how I have slept in his bedchamber, though on the look-out. It frets him, it alters fings, now he knows. He ain't abroad in the country no more wiv Mr Hayton he had knowed years. *Thus*, we did come back the very nex day, not goin to Harwich, much cash spent to get us home, an I don't know what will come of me.

Mrs Lambton ain't shocked at that, neither.

Her head tilts more to one side. 'Did you continue your writing, Jessie?'

'Where I could, Miss.'

'Good. And so—'

'Miss, I ain't got it wiv me, seein as you said it was just for me, them words there.'

'Oh yes. Yes. Now…'

We have come in here so Mrs Lambton can tell me many bad fings goes on in this country known as politics. Women an little ones is harmed most of all. Women don't get to vote in politics, so cannot be changed. All the women can do is hold meetins amongst theirselfs, vote wivout the men, an so get a fair outcome.

Mrs Lambton leans forward, like speakin low to a friend. That fish-hook curl of hair swings over one eye again, anglin for a catch.

'Jessie, you are a clever young woman. Are you sympathetic to our cause?'

I am glad she finks me clever, but brains is little use when she talks in big words. I pulls a face, sayin naught. She ain't pleased I am slipped off of her hook.

One last bit of bait she dangles afore me: 'So what do you think of your Master?'

'That he ain't happy, Miss.'

'But you misled him.'

'Wiv respeck, Mrs Lambton, he is unhappy in other ways.'

She rubs her wrist back and forth, round, over and about—some pain in there what won't come out. 'Jessie, had you ever considered that some men might prefer a solitary existence, that they like being alone?'

I plays daft. But she knows me well; just smiles, an arks no more about his nibbs.

'Let us next read together from a novel, Jessie—a step further in your learning. The author is a young relative of mine.'

Spoke like a promise, but Mrs Lambton is a deep one. She has got a plan, I knows it.

*

Madame to the door in Little Compton Street. *Oh, it's you again.*

Entry denied. Furthermore, pointless: La Parisienne no longer available. The new resident, Miss Shang-Hai, virtuoso with the whip, gains admirers. Alas for romance, how times change. The place itself has come finally to represent unwelcome scenes of uproar, of low-life indignities served publicly upon me, and I must turn away from it for good.

'If you truly wish to know, she is gone to the Dials, not far from here, behind the White Lyon. One of the residents is close with the landlord, and kindly kept the Frenchwoman company, to see her introduced and in passable lodging there.'

'Thank you.'

'Three days gone. We like to look after our own, even when sick.'

'Sick?'

'Well, what do you expect? They can't stay here!'

Desire can fade, but I have further purpose, and must find her. Hence, having walked the length of Soho's several thoroughfares, how to locate White Lyon Street? Seven passageways lead from the centre, and the buildings' contents, their odours, creatures, and inhabitants have spilled into whatever public space is for claiming. As sunset nears, lavender bags, linnet cages, wart cures, woven baskets, tied puppies, knives, bed frames—everything unsold must be returned within. What lodging may be 'passable' in this quarter, whose plan resembles another broken carriage-wheel, going nowhere, and each spoke a chaos?

White Lyon Boots & Shoes indicates the street, but no inn visible. Hazardous to make oneself known to watching thieves by asking the way to a tavern. Yet equally hazardous to wander these bazaars in search of a destination which may not exist, and to look perplexed or lost, thus risking the attentions of skulduggers.

When in unknown territory, buy something.

Buy something, and ask.

At day's end, I discover merely blackcurrants remaining. Three farthings, that I may set forth more certainly. *There is Little Lyon Street and Great Lyon Street, sir, either side the Dials hub. This side is Great Lyon; you needs Little, acrost the way.* Ah! The naming principle is diameter first, then radials. Thank you, my good woman. Something of that sort. *It is no trouble, sir.* Smirk.

*

Led down to the White Lyon's cellar entrance. At the first screened gap along the corridor are signs of human occupation. Small movements, a hand let fall in the dripping near-silence.

'Just here, sir,' as if the Minotaur awaits.

Tap-tap on the osier screen, bringing a shower of dust.

Cough, flapping with a hand. 'Anybody there?'

'Who is it?' Her voice.

Drag away the screen from the doorframe. A pattern of weak light falls from a cast-iron grille set in the wall, just below the ceiling within, just above the stony ground without. Difficult to breathe: a mossy pondweed vapour, sunken and now disturbed, swirls upward from the damp. In the shadows of one corner lies a pale figure, the straw palliasse propped inches above the floor. Nearby, the blue upright grooves of an apothecary's bottle, a pair of soft shoes, the hand-mirror and brush tucked into them. Tinder-box and candlestick, no candle. *Passable lodging.*

'Madam, good evening.'

'Oh sir, I cannot assist you here. I no longer have that role.'

'Yes, well it is not, um, please do not... That is, I bring you blackcurrants. Do you have—?' No, she does not have.

The berries' aroma already rising. Rest them—not in her lap like that, man! Rest the blackcurrants next her. It is no idyll of nymphs and swains.

'I was told you are in some distress.'

'I became unwell...'

Wait, listen.

'... and was made to leave.'

Her head rests upon the shawl she wore when I first visited Little Compton Street. Now that La Parisienne is near, sores are visible upon her face, about her mouth. Scarce any before. Lips cracked as dry creek mud, eyes staring, five weeks since I last saw her.

'Would you tell me how the sores, um, there,' my fingertips visiting my own cheeks, 'in fact arose?'

'Not only there.'

She reaches down, draws the rippling material of her shift high to her naked belly.

'Ah. I see... Yes.'

Her eyes are closed.

Gently, gently, cover again the red tangled mass of her groin. Lean forward, closer to those dark pustules by her mouth.

'Madam, I believe you need help. Perhaps I can find assistance for you.'

'Ce n'est pas nécessaire, M'sieu.'

Listlessness, or hopelessness. 'You have missed your husband all this time?'

'Yes. And my children.'

'Indeed. Your husband made the fine mirror and hairbrush you have here, didn't he?'

She opens her eyes, regards me for a while, pushes back hair from her forehead with the palm of a hand—the saddest of gestures.

'To help him pass the time in gaol. We had journeyed long days to escape Napoléon, and when at last a barque carried us to England, we were not believed, M'sieu. They thought my Guillaume was a spy and took him from me, prisonnier-de-guerre. I was left with the children alone in this city. He was just a quiet man, Guillaume. He made chairs!'

'Indeed, wretched fortune, Madam.' Growing darkness obscures whole areas of this space. 'I shall fetch you candles and perhaps bread: something. As you know, I have had cause to visit you on several occasions at Little Compton Street, yet in all that time failed to learn your name.'

'Claudette. I am Claudette Mertens, de Charleroi en Wallonie.' Some resurgence of pride there.

'But you lived in France?'

'Guillaume was from Picardie. When we married, I took his name, St. Cloud, and went to live with him en France. Is there something wrong, Monsieur? Your hand trembles. Are you again unwell?'

St. Cloud. Her married name a hammer-blow.

*

I could easy fetch a grown-up's chair, but don't fink Mrs Lambton wants me to. From the way she watches, this little chair is a treasure to her, an I must take care not to bust it, for that her daughter is either dead or gone away. An so I cottons-on to what I might have seen afore: the widow Lambton would mould me in her daughter's stead.

Her feet is just acrost the floor from mine. No hoppits.

Miss has chose a story-book, *Frankenstein,* for us to read bits from. This time she will read to me. I follows after—makes a change. I never been read to for the likin of it. Ever it was tests. How do you get understandin if you can't arks for fear of lookin foolish, nor did grow up in words like high people?

Frankenstein is a man o learnin, but foreign. He looks at livin flesh an rotten dead bodies, an so is good to read about. From doin this a sudden light breaks in upon him. He finds out how to make the bloomin cheek of life. Mrs Lambton nods toward me neaf her curl, finkin I should know all bout such men. Speaks of grave-robbers, what don't mean much to me; people what breaks into houses is different.

Frankenstein wanders in a great storm, callin *William, dear angel! this is thy funeral, this thy dirge!* He is essited, tho it be his brother's funeral in the rain. They must have other ways than us in Frankenstein's country. He sees a figure in the gloom behind a clump of trees, an great lightnin-flash soon after. It is frightnin the way Miss says it.

The lightnin discovers a hideous giant more than belongs to humanity—the filthy wretch what this man o learnin did give life to. Straightway Frankenstein knows the great demon he made killed his brother angel William, an must go lean on a tree. I arks Mrs Lambton what is goin on here. Is Frankenstein right about his brother killed by a giant in the gloom?

Jessie, we read onward to discover, says she. Knows but will not say. It is what teachers do in my sperience.

Well, this big wretch passes by the man in the story, climbs a hill an ain't seen no more. The storm goes over, but Frankenstein is drenched just the same. Much is spoke wiv feelin, like *this thy dirge,* an by night he is *anguished* from evil an despair. It is an improvin book, different from all else, an I reach for understandin, but a start.

Then Miss gets me to read, like in a proper lesson, though

doin the part what she did read out. It comes to me more easier for hearin them words the first time round—like real readin. When I gets to the end she claps her hands together, bobbin about like a canary, an I am proud.

Well, Jessie, you seemed to enjoy Frankenstein, says Mrs Lambton. Shuts it wiv a beamin smile like never afore, as much pleased wiv herself as wiv me. The story-writer Mary is some kin of hers: *scarce older than you, Jessie, perhaps eighteen years of age when writing her tale.*

'What, Miss?' says I in foolishness, 'I fought all writers was old!'

Books an papers Mrs Lambton done herself is on them shelfs. Her eyebrows goes high into them curls wiv the grey streaks, an her mouth wrinkles to a walnut. She struggles to let pass what I said. *Sit up, girl! To some only is it given.*

'Can we read some more, Miss?'

Too late. She ain't keen. Mrs Lambton leans forward in that way of hers, all close, friendly an fidgety. I can smell ink upon her fingers when she lays her hand upon my wrist. *Jessie,* she says, *you make good progress with your reading. You are a clever young woman. Your Master informs me of your talent also in the graphic arts. I believe it may be time for you to accompany me to the next meeting of our Marylebone women. What say you to that?* She nods her head, leanin back in the chair.

Ain't much I can say. Dare not twice up-set her. She is tryin for what she finks would do me good. 'Yes Miss,' says I, 'if it ain't too long a time, an Mr Daniell lets me.'

Her face brightens. Mrs Lambton has got me wrigglin on her hook at last. Out of pity I have got caught.

*

From the cellar, Doctor Theophilus Phillips climbs the wooden steps to ground level. He rests his medical bag upon the wall.

'Let me be frank, Mr Daniell. We are both men of the world. I neither know nor wish to know what your interest may be in that woman. Hence, perhaps I should mention that stretch-marks on the patient's lower abdomen indicate at least one pregnancy, which may well have come to term. There will be a history. More importantly for present purposes, this woman's condition is quite advanced. Should you wish to improve her chances, have her taken somewhere more wholesome than a cellar. The rapidly whitened hair may indicate shock. Symptomatic is dryness of the lips, such that the skin's surface is cracked and blistered: mercury, Daniell, mercury, and goodness knows what the dosage. Swift intervention may arrest the progress of syphilitic afflictions. Regrettably, it is as common for the patient to pass into a fatal decline. More usual, y'see, for sufferers to conceal than to confess.'

Phillips hands me a slip of paper.

'At any rate, I prescribe those two items. The first involves a little arsenic, which can nullify some of the mercury's noxious effects. Hence, use a trustworthy dispenser—avoid apothecaries and quacks. Have her drink much water. The patient is to begin the course as soon as possible. Apply lanolin or a like preparation to the skin. Severe bruising is present upon her upper body, but remarkably no fracture. And Daniell, to speak plain, the bleeding about her groin results from grievous assault: even if the woman in the basement were to recover, she would be of little use carnally to you or to any man. I have not been able to make a full examination, but in that respect her time is over: a hazard of her chosen profession. Now, my clerk shall send our invoice shortly. To Cleveland Street, is it?'

(She did not *choose* that life, by God!)

Look down to my boots. 'Yes.' Mumbled thanks.

'Good-day to you.' With one hand Theophilus Phillips settles hat upon head, with the other takes the bag, and sighing, departs.

August 1820

TWENTY-FIVE

'The family speaks French, Mrs Lambton, despite the mother's Flemish origin.'

No bushes, um, beaten about. Meanwhile, proper discretion to be maintained regarding my own relations with La Parisienne.

The widow's eye is ever sharp within the hanging question-mark. 'The first indication was the son, Emil. Saint Cloud, you say, the family name?'

'Yes.'

She huddles in a cloth night-shift, mob-cap and voluminous shawl, raising and lowering her heels to occupy them while she sits. The apartment's air but marginally less fetid despite this cooler weather. She is fifty years old. Perhaps they feel it at that age.

'Young Mr Daniell, the workhouse entry records did reveal a puzzling letter S between the children's first and last names. I failed to deduce that it was part of their surname. The dutiful recorder of entries mimicked the French abbreviation, S for *Saint*.'

'Hence my prentice may well have been born English?'

Mrs Lambton inclines her head. 'Petty nationalism, perhaps?' The angle of inclination describes the skew of my thought. 'Our Marylebone Women, Dissenting Radicals all, will accept your young prodigy. I have told Jessie she may attend the Association's lectures. Also, should our proposed lending library take wing, we may require a voluntary assistant, willing to learn. And Young Mr Daniell, may I ask what brought you to perceive a familial connection between this poor Frenchwoman and your prentice-girl?'

My prentice-girl? No! Strikes a false note, invites wrangling. Ultimately a distraction. Let it simply be *prentice*. Blur such distinctions.

Uncomfortable to recount how the dressing-table set of carved bone was smuggled from some stinking gaol or prison hulk to Claudette, in token of her husband's love. Each item fashioned from whatever scraps he found, and each perhaps a measure also of the long weeks' passing. The family must have thought they had escaped tyranny, only to be persecuted here. Something must be, shall be, done: a responsibility accepted. If only I might know the means!

Jingling harness of carriage-horses in the hollow street below.

Mrs Lambton fidgets in restrained animation. 'It fits, does it not? That is, *Quis separabit?* Who shall part us? The mother's gifts to her children; the husband's gifts to his wife? Carved in bone from a solitary cell—beautiful!'

Allow Mrs Lambton her novelist musings, whether beautiful or not. The chair-maker was gaoled as a spy and must have died a prisoner. The mother came back for her son, resigned the girl to the workhouse, was reduced to prostitution, and failed to visit.

'Mrs Lambton, I now believe this woman to be Jessie's mother. She had to abandon her child fifteen years ago. Madame St. Cloud now suffers a severe illness while residing in poor accommodation, and I would like Jessie to meet her before, um, before too long, but… elsewhere.'

Impossible to continue, sitting with my hands clasped tight, and my eyes one word from weeping.

'Young Mr Daniell, you will appreciate the difficulty this brings. The Flemish Walloons are of course Catholics.'

Ah, Catholics! An uncomfortable fact in a Whig Protestant household. What did the widow say? *Marylebone women, Dissenting Radicals all.* Doctrine casts a forbidding shadow. My consideration had been for the person.

Mrs Lambton's embarrassment plain. No Latin, no beads, no relics, no haloed saints, no Popery: little can be done for Claudette St. Cloud.

*

I keeps one pace behind, showin respeck, whiles Mrs Lambton crosses town to her women's meetin. She hops wiv blackbird beak well forward in the damp mornin air. Mr Daniell was not pleased, though naught said. The lane bends with the Tyburn ditch—not ground I knows well, nor wants to, for that I got chased here once. A few more buildins is gone up since then, an much mud flung about.

'Here we are, Jessie.'

The women's meetin-house don't have no sign, bein someone's home. Mrs Lambton says the rules of politics means meetin-up freely can get you sent afore the judge. *We women are makin a stand.* She goes around the back, an knocks.

We are let into a corridor painted cabbage-water green, wood and walls. You might fink it the only colour they ad, but at the end is branches, leaves an ivy spreadin all about from the corner. An oak tree painted in a house is a trick I never met afore. You walks neath branches to get to the room, very pretty. I would stay longer to see how they bend em round corners so not to show from a distance, an *thus* puspicktive eye-trickery, but Mrs Lambton beckons me on.

It is a room wiv a long table an cushioned chairs all about; fank God no dancin. Whiles I am in britches, most women wears plain dresses. The wet hems draw streaks acrost the floor. One might be a gamekeeper: trousers tucked in boots, coarse jacket, an pipe. She ain't took her hat off; we was ever told, take your hat off in-doors.

The Marylebone women use careful manners. Whiles I might do different from their ways, in my eyes they are as much different. Their stand is more like to a last stand—scarce twenty of em, not countin the children—though the braver for it. Mrs Lambton is Lizzie in this company. When told to say greetins to one woman, I am Jessie an she Persephone. But if I was a Persephone, I'd rather be Miss Smith an make do. Apart in one corner stands two East End girls what is *Saved*, an tryin to be polite. My britches makes em smile. *Wise kid*, they say low, *wearin skirts was ever our undoin.*

It is a sober meetin, begun by goin over what they done last time. What to talk about is listed, afore gettin a *show of hands*. It is not all listenin: the women arks questions, some argues, but no fights. Though not her house, Lizzie is in charge so checks the hand-showin. Next, we gets around tables like for cards, an talk of somefink else. Our table is chiles' labour. Some eight-year-old workin in a cotton-mill got killed in a big machine, an the women's group is not only bewailin, but claimin, *Where is the rights of the chile?* I never knew a chile had rights. It warms me to see some here is bold to arks, should they once be let. You can tell the people here got hope. That is the main fing. They ain't forever downcast.

Goin back, Lizzie becomes Mrs Lambton again, skippity an lobbin questions. *Well, Jessie, do you find inspiration? Progress made? Such a fine group of women, are they not?* Yes Miss, says I.

No question of them bein in the right, but as yet no strengf in numbers. It will take years—the women knows it, an shall carry on till heard.

Yet when you scramble for food in muck-heaps, or by night waist-high in the cold river, only to be told next day how you stinks, an feckless poor too idle to work, well, you might kill on hearin that one more time. It is them you don't hear from knows true want.

Mrs Lambton smiles. She is I fink justly proud. 'Come, Jessie. You belong with us.'

I ain't sure where I do belong. You can get caught in a trap, even if not meant for you.

*

'Jessie, I have matters of substance to explain, and, um, to confess. It shall be difficult for us both. Therefore, it would oblige me to be heard. Do seat yourself. Now, I asked you to gather your workhouse possessions of bone, ready to take with us. Have you them? Good. Bread and milk for ourselves and another? Good. Um, well then...'

How satisfying in the chaos of our times to effect a reunion between mother and daughter after years of separation! Regrettably, when the news is broken, the information let slip: *Please remind me upon arrival that we bring cash, since your mother shall need it.*

No feminine swooning by my prentice, no intemperate passions. Simply, Jessie lowers herself backwards upon the workshop stool, one foot upon the rung. That familiar frown again, darker. She sniffs, studying the floor.

'Didn't know my mother still lived, sir, least of all nearby. In the workouse they told me I was a orphan. They was tryin to be kind, Mr Daniell. There was others like me, what would be put into service, but most young'uns had family, an somebody to turn to. I pinned my opes upon the only kin I knowed of: Amy, what had been took away.'

'I have failed you, Jessie, even in attempting to reward you months ago. Chance alone has found me out. Mine was such poor understanding! In recompense, perhaps I may bring you and your mother together. The prentice deserves a better Master.'

'Is that your plan, sir? For me to leave?'

'No, of course not! How can you have so misunderstood, young fellow, woman, young woman? I was referring to my moral flaws, not to your dismissal because I lack capability! Good gracious!'

Where the calm discussion with Jessie about this shocking news? The considerate disclosure? My gentle assistance offered? Strange to see how my prentice watches me again, eyebrows raised, smiling.

'Fank you sir, for all what you do, an for wantin me kept-on. I finds comfort in it.' The smile fades to a frown. Jessie looks aside. 'Tho I ain't sure how I shall fare at this meetin. Wivout no family, I did learn to close myself up. What might we say to each other, sir, her an me?'

'Well, I am confident some natural bond will be struck between you—or rediscovered. So, shall we to Madame St Cloud? I have sought better accommodation for her, in safe hands with the Cath—with her own people. Not far from here. Your mother is unwell, Jessie, and in some distress. Prepare yourself. Oh, and would you mind carrying the—thank you.'

*

'Good day, Mrs Rourke.'

The welcome much as it was yesterday… or less enthusiastic.

'We have done as the Father desired, sir, lodging her at the back. She has slept much and eaten little—not quite taken to sprats. And if I may mention a most delicate matter. Oh, and good day to you, lad.'

An inclination of her head twice to one side hauls us into the parlour. Large crucifix above the fireplace; discreet curtains; an air of fresh polish and old furnishings.

'You see, Mr Daniell, isn't it? Yes well as you know sir the poor fallen woman for I have heard her story of Father Lambert and very affectual it is too bein betrayed in love by a soldier and her rent money stolen and suffering grievous illness while kept in the debtors' prison with her lips all desecrated and bruises and boils from those cruel stone steps and bad food so slippery which as we know from visiting they have there and to be brought at last on her knees a beggar to seek sanctimony at St Cecilia's door though as Father Lambert has explained our Christian duty is not to turn away—don't you think, er, Mr—?'

(Some Priest, that one!) 'Daniell. It is indeed a duty, Mrs Rourke, but something arisen, has it?'

'I would not say arisen.'

'No.'

'I would not say *arisen*.'

'No.'

'It's more...'

'Occurred?'

'Nor yet even occurred.'

(Could be here all day.) 'Been said?'

'Exactly.'

'Thank God.'

'As we must, sir, each and every one. It is a big house, you see, for others are in our care, even a dark fellow we have accepted into our bosom, and it wasn't the sores, sir, it wasn't the sores, putting them off, it's...' whispering now, '...it's that she is *French*, you see, the others don't like it.'

'They don't?'

'Because of the late wars. Now Mr Rourke and myself, we don't mind.'

'Well of course.'

'We don't mind. France is a Catholic country. I expect some mean well, underneath. But others here, ordinary folk, hard times isn't it, ooh *no*! I fear others lack our synthetic understanding. We have put rosary beads in her chamber, and therefore this befallen alien can take her rest and re-vilify herself with us but with better health in a very short while let us hope and we *are* praying for her as we do for all poor souls we put faith in our blessed Mother Mary and in the Lord our Shepherd that this poor lamb shall find new shining pathways to follow.'

'Most certainly. Many thanks. It is appreciated, Madam, I assure you. And may we—just, um, excuse me—may we go through?'

Along the passageway to a small door on the left. Mrs Rourke tap-tap-tap. Leaves us.

'Madame? Um, Jessie, I believe this is your mother.'

Claudette, sitting at the edge of the board where she must sleep, offers us a hesitant welcome. Familiar shawl about her shoulders; her hair brushed and tied at the back. I have not seen her so fearful. The greasy whatever-it-is masquerading as lanolin, picked up in Great Earl Street, gleams upon her swollen mouth and jaw, upon the scabbing there.

Father Lambert has done well: Claudette's circumstances here preferable to that dripping cellar. Yet she seems out-of-place. Amid the beads and tapestries, the highly-coloured icons on the wall, La Parisienne appears more wasted than before. Mrs Rourke must have found her those woollen stockings she wears, tucked into soft shoes.

'My dear.' Her bruised arms reach out to Jessie. 'I am told it is you. After all these years! Please come closer. Please. Do you think we are alike?'

'I ain't sure, Miss. I can't see how we'd know.'

Miss! Jessie is looking to and fro with alarm.

The welcome falters. Claudette lowers her outstretched arms. 'I think I see something of your father in the line of your eyebrows, m'petite—along here, bien sûr—and in the shape of your cheeks.'

Jessie nods, hapless. I should help them. On the stool nearby, the blue apothecary bottle, tub of salve, and Doctor Phillips's preparations; carved bone mirror and brush beside.

'Um, Jessie, you have your keepsakes with you, have you not?'

'Oh yes. Keepsakes, yes sir.'

'Well?' Eyebrows raised, urging the prentice with my hand: *Go on then!*

When Jessie removes the hatpin and comb from her pouch, Claudette sucks in her breath. She makes the sign of the cross.

'Them keepsakes was left me when I was little, Miss. My treasures, see. I held em close. Never fought to meet the person what did leave em. It feels strange, that's all. Strange.'

'Your father, my husband, made them in prison.' Tears well in her eyes.

'Why not exchange your gifts now, and um, look at them?'

(Well done, well done!) They do so with the tenderness my little sister showed for her rag doll.

'What does the writin say, Mr Daniell?'

'Quis separabit. It is Latin, Jessie: Who shall part us?'

'Well he got that wrong.' Everything curls and shrivels, acid upon copper, the sharp fumes rising. 'Sorry. Don't know how I got to say that.'

'Yes, Madame Saint Cloud. Now, I was about to—' spluttering into my hand '—about to ask why Jessie has an English name, when her brother's is Emil?'

The hint of a smile as she regards me. 'Emil was born in Charleroi. Our girl-child, you, my dear, arrived soon after we came into Kent. We named her Jacinthe. *Hyacinth*, you would say.'

Jessie looks to me in horror.

'But the workhouse man, he did not comprehend Jacinthe. In its place he must have put an English name.'

'Miss, why did you come back for Emil, and not take me?'

Bite the lip: my woman of pleasure the mother of my prentice. The items are returned. Quite failed to anticipate this harshness. After long years of separation, no loving reunion or tearful embrace. And Jessie's question is good.

'I lived as a seamstress, without much skill. They paid us little. In winter we might be too cold at first to use needles, and were paid less. A message came, très important: *Monsieur Guillaume Saint Cloud*. My gentle husband was dead, and I did not feel able to go on. But a carter would come to the workshop, saying he liked my look. En bref, offered marriage. I refused him. Again he asked.'

She looks down, rubbing her hands.

'This carter thought it a favour to me. He was old. I did not much like him. Next, he offered also to take Emil from the workhouse, and raise him as his son. *Don't want no girl,* he told me. It was contempt: *Don't want no girl.*'

Now she raises her eyes, dark as Jessie's, who faces her unblinking.

'He would not be persuaded, however much I tried. Alors, I agreed to marry him, and fetched Emil. I loved my son dearly, and soon I came to hate the carter.'

Jessie sighs, near turns away from her mother, and from me.

What torments must afflict my prentice now? The folly of seeking this reconcilement! Why bring Jessie to a Catholic Rescue Home overseen by mournful Rourkes, to meet the mother who twice abandoned her?

'May we know what the carter, that is, the outcome of—?'

'Oh, he died.'

'Good! Um, I mean to say, I suppose—'

'He owed money. I don't know. They wanted it back.'

Jessie leans forward. 'Where is Emil?'

She sweeps her hair, the tears, from her face. 'I was raised in virtue! Truly I was. My heart was broken. I hated myself, but found no way to survive. We were starving, so for a few pence I gave myself to some man. I lost all pride. Many times Emil asked me to tell of his father and la Picardie, my memories of those days. He admired Bonaparte and la Grande Armée. As my son grew older, he became angry with me. One day, Emil said he was leaving. He would cross the sea—*return*, he said—to join them.'

'No-o!' Jessie's bitter cry.

'Fourteen years old.'

'Miss, I heard his name as Amy—hopin all this time we might meet when my workouse days was done. Look after each other. Now my brother is lost, ain't he?'

'I do not think to see him again.'

Those épaulettes, spoils from the field of Waterloo: discomfiting. And when, after the silence following, Jessie's mother says *I have been brought to shame*, my head goes down. I paid for the favours of this woman, now untouchable!

Place food nearby, some coins upon the table, yet dare not reach out. Brought to shame. Finally, finally, Jessie steps forward to hold her mother's hands.

Madame St. Cloud weeps now. 'Forgive me, Jacinthe, I beg you. I cannot forgive myself. Mais n'oublie pas ton père. Think of your father. He was a good man. By God's Grace he knew nothing of what followed.'

Once Mrs Rourke's door shuts fast behind us, the desolation remains; a sense of exhaustion and despair, of grief unresolved. Light rain drifts over the rooftops. My prentice walks close, neither of us speaking. We go awhile in that fashion, over the wet stones and dampened ground.

Jessie turns up her collar. Tears in her eyes. Big sniff. Wipes a hand across her nose.

'One fing I do know: I ain't no blessed Hyacinf.'

TWENTY-SIX

'Thank you for arriving punctually, Mr Daniell. Appointments, this day and age, so forth.'

'Yes, well, I suppose we all—'

'I rent this room professionally when up from Guildford.'

'Bare of illustration, however.'

Garner pauses to consider me. Perhaps a dull room befits a legal man's meetings with clients.

'To the matter in hand. I have here the office file pertaining to the Daniell family. In the interest of us both to close it.'

'Yes.' (What is he talking about?) The gap of the socket fascinates, but the remaining eye challenges. Courtesy requires that the missing organ be ignored. And the dark-veined hole in the bone itself: disregard it. My prentice would be enthralled.

This Henry Garner shows considerable self-assurance. A senior clerk, not a lawyer, an office employee under direction, who must tilt his head in order to peruse the folio sheets before him, yet addresses me as if we were equals!

Garner flicks the vellum. (Musket ball?)

'Time of the essence, etcetera. Now then...'

'Waiteth for no man.'

'Pardon?'

'Um, nothing.'

Cannot seem to hit it off with the fellow.

'Mr Daniell, basic questions to begin. Certain assurances needed, no more.'

He means my name, place and date of birth, my mother's family name, names of Aunt Amelia and dear sister gone abroad, of any other siblings, Father's profession, the local church we attended, the date of my removal to London, and how I came to reside in Cleveland Street.

'Is the apartment yours?'

The single eye fixes me. For a horrible moment, Mrs Lambton's curling question mark dangles there.

'No. Apartments are rented.'

'You pay rent?'

Impertinence! 'Must I answer these tedious questions?'

Garner's response is to wait.

'My uncle permits me to live there, you understand, without payment, although—'

'*Permits* you!' Garner near springs to his feet. 'This is Thomas Daniell, is it? Took you when a boy of ten to India five years, following your father's demise?'

'Why, yes.' Forcefulness: 'If you know all this information, Garner, why ask?'

'And your uncle still lives?'

'He does. Fitzroy Square, nearby.'

Now this bold clerk, so uncommon exercised that my uncle should persist in living, searches with a magnifying glass for some passage or statement in his papers. Garner, head bowed, eye socket mostly obscured, scans with intensity until, locating the line, he sits back in triumph.

'Mr Daniell, I wish you to remain calm. What I shall say may prove troubling. Ultimately some relief, but a shock, nonetheless.'

No more revelations, please God, no more.

'I believe you were exploited when young. Days of innocence, so forth. I shall explain this circumstance and in due course cite evidence, but please do not alarm yourself. Ultimately some relief: hold to that notion. The terms of your mother's will regarding you, your sister and and your Aunt, were never carried out. Hence our office file upon the Daniell estate has remained open, though buried away. You follow?'

'Um...'

'Breaches of trust occurred; various parties involved; inducements paid—shortcomings, shall we say, in legal practice by our Guildford office at the time. Never disclosed. You are not truly a tenant in Cleveland Street, sir: you ought own the apartment.'

'How?'

'You and others were deprived of a large measure of your legal inheritance. Fraud, sir, embezzlement: jiggery-pokery! As rightful heir at twenty-one, Mr Daniell, the major portion of the estate should have come to you.'

'It has not come to me?'

Garner smiles to himself, rubs his knuckles, waits.

'Then who holds this inheritance from my mother?'

'What remains of it, Mr Daniell, quarter century onward, cetera. Not difficult to deduce which family member benefited, along with a certain lawyer now deceased.'

Once I should have been quite rich. Or within reason well off. Or at least more financially secure. Not as I am now, and long have been. At forty years of age, my inheritance has been spent for me by my own uncle. And I offered to pay him rent for Cleveland Street! Hah! Best not inform Garner. Good gracious, no. Rash to expose my foolishness.

'You shall need my help in this, Mr Daniell.'

'I cannot pay. Um, I have debts.'

'There is no fee. Resolve embarrassments with discretion, our general rule.'

'But is not my inheritance beyond recovery, Garner?'

He waits.

All spent, I know it. My uncle's painting had to be sold at Wardle's—the one I retrieved from loyalty!

'Mr R. Morris has approved settlement of any present debts to a maximum of fifteen pounds. Banker's statement necessary. Recompense, so forth.'

Not enough, not enough.

'Then I thank him.'

But Mary and Aunt Amelia left the country in consequence—made new lives across the ocean. Had they received their due, our family might well have stayed together. What recompense for that particular loss? Bile rises in my throat, fists tight neath the table's edge.

The hole in Garner's skull is partly obscured by folds of skin. Stuff of nightmares.

*

Discovered in the lowest drawer, my sister's letter of two months ago. Her reply to mine expresses anxiety for *your state of mind, dear Brother, and bachelor's perceptions of the world at large.*

Must soon respond. I shall mention prospects of full Academician status, the time of decision nearing, and autumnal colours in the trees. Keep to those.

Other matters Mary shall not yet be told: that my friend and colleague is dead, his wife and children given shelter by relatives; that our own family was split to the core by one we trusted; that our inheritance might have rescued us, had we known, had we only understood. Mary must never perceive how I despise myself for having believed Uncle's persuasions not to live as other men, but to thrive without family; that the path to self-respect derives from others' praise and the commerce of my art.

Jessie has shown me otherwise, whose father is dead also, who was parted when young from her mother, and her brother gone to war. Some similarity in those respects. For either of us, what might be the prospect of loving and trusting another, even oneself, in view of such a history? I have clung to shapes and hues and lines, living by assumption—all my care and tenderness bestowed upon appearances. For the rest, a solitary wreck adrift.

Might Jessie have done the same, but for chance? Unlikely, for chance is arbitrary. She has the wit to perceive it.

*

I done more pitchers, usin four colours as told: a hand, palm-up; finger-joints upon a pot handle; some thyme next ivy leaves, all dry and curled from the yard. Also, half a mouse found when peggin-out washin. It had two folded-up legs wiv a little black arse, and was took back down-stairs off of the bread-board when finished. But his nibbs is fretful an ain't got the time to look. Pitchers must wait.

'I am going out, Jessie. By myself, going out. I need to, um, visit my uncle. Hence do not follow.'

'Not follow, sir? Not see Mrs Lambton?'

'No. Simply, I do not wish you to attend for reading instruction today. Now then, um, yes, thank you, the morning-coat.'

He ain't give me no tasks, havin got the ump about somefink; that much is plain. It ain't for my ears, also plain. He don't arks my feelins since we come out that house where was Miss Cloud. You only got one mother, we all knows. Cannot pick nor choose. That meetin wiv her makes my guts roll like to a hurdy-gurdy. Why was I so cold to her? She looked so sick, weepin wiv it, though even then maybe not for me.

I shall go out by myself an for myself, like him, visitin somewheres, for that I am angry. When fings don't happen like they used, his nibbs ain't doin pitchers nor learnin me art, Mrs Lambton less teacher than recruitin sergeant, my own mother but a stranger, an nobody tells you what's afoot, somefink is up.

Back in the mist, along the Tottenham Court Road, over to St Giles an the house where Miss Cloud is lodged. Mrs Rourke's is bay winders at the front an lionhead knocker for bangin the door. I follows the side alleyway far as the back wall. They got a gate barred off, easy to climb; yet I don't.

From here I can see Miss Cloud's winder-glass. No sign of her. She won't be strollin around, even if weller. No matters, I watches. My mother lies sick in that room. I could go up an tap the glass. I could wave to her, that she might see me, even talk fings what proper mothers an daughters might say. I must have had such foughts in mind, else why come over at all? Yet to go there now an see her is somefink I cannot bring myself to do.

I stands at the gate, lookin over.

An old woman comes near. Bad hips, you can tell. Wiv each step her body rolls side to side in heavy seas.

'Good day' says she, lookin me up and down when I shifts out the way. Only a short whiles for her to pass by, but enough. I turns from the gate. Cannot go back now, nor never.

An I am fillin out. This guise ain't workin for me no more, but I don't much want skirts. I knows what skirts can bring upon you.

*

Stride forth in the dampened air. Turn the familiar corner into Fitzroy. No languishing. Ablaze to confront this deceiving uncle. Today the reckoning!

Forcefulness. Storm the stairway's echoes! (Wheezing by the next floor.) Batter the traitor's apartment. Rat-a-tat-a-tat-a-tat!

Mrs Lambton bewildered, less spirited than is customary. 'Young Mr Daniell, it is fortunate you call in these circumstances.

I would—oh, I see. Later, you prefer? Yes, but— Why certainly, if alone is your wish. I merely thought to—'

Into the bedchamber, its drapes half-drawn. Uncle sleeps, or affects as much. Yet he shall hear me before he dies. I am done with him.

*

Above St Giles is busy little lanes comin out like a net, full o carts an carriages an people makin their way. The drover amidst em wiv five beasts has got his work cut out. I ain't in no hurry to get back to Cleveland Street—that is somefink new.

Sometimes others sees me now to be a woman in man's apparel, an say hurtful fings. When I goes to the women's meetin I am made welcome, but their talk is above my head. Mrs Lambton an me do readin, an I got paper to write upon, but she can't much keep up the lessons now the old man is too sick. She must fear for what follows. An even though I got a mother, it don't feel like Miss Cloud is mine. The Amy I been waitin for all my life was Emil in that basket beside me. He might be dead already—just a boy playin war, an so sad to fink of. It is too late for us all. His nibbs is kindly, learnin me bout the paints, yet I gets lost in his foughts. *Thus*, I learned more, but might never be a proper artiss prentice. To keep from forgettin, I can put fings down on paper. It sets em more clearer in my head. But if I ain't got the words for what never goes away, what I know is real yet somehow lies too deep, then I cannot tell nobody. There ain't no pitcher I can draw. Was I to have a skirt, he would not like me to wear it in-doors. I got to own up to myself: all put together, this ain't right, an I don't know what might be.

A woman is strugglin to shift two tubs out the way in this busy lane. Behind her, a heavy waggon carries trees long enough to poke over the end. You can tell they ain't from these parts. One has got big fick ox-tongue leaves, an knobbly bits at the joins; the other's leaves is blue-green, covered in fur. The roots o them big trees is wrapped in sacks.

'Where you headed, mister?'

'Soho,' he says, 'Now bugger off.' He looks again. 'Beg pardon, miss, I'm sure.'

When the waggon gets goin, a wheel jolts acrost a hole, an into the muck falls a twig wiv two leaves. I picks it up for my art.

It is how fings happen, good as well as bad.

*

He struggles to waken at my approach.

'Do not sit up, Uncle.'

'William. You, boy?'

'Oh yes.'

'Faded, in some way.' Thomas lies still. Liquid from his eyes, and nose, and mouth. The right eye opens: a fluttering near-drowned moth. 'What brings ye?'

'A story, Uncle... *Once upon a time*, you remember? Well, once upon a time, your brother's children loved your make-believe. Those tales beguiled us, for they might just be true, as Mary and I wished them to be. Our delight was well-known, and Father was no story-teller: his grimness did not invite children close.'

'What is this?'

'You built a stock of faith in our hearts, Uncle. Sadly, traded. All spent. You say my mother would have married you. She did not. Clara could have become your mistress, as entreated. When five years a widow, she did not. Clara, you claim, would have joined you in India at a fitting time. Till death itself she did not. You lied about her love for you. Good God, man, you tried to steal your own brother's wife!'

His breath comes shallow. 'Confessed as much.'

'That is enough, is it, to confess?'

No answer, his head turning, restless.

'In my tale, you seek in vain to overcome exclusion from the family, your brother's wariness in your company, and Clara's constancy, while Mary and I witness our mother's widowhood. Without understanding her distress, we sense it: how often Aunt Amelia visits, and stays; the neighbours' solicitude; the ministrations of Lawyer Morris, gaunt as winter birch, all peeling bark.'

'A lawyer to execute the will? How odd!'

(Forcefulness) 'Save your sarcasm! I have seen the records. The lawyer must ensure no jackdaws pick over a dead man's goods: an inventory must be made, assets established, debts settled, all accounted for, and the will's contents declared. You see, Uncle, what knowledge I have gained!'

'You forget the pension. John did not die in action... Admiralty loth to pay.'

Use Garner's tactic: watch and wait. Listen to the furring of Uncle's breath. One learns.

'Took months.'

'But Uncle, you had no patience. You would journey with me to India! My presence warranted funds, and Mother's interest besides, persuading her to agree your foreign tour. My artistic education would be the line to reel her in!'

'No-no-no.'

'Lawyer Morris transferred sums to you *before* the estate's worth was known. Tut-tut. Unlawful. Hence, large payments to your crooked accomplice, and for the passage to Bombay, our travels, and voyage home.'

'Cannot fool me, William. Ye pipe another's tune.'

'*Let us live by our art, lad,* you'd say. More make-believe: the sales of your water-colours could not support our long journeying across that great territory. I was ten years old! Had no notion that you took from Mother's inheritance. Was a penny left?'

A fit of coughing assails him, worsens, bubbling within.

'Once upon a time you must have loved her, Thomas. That,

at least, rings true. Mother's death shocked us all. But the guilt fell to me, y'see, of having stayed so long abroad. Took my parents for granted while they lived, and at fifteen years of age stood by their English graves feeling robbed, at fault.

So to another tale of yours, in which my loving, lying uncle guides and nurtures me to adulthood, whereupon corrupt Lawyer Morris shall safeguard our family's interests. Ha! What grudging sum was spared for my aunt and sister? Amelia could not stomach it. Sailed far away for good, and young Mary with her. Gone! Your thieving severed our family!'

'You believe this? Ever the fool.'

'I discovered your tricks from a lawyer's clerk, a man who tells no lies. Twice you kept his messages from me. Mother's legacy was intended for her children, yet you took this apartment, lodged me in Cleveland Street, and made what should be my workshop yours, naught said. The legal file which would have betrayed you was hidden away unclosed. Once more, old Lawyer Morris took his cut, and graciously I was permitted tenancy of my own property! A neat scheme.'

'Young Mr Daniell, please come away!'

(Ignore her in the doorway.)

'And even then, even then, all you had stolen was wasted. You are a deceiver to the end of your days, Uncle—beneath contempt! I hate you for it. Nor do I understand these tears of mine. Hear me, man? *You hear?*'

Grab him, shake him by the shirt, rattle his throat. That sour, mocking smile!

'What, defy me? I shall—'

Mrs Lambton pulling at me.

'Leave me, woman!'

'No! Young Mr Daniell, he's an old man. I beg you, let him be. Are you so unwell?'

TWENTY-SEVEN

His nibbs holds Mrs Lambton's note.

'Jessie, my uncle is dead.'

'A pity, sir. He did give me water-colours, an good brushes.'

'In the early hours, it was. Mrs Lambton writes here that she watched by the fireside, yet by dawn was fallen asleep. Upon waking, found him cold.'

Mr Daniell don't say no more for a whiles, rubbin his frown.

'I visited him yesterday. Told you, did I?'

'Yes sir.'

'I was enraged by his thieving. Overwhelmed.'

His nibbs has got the shakes again. What has he done?

'Mrs Lambton urged me to let go, in fact.'

'I speck you did, sir.'

'Well of course! Did you think? He died *hours* afterward, Jessie! *Hours!*'

'Yes, Mr Daniell. Early hours, in his sleep, like you said.'

My words has come out wrong. It is a trick they got to make people fink otherwise from what you meant, yet cannot take back. His nibbs stares hard at me, eyes wild.

'Do not let it fret you, sir. I knows you saved my life on the cliff that day.'

He is gone fearsome quiet. I ain't movin a muscle, for that he might do anyfink.

At last he sniffs, an wiv them tremblin hands folds Mrs Lambton's note. Sharp he glances at his work on the bench.

'Is there tea in the tin, Jessie? Shall we share hot tea?'

More vexed wiv hisself than wiv me.

*

'When the time came, it was relief, Young Mr Daniell.'

'To you, Madam?'

'Perhaps to Thomas, also. For months he was unwell, even before losing use of his arm. I am exhausted.'

'Mmm.'

'Mercifully, one has interests; endeavours. Another rock-cake?'

(My stomach fair plugged with her putty-dough.) 'No! No, thank you. Quite enough.'

'Kind friends assure me that uniquely my rock cakes only finish rising when eaten.'

'Your friends are kind indeed, Madam. Now, you may wonder why I call today…'

Mrs Lambton's head inclining, the curl obscures an eyebrow. 'Young Mr Daniell, I would have anticipated your visit, had I not witnessed your aggression toward Thomas while he lay helpless.'

'All was not as it seemed.'

'It *seemed* horrific.'

'Thomas embezzled the legacies of my parents.'

'What! His own family? Surely not so! Was that the reason you assaulted him?'

'Confronted him, Mrs Lambton. Righteous anger. May I ask if, insomuch as you know, he lacked funds entirely?'

She ceases movement. 'I believe so.'

'Is that why you offered *Procession to Madras* for sale at Wardle's?'

'Oh-h!' Hand swift to her mouth.

'Mrs Lambton, I bought it back.'

'May God forgive me.' She shakes her head. 'Thomas would pass me monies for household expenditure, and I listed all the purchases. He said other bills and expenses were paid via the bank. But of late I received household monies less often. At first, I overlooked an old man's forgetfulness, spending what little my writings earned. We could feed ourselves, maintain the hearth, make few demands.' A hapless gesture. 'Young Mr Daniell, your uncle was bed-ridden. Fearing to hurt his pride, I took a painting from the back room. It fetched little to support us.' A bitter smile as she dabs her eyes. 'A pitiful sin. Squalid, don't you think?'

My thieving uncle's legacy to all is shame and sorrow.

*

I gets shown the body laid straight, soon to be boxed an took away. Mrs Lambton's apron an them gloves upon the pail smells of somefink strong. She moves quick as ever, but no hoppits. His chamber is more tidier, potions gone, curtains pulled back. Still the sickness hangin.

'He died in his sleep, Jessie.'

The old man's skin is mottled, like them fancy papers stuck inside her book-covers. Yeller nails on his crinkled fingers. I seen bodies from the water. Flesh goes blue.

'Come,' she says, leadin us out the bedchamber, 'Quite enough for a youngster.'

In her private study I squeeze tight into the child's chair. It ain't got smaller, I got bigger.

'Miss, can I arks somefink bout your own private self?'

'Something personal, you mean?'

'Yes Miss, personal, bout your daughter what grew up in this chair.'

'At six years of age she grew feverish. Died within the fort-night.' Her look is cold stone. 'Is that enough?'

'Sorry, Miss, for my rudeness.'

Settles that. In the quiet after, I reads spine-words upon her books till peace might return.

'Now,' she says, 'Let us continue.'

Mrs Lambton arks me to read. Hard to tell her mood whiles she listens, but flitty, not deep in grief sacred to memories beloved at peace on headstones. More akin to that news-paper parrot flapped out the winder. Yet it is all show. We both knows it. I been stupid to arks. Wiv the old man gone, where might she fly to? Her an me both. It gets more tougher the nearer you gets to free.

The story for readin is a report of a Grand Event wiv a interlude. In news-papers there is always interludes. You gets told who went, like they was your pals in battin order, an *A good time was had by all*.

'Miss, do you give me easier fings to read now?'

She smiles quick. 'Not knowingly, Jessie. Greater ease of reading comes with practice. In that way fresh words become old friends, seen in one's head.'

I can see words in my head. Old friends. I like that finkin.

'Now, young lady, I understand the meeting with your mother passed coolly?'

'Yes Miss.' All nice fings an friendly words afore she darts a test question. Mrs Lambton waits, but won't catch me that way. Livin wivout words nor friends, you easy spot a question wiv more behind it.

Mrs Lambton does a big sigh. 'Well, Jessie, I wish you to obtain permission of your Master to accompany me upon a brief excursion tomorrow. It is time.'

'Excur—'

'A pleasant journey. We walk to the home of an acquaintance.'

(*Time*? Why must they talk so riddled?)

*

At Cleveland Street, his nibbs ain't mopin for old Thomas like for Mr Hayton. He kneels in a patch of daylight, shiftin pitchers acrost the floor. Picks one up an looks at it, puts it back, picks another, frowns, stands it aside.

'Ah, Jessie, I have news.' He gets to his feet. 'The Royal Academy invites me to submit works for their consideration. They wish to appoint a new member having full rights. Full rights! What say you to that?'

'Very good news, sir, I speck. You have been opeful waitin. An

I ave heard of rights, like rights of a chile, rights to freedom. *Rights denied shall be wrongs defied*, I heard.'

'Where heard?'

'At the women's meetin, Mr Daniell.' He don't like that.

'Jessie, these would be my rights of full Academy membership; unavailable to others.'

'Yes sir.'

'One must belong in the first place, y'see, to be entitled to full rights.'

'Yes sir.' (I got him rattled, don't know why.) 'I see you done nice pitchers here of plants in among em, sir.'

He looks acrost. 'Some years ago, now. Those are first drafts, experiments.'

'You don't get them plants round ere, Mr Daniell, do you? Blooms like that? They're from foreign.'

'Indeed—from western Africa, mostly. A merchant returning with them before the French wars had seen sketches of mine somewhere. Paid me to paint them.'

'Very nice, sir. Where was they put?'

'The plants? In a London garden. Many cannot have survived beyond a few months—including the collector himself, I believe. Joseph Banks gathered many more for his Soho library.'

'Library? Ain't that for books, sir?'

'It is science, Jessie.'

(They all talk in riddles.) 'So you won't use them flower pitchers for the membership fing, Mr Daniell?'

'No. The Committee expects fresh work.'

He kneels again, hum-hummin to hisself. I have took enough of his time.

'Oh, Mr Daniell, sir, Mrs Lambton arks, can I go to her again the morrow?'

He looks back far as his shoulder. 'Oh, very well. She may need comforting.'

He ain't seen them pitchers o mine. The last is a flint lump wiv a eye-hole, done from a sketch brung back. Ain't *viewed* em, what they say, or is that only framed ones? You can keep pitchers flat neath the tray-basket when dried. An I am keepin em.

*

These my first swift explorations in line and colour from our eastern tour: faces, postures and groupings, woollen caps, smoke-houses, rigging, osier baskets. They crowd the page. And further annotations. Three engrossing hours; stand slowly.

Doubtless Willem van Brielle anticipates a handsome view of his New Horizons brig leaving Harwich harbour for Helvoetsluys, hoisting sail in the Stour estuary with the Suffolk shore and the Orwell's confluence beyond. Something of that order.

Salt in my wound.

I must depart before roadways become swamps, before October storms wreak havoc about our coasts. The Dutchman would not thank me for depicting his two-master spread upon the waters off Harwich, a crushed moth in full view of the fortress military, and his passengers huddled in a skiff!

Now that van Brielle has paid the half of my estimate for the Harwich venture (Garner's suggestion), the bank permits me to withdraw funds. Lawyer Morris shall settle card-mount debts, so that I may exhibit, while meeting Dr Phillips's fee for attending someone, um, overly well-known to me. I shall pass what I can to the funds for Ruth Ayton. Yet Thomas's plea, *look after Lizzie for me*, transfers the yoke to my shoulders: Mrs Lambton, haunting the place.

Above all, Jessie's circumstance must be thought upon. I would better understand my prentice could I but broach the topic with her. To work and work and work is not enough. I thrash about blind, accepting responsibilities without the means. Familiar tale.

*

Mrs Lambton stops sudden whiles we are upon this outin she did speak of.

'Jessie, you are a woman and regard yourself so, despite your apparel and unfortunate appearance.'

'I ain't got a woman's hips, Miss. I goes straight down.'

'I referred to your hair,' all prune-face. 'But your upper body is now more womanly.'

'This jerkin buttons-up tight.'

'Hence we visit Millicent, a member of our Association. The key to others' respect is self-respect, Jessie.' Them little feet mouses away again.

'Yes Miss.'

'Without the sin of pride. Marylebone's members sometimes have been humbled to meet ragged women loth to admit their need, for shame to be so reduced.'

'Yes Miss. Once I—'

'Yes?'

'Well, I jus knows that feelin.'

'It is surprising common, Jessie.'

We goes a few more paces down Bulstrode Street, Mrs Lambton lookin straight ahead. Is she finkin of herself?

One flick of that big black curl brings her eye round to pin me.

'Millicent resides in the terrace ahead. A dressmaker. You shall see her collection, Jessie, and perhaps acquire the apparel you need.'

'A skirt?'

'Part of our Association's charitable purpose.'

Millicent might be younger than Mrs Lambton. Little hugs all round: them two knows each other well. Millicent talks quiet, livin in quiet herself. She's got a way of arksin sharp questions whiles doin somefink else.

'Do men regard you more of late, Jessie?' (Straightenin a slipped tableclof.)

'Yes Miss.'

'Please call me Millicent.' (Takin cottons from a drawer.) 'We are all sisters.'

Sisters? She cannot mean what he says, even if it is Marylebone.

'This apparel don't fit so well, Miss Millicent. I am fillin-out up top.'

'Your guise no longer succeeds, therefore.'

'It was for ease of mind. Now, bein a artiss prentice, I got this jerkin—new, barrin mends.'

'Well, let us remove it… There we are.'

Millicent holds a tape, lookin me up an down. Lifts an arm, measures from neck to shoulder, acrost the chest, around waist, hips, an down the leg. I stands dumb an stiff as a wood doll.

When Mrs Lambton speaks, it is to her friend. 'Don't you think the difficulties in returning to the fold from hiding, or from any form of exile, are ill-understood?'

Writin numbers, Millicent smiles. 'Well, you should know, Lizzie dear, how grief may bring reclusiveness. Hmm?'

Them words ain't welcome acrost the room. I keeps my mouf tight shut.

Soon I must reach seventeen years. September, they guessed for me when found at St James's door. I ain't wore a skirt since leavin; to wear one now don't seem right. A skirt brings back all I scaped from. Women-prentices ain't never heard of, workouse girls is meant for service, an servants work long days so the likes of Mrs Veebee can have her pastimes.

Well, I won't.

Millicent fetches somefink grey-green, blossomin out all round, for me to try-on afore a tall mirror in the next room. It is a shock how others must see me. I ain't never seen myself full-size so clear an sharp, like lookin inside a light-box. Still skinny as a pea-stick, all elbows, long scar acrost one leg—never a beauty, an yet much different. Not the apparel, but me: I am changed in myself. What others might speck of me, changed, an them wore-out scarecrow-britches cannot hide it.

They are talkin quiet in the big room. The old man *called to the Lord,* an *What might you do now, Lizzie?* an Mrs Lambton bein brave bout *an up-stairs chamber offered at Drury Lane.* Then a snip of scissors: *My dear, you know we have walked this path before.*

'Young lady, shall you soon come out?'

'Yes Miss.'

You sweeps the floor wiv this skirt as you goes, meetin fings afore gettin there yourself. I fears to step upon fanciness an go arse over tip, but Mrs Lambton just says practise. Top half, my shirt is tucked-in; over it, a little grey jacket smellin fresh mofballs, wiv quite short sleeves stitched back, like for scrubbin steps. Millicent calls it fashion, but none wearin it would ever dream of haulin a bucket. No more might I glide all lady-like at some dance, save when stood on wheels.

Mrs Lambton ain't so strict on the way back. 'Are you not free to be yourself, Jessie?'

'Yes, Miss.'

'Women can be free together.'

'Mrs Lambton, have you heard tell o plant libraries?'

'The Joseph Banks, you mean? Soho Square? There may be others. Why?'

'Plant libraries is a strange fought, Miss. That is all.'

*

Progress! *The Fleet at Fraserburgh*, sold. Foul smoke rose in columns from the tar-boiling there. Sand-coloured stains across the sky. Required much subtlety when tinting. The four and a half guineas yet to arrive.

'I appreciate your invitation, Young Mr Daniell.'

Colbert's Tea Rooms in Seymour Lane is Mrs Lambton's choice. Unfamiliar to me—as to most, one would assume. Thomas's housekeeper, *not* his widow, scorns the absurdity of self-indulgent mourning. Colbert's is her prudent means to avoid gossip about private meetings with the deceased's nephew, fraudulence and scandal looming. The old man's slow decline wearied her; now she may return in modest ways to society.

Lost me half-way through.

'I sought our meeting, Mrs Lambton, because my prentice is now a woman.'

She leans forward: 'Revealed.'

'Revealed?'

'Revealed to be a woman.'

'That aside, I would discuss Jessie's future. How I—she—we, together—may cope, and make something of this mess.'

'Is that how you regard the circumstance?'

'Madam, I have noted certain thoughts and expressions, um, expressed by Jessie, the whole tenor of which is Jacobin revolutionary.'

She near chokes upon fruit cake. Swallows tea, pats her throat. Have I struck home? Rather, Mrs Lambton conveys amusement. Ill befits women to patronise.

'Madam, it is the seditious influence of female education!'

'Sir, you wish to fashion a joint arrangement for Jessie's future?'

'Yes.'

'Then let us begin afresh: devise a plan to serve all.'

'Very well. Now, Mrs Lambton, Jessie has a talent for art, shown in her sense of colour, form, and striking presentation, especially of natural or botanic subjects.'

'You have told her this?'

'In a general way.'

'I would say Jessie makes great strides in reading with insight. Her achievement is remarkable, though she under-estimates it.

Young Mr Daniell, perhaps we may base our plan upon these findings?'

'I shall command more tea, Mrs Lambton.'

'Most welcome, most kind.'

Sweetness and light.

Did not some Jacobin woman murder a Frenchie in his bath?

*

It is chance to be born of a foreign mother, new come to this country; chance for my father to be fought a French spy, an did send treasures afore dyin in gaol. An it is chance I grew up a girl, alone in the workouse wiv naught but them treasures, whiles my brother was chose. By chance Faith Morlake was born a slave, an sold like a beast till freed by that bargeman, an for us to meet, what ferried us to Mistley acrost the river in spite of all. An it was plain chance in the Aymarket when I saw the purse nicked an brung it back for a reward, an Mr Daniell wasn't no street sketcher but a proper artiss much highly fought of all round, an made me his prentice.

I fell off of that cliff path, but for once another did care for me, an I was held safe. There is chance in all fings. It don't carry meanin. Chance can save you, or leave you wiv your back broke. At the time, arksin yourself what to do won't bring much clear answers.

On the other hand, Mrs Lambton wants me for her daughter.

His nibbs is lonely an fearful, yet cannot speak of it.

Them fings ain't chance.

Nor is it chance that all sees me now to be a woman, an less free.

Thus, I must do somefink; make my own way, whatever chance might bring.

But how?

September 1820

TWENTY-EIGHT

Down Newman Street, acrost Oxford Street, an a few yards further, Soho Square. I can read the wall-plate. They railed-off the garden in the middle to stop cattle an vagrants. The houses all got tall chimbleys an four floors, to cope wiv the servants.

But none about. I might never get spoke to, standin here wiv seven pitchers tight neath my arm, another helpless woman abroad in a skirt, an the sky close to rain.

Metal wheels rumbling behind, steady horses' hoofs. Not a carman wiv the night-soil, not by day, not here. It is a waggon pulls up, carryin a plant in a big pot lashed upright. Beside the carter, two young women grinnin wiv a man. *Cavortin* is Mrs Lambton's book-word for it she did once read me, all onion vinegar.

Soon as the cart is halted, them young folks is down an into the nearest house. Her wiv the dark hair turns at the door, foots the stop acrost, an waves to the carter. Smilin to hisself, he takes out the tail-pegs.

'Scuse me, is this the library place of Joseph Banks?'

'Not any more.'

'Oh?'

'Died months back.'

'So it ain't a keepin-room for plants no longer?'

He points to the big pot. 'What's that? Now I must get on.'

'Need some help?'

The carter looks me up an down. 'Don't bother me, there's a good girl, else I might ave to put you over my knee.' He laughs till he has to stop an cough somefink.

The dead man's doorway is open waitin, the gay young free-some ain't left nor been chucked out, an quick from devilment I follows after.

*

Heartening to stand at my press with inks, pigments, brushes and tools ranged nearby, and fair progress made. I may snatch a morsel to eat before returning to those sketches. Which the first for etching? Mistley shall be a delight—the Stour in late afternoon's sunlight, the strand where Morlake rowed us ashore from his barge, the merchant's store. I have it bright in mind.

Jessie's traced light-box image of Southwold harbour suggests more the power of a great sea: how the water's plunging weight pitches high the fisher-boat; how, in the angled, streaking rain, her two-man crew maintains safe passage through the harbour entrance; how gentlemen ashore grip top-hats tight gainst the gale.

The little-known Suffolk coast shall do well. Areas of dark and deepened hues to be bitten longer in the acid bath. Twice or more run through the press. Tonal variation, swirling in vaporous cloud. My images of harsh coastal life shall challenge Constable's pastoral idylls!

I yearn to experience again that grip of hazard when turning the wheel, maintaining regular rotation, gauging the resistance neath my hand; and, lifting the covers from the print itself, to disclose at last a unique shadow-country of Southwold's blustery bay. Those raised intaglio lines, fine black filaments of a woman's hair!

Gather all my sketches, tracings and notes to store safe from water-splashes: the old villain's good advice, all those years ago.

*

Doors on each side, all closed, no busy servants to bump into, an the young'uns gone into rooms. Two steps up them stone stairs could put me in gaol. The further I goes creepin, past the table an the big china vase, the coats, the pitchers hazy upon the wall, the gloomier it gets. At the end, double doors is open wide upon a place kept dark. The middle of this house smells of new-dug earth. Them curtains I seen in coffin-makers, too tall to reach the top of, too heavy to shift easy. Nerves all a-jangle now.

I can hear the carter unloadin that big pot. Soon he will be at the door. Somebody will come, an I might just—

'Greetings.'

'Agh!' The gent's voice straight brings back others what did step out the shadows, all whiskers too near my face. I got no clear way past him. Shrink down, tense an hunched, ready to be struck.

Yet the blow upon me don't come.

'Hey now, what is this?'

It ain't the voice of one tryin for anyfink in false fellowship. This man don't move, watchin from the gloom.

Well, you can't stay crouched for long. Feels stupid. So I lifts my head an then my shoulders, till upright, still wary.

'That is better. And you are?'

'Jessie, sir. Jessie Cloud.'

'You know my daughter?'

'No sir.'

'You merely wandered in?'

'I been wantin to come, but was told you was dead, sir. I brung wiv me this greenery what fell off of a tree bein carried, an—

It must be the carter pullin the door-bell.

'Emily! Emily, come down, will you? Well, Jessie, let us raise one or two blinds for a while. Now then… Yes, here we are.'

He cranks a handle an up comes half, and then another. We are in the corner of a high hall. Rows of shelves holdin boxes an trays; little ladders here an there, chairs next the wall at a long desk by the daylight. Out-doors is some wild place under glass, like a crop let go, yet all different crops.

A woman tyin her apron rushes into the doorway. 'Sir?'

'Ah, Mrs Cadge, I have an unexpected guest. The carter is arrived and my daughter out of earshot. Would you sign for what he brings? In the vestibule, for now.' He turns to me. 'Do you know the purpose of this place, Jessie?'

'Yes sir, a library of plants from foreign, brung together.'

'Where did you learn about us?'

'What I picked up, sir, from Mrs Lambton an Mr William Daniell, an from seein the carts.'

'William Daniell is an artist of considerable standing. Do not play with truth.'

'Sir, I am his artiss prentice, an very proud.'

'Aah!' Now I sees him grin wide.

'A foundlin from the workouse, sir.' He don't grin no more. 'I have learned depf of shadow, tints, an the light-box. Also, how to do resin. I went wiv Mr Daniell far as the North Sea, what shows puspicktiff, an bettered my readin by Mrs Lambton in her own private study.'

The man watches plants bein watered. 'Jessie, the herbarium, so-called, belonged to Mr Banks: his scientific collection from around the world. I am Robert Brown, twenty years his librarian. This collection he left to me. Joseph was a rich man; I am not. Our work here is far from done. It shall never be done. The herbarium is a living thing, changing as it grows. Demands upon us grow, also. *In which conditions thrive these plants? How group them? Where put them to use?* You follow?'

'I fink so, sir.'

'Larger premises, more employees, shall soon be required.'

Talkin to hisself by the finish, what vexes him day in, day out. He might be another like his nibbs.

'What is upon them shelves, Mr Brown?'

'You shall see. Come.'

Past two rows, down the third, an goin along all them shelves makes plain how much they got here.

'Now, Jessie, this will do. Take it to a table, will you?'

He comes after wiv a covered tray.

'Look at these. Handle them with care.'

I goes slow, fearin clumsiness when takin somefink from the box. Looks soft, but is hard. Lookin weighty, feels light in the hand. Seems dead, just might be livin.

'What is it, Mr Brown?'

'Tree fungus, from the Malay Peninsula.'

'Nice colours; like a big shell on the beach, or a carved flower.'

'These were cut within deep forest.'

I lays it gentle back wiv the others. One box out of all around. Now he takes the cover off of the tray. 'We are yet to study these items, Jessie. They are as they arrived.'

Bones, assorted. I can read that. I sees snake in there, rat-skull, a paw of some bigger creature, an tiny bones wiv soil yet upon em.

Mr Brown is by my shoulder. 'From Barbados, three years ago. We try to record everything, each in its place, every box its number.'

'How do you know what them fings is?'

'It is the reason we keep records: from description and location through comparison to formal identification, to catalogue, y'see?'

I don't see. Fink he knows it. He ain't daft.

'Are these your works upon the table, Jessie?'

'Not good enough yet to call em works, sir.'

'May I see them?'

I stares at him, just for bein arksed.

*

We depart for Harwich within the fort-night. Of late, storm-tides about eastern coasts flood my dreams, rolling Richard's body in the shallows, carrying all away. Jessie despatched to fetch more pigment. A winter's etching and tinting may calm this wretchedness. I must keep faith. How may this prenticeship continue? Fast in my pocket is Garner's letter, urging a decision upon the Fitzroy property. I am decided, yet loathe the answer.

Mrs Lambton is now arrived to further our discussion. Her customary, restless movements, the lock forever curled before her eye as we share more tea. My prentice has assured me, *them fruit buns won't never be missed.* Incorrigible.

'You see, Young Mr Daniell, we concern ourselves here with Jessie's future, along with our own.'

'Our own, separately.'

'Separately. Housekeepers have no rights under the law. With Thomas's passing, I lose my home.'

Said without passion. Would she have me forswear regulation?

'Mrs Lambton, Thomas bought the Fitzroy apartment with my family inheritance. The rest is spent. I may have to sell the property, and, and, I regret would have no role or room for you in Cleveland Street.' *Look after Lizzie when I am gone.* An albatross around my shoulders.

Her gaze takes in the smeared upholstery, my printer's blackened apron, mash-tub, waste-bucket. 'Young Mr Daniell, no need of your regret. I am done with such arrangements.'

'Oh!' Conceal my relief with a mouthful of bun.

'The Marylebone Sisterhood shelters its own. We are strong, providing for one another alongside those in peril.'

'Mmm.'

'A friend offers me accommodation.'

'Good! I have been—'

'And our Association shall contrive an arrangement for Jessie, also.'

'Impossible.'

'You would not permit it?'

'She would not agree it.'

'A moot point. Young Mr Daniell, I had no inkling that your uncle had defrauded you and your sister when young. During the eleven years I knew him, he continued spending boldly what was not his! As I have told you, our shrinking household income alone indicated a discrepancy between pretence and truth. I blamed the wars; those, and poor harvests. Also, Young Mr Daniell, I suspect that your own health has worsened. May the release of funds lessen your anxieties, and the Lord afford you greater tranquility of spirit.'

'Generous thoughts. Thank you. I fear my anger erupted when confronting Thomas.'

'I feared you would murder him.'

'Thankfully, you were present.'

'And he died in his sleep. You see, I knew Thomas differently. Or thought so.'

'Indeed, Mrs Lambton, your loyalty and service to my uncle are poorly rewarded. Would you agree to select a work of his as a keepsake? And I shall contribute one of my own, should you, um, should you…'

'Young Mr Daniell, how considerate!' Putting down her cup, she smiles. 'I would prize a work of yours: an artist so widely acclaimed.'

*

I fink Mr Brown, bein Scotch, must have give up his kilt for London, seein no need. What he does is sort plants into *varieties*, like people in families, an *records* it down for botany science. Mr Daniell's paintins of plants have got labels what do that. It would take weeks just to look in all them library boxes. They got pressed plants, mosses, toadstools, big fruits startin to wrinkle, an seeds to plant whiles not sure what they grows into. An I got showed a microscope. Mr Brown did speak of big lenses to look at little fings. I watched tiny creatures in water: could put you off drink for ever. On a plant leaf was hairs not seen in real life. Plants like that have *cells*.

The freesome helps Mr Brown in the library. It is his Emily, her friend Cora, an Martin, a clerk to write it up tidy. The women did say hello an was nice to me despite bein educated. Cora did wear a short skirt over britches, so you could not help but see her ankles an calves cavortin when up a ladder. Mr Brown paid no heed. He is a odd bird all round. I fink he would lose hisself like Mr Daniell, if not saved by havin family to fink of.

Chance did not get me to Soho Square. I mostly worked it out, tryin to make my own way, an pleased I done it for myself. What might follow? Mr Brown has kept my pitchers, an I wants em back.

When nex day his nibbs arks me to go fetch two dozen charcoal sticks for his journey to Harwich, I can do two fings in one. It is hard to run in a skirt. Women in a dash grab what they can of some big barge-sail bout the knees, whiles pretendin daintiness an never runned afore; when I goes flat-out for Soho Square, folks gawp.

'Good-day, Mrs Cadge,'

'Why the flushed cheeks?'

'It is the skirts, Miss. Can Mr Brown see me, please?'

'Do you never introduce yourself?'

'It is Jessie Cloud, Mrs Cadge.'

'Interesting name. Come within.'

'Fank you. Cloud is French.'

'Cannot be helped. Wait there. Without appointment?'

'Yes, Mrs Cadge.'

'Do *not* stray as you did before.'

She ain't one to be messed wiv.

As she turns, Mr Brown comes out the big hall.

'Ah, Jessie! You are soon returned.'

'I come for my pitchers, sir.'

'Yes. Mrs Cadge, please conduct Jessie to the study.'

Another study. Curtains drawn back. Empty, save two birds restless in a cage.

'You may wait here.' Mrs Cadge nods toward the desk. 'Do not touch the hutia, by chance new-brought from Hispaniola. It ate the plant specimen it came with.'

'I met someone from Hispan—'

Gone. Just me, two canaries, an a stuffed rat from the cane-fields.

When Mr Brown comes in wiv my pitchers, he makes no move to give em back. 'I apologise, Jessie: the herbarium is a busy place.'

'Yes sir.'

'Our labour is both fascinating and daunting.'

'Yes sir.' (Dauntin?)

'The responsibility, y'see, of accurate classification for future generations.'

'*Thus*, Mr Brown, does your daughter work for you?'

'Not exactly. My wife would have Emily safe married!' He laughs, shakin his head. 'But I would speak with you about the task here. Thank you for showing me your paintings and sketches.'

'Oh, you did look at em!'

'Studied them. Your *viola tricolor*, or heartsease; the trifolium; thyme and variegated ivy; scabbed leaves of oak; and of course, species of coastal plant which tolerate salt airs.'

'Them last was growin by the shore sir—done quick, on walks.'

'Then the more revealing. You demonstrate a natural talent for depicting plant-shapes, the distribution of leaves about their stems, and accurate coloration. An artist of William Daniell's distinction would remark the fact when selecting his prentice.'

'Fank you, sir.' Shan't tell how I did get chose: my natural talent for spottin thievery.

*

Mrs Lambton's eye glints, unblinking. 'Young Mr Daniell, shall I call Jessie while you pour tea?'

Damn near insulting. Also, kitchen whispers between them as I pour.

My sorry furniture is re-arranged next the casement above Cleveland Street; the sofa tidied of all card-mounts and brushes.

A young woman enters in smart apparel, Mrs Lambton fussing-by. Find myself almost about to stand, but she is my prentice still. Jessie: the same pale cheeks and troubled, challenging frown. A little discomfited but newly clean, her hair fresh-brushed, somewhat less disorderly. Not some painted molly-boy or two-sexed creature, as I had first feared upon that woeful day. Nonetheless, a young woman may no more reside with me than they.

Look to Mrs Lambton, who returns my gaze.

'Well, Jessie, let us take tea.' Cup rattling in its saucer. 'This shall be informal between us. Mrs Lambton and I have been thinking about the future together.'

'Her future,' Mrs Lambton murmurs

'Your future, Jessie, um, thinking together about.'

'Does not her costume look quite the thing?'

'Oh yes. Very…'

'Impressive?'

'Impressive, doubtless.'

'I ain't wore a skirt for eighteen months, when several ways younger.'

'Therefore, Mrs Lambton and I shall put to you some possibilities.'

'Like plans, sir?'

'Yes, Jessie.' (The widow, intervening!) 'Necessary plans, following Mr Thomas Daniell's death.'

Regard Mrs Lambton with severity. She sits back.

'Now. Plans. It seems I own the property in Fitzroy Square.'

'Well, that's good news, sir.' Jessie's frown deepens. 'Ain't it?'

'My uncle left debts unpaid. I have bills also, as you know. The press is bolted here in Cleveland Street. My sister does not intend returning to England. Hence no accommodation required. I must sell it, Jessie.'

She frowns. 'Mrs Lambton, where will you go? All them books, an no private study?'

'Bless you for caring so! My dear, a housekeeper's position is ever insecure, and Thomas was long in decline. I shall go live with my friend, Millicent. Books and all.'

'Oh, that is *nice*, Miss.'

(Mutual congratulation in female fellowship is all very well, but the plans for my prentice are not explained. Does Mrs Lambton forget?)

'You see, Jessie, my arrangement with Millicent makes available a top-storey chamber at our Association's building.'

(Ah!)

'Me? For me, Miss?'

'Yes, Jessie. A room of your own, within the protective companionship of Marylebone women, dedicated to the cause! And instructive materials to read! Thomas's death was distressing, yet I discern God's hand in the turn of these events.'

(Cannot follow her skip-logic there. Some religious bee-hive establishment?)

'Not by chance, then, Miss. How would I make earnins?'

'We adopt roles, tasks, functions according to talents. Some occupy themselves through crafts. And we value our mothers of the next generation.'

Jessie nods. 'Fank you, Miss, for takin such care.'

'Are you concluded, Mrs Lambton?'

'If you wish.'

'Jessie, I do not abandon you. As my prentice, you shall gain further skills in etching, and your attendance upon me shall be paid. You may use your income to rent bed and board nearby.'

'Not stay here, then, sir?'

'I cannot. My error was to accept what your appearance suggested, without, um, closer appraisal. However, the apprenticeship shall be maintained—even a further coastal tour, however managed. One grows used to youthful companionship: this obstacle of your womanhood may be overcome.'

We are thanked. *Much to fink about.* May she go now, with these things in mind?

Mrs Lambton's eyes hooded as a roosting crow.

TWENTY-NINE

My first sketch of the fisherwoman, needle in hand, before her cabin. The stitched sacking, soon to be turned. Decorated box nearby. Ragged children at her knee. What were her words? *Not locked up, but prisoners.* And here the scene brought closer, enlarged by box technique. The child's bare feet glimpsed among fine-patterned shells at the right of the image.

The woman's proud defiance commands respect. By advancing a yard into the scene I have accentuated it. She looks downward, somewhat to one side. Sunlight emphasising shadow renders my task more difficult, and therein the challenge: to distinguish this woman's expression from sentimental domestic contentment. No comforting portrait of a quaint shelter, but courage here before us, true nobility.

Might this subject gain prominence at the Royal Academy? The hanging committee, thus named, followed by the judging panel—*wrong order*, as Richard observed. Full membership would bring further commissions, a more regular income, greater ease of credit. Above all, pride!

The grey and blue outlines of my water-colour have faded well in drying. I shall line those emptied helmet-shells with strips of peach tint; likewise, pitchy greens and browns of the fisherwoman's cabin beyond, her arms' rawness contrasted with the nearest child's pallid face. All these await my bringing to the work. Dabbed buttermilk, ochre, hints of carmine, to call forth the woman's honesty and steadfastness: her story there.

My own, also. The sketch leans gainst Mother's old kitchen

jug. Perhaps ridiculous to envisage her smiling above. With her hand's ringed finger, *teng-teng-teng*, she would check for warmth of winter soup or jugged hare. Though she appears to me less and less, the warmth remains within.

I am at ease here, my things about me. Yes, steadfast. No more forcefulness.

*

I have fought much how in the workouse we was not people but burdens. They looked for gladness in our faces at bein kept alive. Poor Nat, what others bullied an mocked for lack of brains, did show me the way by runnin out the laundry gates. A gang killed him cruel down a alley days after, but I learned from what he done. Now I got choices, I shall make my own, an not be led.

Whiles Mrs Lambton is clearin the place at Fitzroy, I lends a hand. She ain't finkin of my readin now, but talks of Millicent's house come from a dead relative, an the more better times all round.

'Your little chamber at Marylebone, Jessie, would have served me adequately, being well-furnished, with a tiled fireplace; overlooking the lane—not the river, for its odours can be noxious. Our Association welcomes newcomers. Members join for different reasons: from distressing experience, misfortune, or Dissenting beliefs, but all act on behalf of women generally.' Whiles foldin sheets, she beams at me.

'A fine cause, Miss.'

'So it is!'

'But I must tell you true, Mrs Lambton, I don't fink your group is for me.'

'Not for you?'

'No, Miss.'

'But we have discussed this! Just as you were given apparel, so shall you be cherished, assisted in reading, and educated at our meetings. Accommodation shall be found you, and fruitful occupation. Might a workhouse girl decline these offerings?'

'I ain't a workouse girl no more, Mrs Lambton.'

She puts down the bedsheet an hastens over, takin my hand. 'Oh Jessie, I am sorry! I meant no insult to you. In my surprise, I simply…'

'I know, Miss. Them little kept-back foughts can easy slip out.'

'I am aghast. Are you truly decided?'

'Turned it over time an again. I am true grateful for all you done, an would try to do, but I cannot join you, Mrs Lambton. Feels like I'd be missin a step.'

'It is the artist in you: the embracement of risk. Yet you would hazard your future with one who denies you safe accommodation, because of your womanhood!'

'My future may not be wiv Mr Daniell, Miss.'

'You reject both? Another offer? Not *marriage*?' An when she sees me laughin: 'Thank God!'

'Mrs Lambton, I learned of the Joseph Banks collection. They got interestin paid work what I'd be let do. It is art used for botany science, an I fink I can do it well.'

'Then I congratulate your ambition.' She sighs, walkin away. 'All this for Joseph Banks—one who in government long defended slavery in the colonies.'

'Miss, he is dead now.'

'That vile practice lives on abroad, conveniently out of sight!'

She fiddles wiv fings from the drawer, struggles to close it, all tight-strung angry. An soon we comes to biddin farewell, both knowin how big this change.

'Jessie,' she says, standin close, 'in my own life I have suffered setbacks, blows to the heart. I had to learn resilience—which is strength and resourcefulness, Jessie, a flame within. But you are blessed with it, dear child. I recognise it in you.' The curl of hair narrows her gaze upon mine, that beak approachin my ear. 'Jessie, do not let them snuff it out.'

*

A decade ago, Richard and I declared our purpose to convey *the manners and employment of people, and modes of life* at the very margins of these islands. With time, my prints have tended to emphasise landscape, qualities of sky and sea. They have become *views*.

The working-people in this next volume, the fisherwoman and her children, the mild waggoner by Dunwich, the ugly history graved upon Faith Morlake's person, Mrs Tumulty's harsh countenance, the boy and his gutting-knife—the personages themselves, beyond their labour—speak to me more. To each setting a story. I have seen them so wholly, while failing to discern the young woman beside me! Shameful.

My work has drifted from its truer purpose. I shall depict those unconsidered lives.

Cannot accustom myself to Jessie's swishing skirts. What if printing ink were splashed upon her new apparel? It would never do!

'Jessie, you prepare for Harwich?'

'Yes sir. The luggage packed in your chamber, near ready. The gear in the hall.'

'Thank you. Soon we set forth again!' (Something in her manner.) 'Um, have you spoke with Mrs Lambton?'

'We did talk, sir, yes.'

'And?'

'I told her how much doin the readin has helped, sir, an learnin what a private study wiv books is for, an I fanked her deep. Mrs Lambton would have me like a daughter go to talks. I sees what they try for, sir, wishin to stand for what's only right. But I ain't ready in myself, an must find my own way to it. She did get up-set bout the women's group.'

'Similar female malcontents have declared themselves elsewhere. Whatever their purpose, Jessie, such opinions threaten sound society.'

'We was both sad, sir, at the end.'

'You need not cease meeting her! The wage I pay for your service shall bring you greater independence.'

My prentice lowers her head. Some misunderstanding? Would have anticipated greater jauntiness.

'You disagree?'

'No sir. I don't know what to say next. How to say it.'

'I have to determine your wage, it is true, although otherwise—'

'Sir, I been offered work.'

(What? Cannot be. *Work?*)

'Soho Square, sir, the Banks collection. The chance did come my way. I met Mr Robert Brown. It is plants they record down for the future. From Botany Bay, an all over, ever since, more an more new-found ones keeps comin. They cannot cope.'

'I don't, um, follow. Jessie, I…'

Those hands and slender wrists guide me to the sofa.

'Oh sir, it is the suddenness has struck you. Knew this might turn out bad. Lean back, Mr Daniell. Rest your head on this cushion. You been workin hard.'

'I staggered, nothing more. Finish what you were saying.'

'Long an the short, they seen my pitchers. Techniques learned from you, sir. I been offered a place, paintin whatever they give me, like showin me the world. It is called bein a ill-u-strator. His daughter works there, and me to go alongside. Name of Emily, wiv a stutter, an you must wait for her to finish. Shall I open the window-glass, sir?'

'Where would you live, Jessie?'

'In the house. The old man left his library an bed-chambers to Mr Brown.'

'I see…'

'Mr Daniell, he arks for your permission wrote down, if you will. He finks of you most highly.'

'I had not expected this at all. Your course is incomplete— um, Methods of Etching.'

'I knows, sir. I knows. Should I go finish the packin?'

'Do you need my *permission* any more?'

'Oh sir, you done so much for me! You helped me scape from the streets. You have saved me. Not many gets to choose their jobs. I seen enough of that. I do not fink I could be a proper artiss to know what makes a good pitcher, keepin scenes an faces in my head like you do. I mostly copies one fing plain. Besides, I cannot attend you whiles lodgin elsewhere. The truth is, in your eyes a boy prentice is what's best. It's right for me to go, sir, ain't it?'

'When does Brown need you?'

'Afore Harwich, Mr Daniell, should you agree.'

'Good Gracious, before our tour?'

'Today, sir, is best. Hard for us both to let it run on. You would need this place kept safe, an I got your second key.'

'Ah. Yes. Thank you. It is regrettable, Jessie. Most regrettable. I feel… well I don't know what I feel, but as you are decided, I shall write the note.'

All asunder. (Behind, leaning gainst the wall, Richard shakes his head. Gone.)

When Jessie returns from packing for each of us, I pass her the signed note for Robert Brown. Bid her sit by me. Pointless to dispute.

'Jessie, a while ago, Mrs Lambton and I discussed our differences concerning your future: how to proceed. Prompted me to begin a small portrait—not posed, of course, but from our acquaintance these several months. And um, as you came to me. As you are. My little gift of thanks, y'see, whatever your decision. I wish you well. It appals me not to have read the significance of your features long ago, because I *do* know you, Jessie. I apologise.'

'Oh sir…'

'No-no-no. And, um, well, here it is.'

Wonderful to see her countenance!

'I intended to give it you fully tinted in a frame, but events forestall me.'

Jessie's eyes moistening. One great sniff. She gazes at the sketch, holding it in both hands.

'Fank you, sir. It is lovely. This shall be for my own wall, an my greatest treasure.'

'I have touched-in greys and greens about the head and shoulders. Signed and dated, you know, in case... It brings to mind those Haymarket sketches, um, and—ouf!'

Without warning she has risen, has flung her arms about my shoulders, pat-pat, *fank you from the bottom of my heart,* her wet cheek to my neck, before I am released.

Have never known the like.

*

I am prepared for Harwich: camera obscura, brass-cornered box, travel-bag, purse. Due at the King's Head by dusk. God forbid delay this time: the Dutchman shall require my version of his two-master in full sail, not some milkmaid at a well.

Quiet here, of course.

Of course. And shall be.

House-key upon the table. Her calico shirt and grey jerkin, ironed, folded and piled. However, the breeches gone. She resents skirts! May as well have taken the remainder.

Something scrawled upon the back of Moulton and Clyne's May-time letter:

Dear MR WILLIAM DANIELL

I got no paper so usin this & hope you do not mind
Thank you for takin me in & givin me a chans
I did want to be a artiss one day I wotched you from the side & you
tried to help me tho I did not allways lern what you was teechin

MRS LAMBTON tried hard likewise & I have thanked her
MISS CLOUD skared me she was so ill & bein looked after
how cood I care for one I did not no whom had not cared
for me
she was not mine nor I hers it is a grate pitty
so when you held me from fallin off of that cliff path
it felt like the first time my life mattered to somebody
I cannot say this rite sir but I am yung & now there is much
more things for me to find out & do & places to go
I must make something of myself & you have helped me see it
I luv the portrate you dun of me now that you no me proper
& good luck with the pitchers.

    Your fathflly Jessie Cloud

I have not stood in Jessie's way; rather, I supported her. As a woman
she declares so, and I am glad. Yet how to know? In all we do, how
do we know finally what shall matter?

By my feet, the tray-basket for laundry. I permitted young
Jessie to sleep in it, here upon the boards, as might a dog. No consideration of this circumstance crossed my mind. Whitened-out.
Laughable! I had more to learn than did my prentice. And those
who have gone before, my mother smiling as she sews, my father
pausing to look up from his charts, Richard's sidelong wit, they
would all agree. Gone, not lost. Here within.

So… good luck with the pitchers.

The note from my prentice was weighted with the lobster-
claw. In this light, more green than blue.

AUTHOR'S NOTE AND ACKNOWLEDGEMENTS

The Prentice-Boy is a work of fiction based loosely upon the life of the aquatint artist and printmaker, William Daniell (1769-1837). His uncle, Thomas Daniell, also an artist and early practitioner of aquatinting, had supported William when his nephew was orphaned at fifteen, taking him to India. In later years, William Daniell and the writer, Richard Ayton, toured Britain's shores and their communities, portraying coastal life. Ayton, disputing the project's finances, finally left. A series of eight volumes was published, with Ayton as author. Two scenes during the fictional tour describe images that the historical William Daniell produced. In 1822, William Daniell was accepted ahead of John Constable as a Royal Academician.

Those are the bare bones. Jesse is fictive; the social divisions between rich and poor, the prentice's pauperdom and limited life-chances, are not.

A novel set in the past is usually thought of as 'historical'. Nevertheless, it is also a product of its own time, and our knowledge and understanding of the past are rightly being challenged evidentially, and revised. I began researching and drafting in 2016. When the novel was finished at the end of 2021, much had changed socially and politically in Britain and abroad. The mood became different. Now we struggle as individuals, as families, and as a society to cope with the consequences. And my own feelings and responses have infused the writing: a story taking place two centuries ago draws from the well of the last few years.

I dedicate this book to my wife, Julia, whose understanding, support and involvement have been immense in this as in so many things. I also thank Kate, my daughter, for somehow finding time in her busy life to provide comments upon an early draft, technological advice, and above all, her constant encouragement.

I owe a huge debt of gratitude to Katie Isbester of Claret Press for her thought, consideration, and faith in my work from the beginning. I also thank Petya Tsankova, Yasmeen Doogue-Khan and all at Claret for their friendly professionalism – such a dedicated team!

Several people provided comments and their own perspectives upon the novel at different stages along the way: Lorna Daymond, Tracy Kenny, Henry Layte, Sophie Playle, Iain McDonald, Alan Mahar, Lynne Middlemiss, Martin Kimber, and Chris Brown. The contemporary aquatint artist, Matthew Benington, offered invaluable research information, showing me facilities, equipment and materials used by students at Norwich University of the Arts. Falmouth Art Gallery's welcoming Curator brought out for me two of Daniell's marvellous prints. I am grateful to them all.

ABOUT THE AUTHOR

During a career in education and training, Ray has written several articles for academic journals, and has authored teaching materials. Following his work for a national charity, he gained a research PhD (Leicester 2010). Ray led a campaign in 2013 to rescue a local bookshop scheduled for closure, establishing a group of volunteers who formed a new, not-for-profit community company. Kett's Books has evolved successfully ever since.

A professional theatre company toured Suffolk and Norfolk in 2016 with his play about the life and work of the poet, George Crabbe. In Crabbe's *Peter Grimes* (1810), an Aldeburgh fisherman kills three apprentices 'farmed out' from a London workhouse. Ray's background reading about the period sparked fresh ideas for a novel.

The Prentice-Boy takes place in 1820. A London artist and a homeless teenager tell the story. When this unusual partnership tours the eastern coast, the experience prompts lasting changes in their lives. Ray's interest is to explore perception and misperception in an insecure society, reliant upon appearances and hostile to change. In that world, the poor have little prospect of a better life, and prejudice denies rights to women. However, challenging situations can provide rich and comic opportunities in fiction, no less than in reality itself! As the likeness of our own day to those harsh times becomes disturbingly clear, this book shows how human resilience can become a reliable source of hope.

Claret Press shares engaging stories about the real issues of our changing world. Since it was founded in 2015, Claret Press has seen its titles translated into German, shortlisted for a Royal Society of Literature award and climb up the bestseller list. Each book probes the entanglement of the political, the historical and the everyday—but always with the goal of creating an engaging read.

If you enjoyed this book, then we're sure you'll find more great reads in the Claret Press library.

Subscribe to our mailing list at **www.claretpress.com** to get news of our latest releases, zoom events, and the occasional adorable photo of the Claret Press pets.

FICTION FROM CLARET PRESS

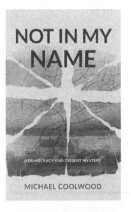